P9-AOO-998

VIRUS

William Harrington VIRUS

WILLIAM MORROW AND COMPANY, INC.
NEW YORK

Virus is a work of fiction. None of the people described here are real, nor are the business entities. No person or business entity here described is a disguised version of a real person or business. Since the same words are often used in the names of businesses in the computer field, some corporate name may seem similar to that of a real business. If that is true—or if a name is actually identical to that of a real person or business—it is absolutely coincidental and contrary to the intention of the author. The entire story is the product of the author's imagination.

Library of Congress Cataloging-in-Publication Data

Harrington, William, 1931–
    Virus / William Harrington.
      p. cm.
    ISBN 0-688-09064-8
    I. Title.
    PS3558.A63V57   1991   90-38780
    813'.54—dc20   CIP

Printed in the United States of America

First Edition

1 2 3 4 5 6 7 8 9 10

BOOK DESIGN BY LISA STOKES

Darius Whitney pulled the stub of a cheroot from between his lips, but he didn't look up from the glowing green numbers and letters on his computer screen. "No, dammit! No! Do you understand the meaning of the word *no?*"

"Mr. Whitney, you're a member of the resources prioritization committee, and Mr. Morgenstern—"

"Out! Get out of here, sonny. I'm busy. I don't have time for any idiotic committee. Let the MBAs jabber away all afternoon around a table in some committee room. That's what they're good for. Me, I've got work to do. I'm trying to accomplish something. Go on, now. Go! And close the door!"

Darius Whitney was not a team player, never had been. An untidy man who insisted on working alone—or almost alone—he kept his office cheerfully cluttered. He filled the air there and in his computer lab with the acrid smoke of his cheroots. He submitted reports only in his own good time—when he had something to report, as he put it. He lost the memos that defined corporate policies and procedures. Consequently he had no concept of organization, no idea where jurisdictional lines were drawn, and so never hesitated to express his opinion on anything that caught his attention.

What was worse, he had no sense at all of hierarchy and had long since made it plain he didn't give a damn.

Why should he? Whitney was the name of the company.

Whitney. Whitney Data Dynamics.

The problem was, he didn't own it anymore.

For three years now Whitney Data Dynamics had been a wholly owned subsidiary of Digital Universal Corporation. Whitney owned 5 percent of Digital Universal, and he had a contract that assured him of a continuing position, a generous salary, and a seat on the board of directors. But he wasn't chief executive officer any longer. The company was run by Nathan Morgenstern and his gang of professional managers—graduates of colleges of business administration—and Darius Whitney was, when the matter was put to him bluntly, an employee.

He had not voluntarily surrendered control of his company. To the contrary, he had lost it. He had pledged his stock to secure the large loans necessary to finance the research and development that had made Whitney Data Dynamics a success. Three years ago he'd had a cash-flow problem and went into default on his loans. The banks and other creditors had put his pledged stock on the market. Digital Universal had bought most of the pledged stock, reorganized the company, and installed their own management.

Whitney was fond of a bon mot of his own invention, which he had repeated so often, it had become a cliché: "Achievement is its own justification."

That, together with "A camel is a horse put together by committee" and "Nothing worth achieving is ever achieved by teamwork," was just about the whole of Darius Whitney's business philosophy, if his aggregated attitudes could be dignified with the word *philosophy*. In his own judgment he was an achiever, a real achiever. *He* had created something, a brilliantly conceived piece of computer software that was all but universally used; and all *they* did was skim profits off his invention. MBAs. Pencil pushers. College boys. Parasites.

Darius Whitney was a recognized genius. He was an eccentric. He was also a bitterly angry man.

"Darius . . ."

He looked up. "Allison . . ." He didn't work *entirely* alone.

"Look at this," she said. She handed him a big sheet of green-and-white computer-printout paper. "The part I marked."

Whitney frowned over the fragment of computer code she had marked. He shoved his unlighted cheroot into his mouth and studied her proffered solution to a programming problem that had frustrated them for a week.

"Might work," he mumbled through lips half-immobilized by the cheroot. "If—If the users are sophisticated enough. Idiots won't be able to cope with it."

They were working on the next software program Whitney Data Dynamics would market: a highly sophisticated project manager, to be called Dynamic Manager.

Dynamic Manager would help businesses control and coordinate the diverse elements of big and complicated undertakings, such as the relocation of corporate headquarters from one city to another.

For example headquarters staff must not abandon their old offices and arrive at the new ones only to find their telephones had not yet been installed. Corporate records would be unavailable while packed in moving vans, so moving had to be scheduled to cause the least disruption to business through delayed access to records. Tens of thousands of such activities had to be coordinated. Whitney was designing software that would be able to schedule and track 100,000 activities and generate both detailed reports and management summaries on every aspect of every activity.

It was ironic, some in the company said, that Darius Whitney should be designing software to help corporate management exert the kind of tight control he himself would defy. It was not ironic to him. He knew little of corporate management and cared less; but when a need was defined for him, he could design a computer program to cope with it. If it was a complex need, he would design a complex program.

He was in fact on the verge of giving Whitney Data Dynamics a decisive edge in a highly competitive field.

Darius's problem was that he had lost control of his company. The company's problem was that the curmudgeonly old man was beyond question a rare genius.

Old man. He was sixty. Some wit said he looked like Leo McKern in the role of Rumpole. His face was wrinkled, and the loose flesh of his jowls was often in motion. He smoked small, smelly cigars, his cheroots, and let them go out—after which he didn't chew on them but rolled them back and forth in his lips and pulled them out and waved them around when he gestured. He liked well-tailored, expensive suits and spent a good deal of money having jackets and vests and trousers draped to fit his lumpy frame; but when his mind became locked to a project, as it usually was, he neglected his appearance and sat at his computer terminals wearing suits in need of pressing, sometimes with smears of gray-white ash on the lapels.

He believed his achievements had earned him a good life, and his definition of the good life included ample quantities of bourbon and wine, good food, and freedom from sweaty exertion—which was what he called jogging, tennis, golfing, or any other activity that fell under the rubric of exercise.

He had no formal education in computer science or in mathematics. He had introduced himself to computers during his many years of service in the United States Air Force, where he had educated himself and attained the rank of master sergeant. He had a natural instinct for numbers and logic. What was more, he had gotten into the computer game when computers were new. The second generation of computer types, university-trained, was rapidly catching up with him; but that was what it had to do: catch up, to match and surpass Whitney's phenomenal talent and wealth of experience.

Allison McGuire was his apprentice. She was thirty-six years old. She had a doctorate in mathematics from Cornell, and her mastery of binary mathematics, acquired the academic way, supplemented Darius's instincts.

Allison was afflicted with an excess of self-consciousness that made her exaggerate her few faults and condemn herself as hopelessly plain, if not altogether unattractive. The truth was, she was not unattractive. She had, in the first place, a trim, boyish figure. Her blue eyes were set in a tangle of fine wrinkles above high cheekbones. Her hands were extraordinary: big and broad, with long, slender fingers. People who asked her if she played the piano were an affliction. She smoked unfiltered cigarettes, two packs a day.

"Want to join me on the other business tonight?" Whitney asked. "I've got a couple of steaks in the fridge."

Darius Whitney lived in a house in Malibu. California Highway 1 intruded between the house and the beach, but the living room, the master bedroom, and a deck all afforded a view of the surf and the Pacific. The house, plus the old-fashioned fin-tail Cadillac he kept running, were two more elements of Whitney's definition of the good life.

Allison McGuire was not. He liked her. He respected her. He felt warm affection for her. And he trusted her. But he had never suggested, much less established, an intimate physical relationship with her. He had never dared hope that she would accept any such suggestion, and he did not want to risk driving her away.

Allison was not divorced. That is to say, she and her husband had never formalized their situation, which was that her husband lived with another woman in Saint Paul, Minnesota, and Allison lived alone in California and called herself by her maiden name. As she had explained to Whitney, her religious scruples discouraged divorce, she and her husband had had no children, and the present arrangement suited her well enough, at least for the time being. Whitney guessed that Allison felt no overpowering desire to establish another intimacy and didn't much care what her husband did to satisfy himself, so long as he didn't expect *her* to do anything.

As for Darius, he was divorced. He had a son and a daughter, both older than Allison, both married and the parents of children themselves. His son was an accountant in Fort Lauderdale, and his daughter was married to a baseball player for the Houston Astros. Darius visited his children occasionally, never more than twice a year—and never when their mother was visiting.

At the kitchen table Darius and Allison ate their steaks and shared a bottle of Chateauneuf-du-Pape. A Bach requiem played on the stereo in the living room. Both of them understood the mathematical foundation that underlay the elaborate structures of Bach's music. They spoke little until the requiem was finished. Even after it was over, they remained silent for a moment.

"Hey, Dare," said Allison then. "Try this one."
She wrote a pattern of numbers on a sheet of paper—

18	46	94
63		61

"What's missing?"

Darius Whitney smiled as he focused on the sequence of numbers. "Pum-pum-pum, tee-tee-tee," he sang under his breath as he pondered, and his smile broadened. After about fifteen seconds he wrote in the missing number with a flourish: 52.

Allison laughed. "Damn! Fifteen seconds! It took *me* a minute and a half."

Darius shrugged. "Well . . . nine squared is eighty-one, reversed is eighteen; eight squared is sixty-four, reversed is forty-six; seven squared is forty-nine, reversed is ninety-four. And so on. Five squared is twenty-five, reversed is fifty-two. You eliminate various possibilities in order and very shortly you come to squares reversed. It would be more difficult if puzzle fanatics didn't use that relationship so often."

"Okay," she said. "Let's talk about the virus."

Virus. It was a word they never used at the office. Though Whitney worked on it in his computer lab there, and Allison sometimes tested small elements of it in the big IBM mainframe computer the company maintained, they never spoke of it, even to each other. The word must not be overheard.

The virus was how Whitney was going to recapture control of Whitney Data Dynamics.

In a sense the scheme was quite simple.

The key to it was Whitney's own magnum opus, the brilliant program called WHIT.

WHIT was a computer-language translator. It was a program that facilitated communication between systems that used different computer languages. In spite of the trend to standardization throughout the industry, there were still many nonstandard computer languages in use, for example in government computers.

WHIT translated on the fly, that is, it translated almost instantly, so nearly simultaneously that users were hardly aware of it.

It came as near as anything in the industry to being a ubiquitous program. Everyone who worked with sophisticated systems wanted WHIT, even some who had no particular use for it. A term had been added to computer jargon: *WHIT-capable*.

WHIT was the irrefutable proof of the genius of Darius Whitney. He had designed and written it alone, at home in his spare time, years ago. It was the foundation product for Whitney Data Dynamics, the company he had established to promote and market it. And now it would be his Trojan horse. It would carry his virus wherever he wanted to send it.

They talked about it a little while they sipped the last of the wine. Then they went into his workroom.

He had an old IBM PC-XT, on which he relied for many simple tasks. He had a ZEOS 386/25, a state-of-the-art desktop based on the fast 80386 processor chip, which he used for more complex work that would have required too much time on the PC-XT. He also had what Allison called the Beast—a computer hacked together by Darius himself and designed specifically to meet his highly personal requirements. He had programmed the two basic computers so idiosyncratically that no one but he and Allison could have used them. But that was a software function; they had modified programs, but the hardware remained standard. The Beast was a Whitney computer, chips and boards and all the rest, put together to suit him. It *did* suit him, but even Allison found it difficult to manage.

Sitting around the room, attached to the computers and to switch boxes with tangled cables, were printers and plotters—that is, printers capable of drawing diagrams—and four separate modems.

The modems were key to a number of his stratagems. The term *modem* meant "modulator-demodulator." It was an electronic device that converted a computer's electrical signals into the audio-frequency tones the telephone system was designed to carry. Darius Whitney had several of them, capable of transmitting and receiving at various speeds.

He also had some illegal equipment—gadgets of his own design that enabled him to use the telephone system, not just without paying bills but to intrude upon supposedly secure communications, especially computer-to-computer communications.

Every week Allison called her parents in Milwaukee. They had no idea she did not pay long-distance charges.

Allison sat down at the 386/25. "If they'd just leave their damned reservations alone, once they've made them—"

"If the dog hadn't stopped to you-know-what, he'd have caught the rabbit," said Darius.

Allison smiled. "Why didn't you say, 'piss,' Darius?" she asked.

He did not respond. She knew why he hadn't used that word. It was one of several he didn't use.

Reservations. They were creating a virus they hoped would infect LANCE, the computerized reservations system used by most of the nation's major airlines and virtually every travel agent. If the virus worked as Darius envisioned it, it would create chaos.

In 1987, when the concept of computer viruses was obscure and even their reality was doubted, Darius had spoken to a meeting of the System Designers Association of America. He had read from a paper partly written by Allison, and he had said:

"Make no mistake about it. Viruses are real. They can do immeasurable harm.

"A computer virus is an electronic version of the elusive, deceptive, maybe-alive-and-maybe-not submicroscopic entity that invades the human body, or for that matter any living thing, and wreaks havoc. The biological virus causes disease, often death. It does so by intruding into living cells and disorganizing them.

"The computer virus is aptly named. It is tiny. It is elusive. It is destructive. It disorganizes computers."

In that meeting some people had smiled tolerantly. They didn't believe. Later they would. Darius went on:

"There is no limit to what a virus can do. It is, after all, simply another computer program, though typically a very small one; and anything any of us can program a computer to do, someone can foul up by inserting into that program a bit of alien source code, a bit of destructive programming. My friends, we all know it is far easier to destroy than to create.

"A virus, once introduced into a computer, can do some very evil things. In the first place it can hide. It can hide, and it can defy every effort to detect it. How? Simple. It can be programmed to watch out for a search—somebody looking for it—and to send out a message that no virus is present. 'Nobody here but us chickens.' "

His audience had laughed appreciatively. And he had gone on to say, "What is more dangerous, once it is established in a computer, the virus can reproduce itself and spread. Established in one computer, it can travel across the communications lines between computers and infect every computer that comes in contact with the host."

They had smiled. Darius Whitney was a genius but an uneducated genius—and look how he had lost control of his own company by throwing money into more research and development before his initial program generated the revenue to support such expenditures. Whitney was an artist. That was the problem with Whitney. He was more interested in the frontiers of the technology than in the day-to-day business of making money from what he created. Where Whitney belonged was on a faculty. Of course there was always the problem of his distressing background: No education. No . . .

"Destruction. Chaos. In *any* computer system. How about the ones that manage securities on Wall Street? How about the computers that check income-tax returns? Hey, ladies and gentlemen, I have considered, believe me, writing a snippet of code that would make the IRS forget that Darius Whitney ever existed. How about the systems that control the exchange of money? I wouldn't mind if my bank's computer were blind to my checks."

Laughter. He *was* joking, wasn't he? He couldn't . . . They couldn't . . . The hackers . . . They *couldn't*—

Or could they? He spoke more seriously.

"What about the computers that control our national defense system? What if the system were rendered blind to an incoming missile?"

13

But the virus couldn't get in. That was the point. Whitney was overlooking the essential. Suppose someone wrote this awful program? How would it be injected into—?

He had anticipated the question. "It rides into your computer in a Trojan horse. Some innocent program. Something you have bought. More likely, something you have *borrowed*. Still more likely, something you have *stolen*. Oh, yes, you know what I mean. Ol' buddy so-and-so just spent ten grand for some great new software. Ol' buddy copies it and gives it to you, letting you avoid paying the royalties you legitimately owe the creator of that program. But . . ."

This sounded like Darius Whitney. He was the creator of a valuable program and resented anyone's copying and distributing it to nonpaying users.

"In *his* computer, ol' buddy's computer, this wonderful new program has picked up an infection. A virus. And now *you* got it! Maybe it serves you right, huh?"

Viruses, he had gone on to say, were propagated on innocent computer programs. Inserted into one program, they could migrate to another.

Already he had been thinking about the virus he would use to recover control of Whitney Data Dynamics—or destroy it.

The opportunity was at hand.

A new version of WHIT was soon to be released—his work for months before he was asked to do the project manager. WHIT 3.0. If WHIT 3.0 left Whitney Data Dynamics with a virus in it . . .

And that was what he and Allison had been working on all these long, after-dinner hours at home. When WHIT 3.0 left Whitney Data Dynamics, it would carry a virus.

They had made WHIT a Trojan horse.

Allison frowned over the screen of the Beast. Darius had created a simulation of LANCE in order to experiment with the virus. It would be relatively simple to infect LANCE so that it would muddle all the airline reservations for a specified day, overbooking some flights and calling others overbooked when in fact few reservations had been made for them. The difficult part was what

Allison had mentioned: keeping the muddle concealed when people changed their reservations. That required something ingenious, and they hadn't yet quite figured out how to do it.

Because they didn't mean just to throw the system into confusion in a general way. They meant to shift *real* reservations from one day to another, one flight to another. It would have been easy just to put LANCE out of business for a few hours or a day; but that wasn't what Whitney had in mind. He wanted people to show up at the airports with valid tickets, valid boarding passes, and find they couldn't get on the flights they had booked weeks, even months, before. That wasn't just crude tampering; that was elegant; that was a challenge.

It was a fascinating challenge. And challenge inspired this pair. It kept them working long hours.

Darius had already written the element of the program that would achieve his purpose. The virus would hide until the day it went into action. After that it would not retreat into hiding. It didn't have to create chaos more than once. Once would be enough. And after it had done it, it would remain visible—not to just anyone, but visible to the shrewd consultants who would be called in to find and disable it. They *would* find it. And they would be able to identify the Trojan horse that had carried it.

WHIT. WHIT 3.0. When the whole world knew that this immensely destructive virus had been propagated by WHIT 3.0 . . . well, WHIT 3.0 would be poison. The company wouldn't be able to *give* it away. Or Dynamic Manager either. And someone would remember that nothing like this ever happened when Darius Whitney was running the company. He wouldn't even have to remind the industry of that; they would remember. And Nathan Morgenstern and his crowd of pencil pushers would be humbled and ridiculed.

Maybe he could buy the company back. It wouldn't be worth much. But the industry would know that Darius Whitney would never let a product leave his shop with a virus in it, and he could rebuild . . .

Well, maybe it wouldn't work out quite the way he hoped. But the virus would do . . . it *would* do something. That was what he counted on: to do something big and dramatic and to ruin the people who had created nothing and *could* create nothing but had stolen from him what he had created.

"Dare," said Allison softly. "Are we working toward a deadline to have this virus ready?"

Darius nodded. "Middle of August."

"What's the significance of the middle of August?"

"That's when people will start making reservations for November twenty-first."

"And what's the significance of November twenty-first?"

"That's the date I'm programming into the virus," said Darius with a sly little smile. "It's the Wednesday before Thanksgiving. The busiest day of the year for air travel. Something like seven million people will try to go home for Thanksgiving by air. And it's going to be chaos. *Chaos!*"

2

—▮-▮-▮-▮-▮—

Lana Lettieri pulled her hand down the side of her cheek and drew a deep breath. This was going to be her worst shift of the year anyway, November 21, the Wednesday evening before Thanksgiving, and to have it start off like this . . .

She sighed. "I'm sorry, sir. I don't have an explanation for it."

The man facing her across the counter was a business traveler in blue suit, black overcoat, and gray hat. Probably he was accustomed to containing his anger, so he spoke firmly, not angrily; but she sensed irritation growing into exasperation, and she wondered if he really could control his temper.

"Now, let me get this straight," he said slowly, with the exaggerated patience of a man coping with a not-too-bright subordinate. "I have here not just a ticket, but a boarding pass. For *five weeks* I've had a confirmed reservation on TWA, New York to Chicago, November twenty-first, five-fifteen. First class. Now you're telling me *someone else* has a boarding pass for the same seat?"

She glanced uneasily toward the crowd milling around Gate 17. "I'm afraid it's worse than that," she said.

He looked at the crowd. It was obvious that no 727 in the world was going to fly all these people from New York to Chicago. They knew it too. It was a tense, angry crowd jostling around the door, as if whoever was first in line was going to get aboard no matter what was wrong. For the first time since she had worked for TWA, she was frightened.

"Well?"

Lana Lettieri picked up the microphone. "May I have your attention, please," she said. "Will anyone with a boarding pass for Seat Four-A come to the counter?"

Six men came to the counter.

Bradley Duncan sat in the captain's seat of the Lockheed 1011 scheduled to take off from Los Angeles to Washington in ten minutes. He couldn't believe what they were telling him. Abruptly he stood up, grabbed his cap and jammed it on his head, and walked back into the first-class section. He passed the rows of empty seats and reached the tourist-class section. The cabin crew was lounging against the bulkheads drinking coffee. The senior flight attendant shrugged her shoulders.

He left the airplane and walked out into the boarding area. The man at the counter shook his head.

It was the damnedest thing he'd ever seen. On the Wednesday evening before Thanksgiving, when every seat should have been taken, United had not a single passenger booked for this flight. Obviously, though, other flights were grossly overbooked, judging from the crowds milling around some of the other gates.

Reservations were handled by a computer system called LANCE, which was owned and operated by a computer company called Info Pro, which was in turn owned mostly by the airlines and some of the big travel agencies. Probably 95 percent of all airline tickets sold in the United States went through LANCE. Most of the major airlines used it to control reservations; some of them used it exclusively. Thousands of travel agents relied on it. Every day tens of thousands—and on the day before Thanksgiving hundreds of thousands—of people arrived at airports all over the country, depending on reservations that had been made through LANCE and were on record in its vast computer memory bank. A failure in LANCE would reduce the whole air-transportation industry to chaos. And from the look of what was going on here, LANCE had failed.

* * *

Two Atlanta police officers trotted ahead of two paramedics, opening a path for them. They had spent the past twenty minutes struggling to clear a way for the ambulance through the tangled traffic jam that blocked every road on and around the airport. Now they had to yell and push to get the paramedics and the stretcher through to the Delta gate. A furious mob milled in the lobbies and concourses. Men cursed. Women shrieked and wept. Babies cried. The situation was not much short of riot—which one of the officers reported to headquarters on his Handie-Talkie.

At the gate two airport policemen stood over a gray old man, who lay on his back on the floor. They had to guard him against people who would have stepped on him in their frenzy to push closer to the counter. The Atlanta officers shoved people aside and finally brought the paramedics to his side.

"What happened?" one of the officers asked a uniformed Delta gate agent.

The young man shook his head. "Reservations are fouled up. I mean, the whole airport, everybody, not just us. It's an unholy mess. And when I had to tell the old fellow it didn't look like he and his wife were going to make it to Philadelphia tonight and maybe not tomorrow. They were going to Philadelphia to spend Thanksgiving with their son and their grandchildren. When I told them, the old man started to yell and bang his fists on the counter. And then he just collapsed. Where have you guys been? He was alive . . . He—He's not now. I don't think."

"Where's his wife?"

The young man glanced at a woman sitting on a nearby chair, alone, under the pitiless white glare of fluorescent tubes. The elderly woman sat with her head down, her hands clasped before her on her lap. One woman, obviously a stranger, squatted before her and spoke gently with her.

"Somebody's responsible for this!" a woman shrieked. It was another woman, not the wife and not the one squatting before her; and it wasn't clear whether she was talking about the old man or about the breakdown of the reservations system. She yelled again: "Someone's responsible!"

The gate agent cringed, as if she had just accused *him* of being responsible, and he said to the policeman, "I *can* put a hundred seventy-eight people aboard this flight. When I quit counting, I had two hundred eighty-four boarding passes. I mean *boarding passes*, not just tickets. And a lot of these people have the idea they'll get on the plane if they just wave those boarding passes in my face and scream loud enough."

One of the paramedics rose. He spoke to the policeman. "He's gone," he said quietly. "Maybe if we could have gotten here sooner—but who knows?"

"We have to take care of his wife," said the officer. He nodded at the gate agent and, before he left him, muttered, "Good luck."

"I'm lucky I'm not at the gate for the New York flight," the agent said, though the policeman was moving toward the wife and did not hear him. "They've got three times as many people—and New Yorkers at that."

Joe Frobisher walked up to the ticket counter at British Air and bestowed a beaming, slightly inebriated smile on an exceptionally attractive young woman. "I've got," he said, "what I suppose is a sort of ridiculous question."

"Yes, sir?"

"Well . . . I came to Kennedy Airport to catch a flight for San Francisco, but the whole American air-travel system seems to be a shambles this evening. Not only that, you can't even get a cab back into town. So, might's well go home, I thought. I don't suppose there's the remotest chance you have a seat available for Heathrow?"

"What class, sir?"

"Whatever you've got available."

"Your choice, sir. We're taking off on schedule, with ninety-five passengers. The aircraft would have been full, but the American carriers aren't delivering the transfer passengers and are not likely to, anytime tonight. I can put you in any class you want. Window? Aisle?"

Joe Frobisher looked toward the windows of the terminal, where the drivers of two cars seemed to be engaged in a contest to see who could blow his horn loudest and longest. He shook his head. "The Americans seem to have got a real disaster on their hands, haven't they?"

"Their airlines-reservation computer system has broken down," said the young woman. "Their whole system has been reduced to chaos."

"So tell us about it," said Vance Reilly, the reporter for Channel 5, facing a portable camera his crew had managed to get into O'Hare International Airport, Chicago.

The young woman with the baby looked up resentfully at Vance, who never, ever managed to unglue his smile, then glanced at the television camera pointed at her. She sat on her suitcase. On the floor beside her was a big canvas bag filled with things for the baby.

"How long have you been here? How long do you expect to have to wait before your flight goes to—to where was it you said?"

"Minneapolis," she sighed. "I've been here since five o'clock, and I could be here this time tomorrow, so far as I can tell. You know, they don't tell anybody anything. Of course not. I'm just a lowly passenger, with a baby I'm trying to take care of, and they don't give a damn."

"You mean you haven't had much help from the airline?"

"Help? The airline won't give us the time of day. And, hey, here's what you can't get in this airport: You can't get a place to sit down. You can't get a meal. You can't get a cab or bus out of here. And you can't get to a telephone to call anybody and say you won't be where you're supposed to be when you're supposed to be there. You can't even get to a toilet."

"You live in Chicago?"

"Yes, I live in Chicago. I was taking my baby home for Thanksgiving. I mean, to see my mom and dad. Now . . . Jesus!"

As she began to sob, Vance Reilly reached out and touched her shoulder. "Hey," he said. "Channel Five is going to take care of you. The station van is parked outside. We'll be leaving in a few minutes. You can come with us."

He turned to face the camera, and the cameraman zoomed in on his face.

"So there's the human side of what's going on at O'Hare. It's pandemonium here. Bedlam. Once again, we're told that the whole reservations system has broken down, that some flights are hugely overbooked, some not booked at all, and . . . well, it's a complete mess. No one knows who's entitled to go on what flights. There've been fistfights at the gates. There are long lines for every service the airport tries to provide. I'm told that right now you would have to wait as long as four hours to get aboard a bus back to the center of the city. A cab? Forget it. Extra buses are being pressed into service, but no one knows when they'll be running. Ladies and gentlemen, let me repeat, if you know someone's here at the airport, don't try to come out and pick them up. You will only add to the traffic jam that is already the worst this airport has ever seen. Stay home. Don't come out here. It will all be straightened out in time. Vance . . . Reilly . . . at Chicago O'Hare, reporting for Channel Five."

An hour and a half after he had walked back through his Lockheed 1011 and confirmed what the cabin crew had been telling him, that he had no passengers, Captain Bradley Duncan was on the land line—that is the telephone, not the radio—talking to Los Angeles Flight Service Station, trying to file a new flight plan.

"I didn't have any passengers, then," he said irritably. "Not one."

He listened for a moment to the voice from the FSS.

"I know. But right now I've got a plane filling up with passengers who want to get to Washington. How soon?"

He listened.

"Are you telling me *your* system is screwed up?"

Tony Rojas stared at his computer terminal. He studied the list of flights using various routes between Washington and Cincinnati. He and his fellow controllers at Washington Center were responsible for routing air traffic through parts of four states and some of the busiest air routes in the nation. They assigned routes and then, on their radar scopes and with the aid of computers, they tracked flights, making sure the pilots did not deviate without permission. One of their chief responsibilities was keeping airplanes safely separated from each other in busy air space.

Rojas spoke into his microphone. "Sorry, Delta. I can't clear you direct. The best I can do is MRB-EKN-HNN-VVG." He was telling a Delta pilot he could not clear a flight direct from Washington National to Greater Cincinnati International, that the flight would have to fly a course marked by the radio-navigation stations at Martinsburg, Elkins, Henderson, and Cincinnati. "You've also got weather over the mountains and are going to need some altitude."

"That's a roundabout clearance, Center," said the Delta pilot.

"I am well aware of that. But you know what's going on. A thousand flight plans have been canceled tonight. Or amended at least. Nothing is flying where it's supposed to be, when it's supposed to be. Except air freight. For three hours nobody wants a clearance to fly anywhere. All of you are canceling. Suddenly you're getting your mess straightened out a bit, and you want immediate clearance on the most direct routes. A thousand flight plans were dumped out of those computers tonight, and a thousand new ones are going to have to go in. Hey, man! We're not equipped to do that in a short time. We have to think about safety. That's the best clearance I can give you."

Rojas cupped his hand over his earphone: an irrational, instinctive gesture, as if he could hear better that way.

The captain was not happy. As a professional pilot, he would not argue with air traffic control, but his frustration came through in his voice. "You mean *your* computers are fouled up too?"

"No. I don't think our computers are fouled up. Just overburdened right now. You taking this clearance, Captain? I've got a lot of other calls."

"There's a rumor that a virus got into LANCE. You sure it's not in your computers too?"

"We're not sure of anything, Captain. Are you accepting this clearance?"

A twin-engine turboprop took off from Macon, Georgia, at 7:35 P.M. The airplane and crew were ordinarily in commuter service, flying passengers to and from Atlanta. This evening twenty corporate executives who had been attending a meeting in Macon persuaded the commuter airline to fly them to Washington National as a charter flight, which would get them home—or within driving distance of home—before midnight.

Washington National was well within the range of the little airliner. It took off with a maximum load of passengers, baggage, and fuel. The two pilots had never flown the route before. The weather was marginal: overcast over most of the route, with snow falling at Raleigh and Richmond. Air traffic control routed the flight on a somewhat westerly course, to avoid the snowstorms. The flight course was Athens-Spartanburg-Greensboro-Lynchburg-Washington. At 9:08 P.M. the pilots radioed Washington that they were lost, in heavy weather, and declaring an emergency. They asked for radar vectors to Charlottesville. The controllers advised against Charlottesville, but the pilots insisted it was their closest big airport. Twelve minutes later the airplane disappeared from the radar screens.

Two networks interrupted their broadcasting to report what they called the first deaths caused by the computer disaster. That airplane, their reporters said, would not have been where it was, demanding that those pilots fly so far off their familiar routes— except that the regular air carriers were paralyzed by what one commentator called a computer freakout.

David Derval grabbed for a paper cup of coffee, but after staring into it for a moment put it aside distractedly. What he really needed was a drink. He was president of Info Pro, the company that owned and ran LANCE, and he was sure this was the worst day of his life.

"So that's it," said Hal Miller, maybe his best technician. "That's the story. It's working great right now, but it could go flooey again any minute."

Derval stood outside the glass wall that separated the control room from the computer room. They were always mysterious, the damned computers; they always were, in spite of all he knew about them, all he had done with them.

"It will take several days to be sure," said Miller glumly.

Derval touched his clasped hands to his mouth. "I thought we were secure," he muttered.

"Nobody is secure," said Miller. "Particularly against what invaded us. Whoever did this is a genius, Mr. Derval. This is no ordinary hacker's virus, and this virus didn't get in by accident. This thing was specifically developed to do what it's done to LANCE. It's been hiding in the system for three or four months, I'd guess, screwing up reservations for November twenty-first and waiting for that date before showing itself."

"It's sabotage," said Derval. "Industrial sabotage."

"We can clean the system," said Miller. "We can put a vaccine in it—you know, a program that will detect viruses and head them off before they get into the computer. I think we can fend off another attack. But first we've got to get it clean. First we have to know exactly what we're up against. Every last bite of virus code has to come out. Then . . ."

Derval sighed and shook his head. "The man we need is Scott Vandenberg," he said. "I'd give anything to have him here right now. I wonder where Scott Vandenberg is tonight—where I could reach him."

"I'd like to have Commander Vandenberg on this job, sir," said Miller. "I'd feel a lot more confident of everything if we could get in touch with him. I don't know of anybody who'd be more help to us with this mess."

"I'll get on the phone and try to find him," said Derval.

At the curb in front of the TWA terminal at Kennedy Airport, Scott Vandenberg signed the chit for the limousine and handed the chatty driver an extra twenty dollars: what he had promised if the man got him from midtown Manhattan to Kennedy by 7:30 on this worst traffic day of the year. Traffic into the major airports was bad enough on the evening before Thanksgiving, but tonight coming into Kennedy was even worse than he had expected—more confused, the drivers impatient.

"You want me to wait a minute?"

Scott glanced around. He saw what the driver meant: The crowd in the terminal was dense and loud even beyond what Thanksgiving Wednesday ought to generate. He had seen the same thing in the other airline terminals they had passed, and obviously the driver had noticed too. All the terminals were chaotic. He had read somewhere that more than seven million Americans would travel by air on this holiday, but even that didn't explain the crush in these terminals.

"I'm tempted to go back into town and take a hotel room," Vandenberg said. "But—"

"Like you said, you've got a date tonight, that romantic late supper in L.A, with that girl you said was—what'd you say? 'Somethin' else?' Yeah, somethin' *else*."

Vandenberg nodded. "Well, if flights aren't running on time, I can always duck into the Ambassador Club and soothe my nerves at the bar while I wait."

"Good luck, then," said the driver. "I'm afraid you're gonna need it."

Before he walked into the terminal, Vandenberg stood outside for a moment and looked at the sky. Something else looked odd: No planes were taking off. Except there went British Air, a 747 lifting off for London.

He picked up his bag and briefcase and walked into the terminal.

Crowded. Yes, crowded but crowded with angry people: red-faced businessmen, their jaws rigid, their eyes glaring; furious women, some crying. A solid mob surrounded the ticket counter. The television monitors that should have been displaying arrivals and departures were blank.

Vandenberg stood for a moment just inside the door, sorry now that he had let the limo go. Obviously his flight wasn't leaving, not anytime soon anyway; and it was going to be difficult even to find out why.

"Hey, uh . . ." He managed to get the attention of a white-haired, bespectacled man in a business suit and overcoat, carrying a briefcase and traveling bag: another business traveler, maybe willing to talk. "What's going on, you mind telling me?"

The man lowered his bag to the floor. "For three weeks," he said, keeping his anger barely under control, "I've had a confirmed reservation for L.A., first class. Now they tell me they're overbooked. Not just overbooked. They've issued four boarding passes for my seat. The flight is overbooked by two hundred seats!"

Vandenberg glanced up at the blank monitors. "Not just your flight, huh?"

"All flights," the man said dully, his shoulders sagging. "And not just TWA. I thought I'd try United." He shook his head. "Same thing. They say the computer system is fouled up. Fouled up. Right. Another goddamned computer screw-up. You can't trust the damned things to do anything right."

Vandenberg nodded. A computer problem. If reservations were fouled up, the problem had to be with LANCE. Something was wrong with LANCE. A plane overbooked by two hundred seats? Four boarding passes for the same seat? That wasn't just a breakdown. The LANCE computer hadn't failed. It was running, but it was running wild, generating spurious reservations.

Scott Vandenberg knew what that meant. He was president of his own small company offering consulting services in the field of computer security, and he was a prominent authority on computer viruses. He knew the symptoms of a virus as well as anyone in the country knew them, and he would have bet a million dollars LANCE was infected with a virus.

He looked at the bank of telephones. People were jammed around them, twenty deep, waiting to place calls to tell families they would probably not be home for Thanksgiving after all. Vandenberg shouldered his way as best he could through the crowd to the locked door of the Ambassador Club. He used his card and went in. Confusion and anger dominated here, too, in what was usually a calm refuge in a busy airport. He ordered a Scotch at the bar and sipped it while he waited for a telephone. Eventually he got a phone and punched in a number from his pocket calendar.

"Info Pro."

"I need to talk to Dave Derval. Tell him Scott Vandenberg's calling."

"Mr. Derval is not available, sir."

"I think if you give him my name, he'll make himself available. Please. Tell him Scott Vandenberg is on the line."

After a minute Derval came on. "Scott," he sighed. "A godsend. I've called your office, your home. Where are you?"

"Kennedy."

"Hey, you're the man I need. I mean, I'm desperate, Scott. You got any idea what a mess we've got on our hands?"

"I'm looking at evidence of it all around me," said Vandenberg. "I'd guess you've been hit with a virus."

"God, have we ever! The system went crazy this afternoon! It's gotta be a virus. The computer didn't put out garbage. It issued real tickets and boarding passes—I mean, ones that looked real, but there were no reservations behind them. It confirmed reservations. I mean, it confirmed reservations that never existed. It put people on the wrong flights! It—"

"That's a virus at work," said Vandenberg. "I feel certain that's what it is."

"That's what Hal Miller says. I thought he was crazy at first, considering our security. But, yeah. I know you're right. This kind of foulup isn't just failure somewhere in the system. Hey, the system *hasn't* failed! I mean, the hardware hasn't. Or the program either, mostly. The damned computer is running, looking normal. But ninety-five percent of what it's putting out is . . . is imaginary. False. Scott, it has fouled up millions of reservations! Can you imagine what this is costing the airlines? And hey! The airline companies are my stockholders!"

"Is it back to normal now?" asked Vandenberg.

"For the moment," said Derval wearily. "Look, could you come out here? I mean, right now?"

"Doubtful . . ."

"Listen, we need you here, Scott. I mean, we need you in the worst possible way."

"I doubt I could do you any good tonight, Dave."

"Listen, Scott. If we've been hit by a virus, maybe it's because the man who made the virus has some grudge against Info Pro. We don't know. We don't know who he is. Maybe he's a guy who wants to launch a competing system. Or maybe he hates Thanksgiving. But maybe . . . just maybe, he's hit air traffic control too. We could be dealing with a crazy, a terrorist. What if there's a virus in the ATC computers?"

"Well—"

"*Think about it.* We haven't got a breakdown here. We've

got a system mishandling information. A damned sophisticated virus. It kept itself hidden for god knows how long, at least eight weeks—from late summer, when people began to make their reservations for Thanksgiving travel—while all that time it was screwing up airline reservations. How can anybody be sure there's not another one hidden in the ATC computers? In fact, they're having trouble. And they're right across the road from us, you know. New York Center is right here in Ronkonkoma. Scott, I think you ought to get out here as fast as you can. Look at what we've got. Look at the ATC machinery too. I'm facing possible bankruptcy here. But across the road we could be looking at a catastrophe: a virus that causes a midair collision. Planes are starting to fly again—"

"You're making assumptions, Dave," Vandenberg interrupted.

"Yeah," Derval admitted with an audible sigh. "But are you going to tell me it's impossible? All you have to do is read the newspapers to know about attempts to put viruses in Defense Department computers—"

"Dave—"

"Man, I *need* you! Anyway you're not going anywhere by airline tonight."

"Okay," Vandenberg conceded. "I won't get to California tonight anyway. But I don't know how I'm going to get to Ronkonkoma either. You can't get a cab out of Kennedy."

The voice on the other end of the telephone line broke into a bitter laugh. "Hell, Scott, we'll send a chopper for you. Tell me where you are. We'll have no end of cooperation in getting Scott Vandenberg out here to work on straightening out this mess."

Since he had a while to wait and since he still had the telephone, he placed another call, to Bethesda. Sally, his ex-wife, now remarried, answered the telephone. Scott spoke with her for a moment, then asked to speak to Judy, their seven-year-old daughter. Sally was good about his calls to Judy; she never raised any objection to his calling as often as he wanted to; and shortly Judy was on the line.

"Honey? This is Daddy. How are you? Well . . . I'm not going to be home for Thanksgiving, as I told you, so I won't be seeing you this weekend. I was on my way to California for Thanksgiving, but Mommy says you've all been watching television and know about the mess at the airports. Well, I'm in a big airport in New York. No, I won't have to stay here all night. Somebody's sending a helicopter for me. Okay. Okay, honey. Sure. I'll be back in Bethesda next weekend, for sure. I'll pick you up. It'll be time for us to do a little Christmas shopping, won't it? Sure we will. Mommy's doing what? I bet she is, and I bet Grandma's sitting in the kitchen watching, making sure she's doing it right. Right? Well, okay. You have a nice Thanksgiving. I'll see you next Saturday. I love you, Judy. I know you do. So, okay. Bye-bye for now. Bye, hon. Bye . . ."

A twinge of regret seized him as he put down the phone. For what he'd lost. Judy. Even Sally. It hadn't been such a bad marriage after all. He carried his empty glass back to the bar and shoved it at the bartender with a nod, meaning pour another Scotch and soda.

Virgilio Cordero sat in a long, heavy black Lincoln in the parking lot at Houston International Airport. It was the middle car of three almost-identical limousines. The other two were his protection.

He was on the telephone, speaking English: "I don't know. Apparently it may be a very long time. I may decide not to fly tonight. I haven't decided yet. But there is something very interesting going on, and I'd be grateful if you would check into it for me."

As he listened to the voice on the other end of the telephone connection, Cordero sipped chilled champagne. He winked at Patricia and glanced appreciatively at the sleek legs exposed by her miniskirt.

"That was my thought too," he said, once more focusing his attention on the telephone conversation. "Obviously this astounding mess has been caused by someone's intervention in the reservations computer system. Breakdown is one thing. Generating hundreds of thousands of false reservations, with boarding passes, is quite another. Hmm? Yes, right. The false reservations are all for real people, whose reservations have been switched around from flight to flight, airline to airline, and—well, all these people are at the airports, expecting to fly and—Hmm? Right. The work of a computer genius. I've spoken with Avianca—you know, the Colombian national airline—and they're getting the word from the various American airlines that it's a virus. No ordinary hacker wrote it. If we could identify that genius and get him to work for us . . . Okay? Let me know what you find out. As soon as possible. This could be very important, Yo. It could be the key."

Patricia had been waiting for Cordero to put down the telephone. She nodded toward a man standing outside waiting for a chance to talk. Cordero ran down the window.

"You have two choices, sir," the man said, bending down to speak through the window. "One, we can fly the Lear. We'll have to make a refueling stop, maybe two. Or you can use the reservations. They're saying they think they can get the flight out of here in an hour. We've located two of the people who claim your seats and we've paid them off. The airline's cooperating with us on that. We ought to have your seats clear of other claims in very short order."

"An hour—"

"Actually," the man said, "it will take an hour to get the necessary clearances for the Lear. The air-traffic-control system is fouled up too."

Cordero nodded. "That, too, hmm? So—"

"Anyway, the airline people really think they can take off in an hour. Nonstop to Bogotá. I think I'd recommend that, sir."

Cordero shrugged. "Fix it," he said curtly.

The man who had been on the other end of Cordero's telephone conversation was Yoshitaka Hara, in Las Vegas. He lived in a comfortable suite in The Sands Hotel—a convenient address for his two avocations: casino gambling and the appreciation of pretty girls. He practiced his vocation from the same suite. The second bedroom was crowded with computer equipment. Hara was a systems designer, a recognized master of computer architecture, languages, and programs. He designed, for example, the computer-controlled routing and switching program for America-Wide Telecommunications, also the computer-augmented inertial guidance system for the Aero 12, the first big jet airliner to be manufactured in Japan.

Unknown except to a few confidants, was his work with computer viruses. His most profitable virus so far was the one that had destroyed UpWrite.

His client, which had paid him a generous fee for his work, was Sig/Writer, Inc., proprietor of a market-dominating word processor called Sig/Writer. That word processor had become, within three years of its introduction, the system of choice in tens of thousands of businesses that relied heavily on word processors, the programs that had made typewriters obsolete. It was the single most widely used software program in the world when, late in 1988, a new word processor called UpWrite threatened its position.

UpWrite was in beta testing when Sig/Writer heard about it. That meant it was being tried by a few selected users outside the company, to see how they would react to it. The reports from beta testing were uniformly enthusiastic. UpWrite was easier to learn, matched all Sig/Writer features, was less demanding of the limited memory available in a desktop computer, and would sell for at least a hundred dollars less than the base price for Sig/Writer.

Sig/Writer employed Yoshitaka Hara to sabotage UpWrite.

For Hara this was not difficult. He obtained a beta-test version of UpWrite and wrote a virus. It was an ingeniously elusive virus, doing its dirty work only intermittently, which made it almost impossible to track. Like the virus Darius Whitney had written for LANCE, the Hara virus for UpWrite was time-oriented. Whitney's virus had been working in background for a long time but spewed its accumulated false information only on November 21. Hara's virus for UpWrite worked on selected hours on selected days; and, having done its damage, retreated into hiding.

What it did was garble the documents—letters, memoranda, contracts, leases, deeds, legal briefs, chapters of novels, whatever—that UpWrite users created. It didn't do it to every document. That would have been too easy. It did it to occasional documents. Users couldn't cope with random destruction.

Like Whitney sending out the LANCE virus, Hara used a Trojan horse. He offered a useful little program, free, to users of three major electronic-message services, known as computer bulletin boards. Thousands of computer users picked off this intriguing little program and put it in their computers. So doing, they propagated

Hara's virus. It spread everywhere, into every computer that used the major bulletin boards and from them into the computers of everyone who shared software.

And it waited there, waiting for UpWrite. The virus infected no other program. But from time to time it queried its host computer.

HAS YOUR OWNER ADDED UPWRITE?

If the answer was no, the virus lay quiescent. If yes, the virus infected UpWrite.

Every buyer loved UpWrite at first. Then it garbled a document. Then another. Irretrievably.

By the time the developers of UpWrite identified the problem and sent out assurances that they could vaccinate their program, it was dead on the market. Bankruptcy.

Yoshitaka Hara accepted a fee of one million dollars for killing UpWrite.

Sitting in his suite in Las Vegas watching the television news accounts of the LANCE debacle, Hara recognized the hand of a brilliant system designer. He remembered the speech Darius Whitney had made about what viruses could do. Whitney? Could it be? But if not, who else?

How would he find out? Maybe it would not be insuperably difficult.

"What do you suppose happened to that charter flight?"

Allison watched Darius, anxious to see his reaction to the question she had contained as long as she could. His attention was fixed on tying a tiny knot in a nylon thread that represented a line in the rigging of the ship model he was building—had been building for as long as she had known him. It was a model of HMS *Victory*, Nelson's flagship at Trafalgar. He had paid $750 for the kit he was using. The hull was not carved from a piece of wood, certainly not from balsa, but was built up, just like the real ship, with ribs and planking. It was almost four feet long, and the masts stood four feet above the model deck. She understood that the ship was his relief from digital mathematics and computers.

"Allison," he said. "If you insist on leaving the television on while you are finishing our Thanksgiving Eve dinner and while I am trying to tie a tiny knot—"

"Well, what caused the crash?"

Darius frowned and spoke gently. "Allison, you and I didn't cause that airplane crash. The reporter says an old man died at Atlanta after finding out he couldn't get on his flight. We didn't cause that either. Are we responsible if an old man so badly lost his temper as to drive up his blood pressure? Are we responsible if some businessmen pressured pilots into flying where they weren't competent to fly, in weather they weren't competent to handle?"

"Pilot error," she said.

He nodded. "So it would appear."

Allison shrugged and returned to her work in the kitchen. Darius, though he pretended he wasn't, was watching the broadcast with intense interest. She could see that he didn't like what he'd heard: that an airplane was down in the Virginia mountains. They had talked and talked about this possibility. And—

No. It wasn't possible. It wasn't their responsibility. They had fouled up the airlines' reservations. They were not responsible if somebody was killed trying to drive where he would have flown, or if somebody used a charter flight with pilots who couldn't . . .

Allison frowned over her preparations for their Thanksgiving Eve dinner. Pilot error. Let's hope that's what it was, she thought. Let's pray that's what it was.

She liked Darius better as he was now: not wearing one of his business suits but looking younger in a pair of well-worn and well-faded blue jeans and a gray sweatshirt. He carried his years better this way. When he was away from the company office and all its petty distractions, he was more the man she thought he was.

Darius Whitney was a great man. She was convinced of it. She was troubled by what the two of them had done with the LANCE virus—as, thank God, he was too—but this man's gift, properly channeled and freed from the organizational pettiness of a company or a campus, could really change the world. She believed that. Her own career had shown much promise but had been stuck dead center by an unhappy marriage and—well, by a lot of things, never mind. The best thing she had done, maybe, was apprentice herself to this man. She was entirely capable of making a good judgment—she had no doubt of that—and she had no doubt she had made one.

If only she could get him to forget Whitney Data Dynamics and work here. His home was a dream laboratory, a clutter of hardware and software for which he didn't have to answer to anyone. Every month he received a score of programs to review, and the disks and manuals were piled everywhere. He got around to trying maybe 20 percent of them, and he sent letters to the creators of maybe 2 percent of them. If he would only charge consulting fees to the people who sent him work for comment, he would easily replace what the company paid him.

But he was an angry man—which in itself was a part of his attraction actually. He did not suffer fools gladly, and he didn't accept injury in the team spirit.

Lately she had taken to patting his shoulder, squeezing his arm, giving him a few signs of the affection she felt for him. Usually he had been distracted and seemed hardly to notice. Occasionally he had put his hand on hers. Maybe, very slowly, they were developing something beyond colleagueship, even beyond friendship.

The Ronkonkoma computer center from which Info Pro operated LANCE was big and state-of-the-art sophisticated, but it was the usual thing and not terribly interesting to a man who had seen most of the computer centers of the western world.

"Commander! Glad to see you!"

Scott Vandenberg had all but forgotten that Hal Miller worked for Info Pro, even though he had himself sent him to Dave Derval with a letter of introduction and recommendation. Chief Petty Officer Harold Miller, an old navy man, one of the last people in the world who would still call Scott commander. Well, it was good to see him.

"What you got, Chief? Virus?"

Miller shook his head. "Well, sir, you know sophisticated viruses as well as anybody in the world. You know what they sometimes do. The last element in a really tough virus is sometimes the erase command. And this one erased itself, so far as I can

35

figure. I can't find it. I'd say it did its dirty work, then erased itself so that we couldn't find it. Figures, wouldn't you say?"

"What checks have you done?" asked Vandenberg.

Miller glanced around. Others were watching, trying to hear this exchange between the rough-hewn Hal Miller and the celebrated Commander Vandenberg that Hal was always talking about.

Scott Vandenberg lived up to his billing. He had been a Navy fighter pilot until five years or so ago. He was tall and undeniably handsome, and he had a sort of easy, confident presence that seemed appropriate to what they had heard of him. Vandenberg was in his mid-forties, with gray hair along his temples and tangles of lines around his eyes and mouth.

"They've been running test routines," Hal Miller said. "An hour ago they loaded a thousand simulated reservations and ran them to see if they would be handled accurately. Of course the system's working fine now. What I've been doing, when I can get a hand on the machines, is run byte comparisons—you know, compare the number of characters in each phase of the operating program against what is supposed to be in there. So far I've found just eight extra bytes—I mean, eight unexpected characters."

"The erase command," said Vandenberg.

"I suppose so, though I haven't had a chance to look at it. The virus had to be a big son of a bitch to do what it did today. We could have detected it if we'd looked. Anyway it's gone now. It erased itself, leaving nothing behind but the command to erase."

Vandenberg had no doubt the virus was gone, if Miller said so. He could vouch for his competence. On the carrier *Constellation*, if Chief Petty Officer Miller told you something had been checked, it had been *checked*.

"How did the virus get in?" asked Vandenberg.

"That's the question," said Miller. "That and how do we stop it from getting in again? I thought we had pretty tight security."

"There's a hole," said Vandenberg.

Miller grinned. "Commander, I hope they're not paying you a big consulting fee to tell us that. Dave Derval's a company president and may have to pay you to cover his ass, but I'm a lowly technician and hope for more."

Vandenberg laughed. "They haven't told me yet what I'm

going to be paid for this night's work," he said to Miller and to Derval, who was now standing beside them. "But I've got a question. The virus erased itself, I suppose. But do you think it's been overwritten?"

"Overwritten?"

"If it erased itself quick and dirty, it may still be on a disk somewhere. I'd like to see it. It may have a signature."

Miller nodded. He spoke to Derval. "We need to shut off every other test and not try to put the system back on line for at least three hours," he said. "What the commander suggests is just possible."

Derval shrugged wearily. "You guys can have it," he said.

"You understand what I'm saying?" asked Vandenberg. "Even though the virus erased itself, it may only have erased itself in terms of accessibility. What really happens in an erase routine is that the erased stuff is left in a sort of limbo on the disk, and it stays there until the computer needs that disk space and writes something else over it. The chief difference between erased bytes and nonerased bytes is that nonerased bytes can't be written over, and erased bytes can. They may still be lying on what we might call the waste can of a disk. The system can't call them out and use them because they've been stripped of accessibility. But the actual bytes may be in there somewhere. You might compare it to pulling something from a file cabinet and tossing it in a waste can. You can't readily find it because it's not filed anymore. On the other hand, until the waste can is emptied, the stuff is still in your office, and you really can go get it if you are willing to poke through the trash. If we poke around in your program files, we may find your virus. We may be able to reconstruct it and take a look at it."

"And the advantage of that is—?"

"The man or woman who wrote this virus is no hacker," said Vandenberg. "And incidentally I wish we didn't use the word *hacker* the way we do these days. A hacker is a competent programmer, not some kid or some crook who uses his expertise to break into other people's programs and do dirt. Anyway this virus has to be top-gun stuff. The people who write this kind of program code are no dummies and no amateurs. But what's important is that most of them leave their signatures on their work. I'm talking about ways they solve problems, the choices they make for getting through a program maze. This programmer may have signed this virus like a check."

"If I get my hands on him, he'll never sign another check," said Derval.

"Okay, then let's talk about why," said Vandenberg. "Why'd he foul you up? If you don't get a blackmail demand, then what did he have in mind? I'd look for that, Dave. How much is he going to demand not to do it to you again? If you don't get a blackmail demand, you're in worse trouble. Then we're up against a nut."

Derval's already flushed face reddened even more. "Nut? What kind of nut? Oh, yeah. I'm the one who mentioned terrorists. God, Scott, could—?"

"Hal can look into the system," said Vandenberg. "You've got me worried about the air-traffic-control computers in New York Center. Since that's here in Ronkonkoma too, just across the road, let's go over and see what's going on."

Across the road the Federal Aviation Agency operated New York Center, the air-traffic-control command post for the busiest air corridors in the world, on computers far less modern and sophisticated than those on which Info Pro managed reservations. Controllers at scores of radar scopes observed—or on a normal night observed—hundreds of airline flights, plus the flight of air-cargo carriers, air couriers, business jets, and small private planes: whatever was in the air. Flight plans for most of these aircraft were in the computers, so controllers could call up the points of origin and destination, the assigned routes, and a mass of other information about every one of these flights.

New York Center was of course linked to Boston Center, Cleveland Center, Washington Center, and every other control center in the United States; and flights were constantly passed along from one center to another, the airplane always remaining on someone's scope, always in radio contact with one controller or another.

Scott stood for a long moment behind a young woman at a scope about twenty-four inches in diameter. It was set only a few degrees off horizontal—tipped just slightly toward her—in a hexagonal desk that also contained the keyboard that controlled her communications. Glowing lights on a console above the scope kept her informed of various conditions in her equipment and in the air environment she was controlling. She spoke quietly into the seed microphone on her headset, listened for responses, and spoke again.

Restful tones of brown and beige surrounded her, together with a light level that facilitated her view of the shifting green and white pattern on her scope. She was separated from other controllers by acoustic panels.

She looked up for an instant. "LaGuardia departures," she said to Scott.

Dozens of others at dozens of other scopes watched and controlled segments of the approaches from every quadrant, into the chief airports in the New York area.

Oddly the computer hardware here was not state-of-the-art. It was federal property, bought from tax moneys, and presidents and Congress had seen fit to skimp on FAA budgets over the years. What they were running here was slow and inflexible, compared with what Info Pro was running across the road. It was an irony that the computers responsible for flight safety and therefore human lives were not as good as the ones responsible for making reservations.

"Commander Vandenberg," said Leighton Drake, the senior man on duty in New York Center. The senior man would have been on duty that night in any case, it being a special night; but Drake was the most senior man at this center. "I'm happy to have you here."

Drake was a gray man: gray hair, gray complexion, gray eyes, gray necktie, gray suit. He was intelligent and competent, but if he had ever possessed any spirit of enterprise, it had been remorselessly crushed by the federal civil service.

"Trouble?"

"Well, our system is overburdened. Scores of new flight plans are being filed every five minutes. But so far as we can tell, we haven't been invaded by a virus."

Dave Derval, who had come with Vandenberg, shook his

3

Doctor Osami Isoroku reached for the last bite of his Big Mac. His left hand fumbled for the paper container. His right continued to touch keys, tentatively, as he stared at the screen and watched the rotating image of a herpes simplex virus. His work was in what he called *real* viruses, the biological ones that killed. He knew about the renegade computer programs called viruses, but that was something different, outside his field. Well, not entirely, since he did work with computers. But outside his cognizance. Computer viruses were playthings for vandals.

What he was staring at was not really a virus but a sort of schematic diagram of one, created by a program he had developed over the past seventeen months and built into Stanford University's huge Cray computer, one of the most powerful computers in the world. A real virus looked nothing like this tangle of points and lines.

Information about actual virus reactions to varying conditions had been incorporated in the program, so that very often the diagram would react as the actual virus did. Suppose you wanted to know how a virus would react to a temperature of 50 degrees Celsius in an atmosphere of pure oxygen. You gave the computer the code for those two conditions, and the schematic of the virus changed. This virus diagram, when those conditions of heat and oxygen were introduced, gradually broke down into a noninte-grated jumble.

41

The exciting thing was that a real herpes simplex virus of this particular type reacted exactly as the computer simulation predicted.

As more and more data were fed in, the computer improved in its ability to predict changes in a virus subjected to an all-but-infinite number of conditions. Months of tests and electron-microscope studies could be duplicated in an hour. No one was yet ready to say that laboratory tests could be omitted; but the computer-generated predictions had proved sufficiently reliable to suggest that certain research paths were more likely to be worthwhile than others.

He touched some keys and restored the diagram. What if the temperature were 40° Celsius? He entered the code for 40°, then the code for oxygen.

The diagram of the virus swiftly disintegrated. Isoroku gaped. The reaction was much too fast. Something was wrong.

More than wrong. The image of the virus disappeared entirely. A message appeared on the screen:

```
DOCTOR DOCTOR! WE BEG YOU TO STOP THESE IN-
SANE EXPERIMENTS! YOU ARE TOYING WITH THE
SECRETS OF LIFE ITSELF! THERE ARE SOME
THINGS MAN WAS NOT MEANT TO KNOW! ANYWAY, DID
YOU THINK US VIRUSES COULDN'T PROTECT OUR-
SELVES?
```

Isoroku attacked the keyboard frantically. He tried to back out of his program, to restart it. That required the entry of an access code, his personal numbers that gave him access to all of Stanford University's computers. In response to his code the computer responded:

```
GOODBYE ISOROKU
```

Osami Isoroku collapsed in tears over his keyboard. A virus. The other kind. The kind that could destroy years of work as surely as real viruses could destroy life. Who? And why?

* * *

With Major General Samuel Warden standing behind him, critically watching his every move, Sergeant Richard Mallory felt anything but comfortable. He glanced over his shoulder, to signify to the general that the computer was ready and that he was ready to receive the general's command.

"Have you had any conversation with Commander Scott Vandenberg?" the general asked curtly.

"No, sir. I don't believe I've ever heard the name. Should I?"

"He tells us our security isn't good enough," said the general. "A smart ass, I figure. I don't know who asked him. I'm damned sure *I* didn't. And I better not hear of any of our personnel talking to him."

"Understood, sir," said Sergeant Mallory.

"I want AMRAT," said the general curtly.

That was the code name for a highly sensitive computer database, containing information about personnel security clearances. It was accessible only to people with high-order clearances themselves.

"Yes, sir."

Sergeant Mallory typed the acronym:

AMRAT

The computer responded:

NO SUCH DATABASE AS AMRAT. ENTER YOUR DES-
IGNATOR.

AMRAT

NO SUCH DATABASE AS AMRAT. ENTER YOUR DES-
IGNATOR.

OPEN AMRAT NOW

YOU ARE IN COMMUNICATION WITH AMRAT-ACCESS
CODE, PLEASE

43

Sergeant Mallory looked up at General Warden. Both of them had access codes, and the question was which one to use. The general's represented a higher level of clearance. He could see files the sergeant would be denied.

"Tell it 242-28-7348," grunted the general. It was the general's code.

```
242-28-7348
```

```
ILLEGAL ACCESS CODE, ABORTING
```

"Type 'sparrow,' " said the general.

Sergeant Mallory did. The word did not appear on the screen, which told him the system had not aborted and he remained in command. The computer would match the word with the access code.

```
TIME PLEASE
```

"443-15-6654," said the general. That was the code for the day. It was changed every day, sometimes more often.

Mallory typed.

ACCESS ESTABLISHED appeared on the screen. Then— QUERY?

"Type 'Monckton,' " said the general.

Sergeant Mallory typed the word and transmitted it to the computer.

The computer replied—no, the virus replied:

GOOFUS WAS HERE!

HO-HO YOUR FANCY SECURITY!

Mary McIntyre, a secretary in a major Wall Street law firm, yawned and twisted her shoulders as she waited for the computer to do its internal checks and load its programs. The computer on her desk was an IBM PC-AT, something of a veteran and yet a friendly, reliable machine with which she had learned to be confident and comfortable. She hadn't the remotest notion of how it worked, in the mathematical sense; but she had thoroughly mastered the programs the firm expected her to run and she had come to think of the computer as an indispensable tool. An exciting tool, with potential she would like to explore further when she had the time.

"I don't know how we ever functioned without the damned things," her boss had said the other day.

And that was amusing, because he had angrily opposed the computerization of the firm.

So had she. She had been afraid she would never ever learn to use a computer. Now she was proud of how well she *had* learned.

She glanced at the screen. The machine had finished its internal tests, apparently was satisfied with itself, and was now executing a program called autoexec.bat—computerese for a program that was automatically executed every time the computer was first turned on, to load working programs and set the computer up for the day's chores.

Mary took a sip from the mug of coffee she had brought to her desk. A few days ago one of the secretaries in the real estate department had spilled coffee on the keyboard of an IBM-AT computer. Oddly enough, no harm seemed to have been done.

Her computer beeped. It had finished the autoexec routine and was ready to go to work.

She tapped a couple of keys and displayed the day's calendar in glowing green. Someone had added a 10:30 AM appointment overnight. They could do that. Mr. Collins's partners could call up his calendar, see what time he had free, and put appointments—*requests* for appointments actually—on his calendar.

Then she took a look at the internal memoranda file. As she expected, Mr. DiFelice had transmitted a memorandum to Mr. Collins explaining why he had set up the 10:30 appointment and asking for confirmation. She punched a couple of keys, and the printer on her credenza printed that memorandum so she could put it on Mr. Collins's desk.

So much for preliminaries. Her first real job this morning was to try to recover some documents from the Barnes litigation file. The documentation for that case—thousands of pages in paper form—was stored electronically in a litigation-support library. Because the documentation was stored in electronic form, she could perform searches in it, looking for the documents relating to specific issues in the lawsuit.

Yesterday Mr. Collins had listened to the deposition testimony of Daniel Barnes, who had testified he had never met a man called Douglas Kinney. Mr. Collins thought he recalled a letter or memorandum in which Barnes had spoken of playing golf with Douglas Kinney. Obviously no one had indexed the letters and memoranda in this litigation library by the names of golfing partners; but because the computer could search the file for words and combinations of words, it could find the document Mr. Collins thought he remembered—if there were such a document.

What she would do was tell the computer to go through the library, looking for any document that used the name *Kinney* and the word *golf*. It was a task that would have taken many hours to do manually. The computer would report results in less than two minutes.

Mary called up the search program. Then she typed in the name of the library she wanted to search—the Barnes litigation file. Finally she typed the search.

For a moment the screen showed nothing but the search, as she expected. Then it filled with a gaudy green pattern, and in the center of that pattern appeared a single oversized word:

GOTCHA!

She frowned. She had never seen anything like it before. What could it mean? She waited for a moment, then tried to key in a command. Nothing. The computer did not respond. The keyboard was locked out. She pressed the Esc key—meaning, escape. Nothing. Then she simultaneously pressed Ctrl and Break. That invariably interrupted whatever the computer was doing and returned it to the operator's control. Still nothing.

She pressed Ctrl-Alt-Del, the signal to reboot—meaning the computer would unload all programs and go through the autoexec program again. Still nothing. The keyboard was locked out. Its signals were not reaching the computer.

Then the gaudy pattern disappeared from the screen, and an ominous message appeared:

`GENERAL SYSTEM FAILURE`

An hour later a very distressed Mary McIntyre was assured that she had not caused—had in no sense whatever caused—the disaster that had fallen on the law firm of Rowlandson, Patton, Collins, Sheen & Krupp. She had only seen the first manifestation of it. Within minutes everyone else in the firm who was using a computer had seen evidence of the dimensions of the catastrophe.

Every word of data maintained by the firm in electronic memory had been erased—litigation libraries, files of correspondence and memoranda, accounting records, telephone directories, calendars, everything. Every bit of operating software was gone—word processors, spreadsheet programs, accounting programs, search programs, desk organizers, everything.

It was as though one hundred desktop computers had been subjected to radical brain surgery. They remembered nothing. They knew how to do nothing.

In technical terms, all the firm's hard disks had been erased. All the electronic memory, in one hundred computers, was blank.

The computer-hackers' cliché was that hardware without software was good only for anchoring boats. In the law firm of Rowlandson, Patton, Collins, Sheen & Krupp, on Tuesday afternoon, there were no computers—only anchors.

"What the hell's going on here?" Dudley Collins demanded of the sweating office manager.

"It's a virus, Mr. Collins. We've been hit with a virus."

"What the hell's a virus, and who hit us with it?" asked the flush-faced lawyer.

* * *

Osami Isoroku's program was not lost. He was the victim of a practical joke by a pair of graduate students at M.I.T.—friends of his, actually, with whom he had created half a dozen droll computer viruses in years past. Having played its cruel joke, the computer virus disappeared without a trace and without having done the slightest harm to Isoroku's work or anyone else's—just as Isoroku's own viruses had done.

Until the two from M.I.T. bragged of their exploit, Isoroku's department was inclined to think he had suffered a delusion brought on by too-late hours and too little nourishment. Then everyone began to worry about how the virus had gotten in. The professors detested the idea of calling in an outside expert to look into the problem. That implied an admission they didn't want to make. After hours of argument, a small majority voted to ask for a few hours' consulting time from Scott Vandenberg & Associates. Vandenberg charged only for two hours' time to clean their system and establish safeguards against future invasions.

Four days after the GOOFUS incident at the National Security Agency, the technicians had to report that they could find no trace of the virus that had displayed the impudent message. No data had been destroyed. No program had been tampered with—so far as anyone could tell. The virus had erased itself, they supposed.

Not so. A week later, while a general and an admiral were staring at a diagram of the trajectory of a Soviet rocket that had been fired from a site on Lake Balkhash, the trajectory disappeared and a smiley-face grinned at them from the center of the screen.

A moment later the smiley-face disappeared and the diagram returned.

The brazen little face continued to appear, here and there, now and again, sometimes every hour, sometimes not for a whole day. No one could find the virus that caused it, but the intermittent appearance of the face was proof that the virus was somewhere in the NSA computers, cleverly hidden. That it had done no harm so far—beyond mocking the agency and its technicians—was not evidence that it wouldn't someday.

Worse, no one could discover how the virus got in. Or how to prevent invasion by another one.

The National Security Agency did what any government agency would do in the circumstances. It denied that any virus had ever invaded its computers. Officially no virus had infected the computers of the NSA. When a congressional oversight committee learned that NSA was overhauling the security that protected its computers and asked why, NSA responded that the work was strictly preventive and not a reaction to a penetration of existing security. In response to a specific question, an NSA spokesman specifically denied that the agency had retained the services of Scott Vandenberg & Associates—and in this, too, the agency lied to Congress.

"So far as I'm concerned, this is a waste of time," said Dudley Collins. "With all due respect to you, Mr. Vandenberg, I think we ought to drop this and forget it. What these people call a 'virus' has cost this law firm a million dollars. It'll come to that when we get the numbers together. So far as I'm concerned, we can go back to typewriters and adding machines."

"Dud, c'mon. We can go back to horses and buggies too."

Collins fixed a scornful, even hostile stare on Jeffrey Stamm. "Sure, Jeff," he said. "I've noticed for many years that people who buy Cadillacs and Volkswagens always speak up sooner or later to justify their odd purchases. And it's the same way with computers. We bought them, and—"

"We're not dumping them, Dud," said another partner, William Patton, firmly. "So forget it. When we send lawyers to Chicago, they have to fly. You can't go by train anymore. When we send documents to a firm uptown, they are transmitted by fax. We don't send out bicycle messengers anymore. And we are *not* going back to typewriters and adding machines. That's not a point for discussion, so let's don't waste time on it."

"In other words, we're computer-dependent," muttered Collins.

"You're damn right we are," said Patton. "So is General Motors. So is the New York Stock Exchange. So is the Internal Revenue Service. If a client walked in here and saw secretaries typing on typewriters or adding up numbers on adding machines, we'd lose that client. This is not 1950, Dud. So let's drop the 1950 crap."

Dudley Collins thought he looked like Henry Stimson. He wore a clipped white mustache to enhance the resemblance. He was not a stupid man. He was known for tossing outrageous statements into a discussion just to see if others could rebut him. He turned now to Scott Vandenberg and said,

"We shouldn't waste any more of *your* time, Mr. Vandenberg. I imagine we're paying for it at a good hourly rate. So tell us why we lost our whole computer system and what we can do to prevent it happening in future."

Scott Vandenberg had been sitting at the foot of the conference table, bemused by the conversation so far and wondering when he would be asked to say a word. It was true they were paying him for his time—at the rate of $250 an hour, to be precise. He reached for the vacuum carafe in the middle of the conference table and poured enough fresh coffee to warm what remained in his cup. He was amused to notice that the initials of the law firm, with a tiny figure of justice, were imprinted on the cups and saucers. On the paper napkins too.

"The answers to your questions are not terribly difficult, Mr. Collins," he said. "You are the victims of a computer virus that I've seen before. I can purge your computers of it without too much trouble, really. I—"

"We called in Mr. Vandenberg, Dud, because he's got a track record for sanitizing computers that have been infected by viruses," said William Patton. "He's the man who rescued Logan, Bartholomew. He has first-class credentials—which you'd have seen if you'd bothered to read the agenda for this meeting."

Vandenberg tried to pretend he hadn't heard the interruption. "I can tell you how to prevent this virus being introduced into your computers again. What's more important, I can make your computers almost immune to future virus infection. But notice I say

50

almost immune. If somebody is sufficiently determined, he will do it to you again. I can also tell you how to preserve your programs and data so that you can make a quick recovery from another infection."

"Somebody wanted to hurt us," said Patton darkly. "I think what I most want to know is, who did it?"

Vandenberg shook his head. "The virus came in by accident," he said. "Nobody specifically infected your computers."

"Accident?"

"Yes. It's a common virus. I've seen it before, in corporate computers, in a government computer—though, I must say, never in a law-firm computer before. I don't think we will ever know who started it. It was created a year or more ago, and it has spread all over the world. It was started by one person or by a group. Whoever it was, they probably never heard of you."

"Oh, come on!" protested Jeffrey Stamm.

"Well—"

"Start off by telling us what the hell's a virus," interjected Collins.

For a moment Vandenberg drummed the fingers of his right hand on the table and glanced around to see how many others wanted to hear the definition of a computer virus. They all did, so far as he could tell. "Forgive me if I make this too simple," he said.

"Can't be too simple for us," said Collins.

"Okay. A computer is a machine that follows instructions. A set of instructions written in a binary code that is cognizable to a computer is called a program. Without a program a computer can't do anything. A virus is an alien and harmful instruction surreptitiously introduced into a program. It can destroy the program. It can destroy data stored in a computer's memory. It can erase disks. It can actually damage the computer itself. And one of the worst things it can do is cause the computer to alter data, to falsify it. That's what happened on the Wednesday before Thanksgiving. A highly sophisticated virus scrambled the reservations information in LANCE."

"And this 'Gotcha' virus that hit us erased our data?"

"Exactly. It erased your disks. Your computers lost not just your stored data but your operating programs. And that, I have to tell you, is largely your own fault. It is absolutely essential, gentlemen, to back up your programs and work product on separate disks or tape. If you had done that, your loss would be something like one percent of what it is."

Dudley Collins turned to the office manager. "Why the hell wasn't everything backed up?" he asked.

The office manager shook his head. "Mr. Collins," he said nervously, "I've tried everything to encourage our personnel to back up their work. Everyone has strict orders to back up at the end of every day. But they won't do it. Eight months ago we even fired a secretary for failing to back up her work. For a week or so after that, the others did it faithfully. Then they went back to their old habits."

Collins snorted. "Well, why don't we fire everyone in the office who fails to back up their computer work?"

"That would include nearly every lawyer in the firm who uses a computer," said the office manager. "They won't do it either."

Collins stared at the office manager, his face a picture of frustration.

"It's nothing unusual," said Vandenberg. "Backing up is a discipline, and many people resist it, especially professionals: lawyers, doctors, accountants . . . I know of at least one law firm that took a worse hit than you've taken, for the same reason."

"Well, how did the damned virus get in here?" asked Collins. He was lighting a cigarette. He frowned over the flame and the cigarette. "Just how did this goddamned germ get into our computers?"

"One of the evil characteristics of viruses is that they can be written to be self-propagating," said Vandenberg. "That is to say, they include an instruction that tells computers to copy them. Usually the instruction is to copy the virus into a particular program. Your virus was probably instructed to copy itself into your word-processing software. Also, it probably included an instruction to itself to lie dormant for a specified period of time."

"You still haven't said how it got in here."

"I don't know how it got in," said Vandenberg. "I'd be surprised if anybody knows. But I'm sure entry wasn't difficult."

"Have we done something careless?" asked the apprehensive office manager.

Vandenberg shook his head. "Probably not. This 'gotcha' virus usually comes in one of two ways. First, you use your computers' telecommunications function to send and receive electronic mail, maybe to check market quotations, maybe to make airline reservations, and so forth: all kinds of marvelous things you can do by hooking one or more of your desktop computers to telephone lines. Also, it is not unlikely that some of your people have used their computers to communicate with so-called computer bulletin boards. Do you know what a computer bulletin board is?"

Collins shook his head. "No, and explain it at sandbox level, please."

"Okay. A computer bulletin board is what might also be called an electronic maildrop. It's a computer, of course, connected to telephone lines; and only computers can communicate with it. You can use your computer to leave a message on the bulletin board. It can be a message addressed to some particular person you know will check the bulletin board, or it can be a general message for everyone who uses that bulletin board. Computer types exchange tips about hardware and software—how to make things work better, and so on. People have been known actually to make dates through a bulletin board."

"Like CB radio, only for smarter people," Collins suggested wryly.

"You got it," said Vandenberg. "One of the things people do with bulletin boards is import free software. It's experimental stuff mostly, some of it very useful for a limited class of work, but not good enough to justify a full-scale marketing effort. The programmers put it out on the bulletin boards and say, 'Hey, take this and try it. If you like it and want to use it, send me fifty dollars.' Most of it is honest. But some of it carries a virus. The first thing you need to do is find out if anybody in your office has been using a computer bulletin board, also if anybody imported any free software."

"Would any of our people have done that?" Collins asked the office manager.

"No, sir, I don't think so."

"Another common source," said Vandenberg, "is the use of gift software. Somebody, say in another law firm, buys a program, likes it, talks about it, and offers a copy to someone in your firm. Typically the giver copies it off his hard disk onto a floppy and gives you the floppy. If *his* computer had picked up a virus, from a bulletin board or anywhere else, it might be riding in this program he's giving you."

"This virus was apparently in every computer in the office," said Jeffrey Stamm. "How did it spread?"

"In the first place," said Vandenberg, "the virus was probably written to infect a particular software. I suggested your word-processing program. The virus probably carried an instruction to look for a particular program. If you hadn't been using that program, it might have erased itself. But you were using it, and the virus copied itself into it. Now, you're running a local-area network here. That is to say, your computers are linked to each other and to a central memory bank. Once the virus was in one desktop computer, it would quickly spread through the network and infect your other computers."

"And it just sat there," mourned the office manager, "waiting for December eleventh."

"Actually," said Vandenberg, "it was probably written to wait a specific number of days, not for a specific date. That would give it a chance to propagate itself to all your computers before it showed itself."

"I imagine," said Collins, "that my colleagues have retained your services to—how would you put it? Vaccinate us?"

"That's exactly the term," said Vandenberg. "My associates will spend some time in your offices. They will make sure all your machines are clean. Then they will put vaccine programs in all your computers. After that, they will set up security procedures to prevent another invasion and to contain it if it should get past our vaccines. I can't promise you absolute security. I can promise you won't again be injured by accident."

"What security procedures?" asked Collins.

"Well, for example, we will recommend that only computers that *need* access to outside information be equipped with modems," said Vandenberg. "Most of your desktop computers don't need telephone-line connections, and you reduce the risk of infection if you limit access to those lines. Probably it would be a good idea to disconnect the computers that have telephone lines from your internal network. That will isolate those computers. If one picks up a virus, the infection will be isolated in that one computer. Also, you should make it an absolute rule, no exceptions, that no computer disks be carried into the office. No disks should be put into your computers except blanks that come in sealed packages. Rules like this—"

"Okay, but how do you vaccinate?"

"There are a number of ways," said Vandenberg. "For one thing, we'll set up a program that runs a periodic byte count on your computers. You understand that the term *byte* means a character—a letter, number, symbol, or space. We can easily count the bytes in all your legitimate programs. We put those numbers in for a standard, and then periodically—at least once a day—we automatically compare those numbers to the number of bytes your programs actually contain. If there are any extra bytes, that sounds an alarm, and then we examine those extra bytes to see what they are."

"Somebody can still foul us up?" asked Collins.

Vandenberg nodded. "Typically senior members of your firm, Mr. Collins," he said. "You set up rules. Junior employees feel compelled to follow them. Senior partners don't. Most viruses I've seen that got into a system after it was vaccinated were brought in by vice-presidents. Impose discipline, make everybody abide by your rules, and you will have tight security. Viruses are introduced by *people*, almost invariably. Control people, you control viruses."

"How does that explain the LANCE disaster?" asked Collins.

"We haven't figured that out yet for sure," said Vandenberg. "But remember, the LANCE computer *must* interconnect with thousands of telephone lines. Most of your computers don't need to."

Scott Vandenberg sat at a desktop computer in his office in Bethesda, Maryland. When he glanced away from the glowing, color-filled screen, he could see snow piling up on the windowsill to the right of his desk. It was well past midnight, and he was wondering if this sudden snowstorm was going to make it difficult for him to go home later, or to get to New York, where he had to be by tomorrow afternoon.

His computer was a Dell System 310. The screen sat on a swivel on top of the central processor, and he had it turned slightly away from the window, since he liked to lean back in his chair when he was pondering and glance back and forth between the screen and the view outside. He liked bright colors on his computer screens, so although the work he was doing could have been done just as effectively on a black screen filled with green or amber characters, his screen was blue, filled with white characters mostly, with red, green, and yellow to highlight some of the messages. In the quiet of the office, where of course he was alone at this hour, the only sound was the low, whispering hum of the spinning disk in his hard-disk drive.

Scott was another one of those people who had been all but mesmerized by computers. It was not a thinking machine of course; it was a tool. A powerful tool that a thinking person could use to extend and amplify his intellect and personality. The limits were not machine limits. What a person could do with a computer was limited chiefly by his imagination and intelligence.

From time to time, whenever he could get to it—and therefore chiefly at night and on weekends—he had been writing a virus of his own: one to test the new defenses built into LANCE. The crew at Info Pro knew he was doing it, but they didn't know how or when he would try to penetrate their security.

Tonight he had tried four times. Four times LANCE had refused to accept his call. For the past hour he had been tinkering with the virus. Now he was ready to try again.

He had built the virus into a communications program. Tapping keys, he commanded the computer to set that program up to run. The display for the program appeared on his screen. He typed in another command:

LANCE

Lights began to blink on the front of his modem, the communications box that allowed the computer to communicate over telephone lines. He had written his program to call LANCE over Tymnet, a telephone network for computer communication. That was a local call here in Bethesda, and Tymnet would switch it through to Ronkonkoma, Long Island.

The call went through quickly. Fewer lines were active at this hour.

As red lights flickered nervously on the front of the modem, the LANCE sign-in message appeared on the screen:

`LANCE, YOUR ID?`

The travel agency his company did a great deal of business with had disclosed its identification number to him—after he had explained what he was doing and why. He typed:

`472QSY3545`

LANCE accepted his identification, as it had four times before. It began to display options and instructions, telling the "travel agent" how to look up a flight schedule, then how to make a reservation, and how to issue a ticket and boarding pass.

Scott followed the instructions and booked himself onto a flight from Miami to New Orleans—a flight the computer said was full. His virus worked this time, as it had failed to do four times earlier. He and another passenger had boarding passes for the same seat.

The other passenger was named Margaret Disney. He gave LANCE an inquiry:

What is the status of the Margaret Disney reservation on Delta 244, January 21?

LANCE replied:

`CONFIRMED`

Bright winter sunshine glittered on heavy frost, and wind-borne crystals of ice stung Scott Vandenberg's face as he walked across the parking lot and into the Info Pro computer center on Long Island. It was just before noon.

Dave Derval and Hal Miller met with him in a square little conference room just off the computer room. It was like all the meeting rooms in computer centers: glaringly lighted by more fluorescent tubes than the space required, furnished with plastic chairs and a Formica-topped table, neat and functional. Two walls were covered with the obligatory green chalk boards, and the diagrams and numbers from the last meeting were only smeared, not erased.

"You didn't get through," said Derval. "We detected your tries. Four of them."

"Five," said Scott.

Dave Derval slackened. He was a heavy man, carrying a burden of soft flesh. His bulging neck filled his loosened collar. Five or six years older than Scott, he looked twenty years older; and since November 21 he had looked not just exhausted but defeated. He shook his head wearily.

"Are you telling us, Commander, that you managed to penetrate us?" Hal Miller asked.

"I penetrated you," said Scott. He took from his briefcase the ticket and boarding pass he had picked up from his travel agent the morning after the snowstorm as he was on his way to the airport to catch a shuttle for New York. "That seat also belongs to one Margaret Disney. Better cancel it out."

Miller accepted the ticket and boarding pass and frowned unhappily over it. He picked up a telephone and rang the controllers who were monitoring LANCE.

Hal Miller was a chronically long-faced man. His sincerity fairly shone from his face. Scott watched him talking on the telephone. He understood something about Hal Miller: that this quiet, hardworking little man confidently knew he would survive Derval, LANCE, or Info Pro. He was content here; he was loyal to this company, within reason; but he was one of those independent technicians for whom there was always a job waiting; he was always in demand and probably received half a dozen offers a month. It was characteristic of the new high-tech industries that their personnel were independent and mobile. That was another reason viruses got in—because disgruntled employees felt no overpowering misgivings about damaging an employer they decided was damaging them.

Miller put down the telephone, turned, and allowed himself a faint smile. "Okay," he said quietly. "Your virus worked."

"You detected the first four tries, right?"

"Yeah. You came in in the middle of the night. What was it, Tuesday? The night guys caught it. But they didn't—"

"They didn't do what they should have done," said Scott. "They should have canceled the ID number I was using when they saw I was repeatedly trying to do something phony."

"Well, they didn't catch that exactly," said Miller. "A lot of our customers are computer illiterates. Or just fumble-fingers on the keyboard. If we suspected funny business every time we get somebody sending nonstandard messages, we'd be suspecting twenty percent of our users."

"I want to set up a program," said Scott, "that will put your fumble-finger reservations in a special category. We can write some code that will look specifically for conflicting reservations. What we've got to do, one way or another, is trigger an alert when somebody repeatedly tries to do something nonstandard, like I did."

"Already working along those lines," said Miller.

"Okay. Besides that, having written a virus that made a con-flicting reservation, I have a much better idea what that kind of virus looks like. We can write a program to look for the kind of code I had to write to do it."

"Sounds good," said Derval. "Sounds like progress."

"What I'm talking about wouldn't have prevented November twenty-first," said Scott. "Because that came in in a box, not over the wire."

"You feel confident of that, Commander?" asked Miller.

Scott nodded. He picked up the paper coffee cup that was another typical feature of these little meeting rooms in computer centers—wondering what Derval intended to do about lunch. "I do," he said. "You can build elaborate security at the front end"—*front end* was a term for the communications facility of the computer center, where eight hundred telephone ports were open to receive airline reservations orders from all over America—"but that's not how the November twenty-first virus got in. You bought that virus and installed it yourselves."

"We have absolute prohibitions against importing unautho-rized software," said Derval.

"It was authorized," said Scott. "Your virus came in on au-thorized new software."

"What?"

"The only authorized new software you bought last summer."

"WHIT," said Hal Miller. "It rode in on WHIT."

"We don't know that for sure," said Scott. "But I'm reasonably confident that's where it came from. From WHIT."

"WHIT . . ." Derval muttered. "Brand new, out-of-the-box, sealed. I'll sue the hell out of them if it's true."

"We can talk about that later," said Scott. "Right now I'd like to look at something in LANCE."

They broke for lunch at 1:45. It was Dave Derval's habit, Scott now remembered, to come to the office early, work through the ordinary lunch hour, then finish the workday over his lunch. He would come back to the office after the long break, but only to clear up minor odds and ends.

"You'll like this place," he said as he drove into the parking lot of a restaurant. "And maybe you'll like the company. I didn't mention it before, but somebody's joining us for lunch."

Since the business of handing over the car to a boy, followed by the business of checking their coats, occupied Derval's attention for the next minute or two, Scott had no chance to ask him who was having lunch with them. Not before they reached their table—a booth actually: round, with the high-backed bench covered in vinyl made to simulate snakeskin—did he discover that the person joining them was an attractive young woman.

"Scott, let me introduce Nancy Delacorte," said Derval as the three men—himself, Hal Miller, and Scott—slid into the booth.

Nancy Delacorte nodded and extended her hand. As Scott took it and squeezed it in a gentle handshake, he saw calm but penetrating eyes appraising him. His quick impression was of a woman in her early thirties, with a strong, honest face, a handsome figure, well-dressed in a checked gray wool jacket and trousers, with a black turtleneck sweater. Her long, dark-brown hair seemed to have been whipped by the wind; and maybe the glow of her complexion was the result of the same icy wind.

"Nancy is an agent of the Security Division of the Federal Aviation Administration," said Derval. "She's heading the FAA investigation of our virus problem."

"What happened on November twenty-first is also the subject of an FBI investigation," said Derval.

"I guess I shouldn't be surprised by that."

"No, you shouldn't," said Nancy Delacorte. "There are some serious federal crimes involved. The disruption of the nation's air-traffic system was indirectly responsible for that crash on the Virginia mountainside. You can't call it murder, but—"

"No, you can't call it murder," said Scott. "Maybe I shouldn't be telling you what the law is, but—"

"I leave it to the Justice Department to say what the law is," she said. "What I'm interested in is accumulating the facts, which sooner or later I'll have to reduce to a report."

"We have some facts," said Scott. "And beyond the facts, a lot of speculation."

"Let me explain my focus," said Nancy Delacorte. "My agency is interested in finding out who did what, sure. But chiefly that's an FBI problem. What I'm really interested in is finding a way to be certain it doesn't happen again. What happened on Thanksgiving Eve became an immense threat to the safety of travelers. That's the FAA's responsibility. That's why I'm here."

"I suggested to Miss Delacorte," said Derval, "that after our meeting this morning we would be able to give her some ideas."

A waiter came to take their orders for drinks. Scott ordered a Glenfiddich on the rocks; and Nancy Delacorte, who seemed to find the waiter's request for an order an unwelcome interruption, shrugged and said she would have a Beefeater martini on the rocks.

"What we say," she told them when the waiter was gone, "will be held in confidence. I'd like you to talk freely. We'll go over a draft of my report before I submit it, and if I've quoted any of you for anything you don't want to go on record as saying, we can cut that."

Scott glanced at Derval and Miller and saw that they expected him to lead the conversation. "Okay, Miss Delacorte, we—"

"Please," she interrupted. "We may be working together for some time. 'Miss Delacorte' and 'Mr. Vandenberg' are going to be awkward. Make it Nancy, hmm?"

"Okay. My name is Scott. People call me that or Scotty. I prefer Scott."

"Scott it is."

It was wrong of him, sexist in fact, to judge Nancy Delacorte as the most unlikely federal investigator he had ever encountered. Still, he couldn't rid himself of the thought. She was straightforward and businesslike, yet soft-spoken; and somehow, even when she spoke solemnly, the tone of her voice suggested a philosophical skepticism and irony that was more suggestive of an academic than a federal bureaucrat. Her clothes, the way she wore her hair long and loose, all spoke something very different from what she said she was. Or . . . Well, really, what *should* a young woman working as a federal investigator look like?

"We can make a reasonably decent guess as to who wrote the virus," Scott said. "It *is* a guess, let me emphasize. It's speculation. But there is evidence. I am firmly of the opinion that the virus entered LANCE as part of a software program the company bought, not through the telephone lines."

"Explain," she said simply.

"LANCE," he said, "is in contact with the world through eight hundred telephone lines. A hacker could sit down some evening in a closed travel-agency office and try to introduce a virus into LANCE. And there's a lot of motive to do so. With just a little skill, a hacker could write a virus that would reserve space on a flight for him and make it appear he had paid for it. To guard against that, LANCE was protected by a rather sophisticated security system, before November twenty-first. We've tightened it since, but I am very skeptical that the virus came in over the telephone lines."

"Can you give me an example of how you check for incoming viruses?" she asked.

"All incoming communication is now being isolated for a second or so, during which time the data are examined by a special program. There are certain commands a hacker would have to introduce into the system to infect it, and the security program looks for the code that constitutes those commands. If it finds anything like that, it blocks that communication and will not let it into the system. The terminal that sent the virus gets a message saying the communication was garbled in transmission and asks the hacker to repeat it. If he is stupid enough to stay on line and try again, he gives us time to begin tracing the phone call. That's one of the techniques we use."

"We are particularly alert late at night," said Miller. "Fortunately that's when our traffic is lightest."

"Do you detect many attempts?" asked Nancy.

"Five or six a day," said Miller. "Most of them are crude, the most obvious ways to infect us; and the system stops them at the door."

"Okay. So how did the virus get in?"

"I am all but one hundred percent satisfied," said Scott, "that it came in on a program called WHIT. I asked Hal to inventory every change made in the operating system in the six months before November twenty-first. A major upgrading of WHIT is the only software imported into LANCE from outside during that period. Every other change in LANCE was internally designed and programmed."

"So what's WHIT?"

"A program we didn't absolutely need, I'm sorry to say," said Derval.

"Everybody who works with sophisticated systems wants WHIT," said Miller. "When you talk about your system, you like to be able to say it is WHIT-capable—even if you never have an occasion to receive communication that requires conversion. You like to be able to say, 'Oh sure, my system can talk to yours. We've got WHIT.'"

"We didn't put it in just for the prestige," said Dave Derval. He paused for a moment while the waiter put their drinks on the table. "We're experimenting with a worldwide reservations system. I mean, to be able to offer Americans confirmed reservations on airlines that don't even have American offices."

"Feeder lines, commuter lines," said Miller. "How do you get from Cape Town to Bloemfontein?"

"Even those little fellows use computers to make reservations," said Derval. "But some have odd computer systems. WHIT would make it possible to work with them."

"LANCE has been WHIT-capable for several years," said Scott. "But last summer an upgraded version of WHIT was offered. They bought it for LANCE and installed it."

"And that," said Miller, "was the only outside software introduced into our computers in the past year."

"That upgrade came in here in a sealed package," said Derval. "Either the virus originated at Whitney Data Dynamics Corporation or somebody intercepted the shipment, broke the seals, put the virus on the WHIT disks, and resealed the package, or—"

"It happened at Whitney Data," said Miller firmly. "That WHIT upgrade was on read-only disks."

"You couldn't add anything to the programs on those disks," she said.

"Actually, there are ways of overcoming that," said Scott. "But I think you're right, Chief. The virus came from Whitney Data."

"Why?" Nancy asked. "What motive?"

"I've got a worse problem than that," said Scott. "We were able to retrieve considerable chunks of the virus code out of LANCE. It had tried to erase itself, but it hadn't been entirely successful. I've been examining those chunks of code. My staff has been examining them. We've been comparing them with some other programs. I—"

"Uh-oh," muttered Hal Miller.

Scott looked at Derval, then at Miller. "Did you guess, Chief? I haven't told you this." He spoke directly to Nancy. "You can never be sure of a thing like this, but system designers and programmers develop what we might call signatures. All unconsciously. It's in the way they get around design problems. A designer who gets around a particular problem in a particular way will probably congratulate himself on that and go on to use the same solution when he encounters the same problem again. So, they develop signatures."

"Who?"

Scott glanced from face to face, to all three of them. "The signature argues that the LANCE virus was created by the founding father himself, Darius Whitney."

Darius Whitney had never seen anything like it. He and Allison were avid readers of *People* magazine and loved to watch television shows like *Lifestyles of the Rich and Famous,* but he could not remember anything he had read or seen that suggested anyone really lived like this: like a goddamn *king* a long time after kings were supposed to have been abolished.

Sitting beside a swimming pool that must have been fifty meters long, Whitney took shelter now under a big table umbrella that protected him from the bright sun. He had intrigued the younger men and women around the pool by showing them that a sixty-year-old man carrying a good many extra pounds not only dared dive from the three-meter board but did it with a certain style. Two dives were enough, though, and he sat comfortably, hands clasped on his belly, puffing on a small cigar and scrutinizing his surroundings with close curiosity.

Darius knew little of geography. He supposed those mountains in the distance were the Andes. What other mountains were there in South America? This was a fair mountain itself; they were hundreds of feet above the city; you could see to everywhere, in any direction. It was the elevation, probably, that explained the climate. Bogotá wasn't far from the equator, as he recalled; yet, the warm, dry air on this mountaintop was pleasant, not tropical-overbearing at all. The water in the pool was heated; otherwise only the very brave would have gone in it. Surrounded on three sides by the villa and by a high wall on the fourth, the pool was sheltered from the mountain winds; otherwise even sitting by the pool could have been uncomfortable.

Señor Cordero stood poised at the tip of the three-meter board. He jumped up, came down on the board, and was propelled into the air. He turned over in a perfect arch, dropped straight toward the water, with his body extended, and plunged in with hardly a splash. Darius had learned diving during his years in the Air Force, had dived competitively in a few armed-forces amateur meets, and he judged Señor Cordero a skilled diver.

Cordero was a man of many talents, it seemed. In the silver-gray Mercedes limousine on the way from the airport he had spoken of flying his own airplane. Darius had noted the signature on one of the oil paintings hanging in the sitting room of the suite he had been given in the house. It was signed CORDERO, and Darius assumed that meant Señor Virgilio Cordero. He was also perfectly bilingual. His English was all but flawless.

He was handsome. His body was trim, muscular, tanned, and hairy. His face was long and thin, with dramatic dark eyes and a sharp nose. It was the kind of face that Darius identified, correctly or not, with Castilian Spanish. The man's black hair was high-lighted with abundant silver.

Darius Whitney was conscious of the fact that he was fascinated by this man—but it would have been difficult to be anything less than enthralled, considering what Señor Cordero had and what he was giving.

A part of the señor's hospitality seemed to be a girl, who apparently had been appointed to stay close to Darius. She said her name was Luisa. She was petite and pretty, and if she was seventeen years old, he would be surprised. More likely she was sixteen. She wore only the bottom of a skimpy bikini—as did the other girls in and around the pool.

Whitney surmised that at the end of the day, when he went to his room for the night, he would find Luisa waiting for him. That troubled him. She was so young. But if that was why she was here, she had long since lost her innocence, and if he didn't accept what she offered, someone else would.

Darius was by no means indifferent to provocative female nudity. He found it peculiarly erotic that this girl could show so much of herself so ingenuously. His thought turned for a moment to Allison, and he wondered if she could do it. He wished she were with him. The invitation to fly to Bogotá had been for him alone. Another time he would suggest she should come too.

He drained the last of his bourbon and water. Luisa raised her hand, and with a snap of her finger peremptorily summoned a boy to take the glass and refill it.

"You are from California," she said. "I am always want to go there." She tipped her head and showed a saucy grin. "You take me there, Whitney?"

He, too, grinned. "Maybe," he said.

Señor Cordero climbed out of the pool and walked across the hot concrete toward the umbrella-shaded table where Whitney sat with Luisa. At his approach she left her chair and retreated a few paces to a towel on the grass.

"You prefer not to swim?" asked Cordero.

Darius smiled and shook his head. "It looks too much like exercise," he said.

"It is very good for you," said Cordero.

"I tend to dislike anything that's good for me," said Darius. "Exercise. Diets. Temperance. Was it Woody Allen who said you might not live to be a hundred by giving up eating and drinking and smoking, but you'd *think* you had? My mother, anyway, said you should enjoy whatever you can *while* you can, 'cause you're sure not going to enjoy it later."

Cordero laughed. Then he shook his head. "When you have a generous share of the good things of life, you want a long life in which to enjoy them. So I do a few things that are good for me."

That was all he wanted to say on that subject; it was dismissed; and he adopted a sober expression as he said, "We need not talk business until later really. In fact I don't want to talk business much until an associate of mine arrives. But I do want to ask you a question or two."

"Of course."

"If you don't mind telling me, just what is your position with Whitney Data Dynamics?"

Darius looked up at the boy who was hurrying from the poolside bar with his fresh bourbon and water; also, apparently, a glass of champagne for Señor Cordero. "I, uh, officially I am president and chairman of the board of directors," he said. "For all practical purposes I am an old toad who has been put out to pasture. The company is run by a chief executive officer and his staff. He was hired by the board of directors and has their support."

"Yes," said Cordero, nodding and frowning. "You lost control of your company, hmm?"

Darius nodded. "I lost control."

"How, if you don't mind my asking?"

Darius sipped bourbon. "Nothing terribly unusual, I suppose," he said. "Computers are my field. Business isn't. I developed WHIT. I created a computer utility program that is almost universally used. Today it generates tens of millions in revenue annually. But to market it initially—that is, to get the word out, to make its value known, to make people want to buy it, cost millions. I didn't have millions of course. I went to some lawyers. They advised me to form a corporation, Whitney Data Dynamics, and sell stock to investors. I was supposed to keep enough of the stock in my own hands to assure control of my corporation. But as we needed more money, I pledged my stock to secure more loans. Banks called my loans and took the pledged stock. One day I found myself owner of thirty-five percent of my own business. The next day I found myself an employee of the people who had bought up the other sixty-five percent."

"Digital Universal," said Cordero.

"Right," said Darius. "Whitney Data Dynamics is now a subsidiary of Digital Universal Corporation. And everything is run by masters of business administration, mostly from Harvard. Señor, there is *nothing* that can't be fouled up by a Harvard MBA."

"I understand," said Cordero, calm and smooth, "that you have been given a princely computer laboratory and free rein to develop anything you want."

"Yes," said Darius bitterly. "And anything I develop will belong to them."

"You developed a brilliant new version of WHIT," said Cordero. "All the technical journals call it brilliant. I myself don't read these, but clippings have been sent to me. You did splendid work."

Darius smiled. "I did, didn't I? But that was unfinished business."

"Are you free to develop computer programs for others?"

"Anything that doesn't compete," said Darius.

"Yes," said Cordero. He nodded and sipped champagne. "It is as we were told."

"You've been checking up on me."

Cordero faced Darius with a bland smile. "Indeed we have, Mr. Whitney. We want to make a business proposition."

As the sun set, servants lighted torches around the pool. Señor Cordero appeared in a white dinner jacket. So did another man, an Oriental of some kind. Darius Whitney was embarrassed. He didn't own a dinner jacket, but he could have rented one if he had suspected it would be needed on this trip. He sensed uncomfortably that his dark-blue suit was not appropriate.

A round table was set up near the pool—set with thick white linen, heavy silver, crystal, flowers, candles burning in hurricane lamps. It was set for just three. If only three men were dining, at least three would serve and entertain, Darius noticed. The girls who had been around the pool this afternoon, including Luisa, were in the water. All of them were naked now, and they swam slowly back and forth, their lithe bodies gleaming in the glare of underwater lights. Across the pool, on the concrete, a string quartet played: not guitars but two violins, a viola, and a cello.

Señor Cordero was suave—which Darius attributed to his being Latin and rich—and welcomed Darius without any visible reaction to his blue suit. He lifted a finger to summon a boy to serve Darius a glass of champagne, which he need not have done since the boy was already at Darius's elbow.

"I trust you had a pleasant nap," he said. "Let me introduce you to my friend Yoshitaka Hara. You and he have much in common and will find much to talk about, I am sure."

Yoshitaka Hara shook hands with Darius, without the suggestion of a bow. He was a totally westernized Japanese, who had adopted the demeanor as well as the dress and language of the West, actually of America. In spite of that, he was an archetypal middle-aged Japanese: diminutive, bald, without spectacles but probably wearing contact lenses. Darius had seen somewhere a painted plaster figurine of a little Japanese man sitting in a wooden tub of water and washing his back with a towel. The remembered figure was not unlike Yoshitaka Hara.

"Mr. Hara," said Cordero, "is my computer consultant. These days a man in business needs a computer expert on his staff—do you not agree?—and, much as I would like to have him on my staff, he insists on remaining independent, a consultant. Anyway I think you and he will talk the same language. I hope you will."

They stood by the pool sipping champagne from tall, thin glasses that Darius did not identify with champagne, which he had always drunk from shallow stem glasses.

"If I owned Digital Universal," Cordero said abruptly, interjecting a businesslike note into the conversation, "Darius Whitney would run Whitney Data Dynamics. I would rid the company of the Harvard MBA boys and put the company back into the hands of the man who created it."

Darius picked up a cracker laden with caviar. "If I owned the government of the United States, I'd abolish income taxes," he said.

"I am serious, Mr. Whitney," said Cordero. "And what is more, it is not impossible."

Cordero glanced at Hara and waited for a reaction from Darius.

Darius swallowed his mouthful of caviar and cracker. "The business proposition?" he asked.

"The business proposition," Cordero agreed. "How would you like to regain control of Whitney Data Dynamics?"

Darius Whitney used his tongue to clear his teeth of what he had just eaten. "Well," he said, with a click of his tongue and lips, "I would very much like to recover control of my company. It *is* my company, you know. I created it, just as Picasso created a work of art or Shakespeare created a play, and it is unbearable to watch a bunch of pencil pushers running it."

"That must be intolerable," said Cordero.

"I'll speak frankly," said Darius. "Money, sure. I want money. Who ever has enough, no matter how much he has? But it's something more than that." He paused for a moment as he stared gravely into the eyes of both men. "I expose myself more than I should, maybe. But I set up my company to be—to be . . . how shall I say?"

"An extension of yourself," Hara suggested.

"Exactly," said Darius, welcoming the way the Japanese had put it. "I mean, I wanted to run a company that would be on the front row of things, the way I had been when I developed WHIT and put it on the market. And these people who run it now, all they can think of is organization charts, company policies, 'prioritization,' and of course their favorite thing, the bottom line. They make me sick."

"I think we can understand distinctly," said Señor Cordero.

"To me, a challenge is a great thing," said Darius, "an opportunity. To them it is a threat."

"Understood."

"Maybe I don't need the damned company," said Darius, raising his glass and sipping champagne. "I could do what I do anywhere. But, dammit, I *built* it. And—and I want it back."

"Clearly understood," said Cordero. "Clearly understandable. And maybe we can help you get it back."

Darius sighed loudly. "Obviously, there will be a quid pro quo," he said.

"Obviously," said Cordero. "Clearly there has to be, no?"

Darius nodded. "Clearly there has to be," he agreed.

"Well?"

Hara was direct. He spoke to Darius almost as if he were excluding Cordero from the conversation. "You wrote the virus that caused the Thanksgiving Eve mess," he said.

Darius grinned and shook his head.

"But you *did*," said Hara with a smile. "You see, I know you did. I did a little elementary detective work and found out."

Darius's breath caught and stopped for a moment. He was incapable of subtlety, and consternation warped his face.

Hara was amused. "When I heard of the virus that infected the airline-reservations system, I recognized the work of a genius. I mean, a virus that systematically distorts data for two or three months, all the while concealing itself and its work. Really!"

"What tells you I did it?"

"How many men could have done it? Not many. I reviewed the names. I could identify some who clearly didn't write that virus. One of them is in prison. He didn't do it. Others, well, who had the time? And a motive? I narrowed the possibilities to two or three geniuses. Then . . ." He smiled and shrugged. "I paid a little money for some additional information."

"I had supposed only two people in the world knew," said Darius dejectedly.

"Yourself and your companion, Miss McGuire," said Hara. "But why not your secretary Mrs. Scibelli?"

"She didn't know what I was doing."

"No, but she knew you were doing something special, something unusual. Please, Mr. Whitney. She is on the payroll of Whitney Data Dynamics. An element of her assignment was to watch what you were doing with your time, how you were using your laboratory, and to report to your good friend Nathan Morgenstern, your chief executive officer. The careful Nathan planted a spy on you, Mr. Whitney—as any well-trained MBA would. Probably she was only one of several."

"Morgenstern. That son of a bitch."

"That son of a bitch," Hara went on, "had but one concern: that whatever you were doing should be the property of the corporation and that you not take it outside. He wasn't concerned about your writing a virus, never dreamed you would do such a thing; but he wanted to be sure that you were using your time and the company's computer facilities to develop software for the company, not to develop something you would sell on your own."

"So you talked to Anne Scibelli."

"I paid a few dollars here, a few there, and finally was given the name of Mrs. Scibelli. I paid her more than a few dollars. So, you see, I *know* you wrote the virus. I can only say, Mr. Whitney, that I admire it very much. I myself have done a few viruses. It is not easy."

Darius had regained his composure. He let the waiter refill his glass. "The most difficult part," he said, "was coping with the fact that the reservations data would be accessed hourly, all during the time my program was screwing it up. You understand that—in the absence of something to prevent it—the whole thing would have become apparent the first time a traveler called to change a reservation. If they went into the system to make a change and found six boarding passes issued for the same seat—well, you see the difficulty."

"How did you overcome that difficulty?" asked Cordero.

Darius Whitney smiled: a proud, happy smile. "It wasn't easy," he said. "Part of the solution was that I had LANCE create a special, separate data base for my fouled-up reservations. Then, so it wouldn't occupy a suspiciously large amount of memory, I had it compress my data until the day it was to be used. At four P.M., November twenty-first, my virus erased all the valid reservations data, decompressed my fouled-up data, and substituted my unholy mess for the valid reservations information."

" 'Compressed,' 'decompressed,' " murmured Cordero. "Am I certain I know what that means?"

"Most data can be reduced to a smaller size," said Hara. "It is a matter of establishing a few conventions in the system. Abbreviations. Symbols. A form of shorthand. A program substitutes the abbreviations and symbols for words and numbers. When you want to use the data again, a reverse program reestablishes the original words and numbers. Rather elementary stuff actually."

"But the system had been issuing boarding passes, tens of thousands of them every week . . ."

"I detached the boarding-pass element of the program from the reservations element," said Darius. "That was simple."

"Why was it simple?" Cordero asked. "I would suppose that would be very complicated. How did you know how the LANCE program worked? I had heard of LANCE long before November twenty-first. I knew my airline reservations were controlled by a computer program called LANCE. Indeed I had my New York representatives inquire for me if it were possible to invest in the company that runs it, which seemed to me a desirable investment, on the forefront of technology. But you must have known every inside element of that technology."

The quality of Darius's smile was partly of his self-satisfaction, partly of the champagne. "I had been a part of the design team that created LANCE," he said.

"Which I knew," said Hara. "That made it easier to guess which computer whiz had attacked LANCE with a virus."

"Good work, Mr. Hara," said Darius. "Not many people know of that connection."

"Ah," said Cordero softly. "Because a prophet is without honor in his own country. A very small percentage of the population knows your name, Mr. Whitney. A great many more—"

"I will accept wealth instead of fame," said Darius bluntly.

He turned away from Cordero and Hara and walked to the side of the pool, where he had a better view of the naked girls. The two men followed him. For a time they stood there, none of them really interested at this moment in the girls, yet pretending they were while they collected their thoughts.

"I think . . . I think you like power too," said Hara. "When we talk of a business proposition, it can involve money or regaining control of your company."

Darius shrugged. "Make me an offer," he said, conscious that he need not have been so distressed that they knew he had written the big virus.

"One more element, if you don't mind," said Yoshitaka Hara. "I do not yet entirely understand your motive. Maybe I do. But—"

"Yes," interjected Cordero. "What did you gain by writing this amazing virus?"

Darius turned his back on the swimming pool. He was grinning and once again comfortable. He chuckled. "I read in the trade papers that Info Pro, the operators of LANCE, have hired Commander Scott Vandenberg to find out what happened and how to prevent its happening again. Vandenberg is not the only man who could find out how the virus got into LANCE, but he *will* find out; and when he does, word will go out in the industry that WHIT carried the virus that fouled up LANCE."

"And then your company may not be worth recovering," said Cordero, surprised.

Darius nodded. "When word goes out that WHIT carries a virus, or even that it might carry a virus—Do I need to tell you?"

Cordero frowned hard. "You want to destroy your own business?"

"No," said Darius grimly. "No. I want to destroy the people who took it away from me, the people who've reduced it to a game of tiddledywinks. It's mine, dammit. And—"

"And you'd rather kill it than—"

"You're damn right!"

Virgilio Cordero drew a deep breath, raised his eyebrows high, and fixed a significant gaze on Yoshitaka Hara. "Let us sit down to dinner," he said.

They were served clams over rice, then immense lobsters on plates with huge steaks. White wine. Red wine. More champagne.

The girls climbed out of the pool and sat on the edge in the torchlight, sipping champagne and munching on the hors d'oeuvres that the three men had not eaten. The twilight faded, and the sky turned black. In the clear mountain air the stars glittered icily against the infinite darkness. The string quartet played themes from musical comedies.

For a while Cordero and Hara talked about the food, the wine, the night sky. Darius marveled over it all: over every element of it, especially the conversation. He had thought he knew what he called the good life, but it was apparent to him as he sat here that these men knew good life in a sense he had never imagined. He was reluctant even to try to join in their talk. He thought he knew wine, for example; and he did, knew what he liked and why; but he could not talk about specific vineyards and not about vintage years. They mentioned planets and constellations that shone above, and he had no idea what they were talking about. Then they spoke of politics, Latin American politics, and he kept silent because he could not offer a single intelligent comment. His limitations bore down hard on him.

Let them talk about computers—but people couldn't talk about computers and nothing else, always.

"Tell me, Mr. Whitney," said Cordero finally, "what do you know about the computer system that controls entry into the United States by foreign aircraft?"

"A little," said Darius, glad to be asked about something he knew.

"You worked on it at one time, didn't you?"

Darius nodded. "A little," he said again.

"More than a little, I think," said Hara. "You served in the United States Air Force. For twenty years. You were discharged a master sergeant. That is where you learned about computers: in the Air Force."

"I have an eighth-grade education," said Darius quietly. "Yes. The Air Force introduced me to computers."

Cordero smiled. "Don't be too modest," he said. "The Air Force gave you the opportunity to work with computers, but you are a natural, instinctive mathematical genius."

Darius frowned. "My father," he said, "believed that formal education—what he called schoolin'—beyond the eighth grade was a waste of a young man's muscle power. I went to work on the farm when I was fourteen. When I was eighteen, I enlisted in the Air Force. The old man was furious. He said I'd just learned how to use a shovel right and then walked off to play with airplanes."

"To play with computers," said Cordero.

"Not at first. Not with my education. Eventually, though."

"Yes," said Cordero. "We have looked into your background quite thoroughly. It seems you know a great deal about air-traffic control, as well as about computers. Air-traffic control was your introduction to electronics, wasn't it? And from there—that is, from radar—you moved to computers, where you had a natural instinct that had only barely manifested itself when you worked as a radar technician. You have an interesting combination of talents, Mr. Whitney."

"I guess you want me to write a virus that will allow aircraft to enter the United States illegally," he said forthrightly.

"It can be done," said Hara. "We know it can be done. *I* could do it, but I know too little about how the system works. Aircraft approaching the United States enter an Air Defense Identification Zone—ADIZ. With some exceptions all aircraft entering such a zone must be identified. They—"

Darius interrupted. "All this is reasonably straightforward," he said. "I learned it because I worked on it, but the procedures are published in the federal manuals for pilots. When an aircraft enters an ADIZ, it is picked up on radar."

"Only then?" asked Hara.

"In fact it has been picked up long before that," said Darius. "When I worked on all this, it was much more primitive, but I've kept track of how it works today. Now, when radar contact is established, the position, heading, speed, and altitude of the target are fed into computers, where they are matched to the same information for filed flight plans. Almost always there is a match. Professional pilots flying big jets arrive where they are supposed to be within minutes of when they are supposed to be there. The match is confirmed by checking the transponder code the aircraft generates on the radar screen. It—"

"And if there is no match?" asked Cordero.

"Well, they can try making radio contact. But if they can't do that, then they've got a bogey, and a pair of fighters will be scrambled to intercept the approaching aircraft."

"This is done very rapidly, I understand," said Cordero.

"At some points, especially off the east coast of Florida, the ADIZ extends out only a hundred miles or so. When you have a bogey approaching at six hundred miles an hour, you don't have much time. The computer makes the match and issues an okay or an alert within seconds after the radar information arrives at the center."

"They aren't looking for approaching Russian bombers, I suppose," said Cordero.

"You're right. Those are tracked by a different system," said Darius. "The ADIZ system is chiefly for identifying approaching commercial traffic and private planes. Of late, its chief function has been to intercept incoming shipments of cocaine."

Cordero pushed his chair back from the table and crossed his legs. "Could a virus be created that would make it possible for aircraft to evade the ADIZ system? Suppose the computers took the information about an incoming flight and reported a match with a filed flight plan—when there was no filed fight plan. Could the aircraft then enter United States airspace and, in a sense, disappear?"

Darius was still eating, and his mouth was full. He shrugged.

"We can't," said Hara, "build airplanes that are invisible to radar, as the Stealth bomber is supposed to be. We can't avoid radar contact. But if, when the contact is made, the computer tells the air-traffic controllers that the aircraft is approaching in accordance with a flight plan filed before it took off—well, you see the point."

"Perfectly," said Darius.

"I can offer a great deal of money for that virus," said Cordero. "Or perhaps you would rather talk about Whitney Data Dynamics. I, with associates, could buy shares in your parent company, Digital Universal—maybe enough to take control of Digital. In fact I think I can assure you we can gain control of Digital. Then we could spin off Whitney Data Dynamics to you, in some way that would not cost you ten fortunes in taxes. The details can be worked out. The bottom line—your MBA friends' favorite cliché—is that you would regain control of your company. We can talk about that, or we can talk about cash deposited in a secret account in Bern or Zurich."

Darius frowned. "I want my company back," he said.

"So you can lock the MBAs out of the plant," said Cordero with a faint, wry smile.

"Okay. Call it revenge. Call it any damned thing you want."

"We don't have to call it anything," said Cordero. "Are we approaching a deal?"

Darius nodded. For a moment he looked away, first at the pool and the girls, then up at the stars. "Do I want to know *why* you want to enter the United States with airplanes that evade the control system?" he asked.

"Do you?" asked Cordero cynically.

Darius didn't entirely catch the cynicism. "I don't know. Well—well, yes, I do. I mean—"

"Mr. Whitney," Cordero interrupted. "Latin American politics. What do you know of the complexities of our politics? Some people—some people can't live in their native countries anymore. You know. Elections. Coups d'état. Changes, one way or another. Men who tower at the top of the heap today must sometimes go into exile tomorrow. And your government is not always cooperative about accepting political refugees. It would be worth a great deal to certain people in our part of the world to be able to assure certain other people that they could, if necessary, gain quick and clandestine entry into the United States. All right? It is worth a great deal of money to some people."

Darius Whitney filled his lungs with air, which he released in a noisy sigh. "To be frank," he said, "I am more interested in what I am going to get out of this than what you are going to do with the virus I will try to write for you. And let's understand that element of it. I will *try* to get your aircraft through. It won't be easy, and I can't promise I can do it. But—"

"You will regain control of your company if you do," said Cordero.

Darius smiled. "We can shake hands on that," he said.

"**O**kay, Commander. Let's see what you've got."

Scott Vandenberg looked up from the computer terminal, into the flushed face of General Warden. The type amused him. He wondered if Major General Samuel Warden hadn't learned his clipped tones and stiff bearing from the German officers in old World War II movies—he looked like Rommel in *The Longest Day*. Commander, he persisted in calling Vandenberg. Sure. To remind him of the difference between their ranks.

"I'll show you," said Scott casually.

He put his hands on the keyboard and typed:

AMRAT

"Think you can get into AMRAT? Really?"

AMRAT was the code name for a tightly guarded database relating to security clearances for military personnel. General Warden and Sergeant Mallory had been working with AMRAT the day the mocking smiley-face first appeared on a National Security Agency computer screen. Though NSA denied it, it had given a contract to Vandenberg & Associates to try to find the virus and vaccinate the NSA systems.

Scott shrugged. "Let's find out," he said. "And incidentally, Sergeant Mallory will testify that he didn't give me the codes."

"Damn well couldn't," said the general. "He doesn't have them."

That was interesting. Sometime in the past week they had taken away the sergeant's access to AMRAT. Did they suspect he was the creator of the smiley-face virus?

The computer's response appeared on the screen:

```
NO SUCH DATABASE AS AMRAT. ENTER YOUR DES-
IGNATOR.
```

Scott shook his head. This kind of thing, forcing an operator to repeat his command, was not security; it was game playing. He typed:

```
AMRAT
```

```
NO SUCH DATABASE AS AMRAT. ENTER YOUR DES-
IGNATOR.
```

Scott glanced up at the general and smiled. The system required a third try.

```
OPEN AMRAT NOW
```

```
YOU ARE IN COMMUNICATION WITH AMRAT.
ACCESS CODE, PLEASE
```

"Now what are you gonna do?" asked the general. "You need an access code."

Scott typed:

```
362-23-7965
```

"Dammit! That's *my* code. Highest-level security."

```
ILLEGAL ACCESS CODE. ABORTING.
```

```
NIMBUS
```

```
TIME, PLEASE

323-81-9987

ACCESS ESTABLISHED, QUERY?
```

All of this was foolishness as far as Scott was concerned. The system's repeated contention that it was not getting the right codes, then its request for the time when it wanted another code, might frighten off an amateur but would not stop a dedicated hacker or a determined spy.

```
VANDENBERG, SCOTT R., COMMANDER USN
```

The computer began to display his Navy personnel file—everything from high school on: his educational record, his service record, his security clearances. He hadn't seen it all and kept pressing the Page Dn key and reading.

"All right," the general interrupted. "Point made. So our security is lousy. Is that what you're trying to say?"

Vandenberg nodded. "Something like that."

General Warden blew out a loud, spraying sigh. "The first thing I want to know is how did you get my security codes? They're changed—Hell, that last one wasn't valid this morning. So—"

Scott shook his head. "General, any security code that is given to you also has to be given to the computer. What I've just shown you is that a knowledgeable operator can extract the security codes from your computer and use them himself."

General Warden snatched a chair from beside a table and sat down at the terminal. "A threat to national security," he said darkly.

"I think the people who put smiley-faces on your terminals are rattling your cage, General. If they were interested in breaching security, they wouldn't show you smiley-faces; they'd extract classified information, and you wouldn't even know it. I think what you've been looking at is a warning from people who just chose a dramatic way to show you it can be done."

"*You* did it."

Scott nodded. "They showed me how. I studied your smiley-face virus. Whoever wrote it knows your system top to bottom. It's an inside job, General."

"Then once we catch the son of a bitch, we're safe."

"No. You're paying my organization a generous fee to show you what happened and how to prevent its happening again. I'm going to give you some twenty recommendations. If you follow them, the system will be secure—until somebody else figures out a way to penetrate it."

"Dammit, is there no way to plug all the holes?"

"No. Not for sure. You have to stay alert and keep working on it."

Scott held Judy's hand as he led her up the walk to return her to her mother. It was never an easy moment. No matter how you explained the situation, you could not make a seven-year-old understand. The worst part was that Judy had gotten it into her head that *she* was the cause of the divorce. Since she had no idea how and was not rational on the subject, what could you say to convince her it was not so? He was satisfied that Sally had tried as hard as he did to assure Judy that she had nothing to do with it, but both of them sensed that the child suspected her parents lied to her—as, after all, she knew all parents did; it was part of what adults did to their children.

"Next Saturday?"

Scott nodded. "I think so, honey. You know how it is with Daddy. If something dumb spoils next Saturday, then it will be very soon after that."

Judy nodded. The explanation never satisfied.

Scott reached to press the button for the doorbell, but Judy grabbed the knob, turned it, and opened the door, yelling, "We're here! Daddy an' me!"

He could not stand outside and refuse to enter the house he had lived in for five years. But he did not venture beyond the vestibule, where he waited for his ex-wife or her husband, Frank, to appear and welcome him.

It was nothing awkward, really. The divorce had not made Scott and Sally hate each other. As for Frank— Well, at first Frank had been self-conscious in the role of second husband in a house that still bore the marks of the first husband's style and personality. But Frank had gotten over that, and there was no awkwardness when Scott came to pick up Judy or to return her.

"On time," said Sally when she appeared. She had taken a moment to repair her makeup, apparently, and probably to pull on the lemon-yellow jogging suit she was wearing. She was a blonde. She had always worn her hair to her shoulders, and currently it was even longer, well down on her shoulders. She was heavily pregnant. "I appreciate promptness," she said.

"Has it ever been otherwise?" he asked.

She shrugged. She looked down at Judy as if to discover some blemish on her caused by her afternoon with her father. She was no hysterical woman, and Scott took her reaction as normal, not to be resented; it had to be torture to surrender up your child for an afternoon to a man who was more and more a stranger with every passing month.

Judy hurried off to her room to put away her coat and the present he had bought her.

Sally stood looking at him. "Frank's out," she said. "Would you like to sit down long enough for a drink?"

"I probably should be going," he said.

"Got a date?"

Scott shook his head. "No." He smiled. "And I won't get one for tonight if I don't get home and get on the phone."

Sally knew her question and his answer had been facetious —as both of them also understood that her invitation for a drink had been just common civility, not the expression of any real interest in his staying and talking.

Their divorce was all the more painful because neither of them could find any reason, really, to dislike each other. In particular, he didn't dislike her. She was still pretty, in her New England gawkish way: a little awkwardness of posture and movement, which contrasted with physical attributes that were not faultless, but not far from it. She still possessed the qualities that had attracted him to her.

He remembered nostalgically how proud she had been of their marriage. For Sally it had been glamorous to marry a fighter pilot when her friends were marrying stock brokers. Her pride had actually been embarrassing sometimes. Judy had been born when he was still on active service, and she was eight months old before he saw her. He had bought this house in Bethesda. Sally had looked forward to his discharge, when he would be at home, a commuter just like the stock brokers. He hadn't planned to engage in a business that kept him on the road almost as much as the Navy had.

The immediate cause of their divorce had been his mistake. The ultimate cause had been that Sally had exaggerated the significance of that mistake. The sum of them had been that a cliché ran out of control and turned into a farce.

Scott's mistake had been Lucy. He had met her at a computer conference at the World Trade Center in New York. She was a salesperson for a computer service called NEXIS, and she had shown him how the service could search almost instantly through the billions of words in the morgue files of major newspapers and magazines. She was an arresting beauty, and he had found himself asking her to join him for a drink at the end of the conference session, just to have the chance to appreciate her alone for a few minutes, not to establish a relationship with her. He didn't mean to do anything to harm his marriage, and she didn't mean to do anything to harm hers; but the attraction between them had proved more powerful than their good intentions. For six months they saw each other as often as they could.

And eventually Sally found out.

She did not forgive. Rather, she *could* not forgive.

And Sally had made her own mistake. Two months before the divorce became final, Scott's lawyer broke the news to him that there was no point in any further effort at reconciliation, because Sally was pregnant by Frank Campbell.

Frank's wife was named Peggy. She divorced him. Frank and Sally were married two months before their baby was born.

They all knew each other—Scott and Frank, Sally and Peggy—and they never saw each other without experiencing twinges of regret about the way everything had rushed to an irreparable conclusion. "If Sally hadn't been so damned fecund," Peggy had once said to Scott, "you guys could probably have put it back together. This thing has been a silly damned merry-go-round, and it needn't have gotten started if—Oh, well. What's past is past."

So it was all final. History.

Including his affair with Lucy. He had stopped seeing her in the hope of a reconciliation with Sally, and when that hope vanished, he called her. Lucy was not interested in seeing him again.

And that was why on this Saturday evening Scott Vandenberg was alone.

He was used to traveling alone, spending his nights in hotels, eating alone, often room-service food. The only time loneliness bothered him was when he had to spend a weekend in his apartment. He'd played handball this morning and turned down an invitation to dinner with the Howards, knowing that one or another of Sara's divorced girlfriends would just happen to have been invited too.

He poured himself a light Scotch with lots of soda. He felt no particular compulsion to call anyone. Still, the evening did look long. He opened his briefcase and took out his spiral-bound calendar. Flipping back, he found the note he wanted.

Nancy Delacorte.

He didn't know if she would welcome a call. Still, before they left Info Pro she had given him the telephone number of her home in Georgetown as well as her FAA office number. Why had she done that if she would be offended by his calling?

Nothing to lose.

He punched in the number and waited for the rings. She answered.

"Nancy? This is Scott Vandenberg."

"Oh, hi, Scott. How are you?"

"Fine. Listen, am I calling at an awkward time?"

"Not at all. I'm just looking at a basketball game on television, but I can't say I'm much interested in it."

"Well, . . . uh, if what I'm about to say is out of line, just say so. But I was wondering if you'd like to have dinner."

"When did you have in mind?"

"Anytime. Like tonight."

She laughed. "Tonight? Where are you?"

"I'm at home. Bethesda."

"Well . . . It may be a little tough to get a reservation anywhere good. So, look, why don't you come here, and we'll have a drink and get on the phone and see what we can arrange? Okay?"

"Sounds great. Seven-thirty?"

"Seven-thirty."

She had been right: On Saturday evening all of the grand restaurants were filled. He sat in her living room sipping Scotch while she tried to find a table for them. After calling a few of her favorite places to no avail, she finally telephoned a small place not far from her home, and even there they could not have a table before nine. She put out a wedge of Brie with some crackers and mixed herself a martini, and they sat and talked and became better acquainted.

Scott was pleased at how unruffled she was in a situation that he found a little awkward. It had been inept of him to call her so late to suggest a dinner date that very evening; and she could have been annoyed. She wasn't. She was relaxed and apparently glad he had called.

She was wearing a red, ribbed-knit mini, with its skirt four or five inches above her knees.

She lived in a tiny red-brick house built before the Civil War, with a gas-burning lamp on the stoop. In the living room a federal settee faced the fireplace and a wing chair stood to its right. The walls were papered in a floral pattern, above white-painted wain-scoting. Three small area rugs left most of the wide, pegged plank-ing exposed. Her stereo system, concealed somewhere, played at low volume.

Scott decided her home accorded with his perception of her character and personality.

"One question about business," she said. "Then no talk of viruses and screwed-up airline schedules, okay?"

"Deal."

"Do you have any idea why Darius Whitney flew to Co-lombia?"

Scott frowned and shook his head. "I didn't know he did."

"After you mentioned him on Long Island, I gave his name to the FBI. They initiated a check on him and discovered he was in Colombia. He flew down there about two weeks ago, stayed over a long weekend, and flew back."

"What was he doing? Who did he see?"

"We don't know. You understand he's not the subject of a full-court press. The FBI just did a routine check. He went to Colombia. He came back. That's all they know. I gather your suspicion that he wrote the LANCE virus is not supported by enough evidence to charge him with anything."

"What I explained to you about a system designer's signature in his work is good enough evidence for me," said Scott. "But I doubt you could convince a jury with it—unless you got a jury of sophisticated computer technicians."

"Are we saying, then, that whoever wrote the LANCE virus got away with it?"

Scott shrugged. "My responsibility is to clean out the virus and secure the system against another one. Is the government anxious to prosecute?"

"I would say there's a good deal of interest in building a case," she admitted. "But except for your suggestion that Darius Whitney may have been the source of the LANCE virus, we have nothing to go on. Nothing."

A little before nine they left her house and walked to the place where she had finally gotten a reservation. It was a small, neighborhood restaurant, obviously family-run. He took the family for French, but Nancy told him they were Belgian, and when he looked at the menu he saw that the restaurant offered a cuisine he might not have readily identified and was clearly different from the typical French fare offered in a dozen places in the Washington area.

They were seated side by side on a banquette. Because they'd had drinks at home, they ordered none but asked for the wine list.

"I'm glad you could do this this evening," Scott said to her. "You realize I didn't even know if I was calling a married woman."

She glanced at him, amused. "I wasn't sure I wasn't being called by a married man."

"Not for more than two years," he said. "I have a seven-year-old daughter who lives with my former wife and her husband—in *my* house in Bethesda."

"A divorce," she said blandly.

"Yes."

"I haven't had the privilege," she said. "Marriage or divorce."

"You haven't missed anything," he said. "No, I shouldn't say that. That's cynical. After a divorce is over, you come to resent the drama, what Mark Twain called 'the tears and flapdoodle.' That makes you cynical, I guess. But it's wrong to be cynical."

"I haven't been married," she said, "but I've had a couple of what they call relationships. Those break up with tears and flap-doodle too."

She flipped casually over the pages in the wine list the waiter had put on the table between them. Scott's attention was caught by her profile, dramatically outlined by the light of four candles burning in a candelabra on a table to their left. It curved cleanly from chin to forehead, and on her full lower lip a drop of moisture caught a bright reflection of candlelight.

She noticed his intent stare and smiled. He guessed she was accustomed to admiration.

She handed the wine list to him. "How do you make the transition from fighter pilot to computer guru?" she asked abruptly.

He shrugged. "You get a good education in engineering and math at Annapolis," he said. "You fly awhile. Then when the Navy tells you your flying days are over, they assign you to a computer-equipped—computer-dependent, I should say—department. So . . . you learn a lot about computers, fast. I'd been staring at electronic gizmos and learning something about how they worked for a long time, so the fixation was already there."

" 'Fixation,' " she repeated. "They become a fixation, don't they? I mean, computers?"

He nodded. "Right. They can become that. You have to watch yourself when you're working with a computer. The first thing you know, you're more interested in making the computer do some-thing intriguing than in making it solve the problem you set out to solve."

"I haven't got the bug," she said. "I'm interested, but I haven't developed the fascination for computers that I see in people like you."

Scott laughed. "I'm not addicted," he said.

"But you've done something I'd give anything in the world to do," she said. "I mean, fly a jet fighter. I can only imagine what it must be like."

"It's scary, among other things," he said.

"You must be something of a guru yourself," Scott suggested. "In the field of aviation."

"I love flying," she said. "I love airplanes. But I wasn't educated in aeronautical engineering or anything like that. On the other hand, how do you make yourself an expert on airport security? You spend a lot of time in airports, with your eyes open. Which is a dull subject. Tell me, do you like baseball?"

He chuckled. "Is the Pope Catholic? I'm an American. I like baseball."

"The winter of our discontent," she said.

"Hmm?"

"The winter of our discontent. The ten weeks between the Super Bowl and the opening of the baseball season."

"Nancy . . ."

She frowned, hearing an earnest note in his voice.

"Maybe this is too soon to ask," he said, "but would you mind if I call you in a week or so? I'd like to see you again. Why not say so?"

"I'd like to see you again, Scott," she said softly.

"From the tenor of this newspaper article, I gather the task was accomplished," said Virgilio Cordero to the man who stood unsteadily before him on a pair of crutches.

The man's name was Stepan Yanak, a man only recently employed by Cordero. He was a squat, muscular man with a broad, acne-scarred face.

"It was accomplished, Señor Cordero," said Yanak. "As you ordered."

Virgilio Cordero nodded, satisfied. They were in a suite atop a hotel in Panama City, and the newspaper Cordero had mentioned was a copy of the *Los Angeles Times*, one day old. The article read:

PLANE CRASH, MURDERS IN BAJA
COCAINE FOUND IN SHATTERED SMALL AIRPLANE

A single-engine Cessna aircraft crashed in a remote area on the eastern slope of the Sierra de San Borja Friday afternoon. Although the crash was reported within hours, it was Sunday afternoon before a helicopter flying from Hermosillo spotted the wreckage from the air, on the side of a mountain called Cerro dos Picachos, and was able to direct Mexican police forces to the site. The team of police officers who climbed the slope of the mountain range on Monday morning and came upon the site was murdered to a man—but not before the police lieutenant leading the squad of four got off a partial report on his Handie-Talkie, alerting a far larger detachment of police and soldiers to rush to the scene.

That larger detachment, flown in by helicopter and heavily armed, arrived on the scene Monday afternoon and found

• Lieutenant Jésus Franco and his three men, all dead from heavy fire from automatic weapons that had apparently cut them down with bursts fired from short range.

• The body of Roberto Cardenas, believed to be the pilot of the small plane, dead in the wreckage, not from the crash but from 9 mm slugs in his body. The fuselage of the Cessna was stitched with bullet holes, leading to speculation that it was shot down by fire from another aircraft.

• The bodies of two unidentified men, whose clothing suggest they are United States citizens.

• Cocaine with a street value of possibly as much as $1 million. Some of the bundles had been exploded by gunfire that scattered the white powder over much of the interior of the crashed airplane.

Mexican authorities describe themselves as being at a loss to explain these facts. Speculation is that Cardenas was flying a load of cocaine without the sanction of the new cartel of Latin American drug barons and was overtaken and shot down.

"How much did they have aboard that little airplane?" Cordero asked. "Can you guess?"

"Fifty kilos," said Yanak. "Maybe sixty."

"And where is it now?"

Yanak allowed himself to smile. "Right there on that Mexican mountain," he said. "Didn't move it. Didn't touch it."

Cordero smiled and nodded. "Sit down," he said. "Do you like champagne? Caviar?"

"Don't know," said Yanak. "I've tasted champagne, but you don't hardly ever get caviar on the East Side of Cleveland."

"Where I'm going to send you now, you'll acquire a taste for both of them," said Cordero. "You don't speak Spanish, do you, Stepan?"

"Only a few words, sir."

"I want you to recover fully from your wound. I'm going to send you to an estate in Paraguay. We will see to your comforts there, and I will provide an instructor, and I want you to learn to speak Spanish. It is awkward for a man who works for me not to speak Spanish."

"I'll try my best, Señor Cordero."

"Let's be sure we understand something," said Cordero. "Why did we have to get rid of our pilot and his gunman?"

Yanak shook his head as he spoke in reply. "They failed. They should have shot down the Cessna over the water, so that the wreckage couldn't be examined. But I don't figure that was the reason."

"Good," said Cordero. "Then what was the reason?"

"I figure it was because they rushed off and put in a telephone call to Bogotá first chance they got," said Yanak. "That was stupid and risky. If anybody knows they made a call to Bogotá, the connection to you could be traced."

Cordero's smile widened. "That is why I am sending you off to learn Spanish, Stepan. You don't blunder on your assignments, it's true; but you are also smart. Well, I'm sorry to have to rush you off, but I have other people to see. Recover. And come back and tell me all about it in Spanish."

As Yanak left, Yoshitaka Hara came in. He did not wait to be asked to drink champagne or nibble caviar on toast. He poured his own and picked up a little wedge of toast. In fact he used a little spoon and added more caviar to it.

"It may be just as well if you don't meet the general," said Cordero.

"I've never been much interested in greasers," said Hara.

Cordero subdued a flash of anger and managed an artificial smile. "Be careful of your terminology, my friend," he said. "*Norteamericanos* use that word for many different kinds of people."

"Okay," said Hara insouciantly as he reached for another wedge of toast. "I won't use that word, and you won't remind me of how Japan lost the war."

Cordero chuckled. The subject was closed. "Progress?" he asked.

"Yes. Definitely. The man is a genius. That's a word I don't like to use. It is used too much. But that's what Darius Whitney is."

"Any problems?"

"One."

"Let me guess. Allison McGuire."

"He tells her everything. And she tries to play his conscience."

"Uhmm . . . well, don't worry about it, Yo. We have ways of taking care of little problems like that."

"Otherwise," said Hara, ignoring the implications of what Cordero had just said, "I think it's going well. I hate to admit this, but I could never have done it myself."

"How soon?"

Hara drew a deep breath. "He talks about a beta test, within two or three weeks."

"That soon?"

"Yes. And at that point he will want specifics about how much he is to be paid."

Cordero nodded. "That is no problem," he said. "We will take care of Señor Darius Whitney. One way or another."

6

—∎-∎-∎-∎—

"**M**y god," Allison whispered. "How . . . ?"

Darius Whitney's eyes were bright with fascination and satisfaction: bright and brittle as they snapped back and forth, scanning the screen on what Allison called the Beast, his highly personal computer in his house in Malibu.

The ever-changing display in front of him represented the air traffic approaching or departing the Los Angeles Terminal Control Area. Each little block on the screen contained essential information about a flight.

Whitney squinted at one block:

AA118 ORD LAX ETA2150Z 3497 CAT5 LVG

AA118 meant American Airlines Flight 118.

ORD LAX meant that the flight originated at the airport once called Ordway, now Chicago's O'Hare International, and was en route to Los Angeles.

ETA2150Z stood for Estimated Time of Arrival, 21 hours 50 minutes Zulu. *Zulu* was aviation jargon for Greenwich Mean Time, the time universally used for air-traffic control, to avoid confusion over time zones and daylight saving time. The flight was due in Los Angeles at 1:50 PM, Pacific Standard Time.

The transponder code for this flight was 3497, which meant that an electronic instrument on board would put that identifying number and the aircraft's altitude on radar screens—not just a blip.

CAT5 meant that the flight had been assigned a STAR—Standard Terminal Arrival Route—designated Catalina 5, one of several standard arrival routes that kept aircraft safely separated as they approached Los Angeles International Airport.

Finally, LVG meant that American Flight 118 was now controlled by Las Vegas Center, which would have it on radar and would be in radio contact with the pilots.

Another block read:

```
V VNY SAC D2108Z 3590 V201 PMD
```

A VFR flight (that is, an aircraft flying under visual flight rules) had filed a flight plan nevertheless. It had departed Van Nuys for Sacramento at 2108 Zulu, had been assigned transponder code 3590, and was following Victor Airway 201 to the navigation radio beacon at Palmdale.

"How did you get in?" Allison asked as she stared wide-eyed at the screen. "Are you sure they don't know you're in?"

"They don't know," said Darius.

"Could they trace the telephone?"

He looked up at her and grinned. "Sweet," he said. "When did we last pay a long-distance bill? If they discover that an unauthorized user is on line—which they won't—they'll think the contact was made by the FAA itself, from Washington. That was the first problem to be solved: working my way into the government's own telephone lines." He shrugged as he turned his eyes to the screen again. "Which, of course, was no very great problem."

Allison stared at the screen, shaking her head. "Darius," she said, her voice subdued by awe. "How are you going to do it?"

He put a finger to his mouth. "By adding false information to what we see here. Suppose we had an airplane approaching, say, San Antonio out of Mexico on a published airway. As that airplane is picked up on ADIZ radar, they are going to see a transponder code on their screen. They query the system to see if that code has been assigned to a flight coming in on that airway at that time. The system says yes, this is a Beechcraft Baron coming in on a filed flight plan. So they relax."

"The system says yes when it should have said no?"

He nodded. "We have in effect filed a flight plan of our own. It's in the computer."

"But why doesn't the pilot of the Baron simply file a flight plan the regular way?"

"Because when the plane lands at San Antonio it is going to be swarmed over by narcs, since it's a flight from Mexico. What we're going to have to do is erase our first flight plan shortly after the plane crosses the border. San Antonio may have been told to expect a Baron coming out of Mexico. When it doesn't show, they'll check the computer. The computer will say it has no flight plan for a Baron from Mexico. They'll suppose there's been a mistake. Our airplane will be on its way to, say, Dallas. And the computer will have a new flight plan for it—one that says it's a flight from, say, Austin. And incidentally the airplane is not a Baron. It's something else, maybe a Piper twin. Since the airplane landing at Dallas looks, to the system, like an airplane that has not been on the other side of the border, the narcs won't pay any attention to it. Even if they're looking for a missing Baron, they won't identify it with this Piper from Austin."

Allison sighed and shook her head. "Narcs," she said. "You're talking about narcs. Not about immigration agents."

Darius closed his eyes for a moment. "Narcs. Immigration agents. Whatever. I don't know what they want to bring across the border. I guess I should care, shouldn't I?"

"It's not immigrants, Dare," she said solemnly. "C'mon."

"I don't *know* it's not immigrants. Dammit. Maybe it is. I mean—there is money in getting political refugees into this country. I . . . hell, I don't know. Am I supposed to know?"

Allison changed the subject. "Aren't you creating a hazard?" she asked. "False information in the system could cause a midair collision."

"No. For two reasons. In the first place we're creating an *extra* flight, not hiding one. In the second place the avoidance of midair collisions is a matter of radar observation of the traffic. If a radar controller sees two planes on collision course, he will warn them—whether he knows who they are or not. Hey . . . sweet . . . Nobody's going to die from this."

She sighed. "No. Of course not. Nobody except the ones that die from the tons of cocaine this is going to bring into the country. Dare, we *do* understand that's what they want to bring in. Not refugees. Not politicians going into exile. It's going to be cocaine, Dare. You yourself just said they didn't want narcs swarming over their planes."

"Well, maybe," he said. "Look, I never did really believe they were only interested in flying in political refugees. And they don't think I believe it, either."

"The stuff is poison, Dare," she said. "Every new ton of it that comes in is going to make new addicts. It looked for a while like the Colombian connection was broken permanently. Now . . . a new crowd. A new source. More addicts. More death."

Darius Whitney pondered for a moment, then he said, "I don't make addicts. They do that to themselves. Anyway, if the stuff didn't get into the country this way, it would get in some other way. There's millions in this deal. Why should I stand back and let somebody else collect what's being offered to *me*?"

Nathan Morgenstern, chief executive officer of Whitney Data Dynamics Corporation, put down his telephone. He let his weight settle down into his chair as if he were deflating, which in a very real sense he was.

He had just spoken for almost half an hour with Tad Gilligan, his national marketing manager. He heard what he had expected but still had hoped not to hear.

"We *know* why, goddammit!" Gilligan had growled. "The word's around. We can deny it all we want to; the word is around. Rumor or fact, it doesn't make any difference. They all believe the Thanksgiving Eve virus got into LANCE in WHIT 3.0. Right now, five months after the Thanksgiving Eve debacle, I couldn't *give* away a set of WHIT 3.0 disks."

Nathan Morgenstern shook his head. The general counsel of the company, John Koch, sat on the couch against the wall opposite Morgenstern's desk. The speaker phone had been turned on during most of the conversation between Morgenstern and Gilligan, and Koch had heard the bad news.

"We know," Morgenstern muttered. "That's the damnedest part of it. We know that son of a bitch Whitney did it. We can't prove it, but—"

"Why?" asked Koch calmly.

"Why would he do it? To hurt us, that's why. To . . . hurt . . . us."

Koch shook his head. "Fanciful," he said. "Speculation."

"Somebody's working on it," said Morgenstern. "Somebody good enough to find out. Hired by Info Pro. You ever hear of a guy called Scott Vandenberg?"

"No."

"He's a goddamn expert. He's the one who came up with the idea that WHIT carried the virus. I tell you what we've gotta do. We've got to find out how much Vandenberg really knows. If he's got the evidence, then we file a multimillion-dollar lawsuit against Whitney. If he hasn't, then we file a multimillion-dollar lawsuit against Vandenberg. Either way, we make points. Either the papers carry the story that we're suing an old crud who used to work here, was put out to pasture, and planted the virus for revenge— *or* they carry the story that Vandenberg libeled us by launching a rumor that's not based on fact."

"A question, Nat. Was the virus in WHIT? *Is* it in WHIT?"

"I can answer one of those questions for damned sure," said Nathan Morgenstern. "It's not in there anymore. It's not on any of the disks in inventory."

"But was it on the disks we shipped to Info Pro?"

"The only man who knows won't tell us," said Morgenstern. "There's no point in asking him of course. If he did it, he'd lie."

"*Could* he have done it?"

"Anne Scibelli thinks he could have. She's his secretary. She says he messed around for a long time with something he wanted to keep secret. He could have been writing the virus."

"How serious are you about suing?"

"Damn serious," said Morgenstern. "One or the other. Whitney or Vandenberg. What I think you had better do is contact Vandenberg. Sound him out. See how much he really knows."

* * *

Scott Vandenberg turned his back to the edge of the swimming pool, planted his hands on the tile, and lifted himself out. He walked to the table where they had left their towels, dried himself a little, and sat down. Nancy was at the other end of the pool, and he watched her swim toward him with strong, graceful strokes, moving fast through the water without splashing. She lifted herself easily over the edge of the pool and came to the table to join him. Like most of the women in the pool, she wore a one-piece swimsuit, cut almost up to the waist. Her version was iridescent blue.

They were spending Friday night, Saturday and Saturday night, and Sunday in a luxury motel just north of Fredericksburg, Virginia.

The weekend had been, he hoped, an inspired idea, the suggestion of one of his technicians at Vandenberg & Associates, who said he brought his wife here twice each winter, at least, to get away from the kids. It was what the motel called a champagne weekend. From noon on Saturday to noon on Sunday the indoor pool was closed to children. The weekend was for couples. Rooms, the pool, a champagne dinner, and a champagne brunch on Sunday morning were a package, and Scott had bought Friday night as well.

He and Nancy had separate rooms. He had told her they would when he called her to suggest this weekend; and she had offered no comment but just said okay, it sounded like fun. He hoped they would not use both rooms, but he wouldn't press. He appreciated Nancy Delacorte too much to chance driving her away.

"I should swim more," she said as she sat down a little short of breath. "I do it a lot in the summer, but . . ."

Nancy was staring at a scar that ran diagonally up his ribs to the middle of his chest. "Man . . ." she murmured. "Somebody try to cut you in two?"

"You could put it that way," he said.

"You were a Navy pilot. You aren't old enough to have flown over Vietnam, are you?"

"Old enough," he said. "They kept the war going just long enough to accommodate me."

"So that's a war wound?"

100

"A war injury," he said.

"Don't play games," she said, shaking her head with a wry little smile. "I can't bear the modest warrior ploy. I'm not going to beg you to tell me how you got hurt in Vietnam, but I'd like to know."

Scott was not playing taciturn warrior. All that restrained him from telling about his experience over Vietnam was that he had been asked to tell it too many times, plus the fact that some people, particularly very young people, reacted in a variety of negative ways, ranging from awe to scorn.

"Nixon called our last aerial offensive Operation Linebacker," he said. "In 1972. I'd just got there and was flying a Phantom, an F-4, off the *Constellation*. I didn't do anything glamorous. I never saw a MiG, much less got a shot at one. Our job—my backseat man and I—was to follow our leader, and when he found the target, we'd follow him in and let fly our rockets where he did. We did it six times. The seventh time a missile came up, right at us. My backseat man saw it and screamed at me to swerve out of the way. I did, but the thing exploded under us, and too close. The plane was riddled with fragments. I retreated at the best speed I could get the damaged bird back to the carrier. We didn't quite make it and had to eject over the water. The scar is a cut from a part of the canopy frame. The missile blast had jammed the canopy so it wouldn't open fully. The ejection shot me right through it."

"You were—?"

"Picked up within five minutes. We were within sight of the *Constellation*."

"You stayed in the Navy," she said.

"Until 1984," he said. "I flew the F-14. I put in thirteen years in the Navy. I could have stayed for twenty. But I didn't fly anymore after 1980, so it wasn't much fun. I took early retirement. I'm still a reserve officer."

"In naval intelligence," she said. "When you left flying status, you were assigned to naval intelligence. That is where you first built a reputation as an authority on viruses."

He raised his chin abruptly. "You've seen my personnel jacket," he said.

She nodded, then frowned. "Well . . . probably only part of

it. I don't know if you realize how seriously the government takes the Thanksgiving Eve debacle. We've reviewed everything on record about everybody involved. For a short time it was regarded as suspicious that you were called in to vaccinate not just LANCE but also the system at the National Security Agency. Somebody suggested you might have infected those computers yourself, to get fees for removing the infections."

"General Warden," he said. "NSA."

"I didn't say that."

"You didn't have to," said Scott. "The general has become paranoid. And maybe he has reason. You ever hear of the Chaos Computer Club?"

She shook her head.

"A German group, out of Hamburg. Hackers. But with a serious purpose. Their idea is that governments classify a lot of information the public has a right to know and that it's too expensive and time-consuming to get at it through the Freedom of Information Act and the like. So, they break into computers—industry and government computers—lift confidential information, and make it public."

"What have they gotten into here?"

"NASA," said Scott. "Anyway, somebody in Germany did."

"And General Warden is afraid they'll get into NSA?"

"Somebody at NSA is warning him it's possible," said Scott. "He thinks he's already been invaded, but he hasn't. Somebody inside the agency was putting smiley-faces on his computer screens to show him how leaky his security is. I patched his leaks, but I can't promise a dedicated hacker won't get in. Nobody can promise that. The only way a computer system can be secure is to be isolated, stay off the telephone lines. Which, of course, systems like LANCE can't do. Communication is their life, their reason for existing."

She reached over and touched his scar. "Sorry," she said. "I didn't mean to talk business today."

"You have all the advantage on me now," he said. "You've seen my curriculum vitae, and I haven't seen yours."

Nancy smiled. "Fair enough," she said. "When I graduated from Duke University in 1977, I had no idea what I wanted to do.

Frankly I'd thought I was going to marry a guy I'd gone out with for three years, but that fell through about the time we graduated. I was kind of lost and decided to try being an airline hostess. My parents were against that—said it wasn't what a young woman with a degree from Duke ought to do with her life—but I tried it and was a flight attendant, as we were supposed to call it, for three years, with Pan Am. Pan Am because I'm reasonably fluent in Spanish and can get around in German and French."

"So where's the transition from flight attendant to investigator for the FAA?" Scott asked.

Nancy sighed. "I came within an inch of getting killed," she said. "Terrorists got explosives aboard a flight I was working. The stuff was discovered ten minutes before we were scheduled to take off. After that I watched the airport security in every airport I was in—and I got damned upset about how lax it was. Well . . . I'm the daughter of an FBI agent. Dad's assistant director now. Did you know that? Every time I was at home, I'd complain about the lax security; and finally one day he said to me, why don't you quit bitching and do something about it? You've got a college degree. You've got a pilot's license. You—"

"Pilot's license? Instrument rating?"

She nodded. "I was reluctant to mention it to a jet jockey like you. Anyway, my father suggested I could maybe qualify for an appointment as a field agent for the Department of Air Transportation, FAA. He got me an interview. I took the exam and passed. And that's how it happened."

Nancy put her hand lightly on Scott's. "No more business talk. Only personal stuff. So . . . let's see. I like to sleep late on weekends. I can be quite grouchy before I get my first morning coffee. And I've got a funny little mole in a place you're not allowed to see . . . anyway, not yet."

Later that night he saw it.

Eddy Wentzel was a pro. He was a professional pilot, had never been anything else, had never wanted to be anything else; and he could fly anything, from a Piper Cub to a Lear jet, and a helicopter, too, if anybody wanted him to fly one. Some planes were fun, and the one he was flying now was just that: a sleek, swift little bird, capable of two hundred knots, which was fast for a single-engine airplane. It was a Mooney, painted brown and white, bearing its registration number, N8288J, in large numbers on the fuselage and wings.

Right. A Mooney. N8288J. But the flight plan filed for it said it was a retractable Cessna, number N4234Q.

The whole idea was crazy. Crazy. He could wind up in the slammer. They could jerk his license.

The Colombians were paying him: the Señors he had flown for several times before, who always paid a premium—and should, considering the kinds of things they asked him to do.

For example in November he'd tried to sneak an old DC-3 into Florida from Venezuela without any flight plan. The Señors had wanted to know if you could bring a big plane, like a DC-3, into Florida in the same way that you could a small private plane coming in from the Bahamas. He'd inserted the DC-3 into the traffic stream between Nassau and Fort Lauderdale and pretended he was just a chicken among the chickens and not a fox flying slow and at a low altitude and as a VFR flight—that is, one flying under visual flight rules, with no flight plan filed.

Ha! Fifty miles from Fort Lauderdale he'd looked out the window and spotted two F-14 Tomcats, one right beside him, one above. He was, in effect, arrested in midair, and they'd led him to Homestead AFB. The narcs on the Air Force base had all but disassembled that DC-3 looking for cocaine. And they hadn't been amused when they didn't find any. He had a sense the name Eddy Wentzel went on a shit list that day.

Of course there hadn't been any cocaine. What the Señors wanted was to explore a lot of ways that you *might* make clandestine, illegal flights into the States. They hadn't asked him, Eddy Wentzel, to actually carry any of the stuff. They knew he wouldn't.

This was a new idea, something about faking flight plans. He had explained to the man who handed him the assignment why it wouldn't work—"Look, when you file a flight plan to cross the Mexican border, you have to land at an international airport or at what's called a landing-rights airport—some airport where there is a United States Customs Service station. And you have to file a flight plan. They're watching on radar, and when they see an unidentified airplane approaching the border, they scramble fighters."

But the man had explained that they were going to tinker with the computers and confuse the controllers about what plane was coming in where. It would be okay, the man said. For sure.

Anyway, they were paying him $10,000 to try. And since there was absolutely nothing illegal on board, maybe it wasn't such a bad game.

The flight plan said he was flying from Chihuahua to El Paso. Fifty miles south of the border he radioed El Paso Flight Service Station:

"El Paso Radio, this is Cessna November four-two-three-four Quebec."

"Cessna three-four Quebec, El Paso Radio. Go ahead."

"Three-four Quebec is over Laguna de Patos and will cross the border in about twenty minutes. Can you notify Customs for me?"

"Your flight plan has been filed with Customs, sir. An inspector will come to you on the ramp. You should check our ATIS, sir, and contact Approach."

"Cessna three-four Quebec, Roger. Thank you, sir, and good day."

He had been told to listen to the airport's ATIS—meaning Automatic Terminal Information System—a constantly repeating recorded broadcast of weather and other airport information. He tuned the frequency and listened to Information Bravo, the current data. It gave him the current altimeter setting and confirmed what he could see, that the weather was clear. It also advised that Runway 22 was in use.

He switched his radio to the frequency for El Paso Approach Control.

"El Paso Approach, Cessna four-two-three-four Quebec with you one-eight-zero degrees and fifty miles. I have Information Bravo."

"Cessna four-two-three-four Quebec, El Paso Approach. Squawk zero-four-zero-four."

"Cessna three-four Quebec will squawk zero-four-zero-four."

Okay. They had changed his transponder code to 0404. He

set in the new code. Now he was on their radar screen, clearly identified. His transponder was also linked to his altimeter, so the numbers on the radar screen also showed his altitude.

"Contact, Cessna three-four Quebec. Cleared for VOR-DME approach. Expect to make left downwind for Runway two-two. Report ten miles."

"Three-four Quebec, Roger."

The airport was not busy. The weather was clear, and they were not using the full Instrument Landing System.

This was where the situation was going to fall apart. El Paso Approach had him on radar. They were tracking him and would track him almost to the point where his wheels touched the runway. Somewhere between here and the runway he was supposed to break away, fly off to the east, and become Mooney N8288J. And they were supposed to be left wondering what became of Cessna N4234Q.

The airport was almost four thousand feet above sea level. His approach would carry him over Ciudad Juarez, then over the Rio Grande, and finally over the city of El Paso before he entered the traffic pattern for the airport.

Eddy kept his speed high as he let the Mooney down to 4,500—just 500 feet above the landscape.

"Cessna four-two-three-four Quebec, you are well below the approach course."

"Roger, El Paso. I've got a little problem."

That would be his last transmission to El Paso Approach Control, or to anyone as Cessna 4234Q. He switched off his transponder, hoping that when his numbers disappeared off their scopes they would think he had crashed. He roared over Ciudad Juarez at more than two hundred miles an hour.

The radio towers were clearly marked on the chart. What was more, they carried arrays of blinking red lights that made them distinctly visible at night. In bright sunlight they were thin silvery pencils held erect by a tangle of invisible guy wires angling away from them like nets to catch low-flying airplanes. He was too low. He saw one tower but didn't see the other one.

"Cessna three-four Quebec, where are you? You may be on a collision course with a tall tower. Climb immediately."

Collision course—Son of a *bitch!*

Eddy hauled back on the yoke to climb just as he caught sight of the tower. He was less than half a mile from it and roaring toward it at 3.3 miles a minute. It didn't look like a pencil now; it looked like a mile-wide gleaming steel wall. He threw the plane into a hard right bank.

He didn't know by how much he missed. A lot more, no doubt, than the fifty feet he estimated.

He was a professional pilot, but his hands trembled on the yoke, and for a long moment he did not reestablish total control, as the airplane swept around in a climbing bank.

"Three-four Quebec, what are you doing?"

The angry voice brought him back. They knew damned well what he was doing. The question was: Could they react fast enough to do anything about it?

He rolled out of his bank, lowered his nose, and dived for the Rio Grande. In his dive he picked up speed. The river was a landmark. So was Highway 180, which ran to the east and through the mountains.

He crossed the river, again at only five hundred feet above the landscape and at more than two hundred miles an hour. A bridge flashed past him. El Paso International Airport was to his left. He was below its traffic pattern, but any Piper Cub tooling around at low altitude was a menace to him. Biggs Air Force Base spread out just north of El Paso International. And Highway 180, which was the south boundary of the two airports, stretched away to the east.

Eddy set the Mooney directly above the highway and followed it as if he were driving on it. It would take him through the mountain passes and away from El Paso.

His real destination was Midland, Texas.

In air-traffic-control jargon, telephone calls are land-line communication, as distinct from radio communication. Calls don't have to be dialed; the lines are kept open. As the Mooney disappeared to the northeast, the controllers were busy on their land lines.

El Paso Approach Control to El Paso Flight Service Station:

"Cessna Four-two-three-four Quebec has broken off approach and scrammed. He's not down. I've still got a blip."

El Paso Flight Service: "Okay. I'll notify the Air Force."

El Paso Approach: "He's out of Mexico."

El Paso Flight Service: "Gotcha."

El Paso Flight Service Station to Biggs Air Force Base: "Got a bogie for ya. A Cessna broke off approach after crossing the river. Heading east."

Biggs AFB: "What kinda Cessna?"

El Paso Flight Service: "Uh, lemme check the flight plan here. He . . . he . . . uh, dammit, I don't know! I got no flight plan for any Cessna Four-two-three-four Quebec. There was supposed to be a flight plan."

Biggs AFB: "Well, let us know when you figure it out."

El Paso Flight Service Station to El Paso Approach Control: "Hey, Charlie, what about that Cessna that scrammed? You got a flight plan on him? I got no flight plan."

El Paso Approach Control: "He called in, got a squawk code. Hell, yes, there's a flight plan."

El Paso Flight Service: "Look on the computer. That's what I'm doing. I got no flight plan here for any Cessna November Four-two-three-four Quebec."

El Paso Approach Control: "Yeah? Well, we've got a tape of the conversation between me and the pilot."

Yoshitaka Hara sat on the balcony of his suite in the Sands Hotel, Las Vegas, looking down casually at the swimming pool and the girls who lounged around it. Eddy Wentzel was not so casual. He stared.

The bald little Japanese was nibbling on chips and sipping from a glass of very dry white wine. The red-haired, flush-faced pilot was drinking beer and had just put a fistful of chips on the paper napkin on his TV tray.

"If I understand what you are telling me," said Hara, "the program performed as it was supposed to, so far as it went."

Eddy Wentzel shrugged. "When I contacted Approach Control at Midland, they were expecting a Mooney, November eight-two-eight-eight Juliet. Also, so far as they were concerned, I was a domestic flight from Tulsa—routine flight plan. I refueled and left there VFR, no flight plan. The Mooney's sitting on the private field at Wetumka, Oklahoma, where you told me to take it."

"Officially that little airplane has disappeared," said Hara. "The flight plan, Tulsa to Midland, has also disappeared from the computers."

"That's all very well, Mr. Hara," said Eddy, "but I got away from El Paso, not because the computers were manipulated but because I had a quick, fast little airplane and was able to get down on the deck and off their radar scopes before they could get interceptors in the air. Also, if you don't mind my saying so, I'm a smart pilot."

"That's why you work for us," said Hara dryly. "That's why you're paid so much. Anyway—you don't think the virus we have created works so well."

"No. I hope you don't mind my saying so, but this gimmick was put together by computer types, and I'd guess they didn't talk much with pilots before they started. If they had—"

"I take your point," Hara interrupted. "It's a chronic problem in the computer field. Altogether too often, system designers pursue their own brilliant plans, without ever consulting the people whose purposes are to be achieved by their programs."

"We got away with it this time, Mr. Hara. We might get away with it again. But they know they were snookered in some way, and they'll be more alert from now on. Besides, I was able to fly the Mooney through, but I sure couldn't have maneuvered a big plane that way. What we tried with the DC-3 didn't work. This deal looks like it did, but I still wouldn't say we're batting five hundred. I'm damn glad I wasn't carrying anything illegal in that plane. I'd have been scared to death."

Yoshitaka Hara nodded. "Tell you what, Eddy," he said. "You stay close for a day or two. Check into a hotel here in Las Vegas. I guess you can stand that, can't you? Let me know where you're going to be, and I'll take care of your account. Maybe coordinating a computer genius with a smart pilot—I have some calls to make. Relax for a day or two. I'll be calling you."

"**M**r. President, please allow me to introduce Miss Nancy Delacorte and Mr. Scott Vandenberg," said Philip Broughton, the Director of Air Transportation Security.

The President of the United States, who had been talking on the telephone as they entered the Oval Office and had just put it down, stepped out from behind his desk and strode across the deep-blue carpet toward the people who had entered. He extended his hand, first to Nancy, then to Scott.

"Miss Delacorte, I'm pleased to meet you. As for Commander Vandenberg, he and I have met before. Twice, in fact. You recall the two occasions, Scott?"

"I surely do, Mr. President. Once in San Diego at a meeting of old Navy fliers. Once when I was called in to check the security of a computer system in your campaign headquarters."

"Right. Anyway, thanks for coming. We're very much concerned about this thing you're working on, and I wanted to talk to the people who are on the front line, so to speak."

Vice Admiral Lawrence Buchanan, Chief of Naval Intelligence, was also present for this meeting.

Nancy was there because she worked for Broughton, and he had directed her to come. She had suggested to him that Scott should be included in the meeting. The President had concurred. He wanted to talk to the man who knew more than anyone else,

110

probably, about the threat of a virus attack on the nation's air-traffic security.

A crackling fire burned in the fireplace in the Oval Office. The President gestured toward the couches near the fireplace; his guests took seats there; and he himself sat down in the deep chair facing them and the fireplace, with a telephone on a small table at his right hand. A silver coffee service sat on the table between the couches. The President, by a nod, suggested to the admiral—who apparently was a frequent visitor—that he pour the coffee.

"I've read your report, Phil," the President said to Broughton. "Plus others. I have an FBI report and so on. Larry and I"—he meant Admiral Buchanan—"have talked at some length about this problem. I've talked with the Majority Leader and the Speaker, too. I guess there's a consensus that this situation has got to be met some way."

Scott had anticipated the introductory comments that would necessarily precede substantive discussion, and his attention was only half-focused on what the President was saying. He glanced around the Oval Office. The room possessed a singular mystique that exalted whichever President was using it and by corollary humbled the people who came to see him there. The mystique of the Oval Office could be a formidable resource for a President.

This was not Scott's first visit. He had exchanged a few words here with President Carter, who, in 1980, had called in several naval aviators to obtain their view of whether or not naval aircraft could be used in any effective way in a prospective operation to rescue the Americans held hostage in the embassy in Teheran.

The President continued—

"Apparently everything that depends on computers is subject to this form of attack to which we seem to have attached a shorthand expression: virus. It's a classic confrontation, isn't it? Attack and defense. Development of strategies. It would appear right now as though the attackers have strategic advantage. May we hope, Scott, that the defense will regain the advantage?"

Scott tipped his head forward and to one side and looked up at the President as if he were peering over a pair of spectacles. He smiled nervously. "I don't know, sir," he said. "I'm not sure I'd agree that the offense has a clear advantage right now. The problem is that most computer users don't defend at all, and many of those who have defensive programs to protect them against viruses don't use those programs conscientiously."

"The number of hackers seems to be growing in a geometric progression," said the President.

Scott smiled. "Actually, sir, I wish we could get away from the term *hacker*. It used to be an honorable term, meaning someone who was fascinated with computers and became very good at using them. Now the word is used to refer to nasty little boys who make petty mischief with computers."

"It's gotten way beyond petty mischief," said Admiral Buchanan.

"Theft and sabotage," Scott agreed. "Expensive too. I'm just sorry that hacker has become a word for people who misuse computers. When I was introduced to computers, I would have been proud to get good enough to be called a hacker. Now . . ."

"You say people don't defend conscientiously," the President remarked. "Even if they did, could they keep intruders out of their systems?"

"Almost entirely," said Scott. "But not absolutely. Another element of the problem is that before long there will be fifty million personal computers in homes and offices in the United States alone, and every one of them has the potential to break into a mainframe system—assuming it's in the hands of a dedicated person."

"You've been working with the NSA," said the President. "What's their problem?"

"In my judgment, Mr. President, their virus originated inside the agency. In my judgment, it's someone's way of giving the NSA a dramatic warning of vulnerability. Anyway . . . we've cleaned the system and vaccinated it. If they're conscientious, they won't see any more smiley-faces."

The President lifted his cup and took a sip of coffee. "What do you think of the El Paso incident?" he asked Vandenberg.

"I've made a specialty of computer viruses," said Scott, "and I have to be careful, I suppose, not to attribute every problem in the world to viruses. But I must say, sir, that what happened at El Paso has the appearance of a virus in the air-traffic-control-system computers."

"I'm deeply concerned about this," said the President. "If someone can tamper with the computers that control air traffic over the United States, not only is there a threat to passenger safety, not only does it create an opening for the importation of huge quantities of narcotics, but it may actually constitute a threat to national security."

"Yes," said Scott. "Safety—"

The telephone beside the President rang. "Excuse me," he said, and picked it up.

While the President listened to the voice on the line, Scott glanced at Nancy. She was oddly solemn this morning. She had made a cryptic comment as they sat waiting in the West Wing reception room, something to the effect that she was not responsible for what was going to happen in this meeting. She returned his glance with a long face.

The President spoke a few words to his caller, then put down the telephone.

"National security," said Admiral Buchanan solemnly. That was all he said, as if he meant to remind the President of the focus this meeting was supposed to have.

For a moment everyone was distracted by a log that rolled off the top of the wood burning in the fireplace, with a thump and a shower of sparks. Then the President spoke.

"It's really a rather frightening threat, wouldn't you say, Scott?"

"Potentially, I suppose it is," said Scott. "In fact, though, the El Paso virus—if it was a virus—was not very sophisticated or effective. It seems to have confused the controllers out there just long enough to let a fast little plane escape. I don't think they'd let that happen again."

"The problem," said Admiral Buchanan, "is that someone got into the system and planted false data in it. If someone can do that, then . . . well, you see the point. Maybe that virus wasn't very effective, but the next one may be something far more threatening. We have to stop this before it goes any further. We have to defend this country's air-traffic system against tampering. By whomever."

"Oh, I agree with you, Admiral," said Scott.

113

"What I want to do," said the President, "is create a special task force to cope with this problem before it gets any bigger. I want to put together a team of the best people we can get, to move energetically against this threat. And, Scott, I'm asking you to head that team."

"I . . . Mr. President, I'm flattered . . . honored. And I'll be glad to contribute all I can. But I'm not sure I'm the man you want to *head* the team."

The President smiled. "Everybody else thinks you are. If you are not this nation's number-one expert on viruses, which everyone says you are, then at least you are one of the top two or three. What is more, you have security clearances. We can let you in on things that people generally aren't allowed to know."

"Actually, Mr. President, my security clearances have been allowed to lapse. As I'm sure you know, I left active duty in the Navy several years ago."

"Another point," said the President. "I'm asking you to return to active duty for a while."

"Mr. President," said Scott with a troubled frown, "I started a business a few years ago. I—"

"It will only take a few months, don't you think? I realize your absence will harm your business—though I'm told your associates are capable people and can keep things going, for a short time anyway. I realize I'm asking you for a sacrifice. All I can say is, your country needs you."

Scott smiled ironically. "How can any man say no to the President of the United States when he says his country needs him?"

"We'll sweeten the deal a little," said the President. "You'll get your fourth stripe, your eagles. Also, you may be pleased to know that Miss Delacorte will be a member of your team. You and Miss Delacorte are friends, are you not?"

Scott looked at Nancy. "At the moment I'm not sure if we are or not," he said. "I have a feeling she recommended me."

"She'll be detached from active service with the FAA," said Philip Broughton. "She'll be working for you."

"You can call in other people you may want," said the President. "You can have office space in the Pentagon or—"

"Would it be impossibly irregular to rent space in the building where I now have offices, in Bethesda? I have the computer equipment I need there. We can save a few days, maybe more, by not having to relocate."

"Since your staff will be civilians, I see no reason for you to be at the Pentagon," said Admiral Buchanan.

The President stood. "You can work out these details," he said. "You report to Admiral Buchanan, who will report directly to me. You can have personal access to me if you need it." The President extended his hand. "And thank you. What you will be doing will be secret for the time being, but we'll recognize your services when we can."

Admiral Buchanan shook Scott's hand. "Welcome back, Captain Vandenberg," he said.

Darius Whitney sat in a deep leather-covered couch in a penthouse suite high above Las Vegas, staring at Señor Cordero's back as Cordero studied something in the distance through a pair of powerful binoculars. So far as Darius was concerned, he was glad the señor had become distracted by something and wanted to examine it more closely through binoculars. The questions had been coming hard and fast, and this interruption gave Darius a chance to ponder the difficult problem that was being gradually outlined for him.

Yoshitaka Hara, too, seemed content with Cordero's abrupt engrossment with whatever he saw through those binoculars. He stared at the ceiling.

Wentzel, the pilot, yawned and sipped beer. Subtlety was wholly beyond the pilot, Darius judged. Wentzel heard what was said, not what was implied. Direct threats worried him. Insinuated ones did not.

Only Cordero's friend, Patricia, was curious enough to have risen to stand beside him and try to discover without binoculars just what Cordero was staring at. Her scanty white shorts did not quite cover her bottom, her white high-heeled shoes tightened the muscles in her legs, and her tight red T-shirt outlined her breasts. Beside her, Allison looked mousy in a skirt and blouse.

Cordero's invitation for this weekend meeting had specifically included Allison. Darius wondered why. He wondered if Cordero wanted her here so he could form a judgment: whether Allison was useful and to be trusted, or if she were responsible for the El Paso failure because she had insisted Darius create something that would not be a threat to safety.

Darius was glad Allison was with him. If she did not compare with the decorative young females like Patricia that Cordero kept around for his amusement, she had already demonstrated the power of her mind. She had been taking an active part in the discussions, and she had held her own against Yoshitaka Hara as well as against the ungrammatical and flippant pilot who was here as the expert on air-traffic control.

"You figure it's possible?" Eddy asked, returning to the subject they had been discussing when Cordero got up and went to the window.

"Why not?" asked Darius.

"Look. I know nothin' about computers, but I can tell you how it works—because a pilot has to know."

Whitney took a quick puff on his cigar. "I'd like to hear it all again," he said.

"Okay. I mean . . . starting at the beginning, okay? Radar sends out a beam, a signal, you might say. A pulse. That pulsed beam travels until it hits something. When it hits something, it's reflected back. The radar station is a sender and a receiver. It sends out the pulse and receives the reflection. I mean, you know, they've hit the damned moon with the radar beam, and the reflection comes back, is received by the dish antenna, and goes inside and into the electronics, where it gets to be a beep in some earphones or a blip on a screen."

"In its most primitive form," said Whitney dryly.

"Right. Now. You can tell from what angle the reflection comes back, which gives you the bearing to the target. You measure the time between transmission of the pulse and return of the reflection, and that gives you the distance. Which is still primitive."

"But good enough to target the German bomber fleets approaching Britain in 1940," said Whitney.

"Right. But what we carry in planes today has color screens. Like, at night or in thick soup in the daytime, your radar looks out ahead of you fifty miles or so and, as the word is, 'paints' what's out there. Like, a mountain shows one color, tall buildings another color, and what we're most interested in—thunderstorms and rain—show up another color. You know of course the radar we carry in planes is set up to show us stuff like that but not other planes around us. We don't see the traffic. Only the controllers' radar on the ground sees that."

"Which is what we're interested in," said Whitney.

"Right."

"Okay. The radar in use today is also digital. You know what that means. The reflected signal is fed into a computer in the radar station and is converted from analog information to digital information, which is done because digital information is much easier to amplify and clarify and—"

"And manipulate," interjected Allison.

"And manipulate," he nodded. "Meaning 'manage.' It's like digital television: much clearer. Also, the digital information can be fed into mainframe computers, where all kinds of things can be done."

"And here is the key, probably," said Whitney. "Most of this comes after my time in the Air Force, but I've read about it. The position, speed, altitude, and transponder-code identification of aircraft are transmitted from the radar stations to the Air Traffic Control computers. The controllers can tell in seconds whether an aircraft is a legal flight and whether it is where it is supposed to be."

"You got it," said Eddy. "Like, when I was coming into El Paso. The controllers queried the computer system to see if I was legal. Because you'd bugged the computer system, it looked like I was. But if I'd been a high-altitude flight, coming in at five hundred knots, the radar would have had me targeted long before I had to contact ATC, and the information off the radar would have been fed into the computers. If I'd been an illegal, the computer would have set off an alarm. My numbers on the radar screen would have started to blink, and they would have kept on blinking until the interceptors were on me."

"The problem, then, is to make selected flights invisible," said Whitney.

"That's the problem," said Eddy. "Señor Cordero wants to fly a big plane across the border. Maybe a 727. Maybe even a 707 or a DC-8. The point would be to make it invisible to ATC radar. Your bug has got to disable the radar station itself so the flight doesn't show on the scope, and also to block the information out of the ATC computers."

"He'll still be a blip on the screen, no matter what you do," said Allison.

"No," said Eddy. "Not with digital radar. The reflected signal has to go through the station computer to be digitalized. That's where you've gotta stop it."

"We can't kill the whole system," said Whitney. "Not even for a minute. They'd go on military radar and scramble every interceptor in the country. They'd think Russian bombers were coming."

"Selective," said Allison. "That's the point. How in the name of god are you going to write a program that blocks the signal for one specific flight?"

"Yes, how?" asked Cordero. He put down the binoculars. "I've been watching air traffic coming into and going out of McCarran International out there. It's like—it's like a dance. Every airplane is moving in relation to every other, in a pattern that shifts but is a pattern nonetheless. How can you make the system blind to one airplane without muddling the pattern and causing them to start colliding with one another? There's the rub, hmm?"

Whitney's mind was already mulling over the problem. He withdrew from the conversation and the time and place. He sat there withdrawn, his thoughts turning on the question of how to make ATC radar fail to see one individual airplane. The solution to that problem was the key to his recovering control of Whitney Data Dynamics.

Dinner was served in the suite. The sun had set, and they relaxed at a dining table set with white linen, china, and heavy silver, and lighted by candles. Hotel personnel had come up to serve the elegant dinner. Everyone had dressed, the men in dinner jackets, the two women in cocktail dresses. Allison had bought her dress just before she and Darius flew to Las Vegas from Los

Angeles: a simple black sheath that hung well on her thin figure and in which, for once, she felt stylish and pretty. She had to notice the contrast, though, between the way she looked and the way Patricia's silk brocade dress clung to her svelte body, at the same time both sophisticated and deliberately erotic. Darius had told her how Patricia had displayed herself topless at the pool in Bogotá, and Allison understood perfectly what Patricia's role was.

Immediately after dinner, Yoshitaka Hara asked Darius Whitney to come with him to his suite at The Sands; he wanted to review with him a scrap of source code he'd been able to pick up from a disgruntled employee of the FAA. Allison pushed back her chair and said she would go with them, since she, too, was interested; but Cordero asked her to stay.

"I've only just become acquainted with you, Miss McGuire," he said. "Surely you can spare me a few minutes."

Allison knew that Darius would hardly notice she was not coming with him and the Japanese. He was by now totally preoccupied with his problem, and she knew from experience that he would remain preoccupied until he solved it and that he would talk with her about it only if he got stuck and felt a need for her special expertise. She smiled at Cordero and settled back in her chair. Wentzel had not stayed for dinner, so Allison was left alone with Señor Cordero and Patricia.

"Coffee?" asked Cordero. "Brandy?"

"Please."

Cordero himself poured the coffee and splashed Courvoisier into three snifters.

Cordero smiled at Patricia. "Why don't you lay out a touch of something even more pleasant?" he said to her.

Patricia left the room.

"Do you have reservations about the service Darius is performing for me?" Cordero asked Allison.

"I don't want to see anyone get killed," she said. "I don't want him to be responsible for that."

"Neither do I," said Cordero smoothly. "We haven't spoken directly, in plain words, about the purpose of these flights—though I am sure Darius understands fully, and that you do. Let me say very simply, Allison, that my business would be ill served, extremely ill served, if we caused an aircraft accident. My predecessors in this business didn't care if people died, so long as their business prospered. So war was waged on them—literally. They tried to fight the whole world. That is not my way. I don't want anyone killed in an aircraft accident. I am relying on Darius's genius to prevent that."

Patricia returned and laid out on the table three small squares of glass, each one bearing a thin line of white powder.

"You are familiar with this?" asked Cordero.

Allison shook her head. "No," she said quietly, solemnly.

"Then maybe you'll let us introduce you to it," he said.

Patricia had also brought three short glass tubes, like glass drinking straws. She smiled at Allison, put one end of a tube in her nostril, closed her other nostril by pressing on her nose with a finger, bent down over one of the squares of glass, and inhaled to draw the powder up the tube and into her nostril. She arched her back, raised her shoulders, and closed her eyes.

Cordero, too, smiled at Allison and proceeded to do the same. He, too, closed his eyes, but only for a moment.

"Well," he said to Allison. "Will you try?"

Allison stared somberly, thoughtfully, at the line of white powder on the glass. "I . . . No. I really don't want to."

Cordero shrugged. "It's up to you of course," he said, dismissal in his voice. "God forbid I should press the stuff on anyone unwilling."

"It . . . has a reputation for—"

"Yes, yes, yes," he said, mildly impatient. "In America it is grossly abused. It is odd, isn't it, how the world's richest nation is also its least urbane?"

"I've always been curious," said Allison.

"Then satisfy your curiosity," said Cordero. "After all, what harm from trying it once?"

Allison shook her head. "Maybe some other time," she said.

Cordero put his hand on hers. "Maybe some other time," he agreed. "For now . . . brandy and coffee."

Relieved that he was not offended by her refusal to try cocaine, Allison smiled and sipped coffee.

"I am aware of your contribution to what Darius is doing for us," said Cordero. "I will show my appreciation when we achieve our success."

Ten minutes later, after Allison was gone, Patricia was glad to put a cup of steaming coffee up to her face. She needed, and she knew Cordero needed, the vapor off a hot drink to rise into the sinuses and nostrils and clear them of the sickening powdered sugar they had sucked up their noses.

During his second afternoon at the Pentagon, where he had to spend some time completing the paperwork of his return to active duty, Scott made a call to Hal Miller at Info Pro.

"Chief? Vandenberg."

"Oh, hey, Commander. How's it with you?"

"You'll never guess where I am and what I'm doing."

"I'm sure it's something interesting."

"I'm back in the Navy. I'm calling from the Pentagon."

"Jesus, Commander!"

"They twisted my arm, told me my country needs me. Well, it needs you, too, Chief. I'm calling to twist *your* arm."

"Jesus, Commander!"

"I can't tell you exactly why, but you can probably guess. I've looked at your personnel jacket. I need you on active status so I can expedite your security clearance. It'll just be for a few weeks, three or four months at most."

"Barbara'll kill me."

"She can kill *me*. It'll be in an office in Bethesda. Civilian clothes. You can go home weekends—that is, any weekend when it's not in the fan. I can get you a quarters allowance. I'll ask Derval to keep you on the payroll, at least to the extent of the difference between what the Navy pays and he pays. I think I can motivate him in that respect."

"I can't turn you down, Commander."

"No. Not any more than I could turn down the man who asked me. Okay, Chief? How about a couple of days? Can you report to me at my office in Bethesda on Thursday?"

"Yes, sir."

"Hey, Chief. I'm sorry. But it's damned important. I wouldn't do this to you if it wasn't."

"Sir," said the marine at the checkpoint where he signed out of the offices of the Chief of Naval Operations. "I have a package for you, for which I have to ask you to sign."

"Package?"

"Yes, sir. I'm to show you the contents."

"Let me see the contents, Sergeant."

The marine sergeant lifted an attaché case from beneath his desk. He opened it.

Lying inside was an automatic pistol in a holster, with a tangle of leather straps wrapped around it.

"Sir," said the marine. "This is an officer's sidearm, current specification. It is a 9mm. Beretta, which replaces the Colt .45. There are four extra magazines of ammunition supplied. Also provided is a shoulder holster, which will enable the captain to carry the weapon concealed."

Scott lifted the sleek automatic. "I'm not quite sure why—"

"Admiral Buchanan requisitioned the weapon for you, sir. If you will sign—"

"Okay, Sergeant. I'll sign. The thing may get a little rust on it before it is returned."

"Sir. If you will accept a suggestion, I suggest you carry the weapon to the firing range and take a familiarization course with it. It is a little different from the .45. If the admiral requisitioned it for you, sir, it has to be because he anticipates a situation might arise where you will be required to use it. It has proved a highly effective weapon, sir, but if I may say so, it does need a little practice."

Scott nodded as he scribbled his name on the form the marine presented. "I appreciate the suggestion, Sergeant. I'll put a few rounds through it, first chance. I once did have a sharpshooter badge with the Colt. Maybe I can qualify with the Beretta."

"Yes, sir."

* * *

He stopped at the house in Bethesda to let Judy see her daddy in the uniform of a Navy captain, so he didn't have time to change before he met Nancy for dinner at an Afghanistani restaurant she knew in Georgetown. He was at the bar when she arrived.

"My god!" she said. "Do I have a date with this handsome naval officer?"

They sat at a table in the very middle of the room, anything but intimate. She ordered a Beefeater martini, and he ordered his second Scotch.

"I am at your mercy," he said. "I don't recognize the words on this menu. You choose. You order."

"We'll have an assortment," she said. "Whatever we have, it will be good, I promise."

He sat silent for a long moment, looking at her over the candle between them, as she studied the menu. Nancy was beautiful. He had known that since the day he met her; but the sense in which the word beautiful came to his mind now was a fuller sense; she was more beautiful than he had originally understood.

He had seen all of her—including the funny little mole adjacent to a most intimate place—that night in Fredericksburg; but the sense in which he now thought of her as beautiful transcended that, too, and was something more than his memory of the exquisite elegance of her naked body. He had anticipated the feelings that now filled him, had recognized their growing and returning again and again to interrupt other feelings. But just now, in this restaurant that was no particularly romantic place, he found himself suddenly engulfed in emotion.

"I'm sorry to be so blunt," he said, "but I have to ask. Will you come home with me tonight?"

"I'm glad you're blunt," she said. "On such a subject, subtlety is really inappropriate. And the answer is . . ." She smiled slyly. "The answer is, I think I'd really rather have you come to *my* house."

He awoke the next morning to the smell of coffee brewing in her kitchen and the sound of it dripping into the pot. Nancy came back to the bedroom, naked except for a pair of slippers. She sat down on the bed and with a gentle finger traced a line from the tip of his nose all the way down his body.

She sat above him, smiling. Her long hair was in complete disarray, falling over her face. She tossed her head to throw it back. With no makeup, she was even more beautiful. Her breasts, which he knew by touch as well as sight, were gorgeous: full and heavy, with big dark nipples. She loved to show them and loved to have them touched.

"You like yourself, don't you, you egotistical male?" she teased as she traced circles in the hair on his chest. "Got all the good stuff a man is supposed to have."

He grinned lazily. "Actually I think I'm rather deficient," he said.

Nancy laughed. "Sure you are." She flexed her shoulders and stared down fondly. "Sure . . . you . . . are."

He reached for her hands and took both of them in his. "Nancy . . ." he said softly.

"Scott . . ."

"I love you. I mean, the big thing, the whole deal. I love you."

She closed her eyes for a moment. "The whole thing . . . The big deal . . ." She nodded. "Me too, Scott! Oh, yeah! Me too!"

—▪–▪–▪–▪—

On the Monday morning of the last week in March, Scott and Nancy arrived at the Bethesda offices of the Presidential Task Force on Air Transportation Security a few minutes later than their usual eight-thirty.

Nancy had moved into the office adjoining Scott's. She brought her secretary up from the FAA offices in Washington. She had six cartons of files delivered—and a secure filing cabinet with a combination lock. She ordered a scrambler telephone installed in her office and in Scott's.

They agreed that morale in an organization, no matter how small and friendly, would suffer if it were known that the chief and his principal assistant were obviously lovers, so they took a businesslike attitude toward each other during the day and in the presence of the people who came to work for them. Only when they were alone, only when they left the office in the evening, did they kiss and hold each other and savor the delight of new love.

It was a splendid time for them: the time for observing and learning, when love grows more complete. He loved the crisp professional confidence she displayed in the office, almost as much as the delights of her companionship after they left the office. He loved the idiosyncrasies he discovered in her every night and morning. He was intensely observant and curious about everything she did.

She sprayed her hair. She was untidy in the bathroom, leaving her spray can, her eyebrow pencil, and her lipstick lying around the basin and on the top of the toilet tank. When she pushed down her panties, she stepped only halfway out of them, then kicked them in the air with her right foot and caught them as they came down. She left her shoes lying in the middle of the bedroom floor, so that he stumbled over them in the night.

She didn't expect privacy from him and didn't grant him any. She came in and sat on the toilet to urinate while he was standing at the basin brushing his teeth, a liberty Sally had not taken in eight years of marriage. She sat on the closed lid in the nude, crossed her legs, and trimmed her toenails and talked with him while he was shaving. She jerked back the shower curtain, stuck in her head, and kissed him while he was bathing.

She hated lima beans and wouldn't eat them, said they made her sick. She drank coffee strong and black, day or night. She disliked tea. She liked two gin Bloody Marys with her Sunday-morning breakfast.

She snored.

He was fascinated, too, with her observations of him. She thought it was funny, she told him, that he dressed from the top down, buttoning his shirt and tying his necktie before he pulled on either underpants or pants. He snored, too, she said. What was more, he talked in his sleep, and annoyed her because he never said anything she could understand.

Fifteen minutes after they arrived at the office on that March morning, Nancy came into Scott's office with a document.

"Ought to take a quick look at this," she said.

"What is it?" he asked

"Phil Broughton sent it," she said. "It's a copy of a report he got from the FBI and the Drug Enforcement Administration. Remember that Cessna that was shot down over Baja California last month?"

"I remember."

"The two Americans were identified, by their fingerprints," she went on. "The pilot was named Robert Doak. The other man was Dewey Price—an ex-con, incidentally. And those same fingerprints were found in a Beech Bonanza abandoned at Tucson.

The Bonanza had been modified so you could pull out the rear windows and fire a gun from the plane. The customs inspectors who went over that airplane found a 9mm shell casing in a seam of the carpet. The guys had picked up their spent cartridge casings but had missed one."

"Okay, but what's this got to do with anything we're working on?"

"Because of the circumstances in which Doak and Price were murdered, the FBI and DEA took more than a casual interest in them. They checked the motels around the airport and found out that the pair spent one night in a Ramada Inn about a mile away. And from there, that night, Doak made a long-distance call to . . . Guess where?"

"Tell me."

"Bogotá," she said. "And not only that. The call went to the offices of an accounting firm that's suspected of being a message center for a cocaine baron."

"And you think that because Whitney went to Bogotá—"

"Let me read you a few sentences from this," she said, picking the report up from his desk. " 'We tentatively conclude that the Cessna aircraft was engaged in transporting cocaine and that very probably it was shot down by rival cocaine dealers. That the Mexican officers and Doak and Price, were murdered is another example of the utter viciousness of the men engaged in this commerce.' "

"Who owned the Bonanza?" asked Scott.

"Leased," she said. "Dead end. It was leased by a dummy corporation. Payments were made from a bank account in Los Angeles. That account is no longer active."

Scott shook his head. "Where's the hook to Whitney?" he asked.

"It's getting tougher to smuggle cocaine into the States," she said. "*Los Señores* are—"

"Who are *los Señores*?" asked Scott. "I see that phrase in half a dozen reports from the Drug Enforcement Administration."

"Its like talking about the Five Families in the New York Mafia," said Nancy. "They are supposedly the new kingpins of the Colombian cocaine trade, the ones who moved in after full-scale war eliminated the old ones. It's a different crowd. They use brains more than muscle—though obviously they will use muscle when they see fit."

"It makes sense, then, to think they shot down the Cessna and killed the Mexican policemen," said Scott. "But Whitney—"

"Okay," she interrupted. "A minute ago I started to say, it's getting more and more difficult to move cocaine into the States. So *los Señores* are constantly probing our defenses, constantly looking for ways to move the stuff in, in huge quantities. So, Whitney goes to Bogotá. Immediately we get a virus in the air-traffic-control system, and a plane gets away from us at El Paso. It's possible, Scott—and we've got to be careful because of it— that Whitney is working for *los Señores*. If he is, he's working for the people who shot down that Cessna and killed its pilot, killed a team of Mexican police officers, and even killed Doak and Price, who were working for them."

"So that's why you carry a gun," he said soberly.

"That's why you were issued a Beretta and advised to carry it," she said.

He had discovered her pistol one morning after they had spent the night in his condominium. They were by now so intimate that, finding himself out of tissues, he had felt free to check in her little handbag to see if she had a package of them, and there, in her handbag, he had found a 7.65 mm Walther PPK: the small, easily concealed automatic favored by European plainclothes police.

When he asked her why she carried it, she had laughed and said it was to fend off naval officers who'd been too long at sea. He hadn't pursued the subject then. Maybe he should have.

"Where's your pistol right now?" he asked.

"In my bag. Where's yours?"

He nodded at a desk drawer.

Nancy frowned. "It should be in its holster, and that holster should be under your jacket," she said.

At 11:30 his secretary called and asked him to come to the task force office. He went up. A United States marshal was there and served him with papers.

Nancy came out of her office. "What's that?"

"I've been sued for fifty million dollars," he said.

"What?"

He handed her the papers. Whitney Data Dynamics Corporation had sued Darius Whitney, Scott Vandenberg, and Vandenberg & Associates. It was an odd lawsuit, based on alternatives. The complaint, filed in a United States District Court in California, first accused Darius Whitney of using WHIT as a Trojan horse to plant a virus in LANCE, which ruined the reputation of WHIT and Whitney Data Dynamics Corporation. Alternatively, the complaint said, maybe Darius Whitney *didn't* use WHIT as a Trojan horse but Scott Vandenberg *said* he did. Either through Whitney's computer crime or Vandenberg's libel, Whitney Data Dynamics had been all but bankrupted. The company didn't know which way it had happened, but Whitney and Vandenberg did and could straighten it out in court.

Scott telephoned his attorney. The peculiar alternative complaint was absolutely valid, the attorney said, and Scott would have to fight the lawsuit.

The same paper was served on Darius Whitney at his home in Malibu at about the same time it was served on Scott Vandenberg. Darius had returned home that morning, after being stopped at the gate by the security guard at Whitney Data Dynamics. His violent argument with the guard, during which he had screamed that he was still the founder and a member of the board of the company, was videotaped by a hidden camera.

He was also served with a subpoena requiring him to appear three days later in the offices of a law firm in downtown Los Angeles for the taking of his deposition.

Allison was there when the papers were served. She, too, had been stopped at the gate at Whitney Data Dynamics.

Darius Whitney went to a booth in a shopping-center parking lot and placed a call. As usual he put only a quarter in the telephone and used his blue box to charge his call to the San Francisco bank he had chosen to pay his long-distance bill for the week.

His call was to Yoshitaka Hara in Las Vegas. Hara told him to be calm, do nothing, say nothing. He, Hara, would fly to Los

Angeles as soon as he had reported the matter of the lawsuit to Señor Cordero. Darius should expect to see him before the day was over.

Back home after calling Hara, Whitney stood and watched the ever-fascinating surf for a few minutes, many things turning over in his mind. Then he went to his computer, the one the imaginative Allison called The Beast. Allison stood behind him and watched.

He punched some keys. The screen filled with code: glowing green letters, numbers, and symbols. He studied it for a while. He moved the cursor here and there and made minor changes. At length he was satisfied. He switched to his communications software. He gave it a telephone number, a local call. From the little speaker in the computer he heard the sound of the telephone ringing, then the whistle and squawk of a computer answering the line. With a few keystrokes he transmitted the program he had just perfected. He terminated the communications link. Finally he erased the program, subjecting it to a hard erase that eliminated all trace of it from his computer.

Darius Whitney chuckled to himself as he ambled into the kitchen to pour himself a bourbon and water.

In the Los Angeles offices of Data Dynamics a secretary watched sheets spilling from a laser printer. Something was odd here. She had ordered only one copy of the document she was printing: a somewhat lengthy report to a corporation that had demanded absolute assurance that WHIT was free of viruses; and the printer seemed to be making multiple copies. She stopped the printer and picked up the top sheets.

The document looked right. First page, okay. Second page, okay. Then . . . What the—?

The third page read:

> As the result of this careful examination of every byte of source code, we feel entirely justified

in giving you an unqualified assurance that the software is

26 Then came the woman in the dawning of the day, and fell down at the door of the man's house where her lord was, till it was light.

27 And her lord rose up in the morning, and opened the doors of the house, and went out to go his way: and, behold, the woman his concubine was fallen down at the door of the house, and her hands were upon the threshold.

28 And he said unto her, Up, and let us be going. But none answered. Then the man took her up upon an ass, and the man rose up and gat him unto his place.

29 And when he was come into his house, he took a knife, and laid hold on his concubine, and divided her, together with her bones, into twelve pieces, and sent her into all the coasts of Israel.

30 And it was so, that all that saw it said, There was no such deed done nor seen from the day that the children of Israel came up out of the land of Egypt unto this day: consider of it, take advice, and speak your minds.

entirely free of any illegal source code. We can assure you that on delivery from us the software will be clean.

"You too?" her supervisor said when she showed him the printed sheets. "And more copies than you ordered, I suppose?"

"I checked," she said. "If I hadn't stopped the printer, it would have printed a hundred and twenty-five copies. I ordered *one*."

From along the hall came the sound of a raucous laugh.

"It isn't funny, Bert! We're getting Bible verses in everything we print. Not only that. The print commands are fouled up."

Nathan Morgenstern, the chief executive officer of the company, came striding down the hall. "What the hell's going on?" he demanded angrily.

131

A technician from the computer center trotted toward him. "Mr. Morgenstern! The whole system's gone crazy! We're losing data. We're losing programs. Mr. Morgenstern, we've got to shut down! We've got the goddamnedest virus anybody ever saw, and we've got to put everything on hold until we can clean the system!"

"They've sued me. They've thrown me out of the damned company and *sued me*! Of course, I'll by god sue back!"

Yoshitaka Hara shook his head at Darius Whitney. "No," he said. His voice was gentle, yet there was behind it a tone of decisive firmness that Whitney detected and understood. "No, Darius. No distractions until our work is finished. In fact, being shut out of the Data Dynamics offices may be the best thing that ever happened to you. It absolves you of a secondary responsibility and leaves you free to concentrate exclusively on the work at hand."

"What the hell am I going to live on? They'll shut off my checks too."

"Ah. Well. Señor Cordero is not insensitive to that problem."

Hara reached into his attaché case and pulled out a manila envelope. "Here," he said, "is a letter of understanding between you and a company called Brown & Herbert, engaging your consulting services to create a computer program to assist them in controlling a complex inventory. You notice it is dated two weeks ago. Sign it at the bottom, please, and date it the same day."

"Hara . . ."

"Please."

Whitney picked up a fiber-tipped pen and scrawled his name across the line left for his signature at the bottom of the letter. He dated it.

"Ah. Thank you," said Hara. "And here is your check for a retainer and your first two weeks' services."

Whitney frowned over the check. It was for $50,000, drawn on the Bank of America to the corporate account of Brown & Herbert, Incorporated.

"Now," said Hara brusquely. "What progress?"

They sat in the living room of Whitney's house on the beach at Malibu. Glass doors opened onto a deck that afforded a view of the beach and the Pacific breakers, which this evening were rumbling onto the sand with threatening power. A few surfers in black rubber suits rode the swelling rollers in spite of a cold rain driven by the gusty wind. The water was green, the sky gray-red as the sun set behind the overcast.

Allison sat outside on the deck watching the surfers. She was not sure if Yoshitaka Hara wanted her to listen to the conversation, and she was determined to avoid any awkwardness.

Whitney stared through the glass. "The scenario is as we agreed," he said. "I see nothing insuperable in the overall idea."

"Describe it again."

"Okay. Take the airport where we want to land. We sample the data they're using for that point and that time. We can see what flights are coming in and what transponder codes have been assigned. We pick a code that has not been assigned. We assign it to our flight. Our pilot sets his transponder to squawk that code. Our virus causes the digitalization program in the radar stations covering that area to kill the signal for a flight squawking that code. Our airplane is invisible."

"To ATC," said Hara. "What about military radar, which is going to pick up the blip? Some of that is not digitalized, some of it does not rely on transponders. The military will see an unidentified flight approaching at high-speed and high-altitude, and—"

"And they will feed its position, heading, and speed into their computers, which will match that data to what ATC has communicated to the military about approaching flight-plan flights. We have to make sure that their computers show a legal flight expected at that position and time, flying that heading at that speed."

"You mean you expect to coordinate the virus that makes the aircraft invisible with one that makes the same aircraft look legal to military radar?"

Whitney nodded. "Invisible to Air Traffic Control, visible but tagged legal to the military."

Hara smiled and shook his head. "You can do this?"

"Only because those agencies and their computers constantly exchange information," said Whitney. "They're in contact all the time, by microwave and by wire." He shrugged. "Wire. Actually now by fiber optics and lasers. Anyway, if you can find an entry point and inject your virus, it will travel in a matter of seconds throughout the system. And the virus, once it's inside, will search out the programs it's designed to infect and will infect them. Then it will hide and wait for us to send through the signals that activate it."

"You know an entry point?"

"I can find one. They communicate too many different ways to keep themselves absolutely secure. The communications lines are usually the key, you know. These systems have to exchange information, they have to communicate . . . and when they do, they're vulnerable."

Hara walked to the glass, and he, too, stared for a long, thoughtful moment at the wrathful surf.

"Whitney," he said. "Señor Cordero thinks you should come to Colombia. More or less permanently. Now that you can't work at Whitney Data Dynamics anymore, you don't have a computer facility. Besides, the lawsuit they filed suggests that you may be suspected, suggests that you may be under surveillance. Cordero will equip a facility for you, where you can work without distraction and without the possibility of interference."

"And without the possibility of walking away from the job if I decided I didn't like it anymore," said Whitney.

"No one's thinking in those terms," said Hara.

"I'm realistic."

"Then be entirely realistic," said Hara. "You can't quit. Whether you are here or in Bogotá makes no difference. Señor Cordero's influence extends far and wide."

"Allison?"

"She comes, too, of course. You can have a suite in the villa."

Darius Whitney took a little cigar from a cellophane-wrapped box, put it in his mouth, and lit it with a lighter. "Tell Señor Cordero I will work in the States for the time being. We will have to run tests. To test, I have to be here in the United States. I cannot penetrate the ATC system from Bogotá—at least not without great additional difficulty. Moving to Colombia is not an unattractive idea. It is just not practicable."

"You could be visited by the FBI if you stay here," said Hara.

"Las Vegas, then," said Whitney. "You like it there. So will

I. And we will be close, where we can work together. Ask Señor Cordero to set up a computer facility for me in Las Vegas."

Hara nodded. "I will convey that request."

"I can't make conditions, I guess," sighed Whitney. "I suppose it *is* a request. I'd like to be able to think of it as a demand."

"You are going to get your company back, my friend," said Hara. "You realize of course that the lawsuit means they are in trouble."

Darius smiled. "Yes." He glanced through the glass at Allison. "I am going to be president, and she will be vice president, of a new Whitney Data Dynamics—with no Nathan Morgenstern!"

Thursday evening Nathan Morgenstern, chief executive officer of Whitney Data Dynamics, left his office a little after six. He did not usually get away that early in the evening, but this was an occasion, his anniversary, and his wife had arranged for a dinner at eight, at a restaurant where they would entertain a small group of friends and receive their congratulations on their ninth anniversary.

He drove a silver-gray BMW. It waited for him in the parking space assigned to the CEO, and two technicians leaving the office at the same time were dismayed to see him in the parking lot at that hour. They had supposed he was in his office and would not see them and would not know when they left for the day. He was not above bestowing a smile on them and dropping a bland little remark they could ponder during the evening: something about how nice it was to be able to get away so early.

Nathan Morgenstern held the degree of master of business administration from Harvard; that was the single most important fact of his life. Everyone who encountered him had to acknowledge that he was a supremely competent manager, educated for that profession but also innately suited for it. He was only thirty-eight years old, but Data Dynamics was the third company he had turned around. His record was in place: on the bottom line of three corporations.

Of course he'd had to kick ass—including the ass of that swaggering old eccentric Darius Whitney, who seemed to think that being a computer guru, the inventor of WHIT, made him some kind of god. Morgenstern had had to make Whitney understand that when a corporate manager needed a lawyer, he hired a lawyer; when he needed an accountant, he hired an accountant; and when he needed a computer guru, he hired a computer guru—and all of them worked for the manager and took orders from him. Learning that lesson had made Whitney a spiteful old man.

It was going to be necessary to do something about him, one way or another. Maybe the lawsuit would scare him.

Nat Morgenstern was a compact man, not too tall, not too heavy; rather, he was a taut bundle of energy. He was, above all, a competitor. For him, everyone and everything, no matter what, was competition. He played tennis to kill. He wouldn't have expended the energy except for the possible thrill of pounding an opponent into the court. His car was faster, his pool was bigger, his wife was more beautiful, his children were more intelligent— all these things were the stuff of life for him. He wasn't loved, always, but he was respected. And that was what counted.

He drove authoritatively. In twenty minutes he was climbing into the hills and to the ridge where his house sat and afforded him a view of the city and of the Pacific. He pulled into his steep driveway, opened the security gate with a beep from a radio handset, and eased the car up to the open doors of his garage.

Odd. His wife's Mercedes wasn't there. Where could she be?

He went inside. The house was silent. The kids weren't there either, or the au pair.

A note lay on the kitchen counter.

Nat—

Kids and Emily have gone to a matinee flick and a hamburger dinner. I'll be back at six.

Dawn

At six. It was now six-thirty. He went to their suite, to shower and dress for dinner. When he came out of the shower, a man was sitting on his bed.

"Ho, Nat."

"Who the hell are you?"

Nathan Morgenstern kept a pistol in the night table by his side of the bed, and he estimated his chances of brushing past the intruder and grabbing it. He did not judge them good. Cold, objective calculation of odds was one of his specialties.

"Relax," said the man. "I've brought you a videotape I want you to see."

The man had in his hand the infrared controller for the VCR and the bedroom television set. He pressed buttons, and the tape began to play.

Nat stared at the screen.

"Nat!"

It was Dawn's voice, strained and terrified. The camera was on her face.

"Nat . . . Don't play around with these people. They're goddamned serious. Don't try to outsmart them. Whatever you do. Nat . . . Do what they want."

The camera moved back, and the picture was of his gorgeous, sunshine-blond wife, bound to a chair. "Nat . . . I think the kids are all right. They say they haven't touched them and won't. Unless—*Nat!* Do whatever the hell they want! Nat, please! Just do whatever they say! Nat! Nat . . ."

The screen went blank.

"Wanna see it again?"

He shook his head. "What do you want?"

"I got some papers for you to sign. Notice your lawyer has signed them already. He's a guy with good sense."

The man popped the cartridge out of the VCR. Nat noticed he wore rubber gloves and was leaving no fingerprints anywhere. The man opened a black attaché case, dropped in the video cartridge, and pulled out a sheaf of papers.

Nat did not even read them. He signed each in turn as it was presented to him.

The man left. The au pair and the kids came home at seven. Nat went to the restaurant at eight, as the man had told him to do. Dawn was there, dressed in her loveliest cocktail dress, made up and fresh and smiling. He saw what none of the others saw: the gleam of sweat on her forehead and the fear in her eyes.

* * *

Scott's attorney called and said Data Dynamics had suddenly withdrawn the lawsuit it had filed against him and Whitney. What was more, a brief statement had gone out on the business wires, in which Nathan Morgenstern, chief executive officer, said the lawsuit had been the result of an error and that he hoped it had caused no embarrassment to the defendants.

"Somethin' screwy about that," the lawyer said. "Doesn't make a grain of sense."

"Thank God for small blessings," said Scott.

The lawyer's call had interrupted a conversation about Scott's daughter, Judy. The question was, should Judy meet Nancy? Judy had reacted with undisguised hostility toward the one other woman Scott had introduced her to—with all of a child's suspicion and jealousy toward a new adult, particularly one of the same sex, who intrudes into a parent's life. Yet, Scott had been saying, Judy had to confront Nancy sooner or later, and maybe it was better that it be sooner. It was a decision that required full attention, by Scott at least and maybe by both of them; and for the moment they dropped it.

Nancy couldn't accept the dismissal of the suit as flippantly as Scott did. It troubled her. "Why?" she kept asking. "Why would they sue and then, less than a week later, dismiss the suit? Scott, that doesn't make sense."

The next day Nathan Morgenstern telephoned.

"Captain Vandenberg, this is Nathan Morgenstern calling. I owe you an abject apology. Please accept it."

Scott shrugged at Nancy. When this call came in, they had been sitting in his office discussing a report they did not take too seriously: of an apparent attempt by a hacker to break into the ATC computers in Denver. He had told her who was on the line before he picked up the call.

"I'm not sure why you owe me an apology, unless it has to do with the lawsuit, which has been dismissed."

"It does have to do with that," said Morgenstern. "That's exactly what it has to do with. It's becoming more and more clear, Captain Vandenberg, that you and I both are the victims of a devil, a vicious, scheming devil. My company right now is tied up in knots, by virtue of a virus that almost certainly originates with the same man who planted the virus in LANCE."

"Darius Whitney," said Scott, looking at Nancy and lifting his eyebrows.

"Darius Whitney," Morgenstern confirmed. "He wants to destroy Data Dynamics. I imagine you know why. I was going to ask you to look into our problem; then I learned you have returned to active service in the Navy, to cope with some implications from the Thanksgiving Eve virus. I had thought for a while you and I were on opposite sides of things. Now I know we're not. I'd like to meet with you, Captain. I think we have some things to talk about."

Scott was not immediately receptive. This was, after all, the man who had just sued him for fifty million dollars and even if the suit had been dismissed, it had given Scott an uncomfortable week and cost him the fees his lawyer had charged to begin to investigate the case and make a defense. "Possibility," he said. "What do you have in mind?"

"Does it interest you to know that Darius Whitney has disappeared?" asked Morgenstern. "I went out to his house in Malibu, to offer—quite frankly—to pay him off, to get him to relieve my company of the virus he planted with us. He's gone. The young woman who works with him—and almost certainly sleeps with him—is gone. The house is locked up. They are missing."

"Taking a weekend," Scott suggested.

"I don't think so, Captain. I have some information you should have. Sensitive. In fact, Captain Vandenberg, I am not calling from my office or home, for fear my telephones are tapped. I've taken a room in a motel so I can telephone you in secret. And even at that I'm taking a risk. Darius Whitney is a telephone artist too. He may be recording everything said on your line."

"Mr. Morgenstern—"

"Don't underestimate the man, Captain Vandenberg. Maybe you have the resources to find out where he is. Don't decide anything about him until you see if you can find him. That will be some kind of test, won't it? Don't you think so?"

139

9

—∎–∎–∎–∎—

They said of Eddy Wentzel there was nothing he couldn't fly. He believed it. He was a well-trained pilot; flying was his living, and he worked hard at being good; but beyond that he had an instinct for the union of machine and man and the air, something born in him, as his mother had always said, inherited from God-knew-where, since he was the first in his family who had ever put his hands on the controls of an airplane.

This one was sweet. It was a Lear, one of the older ones, leased by the boss for this job, and it flew like a dream. He used his pocket calculator to figure their true airspeed: just a shade over 470 knots. As fast as the big commercial jets, the Lear jet flew a little faster most of the time. It liked to fly at 50,000 feet, where you got optimum performance out of it, but he was holding it down to 35,000 on this run, the kind of altitude used by the 727s, 747s, L-1011s, and the like. He was, in fact, on one of their airways, flying among them. That would look right to the military radar types—another passenger jet roaring in from the vacation islands, maybe a charter flight, nothing special.

They had picked a good day for this test. More correctly said, they had waited for a good day. The sky was wide open, blue and clear, and from this altitude the ocean and its cays and islands didn't look like an ocean but a soup full of chunks of vegetables.

Oscar Ruark was flying with him again, as he had on the day

140

the Tomcats intercepted the dear old DC-3. Like Eddy, Oscar liked to eat in the cockpit, and he was balancing a plate of pizza slices on his knees. The Lear had a microwave oven and a refrigerator just behind the cockpit, and a head too. All the comforts of home.

Another time this airplane might haul the white powder. Today it was clean.

For half an hour the Lear had been very gradually closing on a big fellow. Now they were close enough to identify the airplane as an L-1011 and to read on its fuselage the blue-and-red markings of Delta Airlines. Puerto Rico to Miami, likely. They would pass it on their left. About three miles away to their right, a 727 maintained a speed almost exactly the same as theirs, and the distance between them remained constant. They had identified the plane with their binoculars. It was a Pan Am.

For Eddy it was always a curious experience to fly in high-altitude, high-speed traffic. The two big jets streaking northward at almost 550 miles per hour were eerily silent. Vapor streamed off their wings and tails, leaving distinct contrails behind them. The sky was marked by the fat and less distinct contrails of airplanes ten minutes or so ahead.

Oscar swallowed pizza and washed it down with a swig of Pepsi. "They must wonder why we fly at this altitude," he said, gesturing toward the 727, then toward the 1011. "They know we do better ten thousand feet higher."

Eddy nodded. When there was coke to fly, the Lear would not be the right airplane. Oscar was right. Seeing the Lear at 35,000 feet, other pilots would wonder why it wasn't up where it belonged. He had to hope they would wonder only casually. The point was to be inconspicuous. A bizjet at this altitude was not inconspicuous.

The panel clock was edging toward 1600 hours Zulu—that is, 1600 Greenwich Mean Time, the time used for all flight control. Eddy nodded at Oscar, and Oscar switched on the ADF—automatic direction finder—and tuned it to the frequency of a broadcast station on the north coast of the Dominican Republic. The needle on the face of the ADF turned and pointed in the direction of the station. Its purpose was to provide a simple form of radio navigation, but pilots could also listen to the station.

141

Oscar cut in the speaker, and the cockpit filled with music the station was broadcasting. Then the announcer began to talk. It was in Spanish, and Eddy couldn't understand a word. Oscar did, though. He listened intently. The clock indicated 1600. Oscar frowned, then nodded. He reached to the transponder controls and reset the squawk frequency.

"Let's hope it's right," said Eddy.

"He repeats the number twice," said Oscar.

The number the announcer had inserted in his chatter had come from Whitney, indirectly. Somewhere in the States, wherever Whitney was working now, he had activated his new virus. Within the past few minutes he had intruded on the ATC computers, scanned the flight plans for south Florida, and found an available transponder code. He had given that number to someone who had telephoned the Dominican broadcast station. The announcer had been well paid to mention the number on the air at 1600 Zulu. If Whitney's virus worked the way he promised it would, any aircraft squawking that code would now be invisible to digital radar. What was more, the military would find, if they checked, a flight plan filed with ATC, showing a private jet approaching Miami from Puerto Rico and squawking that code—customs notified and everything legal.

Eddy didn't know where the computer genius was. That was how the *Señores* worked, like a spy network in an adventure novel. What you didn't need to know, they didn't tell you.

All Eddy and Oscar needed to do now was relax and fly. In a little more than an hour they would know if Whitney's virus was any good.

They passed the 1011, which for some reason was flying a little slower than they were—probably because of the gate schedule at Miami; passengers didn't like to arrive and have to sit in the plane for twenty minutes because a gate was not yet available. The 727 remained on their right. A big 747 was edging up behind, on their right, too, and a thousand feet below them.

As the two pilots watched, the 747 slowly overtook and majestically moved out ahead of them and of the 727, then almost disappeared in the distance. The difference in their speeds—maybe only thirty miles an hour—was so small that three-quarters of an hour passed.

"Aha," said Oscar.

Eddy saw what he meant. The 747, some twenty miles ahead of them now but still indistinctly visible, the sun gleaming off its aluminum, had begun to gain speed. That was because the pilots had lowered its nose and were beginning their descent toward Miami. The 727 was doing the same. Eddy dialed in a standard-rate descent on the autopilot and kept up with the 727.

He set a radio receiver to Miami Approach Control and began to listen to the talk between Miami and approaching flights.

Clear weather or no, traffic approaching an airport of this size flew instrument approaches, using the same navigation and control techniques they would have used in heavy weather. The sophistication of the system, plus precision flying by all the pilots, would keep the traffic safely separated. The airplanes—from whichever direction they were coming—had to form themselves eventually into two parallel lines, one for each of the two east-west runways. All planes would fly prescribed courses at prescribed altitudes, spaced about three minutes apart. They would line up for the runways by following the radio signals from the instrument landing system—ILS—which would bring them into line and hold them at the correct altitudes and rates of descent. In most of these airplanes the autopilots would lock onto the ILS, and the planes could, in effect, fly themselves right to the touchdown point on the runway. Most of the pilots would switch off the autopilots at some point and land the planes themselves, but they would follow the ILS as precisely as the autopilots would.

The system required precision flying by everyone. One incompetent pilot, deviating from his prescribed course and altitude, could foul up the whole system and endanger the lives of the passengers in half a dozen or more airplanes.

What, then, would a plane do that was invisible to ATC radar? If it flew onto a collision course with another aircraft, the controllers wouldn't even know it and couldn't radio a warning. What Eddy Wentzel had to do was going to be tricky. He was going to approach the airport in the stream of incoming traffic, which would grow thicker every minute as scores of birds from all over converged on the big international airport; and to maintain separation from other airplanes, to avoid a disaster, he and Oscar could do no more than stare hard in all directions, relying on nothing more sophisticated than their eyesight.

Traffic inbound from the southeast was being directed to REEFE Intersection—meaning the intersection of two precisely defined directional beams broadcast by two VORs—very-high-frequency-omni-range stations. From REEFE the airplanes would fly northwest until they intercepted the narrow, very tightly defined radio signal off the Miami ILS. This was called intercepting the localizer, which would occur about twenty-five miles from the airport.

Eddy had thought about how he should fly this approach. He had decided that a pilot seeing him ahead but not far enough ahead would almost certainly complain to Miami Approach Control. He had decided he would fly the approach about five hundred feet too high, and maybe two miles behind a big jet. The pilots in the big fellow wouldn't see him and wouldn't guess he was back there. The separation would be great enough for reasonable safety.

As they neared the REEFE Intersection, the courses of the Lear and of the Pan Am 727 began to converge. The prescribed altitude for aircraft over the intersection was four thousand feet. Eddy arrested his descent about twenty miles southeast of REEFE. As he flew level and the 727 continued in its gradual descent, the 727 moved well ahead of him. Eddy brought the Lear into a position directly above and behind the 727, lowered his nose, and recovered speed to maintain his position.

The 727 turned to 320°. Eddy followed.

Now the pilot of the 727 raised its nose and began to slow it down. Eddy slowed the Lear. Speed bled off quickly as the 727 maintained a standard-rate descent flying in a nose-high configuration. The slats rolled down on the leading edges of the wings, and the first flaps came down on the rear edges, changing the shape of the airfoil for slow-speed flying. Eddy could do that on the Lear too.

Abruptly the Pan Am 727 rolled into a sharp left turn. It had intercepted the localizer and was turning toward the runway heading. The airport was some twenty miles ahead. Then the landing gear came down.

Oscar kept looking for interceptors. He was also looking for other traffic.

Eddy's confidence grew. Listening to Miami Approach Control, he had identified the Pan Am flight he was following. He heard the pilots get their instructions. He heard their responses. No one said anything about a bizjet out of position.

"Pan Am one-four-two, contact the tower on one-one-eight-point-three."

"Pan Am one-four-two, Roger. Thank you and good day, sir."

Eddy, too, switched frequencies and began listening to Miami Tower. They were less than ten miles from Miami International Airport now—coming over the southern end of Miami Beach. And here was where Eddy had decided to cut away.

Quickly he retracted his slats and flaps, and with his wings clean he advanced the throttle, lifted the nose, and shot the little Lear into the fast climb that was one of its best features. Soon he was climbing through five thousand feet. He would pass over the airport still climbing, from five to seven thousand, and so pass above all the traffic descending toward or lifting off from the runways.

Oscar relaxed and tipped back his can of Pepsi.

Eddy watched below. Traffic was heavy down there but moving in an orderly pattern. He could see the Orange Bowl to his left. To his right he could see the complicated runway pattern of Opa Locka Airport. Ahead—Well, he couldn't see the ground ahead. His nose was still up, because the Lear was still climbing. But he knew what was ahead. The town ran out, and soon they would be over the swamp, the Everglades.

Oscar screamed in horror. "EDDY!"

A wing was coming at them. Like a huge knife blade, the great wing was closing on them at what had to be five hundred knots. It was a wing—that was all he could see, just a wing—and it wasn't fifty feet from slicing into the nose of the Lear.

Eddy hauled the yoke back into his lap. Their only chance was to pass above that terrifying giant knife.

The Lear all but stood on its tail.

The knife disappeared.

Stalled, the Lear nosed over into a sickening dive. It rolled into a spin. Eddy fought to recover. He moved the yoke to a neutral position and stamped down on a rudder pedal to halt the spin. The dive straightened. He eased back on the yoke.

"EDDY!" Oscar screamed again.

They were plummeting toward a DC-9 that was climbing out from Miami International.

Eddy kicked in right rudder and threw the Lear to the right. It swooped past the DC-9. The ground was rushing up at the Lear. Eddy had a thousand feet left, no more, before the airplane slammed into the swamp.

He shoved in his throttles and powered the airplane to climb again. It leveled out and roared over a manufacturing plant on the western edge of Miami at no more than five hundred feet. But within a minute it was stable, and Eddy eased the Lear into a gradual climb to the northwest.

"Goddammit!" he yelled, not at Oscar, just at the gods. "You can't fly an invisible airplane into a place like Miami! Dammit! Dammit! Dammit!"

Scott Vandenberg read the front-page story from the Miami *Herald.* He knew something of the two near-misses over Miami International from the wire-service stories and television coverage—which was totally inaccurate. The story in the *Herald,* which had been sent to him by courier service from Miami, was far more complete:

> "A cowboy" is the term used by two airline pilots to describe the pilot of the small business jet which ran wild in the traffic over Miami International Airport yesterday and came within a few feet of causing not just one but two, midair collisions that would have resulted in the deaths of hundreds of airline passengers.
>
> "Incompetent idiots" is the name one of them used for Miami air controllers who failed to see the maverick jet and failed to warn them it was on a collision course with them.

146

FAA investigators say they have no clue as to the identity of the pilot who violated every rule in the book and nearly caused a major disaster. He flew his small jet, capable of speeds approaching 550 miles an hour, out of the Miami area to the north and disappeared.

"You've already read this, haven't you?" Scott asked Nancy, who was sitting facing his desk.

"No," she said. "I saw the story on television last night. I've had a call from Phil Broughton about it."

"The first thing that happened," said Scott, still scanning the newspaper as he spoke, "was that a little jet, apparently a Lear, damn near knocked a Continental 727 out of the air. There was a commuter prop-jet ahead of Continental, and the captain couldn't slow down enough to keep normal separation. So the tower ordered him to break off the approach and go around. He put the 727 into standard procedure for breaking off an approach, climbing and turning, and all of a sudden—all of a sudden, here comes a little jet, right at him. The Continental captain said it all happened too fast for him to do anything about it, and the little plane would have taken a wing off the 727 except that it was practically standing on its tail and climbing fast."

"The TV report told that much," said Nancy.

"And the story goes on. I'll read you some of it. 'Passengers sitting on the right side of the Continental 727 report seeing the small jet in an almost vertical position and speculate that its pilot threw it into a steep climb to avoid collision. Two of them praised the pilot of the small plane for quick thinking and expert flying.' "

"The FAA's not looking at it that way, I can tell you for sure," said Nancy.

"I'll read some more. 'The second near-collision was with a Delta DC-9 that had just taken off from Miami en route to Birmingham. First Officer Daniel Whiting spoke for the crew of that flight. They had no inkling of any danger until First Officer Whiting, looking out the right window of the cockpit, saw the business jet plummet past, not more than a hundred feet from his wing tip.

'The instantaneous reaction of the flight crew was to swerve the DC-9 to the left. This maneuver, which they later said was not

147

necessary, threw two flight attendants to the floor in the passenger cabin. They suffered injuries that required the flight to return to the airport.

'Delta spokesmen said this morning that the two flight attendants have been released from the hospital and will return to duty in about a week.

'So fast did the little airplane pass by, and at so low an altitude, that First Officer Whiting assumed it had crashed. He did not see it except for the instant when it dived past, and passengers in the DC-9 were unaware of the near-miss and were mystified as to why their airplane had taken such a sharp turn to the left.' "

Scott handed Nancy the front page so she could scan what he'd read for herself. He turned to an inner page, where the story continued:

> Personnel in the control tower and in the radar center that monitors traffic moving in and out of one of the nation's busiest airports were mystified as to how the small jet intruded into the Miami traffic pattern without being observed. They were equally mystified as to how, after the two airline pilots complained of the near-misses, they still could not locate the intruder on their radar scopes.
>
> An intense investigation continues.

Scott put the paper aside. Nancy picked up the inner pages and finished scanning the story.

"Okay," said Scott. "Was it a virus making a plane invisible to ATC radar?"

"Phil Broughton thinks so," she said. "Anyway, he wants to know. He's all but ordered me to get down to Miami to look into it."

"All but ordered you?"

"Well . . . Technically, I'm detached from the FAA for the time being. I work for you. He wants me to urge you to go down to Miami."

"Okay. And Hal Miller. I want Hal to go too. We'll fly down to Miami and take a look."

148

* * *

Still invisible to ATC radar because of the virus, Eddy Wentzel had flown to the Fort Myers airport. But he had not landed. When he was directly over the airport, he switched off his transponder, then switched it on again with a code that indicated he was a VFR flight—that is, one flying in clear weather under visual flight rules: typically an amateur pilot out for some fun—and he had extended his landing gear and flaps and flown low and slow. No longer invisible, he had looked on the radar scopes like a small plane just taking off from Fort Myers. A little later he had landed the Lear at Gainesville, as a VFR flight from Fort Myers. A line boy had come out with the truck and refueled the Lear, and Eddy had been under no obligation to tell that young man where he had come from or where he was going, so no one noticed that a Lear jet from Fort Myers had landed with tanks nearly empty. At Gainesville Eddy had filed a flight plan for Bogotá, with a refueling stop in Jamaica, and after less than an hour on the ground had taken off again. It had been a long day's flying, so on the flight to Colombia, Oscar Ruark took a turn at the controls.

With Oscar flying, Eddy had tried to sleep. He couldn't. His mind had run back over every second of the terrifying near-collisions over Miami. He had analyzed. He knew what had gone wrong. The question was would they believe it, or would they just think he'd screwed up?

He had landed at Bogotá after dark, skillfully bringing the Lear down through thick cloud and heavy rain to a textbook landing on the gleaming wet runway. Word was waiting for him. He was to report to the villa in the afternoon.

After ten hours sleep he reported to Señor Cordero.

"It's no good," he said.

"I have seen the news reports," said Cordero grimly. "Can you justify yourself, Eddy? Was this an error of yours?"

"The error . . . there's a possibility . . ." said Eddy, conscious of his precarious position. "Next time let's don't take it into a place like Miami."

"Don't I recall that was your choice?"

"Yes, sir. It was. My thought was that it would be easier to hide in heavy traffic. And it would have been okay, except that—"

"What was your mistake, Eddy?" Cordero demanded.

Eddy Wentzel closed his eyes and confessed. "I switched from Approach Control frequency to tower frequency when the 727 ahead of me did. If I'd stayed with Approach Control, I'd have heard him call off the Continental 727 and would have realized he'd be climbing."

"In other words," said Cordero coldly, "the system developed for us by Mr. Whitney worked to perfection. The difficulty arose from pilot error."

Never before in his life had Eddy Wentzel been called on the carpet for pilot error that endangered a flight. That happened to other pilots, not to Eddy Wentzel. With sweat glistening on his forehead, his throat dry, he drew a deep breath and nodded.

"You landed at—"

"At Gainesville, Florida."

"Any problem?"

"No, sir."

"No customs agents, no narcs?"

Eddy shook his head.

"So it works. You did something stupid, but the system works. We can enter the United States from south of the border, evade detection both by Air Traffic Control and the military, and land where we want."

"I'll still suggest we avoid the busiest airports," said Eddy.

Señor Cordero nodded. "Perhaps," he mused. "Perhaps . . ."

A Falcon jet belonging to the FAA landed at Miami International. Directed by respectful controllers to the ramp in front of the Flight Service Station, the sleek airplane delivered Scott Vandenberg, Nancy Delacorte, Hal Miller, and Nancy's secretary to the center of the FAA investigation of yesterday's near-misses.

"We have no new information, Captain Vandenberg," said Marilyn Stiffel, tower chief. "Would you like me to set up a meeting of all those involved?"

Scott shook his head. "Thanks, but I'd rather see people individually as we work through things."

They went up into the control tower.

"I'm sure you understand all this," Marilyn Stiffel said to the group, "but— Anyway, a quick review. The man over there is handling ground traffic north, and that one over there, south. They're talking to the planes that are taxiing. The man and woman on the tall stools are Miami Tower right now—the bald fellow handles all traffic south of the airport, and the blond woman is handling traffic to the north. They're talking to planes in the air, landing and taking off. Planes are handed off to them by Approach Control, and they clear them to land, assuming a runway is clear. They clear planes onto the runways, then to take off, and finally hand them off to Departure Control. Their radar scopes, the big ones above their heads, only cover the airport's control zone and a little more. On a clear day they do most of the work visually. They can see the planes. At night or on a bad-weather day they visualize the situation by watching the information on the scopes."

The big radar scope above the bald man showed its display in orange. The runways and principal obstructions in the area—tall buildings and radio towers—were marked on the face of the scope. The controller could see every airplane within a circle about twenty miles in diameter, including those on the runways. He spoke in a quiet monotone, pausing after each transmission to listen in his earphones to pilots' responses.

"TWA One-eight-zero cleared for takeoff. Delta Two-four-five, taxi into position and hold. American Seven-seven hold short of Runway Two-seven-right. Continental Four-four-three, contact Miami Departure Control. Good day, sir. Delta Two-four-five, cleared for takeoff. American Seven-seven, continue to hold short. Lear Five-nine Bravo, cleared to land on Runway two-seven-right . . ."

Scott and Nancy stood for a long moment, conscious of the monotone, able to relate what he was saying to aircraft they could see on the runways and taxiways and in the air. Traffic was moving in an orderly flow, and even two visitors to the tower—two with experience at this sort of thing, anyway—could fix in their minds what controllers called the picture.

Finally Scott spoke to Marilyn Stiffel. "Did anyone see the Lear?"

"No. As nearly as we can figure, he was well above the traffic. If the Continental 727 hadn't had to break off his approach and climb out, the Lear would probably have overflown the airport without incident."

"Which means," said Nancy, "that he was no cowboy, no drunk, no amateur. He knew where aircraft shouldn't be—that is, ordinarily wouldn't be—and he was deliberately flying through your airspace."

The woman nodded. "When he saw he was about to hit Continental, he jerked his yoke back all the way and climbed so steep he stalled. That's how he missed Continental. That put him into a stall-spin, and he almost fell on top of Delta. But he recovered, missed Delta, and managed to pull out before he hit the ground." She glanced around the tower room. "I don't want to be quoted on this, but he was one hell of a jet jockey, if you ask me. Like you say, he was no cowboy. He was a pro."

"Did he show up on the tower scope?" Nancy asked, nodding toward the radar scope above the controller.

"No."

"It's digital?" Scott asked.

Marilyn Stiffel nodded. "Replaced about four years ago. The image is much clearer."

"Okay. Let's go look at the radar room."

The radar control center for Miami International was in a big windowless room on a lower floor of the tower. There, in the green glow of radar scopes, two controllers stared intently at approaching aircraft and spoke quietly to them through their seed microphones, and two others watched and talked to departing traffic. This radar covered a much larger area than the radar in the control tower.

"What I'd really like to see is the digitalizers," said Scott.

What he had called digitalizers were a group of small computers that had only one function: to convert the often indistinct display on analog radar scopes to the clean, crisp sets of brightly gleaming numbers that appear on digital scopes.

The digitalizers were in a separate room on a lower floor of the tower and were under the supervision of a technician called

Edward Digby. Digby was a black man with skin the color of milk chocolate, close-cropped hair, and a small, neat mustache.

"I'd like to ask you something," Scott said to him. "Do you ever run a byte count?"

Digby shook his head. "No, sir. Wouldn't be a bad idea, would it?"

Scott looked around. An ordinary desktop computer sat on a shelf to one side of the room. It was not switched on.

Digby saw what Scott was looking at. "We could do it," he said. "There's no reason why we couldn't do it. That little computer could do it."

"You're wired, aren't you?" Scott asked. "It wouldn't take but a few minutes to see if you've got stray bytes in your digitalizers."

"Wouldn't take but a few minutes," Digby agreed. "You want to do it?"

"Go ahead," said Scott. "Let's see what we get."

Scott, Nancy, and Hal stood aside and watched Digby make the check. He switched on the desktop computer—an IBM PC-AT. It was cabled to a controller box so it could communicate with each of the digitalizers. Digby flipped a switch on the controller box. He pushed a disk into a slot on the front of the AT. Then, with a few taps on the keyboard, he commanded the AT to copy the operating program out of the digitalizer.

"Okay," he said, glancing up over his shoulder at Scott. "Let's see how many bytes."

With another few keytaps he ordered the AT to display a directory of the program then controlling the digitalizer computer.

```
VOLUME IN DRIVE C: HAS NO LABEL
DIRECTORY OF C:\DIG
DIG.EXE      32915  2-18-87
1 FILE(S)    17328704 BYTES FREE
```

The AT was not equipped with a printer, so he wrote the numbers on a sheet of paper. Then he pulled a floppy disk from the box on the shelf. It was the original program disk for the digitalizers. He ordered a directory of that disk.

```
VOLUME IN DRIVE A: IS DIGITALIZER
DIRECTORY OF A:\
DIG.EXE       31121  2-18-87
1 FILE(S)     330,948 BYTES FREE
```

"I guess we know," said Digby solemnly. He scratched numbers on his paper. "We've got 1,794 extra bytes."

"The virus," said Scott. "Look, Digby, I want to ask you to do something." He turned and looked at Marilyn Stiffel, meaning that he was asking her too. "I want you to keep this a complete secret. Copy the program with the virus onto a blank disk, and I'll take it with me. You copy the original program into all your digitalizers. Also, every time you come on duty, the first thing you do is copy the original disk into the digitalizers—more often, if you see any reason. The other shifts will do the same. The last thing you do at the end of a shift is a byte count like you just did. If you find extra bytes again, call me."

"You got it," said Digby.

"Make a few extra copies of the original disks. This is going to cause wear and tear."

"Right."

Scott spoke to Marilyn Stiffel. "Be sure all the people who work in here do it. Make sure they understand it's a secret."

She nodded. "And you'll be giving the same orders to every tower in the country," she suggested.

He smiled. "That's a secret too. But not a bad guess."

Darius Whitney looked up from the Zeos 386-25 personal computer he had found when he walked into this little house on what was called Toiyabe Ranch, on a low mountain slope just west of Las Vegas. Through the window just behind his computer he could see, first, a small swimming pool inside a tall faded-redwood fence, second, the snowcapped crest of mountains he could not name. There were fifteen or twenty of these bogus-rustic houses scattered around the lodge that was the center of the condominium complex. All of them had high fences around their patios and pools, and he guessed that some of his neighbors were celebrities, come here in pursuit of privacy.

Allison was in the pool. Since she had her privacy for sure, she was skinny-dipping. Darius thought he might try the same himself in a little while. For the moment he was intently focused on his computer screen, watching the development of afternoon air traffic approaching Florida's west coast.

Fort Myers. Not much could be coming in there. Señor Cordero's stupid pilot could probably handle that without causing a disaster. Mexico City to Fort Myers. Not a bad test. A suspicious route. But simple.

Cordero had said the flight into Miami had worked perfectly so far as the computer program was concerned. The fault had been the pilot's, who had switched control frequencies prematurely and had missed an essential transmission. So the program worked. The virus worked. Even after nearly killing two hundred people, Wentzel had been able to fly out of the Miami area, still invisible, still a mystery both to ATC and military radar observers.

Now—This was a fine little computer. It was not The Beast, but it was a capable little machine, for which he had learned respect. He enjoyed the vivid colors on the screen. Since someone else was paying, he had taken bright colors.

Allison's computer was a duplicate of this one. She liked it too.

He wondered if anyone had tampered with The Beast and all the rest of the good equipment he'd had to leave in Malibu. They had brought along what was illegal—the paraphernalia that let them make free telephone calls—and boxes of disks filled with programs; but the highly personalized lab he'd made for himself had had to be abandoned. It hadn't been easy to walk away from machines he had so anthropomorphized that he had sometimes talked to them as though they had personalities. It was as though he had left friends.

What was more, he'd had to abandon his model of H.M.S. *Victory*. If he never got back to the house in Malibu, he would regret losing that model. You couldn't buy something like that, for any amount of money—something you'd worked on with your hands for months.

Virus . . .

He had made his entry into the ATC computers almost an

hour ago. From here he routed his telephone link through Los Angeles Center. His telephone connection looked like a routine connection between Los Angeles controllers and the central computers.

He had made a simple program that scanned the transponder codes assigned. He chose one that wasn't assigned and picked up a voice-line telephone to call Hara in Las Vegas. Hara would communicate the vacant transponder code, which Wentzel was to use, to whoever would radio it to the Lear jet flying across the Gulf of Mexico.

Eddy was comfortable with this flight. They'd worked the kinks out now, and he was confident he would have no problem. Mexico City to Fort Myers to Sarasota. No very complex approach. No heavy traffic. He could see no reason why it shouldn't work this time.

Oscar couldn't either. He was munching on some tacos he had thawed in the microwave.

Their transponder code had been broadcast by a Havana radio station. Havana, Cuba! The grasp of *los Señores* reached everywhere.

He switched a radio to Fort Myers Approach. A phlegmatic voice was talking to just two aircraft. There were more in the pattern, but only two were making instrument approaches on this clear day. The two were coming in from the north, a Continental flight and a Delta flight.

Eddy switched to tower frequency for a minute or two. He could hear lots of chatter between a slightly tense controller and a multitude of voices: the pilots of a dozen Cessnas and Pipers that were circling the airport, at least three of them taking touch-and-go landing practice.

Okay. Eddy slowed down, let out flaps, let down wheels, and descended to five thousand feet. The Lear crossed over the Caloosahatchee River and then over the airport. Over the airport he switched his transponder to 1200, the code for VFR flights, and turned north toward Sarasota.

Fifteen minutes later he called the tower at Sarasota-Bradenton Airport. Five minutes after that he was on the ground.

Oscar Ruark busied himself cleaning up the cockpit, gathering their food wrappers and empty cans. Eddy taxied to the ramp beside the general-aviation building. He shut down his engines.

A dark-blue station wagon sped out from between two hangars and stopped just ahead of the Lear's nosewheel. Two other cars, these with emergency lights on top, pulled up to either side.

"Oh, shit," muttered Eddy Wentzel.

10

Eddy Wentzel had experienced two tough days—first, the flight from Mexico City to Sarasota-Bradenton Airport, arrest, interrogation; then a strip and body-cavity search and confinement in a cell, followed by a drive to Tampa in handcuffs and chains—and now . . . Now this confrontation with some damn Navy captain. He had never been in jail before. He was indignant and angry, and he didn't like this pious damned officer.

"What have you got me for?" he asked. "Illegal entry. That's all. Illegal entry. The Lear was clean. God knows they absolutely disassembled it. And what'd they find? Nothing. *Nada*, as the Spics say. *Nada*. So what's gonna happen? You wanta know what? Nothing. They'll lift my license, I suppose. I can live without it. Cooperate with you, you bastard? Why should I cooperate with you?"

The Navy captain was named Vandenberg, and he sat across a table in the federal detention center at Tampa, handsome in a suntan uniform with eagles on the collar. Probably enjoying the contrast with the ugly orange coveralls a prisoner had to wear, Eddy thought. To hell with him.

On the other hand, the captain was smart enough to understand. It was true, what Eddy was telling him. They had him on a charge of illegal entry. He had flown a Lear jet into the United States illegally, coming through the Gulf Coastal ADIZ without a flight plan. (Some controllers insisted there had once been a flight plan for that Lear, but if there ever had been, it was gone, disappeared out of the ATC computer system.) He'd lose his license. Sure he would. But that wasn't enough to make him talk. No way. Eddy was not going to tell anybody anything.

As soon as his lawyer arrived, he was going to be released on bond. If he had no reason to talk, he would not talk.

"Let me do a little guessing, Wentzel," said the Captain. "Somebody is trying to use a computer foul-up to make it possible to fly controlled substances into the United States. I don't expect you to answer. But think about this. You've fouled up. You've got caught. You've got us on the right track. You can do some time in a federal slammer, or you can do a whole lot of time in a cemetery. You figure?"

Wentzel pushed back his chair and stood. He stepped to the screened window and looked down into the parking lot. Yeah, the Captain was smart enough to have it figured out. Most of it.

Wentzel filled his lungs with air, then blew it out. "All you can threaten is the slammer, Captain," he said. "I don't like the slammer, but I can do it. The cemetery . . . sorry, Captain. No deal. Forget it."

The Captain pushed back his chair too. "Okay, Eddy," he said. "Keep it in mind. Change your mind . . ."

Eddy was encouraged by the speed with which the bosses arranged his release—and Oscar's. As the lawyer said to them, after all, the charges were not hugely serious; there was no reason to hold two men in prison for having flown into the United States an airplane absolutely clean of controlled substances and carrying no illegal aliens.

The lawyer had driven them to a motel. They had checked in, and very shortly a man had knocked on their door. He said his name was Stepan Yanak. He was a solid, evil-looking little man with beady eyes.

"I work for the friends," he said crisply to Eddy. Then he turned to Oscar Ruark and said the same thing to him, in Spanish. "Okay, you guys. Put it another way, I work for *los Señores*. We all do. Problem?"

"Hell, no," Eddy had said.

"Dinner before we set off on a long, boring flight," said Yanak. "Preferences?"

"Where we can look at the girlies, maybe," said Eddy. "Hmm?"

Half an hour later they sat in a roadhouse facing great sizzling steaks and heaps of French fries on hot steel platters on wooden planks. At the suggestion of their corselet-clad waitress, a liter carafe of red wine stood in the middle of the table; but each of them had already drunk bourbon or Scotch and felt it; and the rich red wine stood all but untouched.

On the small stage not far from their table, a lithe black girl, totally naked, wiggled and grinned in a simulation of dancing.

"What was the name of that Navy captain?" Yanak asked Eddy.

"Uh . . . Vandenberg. Vandenberg . . . Yeah, Scott Vandenberg. But hey, man! Tell him nothin' is what I told him! Nuh-uh-thin'! Absolutely."

Yanak nodded. "Only thing to tell him. The bosses counted on you telling just that and no more."

Eddy looked at Oscar, who was sawing back and forth with a steak knife on his great, thick slab of beef. "Count on us," he said uneasily.

Stepan Yanak took a moment to survey the room, where their attention was divided between the succulent steaks on their platters and the naked body on the stage. It was a room that was common in Florida: dark wood and dark-red cushions, fake swords and shields on the walls, electric candles glowing in fake pewter sconces—all very Spanish, in restaurant-supply-house ersatz Spanish.

The bodies were real. The black girl stepped down and was replaced by a pale white girl, who provoked much more applause from the beer-swilling men at the heavy tables. She pulled off the little she had been wearing and danced naked to the whistles and lewd cries of the rednecks at the tables.

"You told him nothing?"

"Nothing, for god's sake. Nothing. What the hell else? Nothing. What else? Nuh-uh-thin' "

"How much does he know, would you say?"

160

"Vandenberg? Too damned much. He guessed pretty much what's going on. Hey, man! Understand that I didn't tell him! He had it figured out. Too damned much, he had it figured out!"

"A Navy captain?"

"Captain Scott Vandenberg, I tell ya. Some kind of special fed, looking into what we're doing, Stepan. That's what he's up to—looking into what we're doing."

Stepan Yanak glanced at the naked girl moving in awkward imitation of a dance. She stepped forward, stepped back, rolled her hips, fluttered her hands, tried to smile.

"Why'd the flight get detected?"

Eddy shrugged. "Whitney's system failed, man. Radar tracked us all the way in. Man, they knew where we were from the middle of the Gulf of Mexico. Y' can't lay this one on *me*! We were on the radar scopes all the way in."

"Are you sure of that?"

"Hell, yes, I'm sure of it. That's what the feds told us when they arrested us at Sarasota: We been following you guys five hundred miles."

They drank half their wine plus two more rounds of drinks and watched three more girls dance. About ten they walked out into the parking lot.

"Airport," said Yanak.

He drove. They left the town and sped into the darkness.

"Man. Hey, man." It was Eddy. "Hey, man, 'fore I get on any airplane . . . actual, before we go another mile, I gotta stop. You know? Gotta stop."

Stepan pulled over to the side of the road. Eddy stumbled out into the dark. They were beside a canal, and on the other side of the canal a swamp chirped and grunted in the night. In the canal a big animal, likely an alligator, harrumphed and splashed. Eddy staggered to the first vegetation.

"You, too, buddy," Stepan said to Oscar. "Let's get it over with before we get to the airport."

Oscar opened the back door and stumbled off the pavement.

Stepan Yanak reached under the seat and pulled out a Mini-Uzi. He got out on the driver's side. He looked up and down the road. No headlights.

Eddy zipped up his pants and stumbled toward the car.

The short burst from the Uzi was a sharp, mad *ri-ip* on the quiet night. Half a dozen 9mm slugs tore through the chest of Eddy Wentzel. Oscar Ruark started to run. The second burst threw him forward. He fell to his knees and crawled a few paces forward before he died.

Scott Vandenberg drove a black Porsche 911. Not all the time. He also had a red Honda that he drove when he had to leave his car in an airport garage or on an isolated parking lot. The Porsche was an extravagance he had indulged in two years ago.

Nancy loved the Porsche. She loved to drive it and was the only person he had ever allowed to drive it. This warm Friday night at the end of April, she circled the Beltway the long way around, just to have her hands on the wheel a few minutes longer.

It was raining hard when she pulled the car up to the door of Scott's garage and pressed the button that opened the door. For a minute they stood in the garage and watched for some slackening of the downpour; and when it didn't come, they laughed and ran for the back door to his condominium.

"Ahh!" she laughed, standing in his kitchen slapping water off her hair and clothes. "Why didn't you warn me it rains in Bethesda?"

"Let's see," said Scott. "Where is it the rain falls? Oh, yes: on the just and the unjust. Which are we?"

"The unjust of course," she giggled.

Nancy scurried around the kitchen, turning the Lucite rods that closed the venetian blinds; then she took off her damp skirt and blouse and draped them over two chairs. In white panties and bra, a black garter belt, dark stockings, and black shoes, she opened the refrigerator and scooped ice cubes into a glass.

"Scotch?" she asked.

"I think I'll make some coffee and have a brandy," he said.

"Sounds good," she said.

He ground beans and started the coffee maker. He slipped out of his wet clothes and walked into the living room to join her, wearing a pair of blue slingshot Jockeys.

Nancy walked around the room, surveying the books again.

162

She liked this room, and they had talked about whether they would live here or in her house in Georgetown. She wasn't sure where they would shelve all his books in the Georgetown house. He was something of a bibliophile, and his library had grown to more than two thousand volumes: mostly history and biography, but a collection of novels, too, plus books on art and books on aviation and computer science.

His officer's sword hung above the fireplace, the only token of his career as a Navy flier. On the mantel stood three photographs: of his late father, his mother, and his daughter.

"Too warm for a fire," she said. "Too bad."

She stood with her back to the cold fireplace, an arm resting casually on the mantel. The rainwater had made her fluffed-out hair fall to her shoulders. Her face glowed pink, maybe from the exhilaration of driving the Porsche and then of running through the cold rain.

The coffee maker burped and gurgled in the kitchen, momentarily distracting him.

Nancy stepped away from the fireplace and withdrew a book from a shelf. "Eleanor of Aquitaine . . ." she murmured, reading the jacket copy. She glanced at the shelf again. "My god, the man's got *two* biographies of Eleanor of Aquitaine. Is she a favorite of yours?"

He nodded. "I think she was one of the most fascinating people in all history. Wife of a king of France, then of a king of England. Mother of two kings of England. But much more than that. Eleanor was her own woman. She fought both her husbands and one of her sons, in war. She went on the Second Crusade, you know—all the way to Jerusalem."

Nancy smiled. "You've got depths I haven't plumbed yet," she said.

"I hope so," he said.

The coffee maker made a hawking sound. He shrugged and went to the kitchen. She followed him. She poured coffee, and he took down small brandy snifters from the cabinet.

The telephone rang.

Scott picked it up, and when he heard who was calling, he turned on the speaker so Nancy could hear the conversation.

". . . and they called as soon as they made the identification."

Nancy did not recognize the voice. The man calling was the FBI agent who had met Scott in Tampa and accompanied him on his visit to the federal detention center to talk to the pilot, Eddy Wentzel.

"Both of them?" Scott asked.

"Both of them. Absolutely chopped to pieces with some kind of automatic weapon. Their lawyer posted bond for them about five o'clock. They left with him. He swears he has no idea what happened. He dropped them at a motel, where they wanted to go. They checked in. The motel clerk says they paid a night in advance, in cash; and after they checked in, he never saw them again. Neither did anybody else that's been found so far."

Scott glanced at Nancy, who frowned and took a sip of the strong black coffee.

"An execution," said the FBI man.

"Right. Thanks for letting me know."

"We're dealing with rough guys, Captain. Be careful."

Nancy had already picked up her purse. She lifted out her Walther. She nodded. "Dealing with rough guys," she said. "Where's your sidearm, Commander? Still in your desk? It's time you began to carry that Beretta."

"What did they do to us this time?"

Virgilio Cordero, stiff and formal in white dinner jacket, stood above Darius Whitney, who sat at a computer terminal and had been staring at the code for a change in the program until he was interrupted.

Yoshitaka Hara had driven Cordero out from Las Vegas, after their dinner in his penthouse, to find Whitney still working at the computers set up in the living room of the house at Toiyabe Ranch. Hara had asked Allison to take a little walk with him, since Señor Cordero wanted to talk with Whitney alone.

"I'm not certain," said Darius. "I've been trying to figure out what went wrong. I've put some damned long hours into it."

That was true. Sitting before the Zeos computer, wearing a white polo shirt and khaki pants, he had neglected to shave today.

Cordero walked to the window and looked out, not focusing

on anything, just staring idly at the night. "Tell me," he said. "Have you ever heard of a Captain Scott Vandenberg?"

"Vandenberg . . . Sure. An expert on viruses. On killing viruses."

Cordero pulled a thin silver case from an inner pocket of his jacket and extracted a long cigarette, mint-green in color. He lit it. Darius had not seen him smoke before. It suggested the man was tense, maybe even angry.

"Vandenberg is a bastard," said Darius. "If he's working against us, we have trouble."

Cordero blew smoke against the window glass. "Would you describe him as the best the United States can send against us?"

Darius pondered briefly. "If not the best, then damned near it," he said. "There are others who may be as good. Nobody's better."

Cordero stared at Whitney, a cold, appraising look in his eyes. Darius could read him and understood Cordero was wondering whether he had chosen the best man for this job after all.

"I guess you've been told," said Cordero, "that our flight from Mexico to Florida was a disaster. Their radar picked up our airplane well out over the Gulf and tracked it to its landing. Our pilots were arrested. The airplane has been impounded. Do you have any suggestion as to why this happened?"

"Are we certain," asked Darius, "that the Havana station transmitted the right transponder code?"

"We recorded the broadcast. It was right."

"Then—"

"I can tell you what happened," interrupted Cordero. "Your virus was identified. The digitalizer computers were cleaned. They are being cleaned several times a day. Or so Yoshitaka Hara tells me."

Darius scowled. "Uh-oh. Then not only can they clean out the virus, they can detect it. We'll have to do something entirely different."

" 'Entirely different,' " Cordero scoffed. "What? And when? How long will it take you to write a new program? And what assurance do I have that it won't be detected and nullified?"

Darius rose from the computer console. He walked to the

kitchen, picked up a small piece of yellow cheese that lay on the counter, then poured himself a splash of bourbon. "Señor Cordero," he said. "I have demonstrated to you, twice, that I can write a virus that makes it possible for an aircraft to penetrate the American system undetected. You are asking for something that is impossible, however—a virus that can reside in those computers permanently and allow you to maintain a regular traffic across the borders of the United States. Viruses can be detected, with byte counts and other ways. When someone suspects the presence of a virus, the operators will run byte counts at frequent intervals. They'll use other ways to frustrate us. We—"

"Do I hear you acknowledging failure?" asked Cordero coldly.

"Not at all. What I'm telling you is, you can't expect to operate regular, continuing air traffic across the borders of the United States, invisible to radar. I can't write a virus that can make that possible. No one can. What I *can* do is make an *occasional* aircraft invisible."

"Occasional—"

"Yes, and that should be enough. We've sent in a Lear jet. We've sent in a Mooney. What if the plane going in were a Boeing 747? Señor Cordero, we haven't talked specifically and directly about what these airplanes are going to carry. Of course I know; I'm not stupid. How much of it would a 747 carry? Say, forty tons. What's that worth? I can't get airplanes through the radar screen twice a day or twice a week, but I can get one 747 through. Or maybe two."

"I would have a lot invested in such a flight," said Cordero thoughtfully.

"You would make a huge profit. Huge. Immense."

"You are confident," said Cordero.

Darius nodded. "I can do it. There's more than one way to skin a cat."

For a long time after Cordero and Hara left, Darius remained staring at his computer screen, while Allison watched and was reluctant to interrupt his thoughts. Scattered around him were sheets of source code he had printed out and marked with a red pen. He had written a simulation of the ATC digitalizers, as she knew; and he was trying to find a way to accomplish his task with a smaller amount of code. He had injected 1,794 extra bytes into their program. No wonder they had detected it. How would they react if they found one-tenth of that? And could he do it?

She sat on a straight chair a pace from him. For a long time she sat and watched and was silent. Then she asked, "Can you compress it?"

Darius shook his head. "I don't know."

"Want to give me a look at it?"

He turned and looked at her. "Umm-hmm, why not?" he said. "In a minute. What did Hara have to say?"

"Nothing much," she replied. "His assignment was to get me out of here while Cordero talked to you. Are you ready to tell me what he said?"

Darius drew a deep breath, stiffening his back at the same time and drawing himself erect. "For a moment I thought Hara had taken you out of the house so you wouldn't see Cordero kill me," he said.

Allison shook her head. "You exaggerate," she said quietly, not excited by his suggestion. "It's not that bad."

He sat staring at her for a long moment. She had worn a skirt and sweater when she went out walking, showing Hara the condominium, the lodge, and the lake. Just now she had changed into dark-blue shorts and a red T-shirt lettered in white across the front—TOIYABE RANCH. She snapped her lighter and lit a cigarette.

"Allison," he said. "Who do you suppose killed Eddy Wentzel?"

She frowned as she thought about that. "Okay. But—"

"Let's not kid ourselves," he said.

Allison sighed loudly.

"Thanks," said Darius.

"Thanks?"

"For not saying, 'I told you so.' You did, and I didn't listen to you."

She rose and stepped behind him. She put her cigarette aside and used both hands to knead his shoulders. Darius looked up into her eyes. She bent forward and kissed him on the mouth. It was the first time they had kissed. He reached for her and drew her down to him and made the kiss strong and loving.

She slipped around onto his lap, and for minutes they kissed tenderly. She felt his eagerness, but she sensed, too, that he was surprised, as she was—pleased but a little puzzled and even a little troubled. For her, in that three or four minutes, the world changed—and she believed it did for him too.

"Darius," she whispered. "I . . . We . . . A whole lot depends on"—She nodded toward the screen of the computer—"doesn't it?"

He blew a loud sigh. "Yeah. It does," he said.

"Too damn much," she said. "And I don't—for right now, anyway—see the way out of it."

He stared at the screen again. "What if the FAA reprograms?" he asked. "They could foul us up good. And now that they know we've infected their system, they just might reprogram. A few changes here and there, only enough to defeat us when we get in again. All I can think of to do is sample the digitalizer program at regular intervals."

"Can we sample all of them?" she asked. "I mean, can we sample what they're running at every airport?"

"We won't have to. The best thing is, they're bureaucrats. Whatever they decide to do in Miami, they'll do in Dallas. Consistency. Consistency is the bugaboo of small minds. Besides that, the happiest feature of their system—from our point of view—is that it is all interconnected. It has to be. Every computer they have has to communicate with every other. When you break into one, you break into all."

She stared at the screen for a moment. "Why don't you erase?" she asked quietly.

"Hmm?"

"Erase," she said. "It's so easy to get the virus in, you don't need to leave it in place. You erase everything else. I mean, you leave no trace of the fake flight plan. So why did you leave the digitalizer virus in the digitalizers after it had done its job?"

He glowered at her. "Because I'm under fuckin' pressure," he grunted.

"Okay, scenario," she said. "Now that they know you've been in, they're going to be alert. So first you've got to do a compare, just before you insert the virus. Compare what they're using with the program you wrote the virus for. If I was those guys, I'd—"

"Yeah, yeah," he said, almost annoyed at how she had all but read his mind. "So we sample the system and compare."

"Okay. Now you insert the virus at the last possible minute. We don't know how often they do byte counts, but they can't do them every ten minutes."

"We need about an hour," said Darius. "About an hour that the airplane needs to be invisible."

"Make the virus signal you when it detects the start of a byte count. Look, we know what they have to do to get a count. Write a little program into the virus that warns you if they are looking for it."

"Right," said Darius. "Also, when it detects the byte count starting, it erases itself. So it's not there when the actual count gets going."

"Now you're talking."

"Yeah. Which means I don't have to compress it, because they're never gonna see it."

She kissed him again. "You got it," she said. "Damn genius."

The tension ran out of him. She could see it running out. He frowned at her for a moment, a little smile under that frown, then his eyes flickered toward his bedroom door. Allison nodded.

Cordero sat down to dinner at a poolside table at The Sands, two hours after midnight. He liked the way everything continued all night in Las Vegas. The streets were bright. The casinos were active. The swimming pools were still alive with two kinds of people: men and women trying to clear their heads, and young women looking for a profitable connection for the rest of the night.

Patricia was with him, wearing a bikini. She had climbed out of the pool when she saw him walk to a table. Stepan Yanak had been swimming with her, and he sat down at Cordero's table in his tight red swim trunks. Yoshitaka Hara, like Cordero, still wore a white dinner jacket.

Cordero ordered hors d'oeuvres and a bottle of Tio Pepe, a very dry Spanish sherry. He settled back on his chair and contemplated the pool, as if the conversation at two in the morning was to be entirely casual.

Cordero nodded toward a girl just climbing out of the pool and said to Yanak, *"Es una muchacha bonita. ¿Entiende usted?"*

"Sí, entiendo," said Yanak. *"No entiendo todo, pero—"*

"Bueno," said Cordero.

He had told Yanak to learn Spanish, and apparently the man was learning. They wouldn't speak Spanish; Hara could not understand it; but it was good to hear Yanak pick up and understand a quiet, casual comment and answer confidently. Yanak might well justify his confidence in him. The repugnant little thug from the mean streets of Cleveland might earn responsibility and its rewards.

Cordero spoke now to Hara. "How important is Vandenberg?"

Hara hesitated for a moment as he judged the significance of the question. "He didn't take long to discover what was going on and interfere with it," he said.

"He will continue to interfere, I suppose."

"I am sure he will. He has been appointed to a presidential task force dedicated to frustrating us."

"How difficult would it be for them to replace him?"

Hara raised his chin. Now he understood the import of the conversation. "Difficult," he said. "Not impossible, but difficult."

"What if we approached him?"

"I doubt that's a good idea," said Hara. "He was a jet jockey for Uncle Sam's Navy for a good many years. An Annapolis graduate, career officer. Also did some service with naval intelligence." He shook his head. "No. I don't think I'd approach him."

"Then—"

"Damned carefully," Hara interjected. "Only damned carefully."

"Captain Vandenberg, you're looking at a man who's *scared*."

Nathan Morgenstern, whose wife sat beside him across the restaurant table from Scott, had already said they had slipped away from their home in California in the middle of the night and had driven to Washington, for fear that buying airline tickets would reveal where they were going. They had said, too, that their children were in the motel, where they had registered under an assumed name, also that the children were watched over by an armed bodyguard. They sat over breakfast: coffee, Danish, eggs, ham.

Scott, who had never before seen Morgenstern, sensed that the self-esteem of this trim, California-tanned, meticulously tailored man had disintegrated. His wife, whose name was Dawn, was sympathetic and kept her hand on her husband's as if to contain his chopping gestures. It made no difference; he chopped away with the other hand; and when his hand was not in motion, it lay on the table and his fingers drummed a staccato, arrhythmic beat.

"Has anyone found him? That's what I want to know. Does anyone know where Darius Whitney has disappeared to?"

"The FBI is looking for him," said Scott.

"And haven't found him," said Morgenstern ominously.

"Haven't found him," Scott agreed.

Morgenstern drew a deep breath. "Captain . . . can I speak to you in confidence?"

"Yes. You can speak to me in confidence."

Morgenstern glanced at his wife. "I have to speak to somebody," he said. "Somebody . . ." Once more he drew breath. "Captain, I sued you and Whitney because I thought one or the other of you had severely damaged my company. I withdrew my lawsuit because my wife was kidnapped and it was made clear to me her life was in danger if I pressed the suit."

Scott's face flushed. *"Kidnapped?* You're serious? Look, you don't think *I* had anything to do with a thing like that?"

Dawn shook her head emphatically.

"No," said Morgenstern. "We don't think that. Not at all. We think you are potentially as much a victim as we are."

Scott grabbed up his coffee cup, unable to conceal the shock provoked by this turn in the conversation. Could he believe these two people?

"Kidnapping doesn't sound like Darius Whitney," he said.

"Who has he allied himself with?" asked Morgenstern darkly. "Who's he working with? Or for? And most of all—*where is he?*"

Scott shook his head. "I wish I knew."

Morgenstern and his wife exchanged glances. "We've brought

you something, Captain," said Morgenstern. "I don't know how much help it will be. Maybe none." He shoved a bulging soft-sided briefcase under the table. "What's in there is computer disks. Copies of everything Whitney was working on in our computer center during the six months before he left us. I don't know if you'll find any clues in there, but if any of that stuff is helpful . . ."

"That could be very helpful, Mr. Morgenstern."

When Hal Miller nodded, the solemnity of it, the rhythmic bobbing of the head, somehow suggested Maine or New Hampshire to Scott: the taciturn somber affirmation of a downeast Yankee. In fact that was where Miller had come from originally, and his many years in the Navy, then with Info Pro, now with the Task Force, had not changed him.

"It works," he said. "Nothing's certain except death and taxes, but I'd lay a pretty heavy bet on this. The programs Morgenstern delivered made it a lot more sure."

Miller had been directed by Scott to try to write a program that would identify the hand of Darius Whitney in a virus. They had already known some of Whitney's habits, his approaches to problems of software design, his favorite solutions. They had used all the software he was known to have designed, compared it, and found a consistent thread running through all of it.

But the disks brought by Morgenstern had tripled their stock of known Whitney designs. Miller had developed a program that contained a sort of intellectual and psychological portrait of Darius Whitney and could identify his work with an impressive degree of accuracy.

"It's like fingerprint checking," said Miller, his enthusiasm raising the level of his voice. "You know . . . so many points of comparison—"

"A conclusion, Chief. A conclusion," said Scott a little impatiently.

Miller started to nod again. "Whitney wrote the digitalizer virus," he said. "Five points of comparison."

"Okay. The next step. Can you run the program against all the internal programming of the ATC computer system, to see if anything in them is Whitney's?"

"I've been working on that," said Miller. "I think we can do it. The first problem is to get cooperation. The FAA types don't want to let us in."

"I'll take care of that," said Scott. "First, I want a detailed written report on what you found in the digitalizer virus."

"That report," said Miller, "is going to say Whitney wrote the digitalizer virus."

"That report, Chief," said Scott, "is going to get us a warrant for the arrest of Darius Whitney. And an indictment."

Nancy began every day with three or four cups of strong black coffee. She ate no breakfast, but she affirmed that she could not begin the day without her coffee. Her caffeine fix, she called it.

Scott had heard her say to a waitress one morning, "If she's having decaf, bring me the caffeine you leave out of hers."

Their morning habits did not clash. He began the day with a large glass of orange juice, with the *Washington Post* in front of him on the kitchen table. The coffee brewed while he drank his juice and scanned the paper. He drank coffee while he shaved, and by this time she was at the table with the paper.

Routine. Habit. On this Monday morning in May it saved their lives.

Scott hurried into the kitchen from the bathroom, carrying his cup. "Here come the guys," he said, and he picked up from the counter the little transmitter for the garage-door opener and pressed the button.

Three seconds later a fiery explosion blew out the walls of the garage, flung off the roof, threw his Porsche across the garage and half over his neighbor's Buick, and shot glass and window framing into six condominiums. A turbulent, smoky fire erupted as the gasoline from two burst tanks ignited and burned.

* * *

No one was killed. A child from one of the condominiums was taken to the hospital for treatment of cuts, but the paramedics said they would have cleaned and bandaged her cuts at home if she had been an adult. Scott was cut on his left arm. His blood ruined his suit, but the cuts were not deep and would not be the source of any permanent damage. A torrent of glass shards had swept across the table where Nancy sat, but none of them had touched her.

Nancy had begun to make telephone calls even before the medics attended to Scott's cuts. A pair of FBI agents were in the kitchen by the time the local police and Maryland state police began to ask questions.

"The garage-door opener?" a fire marshal asked. "You feel certain about that?"

Scott nodded. "When you sift the mess out there, I'm sure that's what you'll find. The detonator was triggered by the door going up."

"Not by the radio signal from the opener transmitter?" asked a Bethesda detective.

"No, because ordinarily I would have raised the door by pressing the button on the garage wall."

"Why'd you open the door from here in the kitchen this morning?" asked the detective.

Scott stood at the window, looking at the collapsed garage, which had fallen on the burned wreckage of his Porsche and his neighbor's Buick. The two hulks were smothered in white foam. Rubble was scattered across driveways and lawns; bricks had been tossed onto the roofs of nearby homes; and bricks had shattered the windshields and dented the bodies of cars. A packer truck from the city's refuse department sat at the end of the driveway, blocked in by a score of fire trucks, police cars, squadwagons, and vans from the local television and radio stations.

"In this neighborhood the city picks up the trash on Monday mornings. I don't like to leave my cans outdoors; dogs upset them and scatter stuff. So, when I know I'll be home on Monday morning, I leave the cans in the garage. The guys usually come just about the time I leave. If they haven't, I push the cans out when

I open the garage door. If I see them coming when I'm still in the house, I open the garage door so they can pull them out and empty them."

"And this morning . . ."

"I was in my bedroom, just finishing dressing, when I heard the packer truck on the street. I came into the kitchen and used the transmitter to raise the garage door. And . . . BOOM!"

"If we had gone out to the garage as usual," said Nancy, "and he had pushed the button on the wall . . ."

"I would guess," said Scott, "that the detonator was in the track. When the door wheels ran over it. . . . The charge was probably hidden in one of the boxes everybody has in their garage."

"Okay," said the Bethesda detective. "Basic facts, please." He flipped a page of his pocket notebook. "Full name, please?"

"Scott R.—for Richard—Vandenberg, Captain, United States Navy."

"Age?"

"I'm forty. I'll be forty-one soon."

"If somebody doesn't murder him first," said Nancy wryly.

"Murder," said the detective. "Okay. Why, Captain Vandenberg? Why would anyone want to murder you?"

"Hold it," said one of the FBI agents. "Sorry, but I've got to intervene. Captain Vandenberg is on special assignment, under the direct orders of the President. What he's doing is classified. The motive for the attempt on his life is related to his assignment. We can't go into it."

Scott knew that what the man said was true. He had known it from the instant he saw and felt the explosion. It was so unambiguously, inescapably certain that he and Nancy had left it unspoken while she was pulling off his coat and shirt and pressing wads of paper towels to his cuts as they waited for firemen and police to arrive.

She had been quicker to react than he had. As soon as she saw he was not critically injured, she had begun to prowl the house, pistol in hand, checking the doors and windows, as if she expected a follow-up attack. She had received the first firemen

and policemen under the muzzle of her Walther, and at this moment it lay by her hand on the kitchen table, on a layer of glittering
glass.

The Bethesda detective had once before experienced the
abrupt curtailment of an investigation, on assertion by a federal
agent that it was secret federal business. He didn't like it, but he
knew better than to argue. He closed his notebook.

The Maryland state police sergeant was more candid. He
threw up his hands. "You gonna keep living here, Captain?" he
asked.

It was a good question. The accusatory looks on the faces of
his neighbors when Scott and Nancy left with the FBI agents suggested that his presence in the condominium was no longer welcome. His neighbors were afraid to have him there. He couldn't
blame them.

"You can't blame me."

Sally had phoned. She was telling him she could not allow
him to visit Judy as long as his life was threatened. Which was
right, she couldn't. And he couldn't insist on visits.

"I can talk to her on the telephone," he said. "How in hell
am I gonna explain?"

"I've already explained," said Sally with that careful precision
in her voice that she always affected when she was determined
not to be contradicted. "I didn't tell her you were threatened. I
told her you'd got another one of those assignments that requires
you to be overseas for a while. I told her you'd be flying again.
She's too young to remember your long absences, but she does
know you were a Navy pilot. I told her you'd been called away
suddenly and didn't have time to stop by first. I don't think you
should call her."

"You've assumed a lot, haven't you?"

"I have a responsibility," she said.

"What about the goddam newspapers?" he asked. "What
about the goddam television?"

"I've managed to keep them away from her so far."

"What about the kids at school?"

"The kids at her school don't know exactly who you are. I talked to the teacher. She's going to cool any talk about the explosion."

"I don't have any choice, do I?"

"No, not really. But neither do I, Dick." She had always called him Dick, after his middle name. She used to say she thought his parents had indulged in something of an affectation in naming him Scott. "I have to wonder if—"

"Don't even think of it," he said. "It's not like that."

But it was like that. The child was under twenty-four-hour surveillance by the FBI, on direct order of the President. They were supposed to keep out of sight. *That* would be a test of their professional competence.

"You do understand?" she asked, uncertainty returning to her voice.

"I understand. And . . . Sally . . . I'm sorry about the whole damned thing. You know I—"

"You seem to be getting along reasonably well," she said. "The woman is a real looker."

"Thanks. I'll tell her you said so."

They had to move into a safe house: a motel, actually, in Chevy Chase. The office in Bethesda was under guard. They moved on varying schedules, in different cars, along different routes. Scott carried his Beretta—all the time, everywhere, and didn't feel foolish about it anymore.

Living under siege, real or perceived, usually draws people closer together. Scott and Nancy had been sleeping together two or three nights a week usually; now they were together every night. Living in adjoining rooms in a motel, they could hardly stay apart. They talked of going ahead and getting married; but they agreed they did not want to have a wedding under armed guard.

On the Thursday morning after the explosion he went with her to the little airport at Gaithersburg, where she flew her biennial flight check. She had told him she had a pilot's license, but she had said almost nothing more about it, being reluctant to talk about her own flying to a man who had thousands of hours in his log books and had flown hundreds of carrier takeoffs and landings in powerful jet fighters.

On this morning she had to fly a single-engine Cessna with an instructor for about an hour, to demonstrate that two years after her last biennial she could still fly safely. It was a requirement for continuing her license.

Scott sat in the rear seat of the Skyhawk and watched Nancy take off, fly the airplane through a series of prescribed maneuvers, including recovery from stalls, fly turns about a point, do three touch-and-goes, and finally bring the little plane back onto the runway in a smooth, graceful landing.

"Kept it up, Captain?" the instructor asked when they were on the ramp beside the airplane.

"As a matter of fact, I haven't. I haven't been at the controls of an aircraft in six years."

The instructor nodded at the Skyhawk. "Take less than an hour to get your license in order, I bet. 'Course you'll then need a physical. Seems to me, a man who has learned to fly ought never to give it up."

Nancy was grinning at him.

Scott shrugged. "You got a deal, man," he said. "Let's see if I can still handle it."

Of course he could. He flew differently from Nancy, differently from the instructor, with far greater emphasis on precision: entering a turn at five thousand feet and coming out of that turn at precisely five thousand feet, neither climbing nor descending ten feet during the maneuver; constantly adjusting his throttle, so that the engine turned over at exactly the same number of revolutions per minute regardless of altitude; touching his wheels to the runway precisely 150 feet from the end of the pavement, not twenty feet off. At the end of half an hour the instructor pronounced himself not just satisfied but an admirer of Captain Vandenberg's flying.

A couple of days later Scott sat in the copilot's seat of an FAA Falcon and took the controls. He was surprised at how satisfying it was to fly again.

"Why'd you ever quit?" Nancy asked finally, having eschewed the question for some time.

"Couldn't handle the physical for an F-14 anymore," he told her. "Contact lenses don't go with flying carrier landings in a Tomcat."

"And if you couldn't fly a Tomcat, you didn't want to fly at all?"

"Something like that."

"The more I know about you—Well, never mind. I love you, you egomaniacal idiot."

"We'll buy a plane of our own," said Scott, reaching to put his arm around her and his hand on her thigh. "Like that Sky-hawk. A couple can afford . . . Hell, we can afford a *twin*. And we'll fly . . ." He stopped, flustered by his enthusiasm. "You know."

"We'll fly to Florida," she said. "To the Bahamas." Abruptly her face darkened. "If we survive."

Allison McGuire opened the door of the house at Toiyabe Ranch to find Yoshitaka Hara standing there, accompanied by a man of menacing appearance whom she didn't know.

"We are sorry to appear so early in the morning," said Hara with the smooth civility he used to cover flawed character. "But we've come on urgent business."

"Darius is still in bed," she said.

"Please wake him."

Allison returned to the bedroom. Darius was indeed still in bed, but he was awake; he had been wakened by the doorbell, just as she had. He sat up, quite naked though covered from the navel down by the sheet he had pulled across his hips and legs when she left the bed. One of her discoveries of the past few days was that Darius did not even *own* a pair of pajamas. She did and had pulled on white cotton ones when she went to the door.

"It's Hara," she said. "Something urgent."

Darius sighed. "With them something is always urgent," he grumbled. "Give me a kiss, my little dove, and I will dress and see what disaster befalls now."

Allison pulled a robe on over her pajamas, though they were modest enough, and started a pot of coffee while Darius dressed.

She had planned to begin the day with a refreshing swim, and she resented being confronted with something urgent before eight o'clock. Darius came into the living room—the room now crowded with computers and communications equipment—dressed in khaki slacks and a dark-blue polo shirt.

"This is Stepan Yanak," said Hara, nodding at the half-bald man with the acne-scarred face—a man Allison had already decided she didn't like. "He works for Señor Cordero."

Darius did not judge him very favorably either, for he only nodded curtly at Yanak, then tipped his head and fixed an anticipatory stare on Hara.

"I have rather distressing news for you," said Yoshitaka Hara.

"I suppose I shouldn't be surprised," grunted Darius.

Hara ignored whatever the comment implied—irony, contempt—and spoke in a hurried but matter-of-fact tone. "The government of the United States has issued a warrant for your arrest," he said.

"On what grounds?" asked Darius indignantly. "What are the charges?"

"Violations of the Computer Fraud and Abuse Act," said Hara. "A multitude of charges, most of them having to do with the Thanksgiving Eve virus and LANCE. Interference with computer services, illegal use of interstate communications facilities . . . Also some charges about threats to air safety. And of course the prosecutors' catchall: conspiracy."

Darius shook his head defiantly, but Allison could see he was staggered by the news. The color of his face changed, and he seemed slack, diminished.

"Also, you are charged with having written the virus that allowed Eddy Wentzel to fly the Lear over Miami without appearing on the radar scopes."

"How could they identify me?" asked Darius weakly.

"They have examined every program you ever wrote—that is, every one available to them, including a lot of work you did for Whitney Data Dynamics in the last year. They identified your individual ways of solving programming problems, and they wrote a program of their own that searches programs, including viruses, for what they call your signature. They found what they identify as your signature in the program that made the Miami radar blind to the Lear."

"Bull," said Darius. "They're just guessing."

"How do you know all this?" asked Allison. "How do you know they wrote this signature program and so on?"

"To obtain a warrant," said Hara, "they had to file an affidavit with a federal judge, describing the evidence that would justify arresting you. That affidavit is a public record and was examined by Señor Cordero's lawyers."

Allison frowned hard. "You said, 'arresting *you*.' There's not a warrant for *me*, is there?"

Yoshitaka Hara nodded gravely. "I'm afraid there is. Co-conspirator."

Darius drove his right fist into his left hand. "Damn! What can we do?"

Allison saw that he was close to tears. She was, herself.

"Señor Cordero asked me to tell you that everything will be straightened out. It may take time, but it can be straightened out. In the meantime, you must fly to Bogotá. You must finish the work there."

"Why not here? No one knows where we are."

Hara shook his head. "No one generally. But we have not been so clever as to hide you if the FBI really wants you. No, you can't stay here."

"We can't fly to Bogotá either," said Allison, controlling her voice only with effort. "They'll be looking for us at the airports. Our passports—"

"You won't need passports," said Hara. "Everything has been arranged. Just go with Stepan and do what he tells you. Everything will be taken care of."

Darius fixed a disconsolate stare on Allison. She knew his thoughts: the same as hers—that they were prisoners, that probably they couldn't refuse this man Yanak, who was an enforcer if ever she saw one. For a moment she wondered if there really were a warrant. Cordero had always wanted them in Bogotá, where he would have them under his thumb. But as if he had read her mind,

Hara took the papers from the inside pocket of his sand-colored jacket and handed them to Darius—copies of the warrants.

"We haven't got much time," said Yanak, speaking for the first time. "Let's get your stuff together."

"When are we going?" Darius asked.

"Now," said Yanak.

Hara returned to Las Vegas. The taciturn Yanak drove Darius and Allison south into Arizona to the Mojave County Airport, where they found a small, high-winged, twin-turboprop airplane waiting. The three of them boarded, carrying only two suitcases: one held such personal possessions as Darius and Allison had been able to grab in the hectic twenty minutes before they left the house; the other contained the invaluable disks and printout sheets that contained the new virus. The plane took off and soon was above the clouds. It landed twice to refuel. It reached Bogotá at sunset.

Exhausted both emotionally and physically, Darius and Allison accepted whatever Stepan Yanak suggested: a mysterious run around Colombian immigration, without showing their passports, quick transfer to a limousine, and a silent, somber ride to the Cordero villa.

Neither had said to the other that the villa would be their prison. They didn't have to say it. They knew it.

They were installed in a suite in the villa, with windows overlooking the swimming pool. The computer equipment they found waiting for them matched exactly what they had left at Toiyabe Ranch. Señor Cordero spent whatever had to be spent and provided whatever was needed. This also included clothes for both of them, including the dinner jacket Darius would be expected to wear each evening as well as two silk cocktail dresses for Allison.

That night they did not go down to dinner. Señor Cordero, it seemed, was not there, so they weren't expected. His arrival the next afternoon was the occasion for much excitement, as if a feudal lord had just returned to his manor—which, as Allison observed, was pretty much the way it was.

They were called down to dinner that evening. The Señor heard a report on their progress in writing the new virus. He listened, but it was apparent that he understood only the basic out-lines. He needed Yoshitaka Hara to hear their reports and interpret them. Only one element of the conversation was significant—

"Miss McGuire," Cordero said when they were almost ready to leave the poolside table. "Stepan is going to fly up into the mountains tomorrow, to deliver a message for me. By helicopter. I suggest you fly with him. I know you will find the trip interesting. It is in fact an opportunity few people have, one that may not come again—to see some of the most primitive jungle remaining intact on the continent."

Darius could see that she was uncertain about how to respond. He tried to help. "She has had a hard couple of days," he said.

"Please," said Cordero. "She will enjoy it. She will remember it for a long time."

Allison left the suite early in the morning. Darius tried to sleep but could not and got up not long after and called downstairs for coffee. The kitchen sent up more than he asked for: a pot of coffee, Danish, and slices of fruit. Dressed in an outfit that had been provided for him—a khaki safari jacket and slacks—he sat down after breakfast at one of the two computers and began to reconstruct the work that had been interrupted by the call to come to Bogotá.

He could not work. He was distracted by a thousand different thoughts. Above all he wondered why Cordero had insisted that Allison go with Yanak on the helicopter trip to the mountain jun-gles. He tried to sort out in his mind the whole situation back home: the criminal charges against him and how he would resolve them. He lit a cigar and paced the suite, pausing occasionally to stand at the window and stare down at the pool, where some of the Señor's decorative girls were already lounging around.

Erase the digitalizer virus. That was the key, as Allison had suggested. He would insert it when it was needed, and as soon as it did its work, it would erase itself. Then let them do byte counts. If they counted while the virus was in place and working, they would detect it. If they missed it during the single hour when it was needed, they would miss it entirely. The digitalizer virus had to infect the equipment at only one airport. The byte counts would have to be done airport by airport, and they couldn't do constant byte counts. They couldn't because every byte count interrupted the digitalizer for a short time. They would do them periodically, maybe three or four times a day. And he would sneak in between them.

The other element of the key was to detect the byte counts. And that he could do. Having targeted a digitalizer, he would monitor that one and would know when it was subjected to a byte count. He would know what windows were open to him. Once a count was done, he could be confident it would not be repeated in the next hour. That hour was his window of opportunity.

He sat down again at one of the computers, inserted a disk to mount one of his experimental programs, and began to compare what he had against what he needed.

Late in the morning he was interrupted by a soft knock on the door, and a moment later Virgilio Cordero entered the suite.

"I want to make sure you have everything you need," said Cordero. He was wearing a short robe, apparently over swimming trunks, and was smoking one of his odd, mint-colored cigarettes. "And to invite you, when you want to take an hour off, to come down to the pool."

Darius shrugged. "I can't inject the virus into the system from here," he said. "Sooner or later I have to return to the States."

"It can be arranged," said Cordero.

"What? I go home a fugitive, wanted by the FBI? I sneak in, sneak back out?"

Cordero walked to the glass doors and stepped out onto the narrow balcony. "I understand your concern," he said over his shoulder. "But time is long. The world is complicated. We always find ways to do what we want to do. Or . . . we find alternatives."

Darius pushed his chair back and rose from the computer, rubbing his eyes with his fists. "So much for recovering control of my company," he said. "Whitney, the fugitive from justice—"

"Darius. Your company is a small matter. For you. Not for me. For you. You talked to me about flying a 747 into the States undetected. You were talking about half a billion dollars. Maybe we buy up the stock in your company. Maybe you buy it, out of what we pay you. Or maybe you won't care about it anymore when you are personally worth more money than the value of all the stock in the *parent* company. My friend, you are going to be a fabulously wealthy man!"

Cordero's back was to him, so Cordero didn't see the look on the face of Darius Whitney—which would have told him that Darius didn't believe a word he was saying.

Darius had a new motive for putting the best of himself into the work: Probably his life, and Allison's, depended on it.

Allison was both fascinated and sorry she had agreed to the morning's flight to this remote mountainside factory. She had thought about it during the night, when Darius was sleeping, and had concluded she might as well go. Darius had enslaved himself to the new project; and in spite of the fact that she had contributed an important suggestion to it, he would exclude her from the work until he needed her again. She had accepted all the elements of the suggestion and had boarded the helicopter with Stepan Yanak not long after dawn, supposing they would return in the afternoon.

She wasn't sure where she was: in Colombia, Ecuador, or Peru. They all looked the same from the air. She sat on a wooded hillside in stifling, humid heat, wearing shorts and a halter and not well protected against the insects that infested this upland jungle, and watched the dull, sweaty labor of the first steps in making cocaine.

Yes, it was cocaine. Señor Cordero didn't even pretend anymore that the air cargo would be anything else. He talked about it not as a viciously addictive narcotic but as a product people used for sophisticated pleasure—one that *Norteamericanos* couldn't control.

Sweat streamed down the bodies of the wiry little men who carried bundles of newly harvested leaf toward the crude wooden troughs. The old story was that Inca couriers could run for days through the mountains, eating almost nothing, drinking almost nothing, sustained by the coca leaf they chewed. These small men were supposed to be descendants of the Inca. Each man's cheek swelled with a wad of leaf, like the half-chewed cud in the cheek of a tobacco chewer. Their bodies were hard and thin, with stringy muscles showing like hard cords in their arms and legs. Their tattered shorts and shreds of shirts hung loosely over their narrow chests and hips.

In the trough—it was unbelievable—other tiny men, and some boys, about half of them naked, the rest nearly so, tromped monotonously in a mixture of leaves and water, breaking down the leaves as the first step in the long process of converting green leaves to white powder. The men and boys chewed leaves and danced around the big trough, raising their feet knee-high and stomping down into the thickening mixture. They didn't sing. There was no rhythm. They trod and were self-absorbed. Water thick with the juices of the leaves was constantly drawn off.

Besides the leaves they shoved into their mouths, the men also intermittently pulled from their pockets what looked like chunks of dirty gray chalk; and they bit off bits of this and chewed it with the leaf. That was the magic combination: the coca leaf plus some sort of alkaline that helped the digestive juices in making the body absorb the chemical.

"It's like nicotine, you see," said Stepan Yanak. "The good of it is in the leaf. The question is, how do you get the good stuff out of the leaf? They chew it with their bits of chalk and get a little lift out of it. For more sophisticated people, it's extracted and refined and offered as the pure stuff."

The leaf substituted for food apparently. The workmen were energetic, unsparing of themselves, even though they were hollow-eyed and emaciated.

"They harvest the leaves for miles around," said Yanak. "The mountainsides—"

"Sure," she said.

She was tired and hot and tormented by bugs, and she was ready to go back to the villa. The noisy, shaky helicopter had taken a lot out of her, as did the half-hour ride in an old car filled with gasoline fumes, and now she sat and sweated; and though what she was seeing was interesting, she had seen enough.

"They've got no other way to make a living," he said. "This is what they do. This is how they live. Otherwise . . . starvation."

Allison sighed. "How soon we leaving?"

Yanak grinned. "Ah. I've got some business here. Gotta see

a man coming in tonight. They've put up tents for us. I mean real tents, with mosquito nets and all. You haven't lived till you taste the pork they roast, with vegetables I can't even name but are great! Plus wine. Plus . . . You'll see. We're going back tomorrow sometime."

He'd been right. Much as she resented spending the night in this squalid camp, she found herself treated like a queen, and she had to admit that Señor Cordero himself could hardly have offered a more mouth-watering meal. She had never eaten such . . . pork? She was reluctant to ask what it was. And vegetables, maybe fruits—who knew?—the like of which she had never tasted. Also wine made from god knew what, but utterly delicious. Around a big fire.

A boy, maybe fourteen, certainly no older, oiled her, to keep away the bugs—just as he did Yanak and the men sitting on mats on the ground in the light of the fire. He pushed his hands under her halter and down into her shorts, to spread the oil over as much of her as possible—without, so far as she could tell, taking the slightest prurient interest in where his hands touched.

Naked boys, their bodies oiled, danced to the thin music of an ill-tuned, ill-played guitar. If any of the men found this dancing erotic, as she did, they showed no sign of it. Their attention was focused on their food and on the exotic green wine, of which they partook gravely and sparingly. Obviously they did not eat and drink this way except in the presence of the representative of the Señor and the woman, and they hardly knew how to enjoy it.

The arrhythmic thump of men and boys stomping in the trough never stopped. They worked all night apparently. She was seized with a sense of primitive timelessness, imposed on her consciousness probably by the vast black night overhead, with more stars than she had ever seen before; by the firelight; by the capering dance of the naked boys; by the grave and meditative faces of the workmen who ate and drank and watched the dance.

Though everything they did was for making cocaine, they had none. They chewed the leaf, that was all. She tried it. It was mildly pleasant, she thought, but did not threaten addiction, at least not to her. But the long, hot day and the food and drink had made her drowsy, so when Yanak suggested they retire to their tents, she was ready, even though it was only eight o'clock.

The tent was as Yanak had said: tight, secure, furnished with a camp cot surrounded by mosquito netting. There was no lantern or other light inside, and when she closed the front flap, it was absolutely dark, until her eyes adjusted and she could see tiny holes in the canvas, points of firelight like yellow stars. The inside of the tent stank of insecticide, which had been sprayed just before she came in. She lay down on the cot, pulled the sheet up over her, and was asleep within minutes.

When she awoke, she had no idea how long she had been asleep. Maybe an hour. Maybe only a few minutes. Maybe it was almost dawn. She tried to see the time on the faintly glowing face of her watch, but her eyes weren't yet ready to focus.

Voices had wakened her. She realized she had heard voices: harsh voices. Now it was quiet outside, except for soft weeping. Someone was crying. Not a woman. A man.

Then she heard a voice again, strained, pleading. "Let me go back and tell them. When they know . . ."

"They'll know." That was Yanak's voice. "They'll understand."

"Take me to see the Señor, then!"

One shot. She heard one explosion. Then silence.

In the morning the camp was strangely silent. Had it been a dream? A nightmare? The men stared sullenly at them as they prepared to leave. Yanak grinned at her and winked. The car took them down the mountain and back to the helicopter, shortly after dawn.

Yanak had killed someone. She couldn't doubt it. For what other reason had they stayed overnight? Why else had Señor Cordero sent him here? And why had they insisted *she* come, unless it was to hear the murder and know what they were capable of? They expected her to tell Darius of course. It was a warning. And she would tell him. What else could she do?

Hal Miller reported to Scott Vandenberg. "Okay, Captain," said Miller. "The digitalizers are free of viruses. I mean, the ones in Miami are clean, and so are all the others we've checked—

mostly at airports in the south. They're running the byte counts at regular intervals now."

"Have them make that *irregular* intervals, Chief," said Scott. Since Miller persisted in calling him captain, he had adopted the habit of calling Miller chief—for chief petty officer. "Okay?"

"Yes, sir. Now . . . We've come up with something interesting. The Whitney-detection program found several examples of apparent Whitney programming. That got everybody excited. But when we looked into them, we found they were Whitney all right—but programs he wrote for the Air Force and the FAA during his years in government service."

"You're kidding."

Miller grinned. "Parts of the ATC computer system are Whitney programming, after all these years. Small parts, but there you are."

"But no recent Whitney signatures?" Scott asked.

"No, sir. But something else in the main ATC program suggests it may have been invaded. The main program is free of viruses right now. The byte counts demonstrate that. But the way some of the programs are distributed over the disks in some of the main drives make it look like something else was in and has been erased. I mean, it looks like a Trojan horse may have been in, dropped a virus and erased itself, and then the virus erased *itself*."

"In other words, the programs should have been reasonably compact, and—"

"Yes, sir. Some of the operating software is scattered around the disks as if something intruded and was then erased. Of course, whether that was Whitney work, no one could possibly tell."

"Good work, Chief," said Scott. "Keep on it."

Nancy Delacorte arrived in Los Angeles on a Monday morning. For some reason, morning sunshine always seemed whiter on days when a thin smog hung in the air. She pulled a pair of sunglasses from her handbag as she walked out of the United Airlines terminal and caught a cab. It was hot, too. She wore a white linen suit and decided she would be carrying the jacket over her arm before very long.

Ben Niessen, the man she had telephoned from Washington

last week, came down to meet her in the lobby of the headquarters building of Pacific Bell, for which he was chief of corporate security.

"Well," he said in the soft accent of a transplanted Alabaman. "I did not hear in your voice when you called that I was to have the honor of welcomin' so charmin' a young lady to California."

"I had no idea I would meet so gallant a gentleman," she replied.

Niessen laughed. It seemed to please him that she could receive and return banter like this. She noticed that his eyes dropped three or four times to her legs, advantageously exhibited by her short, tailored skirt. She judged his appraisal innocent just the same. Like many southern men, he played an artless little game and didn't expect her to take it seriously.

His next words were earnest enough. "I have been lookin' into what you suggested," he said. "I think we can do what you have in mind."

"You talked with your technical types?"

"Yes, ma'am. We have not tried your idea yet, but they say they can maybe come out with the information you need. Would you like to go on to our computer center?"

"I would, yes."

The center was on the twenty-fifth floor: a typical brightly lit big room, air-conditioned, humidity-controlled, and quiet, except for the hum of stacks of disks spinning ceaselessly in their drives. The technicians were typical too: intense young men and women who seemed in competition with their machines.

"I am goin' to ask Miz Delacorte to explain what she has in mind, so you can hear it in her own words," he said to two technicians, a young man and a young woman, when they were seated at a folding table and paper cups of coffee had been put in front of them.

"All right," said Nancy. "I know you're plagued with what we call blue boxes, devices contrived by computer hackers to break into your codes and enable themselves to make free long-distance calls. As I understand it, a blue box makes the audible tones a touch-tone phone makes, only it beeps out the codes that control the telephone switching and billing systems."

"We've got the worst of it under control," said the young woman. Her name was Jane. "We've made the system harder to cheat."

"Except maybe for the most sophisticated hackers," Nancy suggested. "And Mr. Niessen tells me you maintain a record of the calls these people make."

The young man—he was Dave—nodded. "That's how we've caught some of them. They can cover the way they originate their calls, but sometimes we can identify them by the numbers they call."

Niessen chuckled. "He calls his mama twice a week, his girlfriend every night, you get so you can guess who he is. A little inquiry. . . . The FBI takes it seriously. Theft of telephone service."

"The college students who used to call their mothers and girl friends can't get into the system anymore," said Jane. "There was a time when all they had to do was put a number generator to one of our phones and let it transmit number after number until eventually it hit a code. We're more sophisticated than we used to be. It's much tougher to break the system."

"But some still do it," said Nancy.

The young woman frowned uncertainly.

"It's all right," said Niessen. "Miz Delacorte is a federal investigator, as I told you. It's all right to tell her what's goin' on."

"In our service area," said Jane, "we've still got six or seven functioning blue boxes. They've used computer programs to crack our internal codes. The way that usually works is, they somehow get their hands on just one code—somebody in our company gives it or sells it to them—and from that one they can figure out others."

"It takes some pretty sophisticated computer work," said Dave. "Not just any hacker can do it. Which is why we only have a few hackers stealing from us now."

"But you do keep a record, don't you, of every call you identify as originating with a blue box?" Nancy asked.

"Oh, sure," said Niessen.

"I want to look at hacker calls originating from Malibu," said Nancy. We're looking for a fugitive. He's a businessman. Everybody today leaves some kind of paper track. Especially a person in business. The FBI checked this man's track, and I reviewed what they found—which of course included telephone bills. It seemed very odd to me that the man we're looking for paid no long-distance charges. I thought it unlikely he made no long-distance calls. And since he's a highly sophisticated system designer and pro-grammer—"

"We call him Beach Boy," said Jane. "The calls originate from telephone booths all around the Malibu area."

"How many calls to the four-one-four area?" asked Nancy.

Jane grinned. "Hey! You got it. About once a week, to the same number in Wisconsin. A company in San Diego complained it was being billed for calls to Wisconsin and didn't have any contacts in Wisconsin. So we began to look at that number from the other end."

"That was his girlfriend calling her parents," said Nancy.

"Callin' an old-fashioned pharmacy in Milwaukee," said Niessen. "One with a soda fountain and tables. We sent an in-vestigator to ask about it, and the man who owned the pharmacy denied he ever got a call from California. The number was a pay phone in the pharmacy, and the man said teenagers sometimes got calls on that phone, but he didn't know who called them."

"What's the man's name?" asked Nancy.

"McGuire."

Nancy nodded. "Our man keeps a girlfriend named McGuire."

Dave had opened a book of computer printouts. "Slacked off," he said. "No calls at all for several weeks."

"Besides Wisconsin, where did he call?" asked Nancy.

"You know, most of the calls—almost all of them in fact—were to Wisconsin, until recently. San Francisco a couple of times. Las Vegas. And then, here's one. An international call. Fifty-seven-dash-one."

"What's that?"

Jane pulled down a telephone directory and looked at the table of international dialing codes. "Fifty . . . Hmm. Bogotá, Co-lombia."

"Great! Now we're getting someplace. Can you find out who he called in Bogotá?"

"Sure. We'll call Bogotá. They'll tell us."

Dave was still running his finger down the columns of numbers on the printout. "We've got five . . . six calls to Nevada."

"Figured he was calling his bookie," said Niessen.

"Let's find out who he *was* calling," said Nancy.

"Sure. We can do that," said Niessen. He picked up a telephone, punched in a code, and read the number from the printout to someone. He put down the telephone. "Las Vegas," he said. "A Japanese fellow, apparently. The name is Yoshitaka Hara. Mean anythin' to you?"

12

—▮-▮-▮-▮—

Sometimes the simplest ways of doing things were the best. Sometimes it was best to add just a small measure of complexity to simple things, to be sure they would work.

The simple way of getting Darius Whitney into the United States, to New York, was to fly him in on a regular commercial flight. It was simple enough to obtain a forged passport for him— simple anyway if you had Cordero's resources. To make it more certain, Darius flew from Bogotá to Rio de Janeiro to Dublin to London and then to New York. On an Irish passport in the name of James McMurtry.

He had grown a mustache before his passport photo was taken; and he wore it now, a bit more straggly. He traveled first-class, ostensibly alone, actually with Yanak sitting a few seats away from him and following a few paces behind in line when he went through passport checks. It was all very clean. He walked out of the British Air terminal at Kennedy Airport and caught a cab. He checked in at the Summit Hotel on Lexington Avenue. It was only when he was in his room that Yanak caught up, knocked on his door, and came in to tell him he was to meet Yoshitaka Hara for dinner.

Yoshitaka Hara was staying at the Grand Hyatt Hotel, on Forty-second Street next to Grand Central Station. When he emerged

195

from an elevator and walked across the cavernous lobby, he was immediately spotted by a man sitting behind a newspaper: an FBI agent with a tiny radio transmitter cupped in his hand. Inconspicuously, just by pressing a button, the agent sent the signal that Hara had come down from his room. No one, not even the woman sitting beside him, was alerted that the man was sending a signal.

It was clever. Too clever. They lost their man, then and there.

The signal transmitted by the man in the lobby beeped in the receiver another agent wore on his belt. He was on the sidewalk just outside the hotel. He put a bigger transmitter to his mouth— this one a voice transmitter, not just a beeper, and not inconspicuous at all—and told the cars to move closer, that their man was coming out.

That agent surveyed the cabs available and the people waiting for them. Yoshitaka Hara, he figured, had a short wait for his cab. That's what he told the men in the two cars.

The agent in the lobby folded his newspaper, stood up, and walked casually toward the escalator leading to the lower lobby on the street level. He reached the top of the escalator just in time to see the slight, bald Japanese turn right and walk briskly toward the exit into Grand Central Station. Hara was not going out onto Forty-second Street.

The agent could have trotted down the stairs adjacent to the escalator, but he didn't; probably from habit, he stepped onto the escalator and found himself riding down slowly, blocked ahead by a party of happy, chatting men and women, blocked behind by two men laden with luggage. By the time he reached the bottom, Hara had exited into the shop-lined corridor leading to the station.

The agent was faced with a decision. Should he run out on the street and explain to the others, or should he trot after Hara? He chose the latter. He forgot about being inconspicuous and ran after Hara, repeatedly pressing the button on his transmitter to alert the others.

He caught a glimpse of Hara just as he passed through the glass doors and into the big railroad station. In there, as the agent well knew, there were a score of ways to go. He ran, but by the time he pushed his way out into Grand Central Station, he was confronted by jostling crowds, a thousand people in a hurry—and no sign of Yoshitaka Hara.

The agent in charge was forced to telephone Nancy Delacorte and tell her they had lost their man.

Hara had not the slightest suspicion that he was under surveillance or that he had caused anyone distress. He was on his way out to dinner and all he was doing was what any sensible person would do to travel twenty blocks north in midtown at eight in the evening: He was boarding a subway. He walked down to the Lexington Avenue line and stepped onto the first northbound train.

He had told Yanak to send Darius to a small Hungarian restaurant he had discovered a few months ago and favored. He was waiting when Darius arrived, sitting at a candlelit table literally in a window, on show from the sidewalk.

"Should we be sitting here like in a store window?"

Hara grinned. "Do you think every New York cop has been shown a picture of Darius Whitney and will recognize you if he sees you?"

Darius glanced uneasily out the window, at a quiet residential street where it was still not quite dark. People walking past the restaurant stared in curiously.

Hara picked up the short menu and glanced over it. He grimaced contemptuously when Darius ordered a bourbon and soda. For himself Hara ordered a bottle of Bikavér, a heavy red wine he intended to drink with a small portion of *rabló-hus*, robbers' meat, which would be his appetizer.

"I understand the new programs are ready," said Hara.

Darius nodded. "That's why I came to the States," he said. "To inject them. You can't do it from Bogotá."

"No," said Hara quietly. "Of course *I* could have injected them. How are you planning to do it, anyway? Through the FAA itself?"

"Through Kansas City, I think," said Darius. "Being so far from the borders, they are not terribly security-conscious there. I'll inject into Kansas City Center and let the virus propagate through Kansas City's contacts with other centers."

"I can do that," said Hara. "You didn't have to come here."

"I suppose so," said Darius. "Technically you could. It's better that *I* do it, and test everything."

"Your trip here involves minimal risk," said Hara. "Even so, I am directed by Señor Cordero to keep a full copy of everything."

Darius shook his head. "No one receives any copy of anything," he said, "until I know that a substantial part of my money is on deposit in Switzerland."

Yanak grinned. "Don't you trust us, Darius?" he asked, as though it were a big joke.

"No," said Darius. "I don't."

By the time Hara returned to his hotel, Nancy was in the lobby. The agent who had lost him nudged her arm as Hara stepped off the escalator.

She checked her watch. "Three hours and forty-five minutes," she said. "I'd guess he's a little tipsy. Okay. Now what?"

The senior agent in charge of the operation approached. "He's going up to his room," he said. "No problem. Everything's installed."

During Hara's absence they had installed listening devices in his room and locator transmitters in the linings of his luggage. In a van outside, receivers were beeping away busily, assuring the FBI and the FAA that Yoshitaka Hara's luggage was still in his room.

"It was stupid to have lost him over the last four hours," said Nancy to the senior agent. "I'd give anything to know who he saw during that time."

"Maybe he just went out to dinner," said the senior agent. "He looks well fed and happy."

She nodded derisively. "Sure. So did Benedict Arnold during that last breakfast with George Washington at West Point."

The agents did not lose Hara the following afternoon when he left the Grand Hyatt Hotel in a cab, went to Kennedy Airport, and boarded a flight for Colombia. They could do nothing about it. They did not have enough against him to stop him. Immigration agents at every airport were alerted to look for his return.

Not knowing that Darius Whitney had reentered the country, the FBI was not looking for him. When he flew from New York to Las Vegas and went to Hara's suite at The Sands, letting himself in with the key Hara had given him at dinner, no one noticed that either. The agents who had been watching Hara's suite had been advised he had left the country, so they had relaxed their surveillance for a day or two.

In Hara's suite Darius spent a night and much of the next day using Hara's computer equipment, seeking access to the ATC computers in Kansas City. By the middle of the afternoon he found an entry—by sending his call from Las Vegas through Washington Center and making Kansas City suppose the call was a program adjustment from the FAA. He injected his new programs. Within three hours they had spread to every element of the nation's air-traffic-control system.

Stepan Yanak caught up with him in Las Vegas. Together they flew to San Francisco, then to Vancouver, and from there to Montreal and an Air Canada flight to Ireland—where the immigration man welcomed Mr. McMurtry, bearer of an Irish passport. Exhausted, Darius slept fourteen hours in a Dublin hotel, then caught a flight for Buenos Aires and Bogotá. Allison threw herself into his arms as he returned to their suite.

Judy Vandenberg's teacher was a twenty-eight-year-old woman named Carol Amanda—Miss Amanda to her pupils. Judy was up to her elbows in paste and water, energetically smearing papier-mâché over a lump of clay she had fashioned into a little head, when Miss Amanda came to her side and quietly told her to wash up. Someone was in the principal's office to see her.

The teacher said no more than that. The word on the telephone from the office was that the child's mother had been injured in an accident and that her uncle was there to take her to the hospital.

Like any seven-year-old, Judy was neither hurried nor efficient at washing paste from her hands and arms. She dawdled. Miss Amanda was reluctant to hurry her and spoke gently. Judy took her time.

At the office the man waited. He was a heavyset, graying man, wearing a light-blue Izod golf shirt under a loose nylon jacket. He smiled wanly, as if the news about his sister were dreadful, but he chatted amiably with the secretary behind the counter just the same. So amiably in fact, even with tragedy submerged only shallowly under his voice, that the secretary did not follow the standing policy in all these cases: to call the child's home before letting any child leave the school in the custody of anyone other than a parent.

At last Judy arrived. Miss Amanda led her by the hand into the office.

"Your uncle is here for you, Judy," said Miss Amanda. "He wants to take you—"

"He's *not* my uncle," snapped Judy with a petulant little stamp of her foot. "Not."

The secretary reached for the telephone. The man pulled a pistol—a snub-nosed revolver—from under his yellow nylon jacket.

"No, no," he said. His voice was firm but just as sadly amiable as before. "Just jerk the wire out of the phone. Give it a good yank. C'mon. And don't play around. Either one of you."

"See? He's not my uncle," said Judy.

The man looked down at the child. "Judy," he said softly. "Do you watch much TV?"

Judy nodded.

"Then you know what guns do to people, don't you? Like this one. Now . . . you wouldn't want me to shoot your teacher, would you?"

Judy's eyes widened—with fear, yet with total comprehension—and she shook her head.

"Okay. So we're going for a ride in the car, you and me. Nobody's going to hurt you if you're a good girl. And you'll be home by tonight. By dinnertime. Okay?"

Judy shook her head.

His face hardened for an instant, before he understood. Then he smiled. "Not okay? I understand. But you'll come along with me, won't you? So nobody gets hurt. Right?"

The little girl nodded.

"Mommy told you not to go in cars with strangers. And she's right. But I'm not going to hurt you. This is different. I wouldn't think of hurting you." He glanced at the terrified teacher and secretary and added—"I really wouldn't. I won't. Just don't do somethin' stupid. The same promise doesn't go for you."

Carol Amanda was willing to be a heroine, even a martyr, she thought—if it would help. But how would it?

The man looked down at the little girl. "Why don't you call me Uncle Burt? I'm gonna be like an uncle. Now, give me your hand. It's gonna be okay, honey."

The big man in the gray slacks, blue shirt, and yellow jacket backed out of the office, leading the tiny child in her pink shirt, white pants, and pink sneakers. The teacher began to cry.

The secretary waited no more than two seconds, then burst into the principal's office, where there was an intact telephone.

"Uncle Burt" pushed his pistol back into the holster on his hip under his jacket and strolled casually along the corridor toward the door. "Judy, it's gonna be okay," he said. "Some folks have got some problems, and this is gonna help them get them straightened out. And it'll all be straightened out in just a little while. We'll have some ice cream and maybe some hotdogs. You like hotdogs?"

"Pizza," she said.

"Pizza it'll be. You and me may not have such a *good* time, but it'll be okay."

They walked out onto the school grounds. A drizzle was falling. The walk toward the street sloped gently down across a weed-choked lawn. The man lifted his chin high and searched the street for the black Chevrolet that would pick them up. He didn't see it. He kept walking as fast as he could without forcing the little girl to run and be conspicuously rushed. Where the hell was Duke?

"FREEZE!"

The man spun around, releasing the child's hand as he snatched back his jacket and jerked out his revolver. He thrust the muzzle toward the short, slender man who had yelled at him—a man dressed in a dark-blue nylon jacket and baseball cap, both emblazoned with the letters FBI in white paint. Before "Uncle Burt" could pull his trigger, he was lifted off his feet by the explosive impact of a second agent's heavy, high-velocity slug, which struck him just between the shoulder blades, severed his spine, and burst all his vital organs. He did not topple forward; he was thrown forward and sprawled on his face.

Judy shrieked.

"Not unless it were extremely important," said the President. "No part of it, unless it were extremely important."

"What could be that important?" asked Sally weakly. "Judy—"

"Mrs. Vandenberg—"

"I'm not Mrs. Vandenberg."

"Of course not. Sorry. Mrs. Campbell. I do want to make the point with you, however, that the work Captain Vandenberg is now doing is vital to our country. In more ways than one."

The President had asked Sally and Frank to come to the White House, to meet with him and Scott in the Oval Office, where he could make a personal appeal to them to agree to move into a government safe house.

"Where?" asked Frank Campbell. "I ask because I'd hope to be able to continue to go to my office."

The President nodded. "To be perfectly straightforward with you, Mr. Campbell, it is really inconceivable that anyone would try to harm *you*. Or even Mrs. Campbell. It's the child that we have to protect. The man who tried to kidnap Judy obviously worked for somebody who thought they could influence Scott by holding her hostage. It is unlikely they'll try again, but we don't want to take any chances. The house we have in mind is within commuting distance of downtown Washington."

"What about her school?" asked Sally. She was heavily pregnant, no more than a few weeks from the birth of her next child.

"School's out next week," said Scott.

"And this will be over before it starts again in the fall?"

"One way or another," said Scott grimly.

Sally drew a deep breath and stiffened. She spoke directly to Scott. "You had no right to involve yourself in anything so dangerous to Judy. And you, Mr. President . . . You had no right to ask him. His commitment involved other people, that he had no right to commit."

"Sally—"

The President interrupted. "If Captain Vandenberg is successful," he said, "he may save the lives of thousands of people. If he is not, we may lose that many."

She turned her head toward Scott and for a long moment regarded him with an expression that mixed annoyance, frustration, and grudging admiration.

"I'm sorry," Scott said quietly.

"Children . . ." Sally whispered tearfully. "You can never know. She says nothing about what happened. It's as if being kidnapped and seeing your kidnapper shot to death before your eyes was nothing very special. I wonder if kids don't see so much like that on television that . . . I wonder if she thinks that man got up later and went to wash the fake blood off. Or when she actually realizes that—"

"We're lucky so far," said Frank.

"But we don't know what impact it will all have later," she said. "She hasn't had a nightmare about it yet, but she will. I just know she's holding something in, something that will come out." Sally wiped away a tear and shook her head.

"The safe house is very pleasant," said the President. "On a golf course. The security arrangements are inconspicuous."

"At least you'll get to visit her again," Nancy said to Scott.

They were in the back seat of a car driven by an FBI agent, on the way from the temporary offices in Bethesda to the motel that was their safe house.

"Right. She'll get visits from daddy, the man who's responsible for her not living in her own home anymore."

Nancy understood she could not discuss the subject with him. She stared out the window for a while, at the lush green of June that would shortly be burned brown by a Washington summer.

"Who did Whitney call in Bogotá?" Scott asked.

"We don't know yet. The Colombians say the number belongs to a firm of accountants, and the accountants say they don't know who might have called them from California."

"Are they lying?"

"Are the ayatollahs Muslims?"

"Who do we have down there?" Scott asked. "CIA?"

She nodded.

"Can we use them?"

"I know the President would rather we didn't."

"Then somebody's going to have to go down there."

"Exactly. Someone who speaks Spanish."

"Nancy . . . No. No, for god's sake!"

She faced him, fixing her eyes on his. "Alone, too," she said. "Alone."

He kept shaking his head. "No . . . No. We'll have to think of a different idea."

Virgilio Cordero had partners. One of them was a Peruvian named Plutarco Candelario. The Peruvian had come to Cordero's villa with some challenging questions.

"I am most anxious to know," he said, "why the American government has officially inquired about the confidential telephone number. Whitney is of course the problem. He placed a call from the States."

"He made the call from a public telephone booth," said Cordero. "It cannot be traced to him."

"It was nonetheless a foolish thing to do. A risk—"

"Whether it was or not," interrupted Cordero, "we can't do what we are planning to do without him. He assures me he has successfully infected the American ATC system again."

"Has he then outlived his usefulness?" asked Candelario.

"No, Plutarco, he has not," said Cordero. "Our Mr. Whitney is no fool. Some essentials of his virus program are in his mind. And only in his mind. He has openly declared his distrust of us, and he has built self-protection into his design."

"What do you mean, a trap?" asked Candelario irritably. "What kind of trap could he build?"

They were sitting in the library, in the big leather chairs, where Cordero had provided vintage brandy and a variety of cheeses. As he thought for a moment, he used a short knife to cut a bit of cheese.

"Suppose . . ." he said. "Suppose his virus expects a communication from him at intervals. Suppose it doesn't receive it and disables itself. Suppose it displays a message on every ATC screen in the United States, saying 'Watch out for a horrible virus put in here by Señor Virgilio Cordero of Bogotá.' "

"It sounds to me," said Candelario with a measure of scorn in his voice, "as if you have put yourself at this man's mercy."

"Not exactly," said Cordero. "The man is venal. And in some respects he is a fool. Watch me this evening. Watch me regain his trust."

At dinner that night each man was accompanied by a young woman—Cordero by Patricia, Darius by Allison, the others by members of the group that every evening lounged around the pool or swam nude in its lighted waters to divert Cordero's male guests. Flaming torches lighted the area.

The men wore white dinner jackets. Allison wore a cocktail dress of shimmering light-blue silk. She had been encouraged by Patricia, who had come to the suite to see if she needed help with her dress, to wear nothing under it; and it hung fluidly over her slender body, revealing and yet modest. Patricia wore a knee-length dress of black lace that mocked modesty by shifting as she moved, serendipitously revealing and concealing.

A roast suckling pig turned on a spit over a fragrant wood fire. As the small group drank before dinner, an Indian man and woman, dressed in loincloths and feathers, danced sinuously to the beat of a drum and some kind of stringed instrument that was plucked to make haunting, whining music.

Darius stood by the pool smoking a cigar and watching the dancers with an empty gaze that told anyone who looked closely that he hardly saw the performance, that his mind was somewhere else.

Cordero approached him. As if he had signaled, Hara and Yanak broke away from their companions and came after him. Allison rose to go to Darius, but Patricia quickly engaged her in conversation and delayed her.

"Come and have a seat, my friend," said Cordero to Darius, pointing toward the table where Plutarco Candelario sat with an olive-skinned girl.

The girl rose and hurried away as Cordero led Darius to the table. Cordero introduced Darius to Candelario. Candelario's English was weak, but he managed to tell Darius he had heard of him and admired his work. Darius smiled distractedly and sat down.

"Are you ready for the big effort?" Cordero asked him.

Darius tossed back the last of a bourbon and water. "I don't see why not," he said.

"There will be a major investment at risk," said Cordero.

"For both of us," said Darius.

"Yes. We are thinking in terms of entering the States through New York."

"New York! What happened in Miami would be ten times worse in the New York Terminal Control Area. You—"

"We won't land in New York," said Cordero. "I think, though, that a big plane coming in from the northeast is much less likely to look suspicious than one coming in from the south. Can your virus blind New York radar?"

Darius had kept the straggly mustache he had grown for his photograph on the forged Irish passport and now twisted one end of it between a thumb and forefinger. "Why not?" he asked. "One entry is the same as another. The key lies in the airport you choose."

"We have been investigating that. So you are ready, then? We can arrange the flight?"

"As you wish," said Darius.

Cordero nodded and smiled at Hara and Yanak. "No more tests," he said. "We are ready to go."

"We are ready to go," Darius agreed.

"In that event," said Cordero smoothly, "it is time to think about your fee." He handed Darius a small slip of paper. "Note the number," he said. "That is your account number in Zuricher Handelsbank. You will notice that the balance on deposit, withdrawable with the number alone, is sixty-five million Swiss francs. That is a little more than ten million dollars. Do you regard that as an adequate fee for what you have done so far?"

Darius stared at the printed deposit slip—for that was what it was. "Yes," he whispered. "Quite adequate."

"I will double it when the plane and cargo land safely," said Cordero. "After that—Well, we shall see how things go."

Darius's tongue, licking his lips, touched his mustache. "Thank you . . . It—It *will* work."

13
—■-■-■-■—

Attending a breakfast meeting at the Pentagon were Vice Admiral Lawrence Buchanan, Chief of Naval Intelligence; Philip Broughton, Director of Air Transportation Security; Captain Scott R. Vandenberg, Chief of the Presidential Task Force on Air Transportation Security; and Nancy Delacorte, Deputy Chief.

Scott wore his uniform.

Nancy and Scott sat on a couch and Admiral Buchanan and Director Broughton sat in upholstered chairs, all facing a coffee table set with a silver coffee service and flatware and china in the anchor patterns that were used aboard ships.

"You are satisfied, then," said Admiral Buchanan, "that Darius Whitney is in Bogotá and is working on a virus to let South American cocaine dealers fly shipments into the United States, avoiding radar surveillance? You're sure you haven't jumped to conclusions?"

"Sir," said Nancy. "Yoshitaka Hara is also in Bogotá. He flew there from New York the day after we lost him in Grand Central Station. He hasn't returned. For a couple of days, though, someone lived in his suite at The Sands."

"A girlfriend maybe?" the admiral suggested.

"No. A man. The maids and room-service personnel saw him. The man they described was almost certainly Darius Whitney."

"Now, wait a minute," said the admiral. "If the FBI was

watching Hara's suite in Las Vegas, why didn't they ask this fellow who he was? Or photograph him, at the very least? Or tail him?"

Nancy smiled and shook her head. "When we told the FBI team their man had flown to Colombia, they saw no need to watch his supposedly vacant suite. And they didn't."

"And later the FBI questioned the hotel people?"

"Yes, but only casually at first—because they knew Hara was out of the country."

"What was Whitney doing there?" the admiral asked.

"Using Hara's computer equipment," said Nancy. "We have a continuing tap on Hara's telephone lines, pursuant to a court order we got earlier. Since the FBI knew Hara was out of the country, the taps were monitored only by recorders. Anyway, whoever was in the suite made a lot of telephone calls, mostly getting busy signals, then getting computers that screeched on the telephone line and then hung up on him."

"Could that have been him trying to get into the ATC computer system?"

"Absolutely," said Scott. "And I have little doubt he succeeded. I'm afraid his virus is in the ATC system right now."

"What's it going to take to find it?"

Scott shook his head. "We're working on it. I have Miller at it, and I've put my whole private crew to work on it. The quick and dirty way of finding it hasn't worked. It's going to be devilishly difficult to sanitize the ATC system. Whitney has programmed this virus to hide, probably to detect efforts to find it, and to give false indications to make searchers overlook it."

"But I thought the digitalizers are *small* computers," said the admiral. "How could Whitney hide something in those little machines? And why—"

"Sir," said Scott. "We're talking about two viruses. The one that fouls up the digitalizers has to be inserted in one little computer. And you're right, it won't be difficult to detect—*if* we know which one of the thousands of digitalizers is infected. The second virus, the big virus, is the one that goes into the main ATC system and creates the false flight plan that causes controllers to think they have a legal flight coming in."

"If it's another virus that makes ATC radar blind to selected incoming flights," said the admiral, "then we'll have to rely on military radar that isn't digital."

"It's the digitalizer virus that makes digital radar blind," said Scott. "That's why the Miami controllers didn't know they had a Lear over the airport. Military radar knew he was there, but the big virus had made him look like a legal flight."

"Well . . . Since we know what they did at Miami and how they did it, why can't we adopt countermeasures?" asked Admiral Buchanan.

"We have to anticipate they've made the virus different and more sophisticated," said Scott.

"We have two major problems," said Director Broughton grimly. "Apart from the fact that they'll flood this country with cocaine, their invisible flights intruding into crowded airspace will sooner or later cause a midair collision. I need hardly tell you how many lives—"

"There's just one solution," said Nancy. "We're going to have to go after them. We can't just sit here and wait for them to do it."

"What do you mean, go after them?" asked Admiral Buchanan. "You aren't suggesting we send a hit squad after somebody?"

"No," she said. "But we know where the flights are going to originate—almost certainly in Bogotá."

"Why Bogotá, necessarily?"

"Because they are going to use a big airplane," she said. "It shouldn't be impossibly difficult for someone on the airport to figure out which airplane will be the illegal."

"I don't see how you could identify the aircraft," said the admiral. "That's a busy airport."

"A process of elimination," she said. "You can eliminate the bizjets and business twins. They can't carry enough cocaine on one of those to justify the expense and risk they've taken. I figure they're coming in with a freighter. A big one. You can eliminate the scheduled carriers with hundreds of passengers on board. They're going to land at the passenger terminals of major airports. Anyway, the load they can carry *plus* the passengers and their luggage—"

"But a lot of cocaine has come in that way," said Admiral Buchanan. "In luggage, in cargo, in—"

"If they were going to keep using that old strategy, they wouldn't be bothering to make aircraft invisible," said Nancy. "I think they're getting ready for a coup! Nothing less would warrant what they're doing. So I say they're coming in with a big freighter, loaded heavy with the stuff—hundreds of millions of dollars worth. And they're going to have to land where they can unload before we catch up with them. That's not at the general-aviation terminal of a major airport. They'd be caught there, for sure. They're coming in where they think we won't expect them."

"You're looking for a 707 or a DC-10, I suppose," said Broughton.

"It's got to be able to carry a big load—and I'd think fly the route nonstop—and land on a smaller airport. He'll come in with the traffic approaching a major airport of entry. Then he'll break away and make a run for an isolated smaller airport."

"I hear a lot of assumptions," said Admiral Buchanan. "Assumption piled on top of assumption. Still . . . I have to say, I follow your logic and can't find a fault in it."

"We can go after him three ways," said Scott. "First, I'm going to keep working on the virus. Second, we can identify likely airports and put them under surveillance. And third—Well, I'm hesitant about this, but Nancy—"

"I go to Bogotá," she interrupted, "and see if I can identify the aircraft before it takes off. I speak fluent Spanish, and I've been trained in the conduct of clandestine operations. I—"

"Damned dangerous," said Admiral Buchanan. "Let's not forget who we're talking about. The Mafia used to send hit men to kill their enemies. The Latin American cocaine dealers kill their enemies plus their families, just for emphasis. And they've tried to kill Captain Vandenberg, then to kidnap his daughter. What do you think they'd do to you if they caught you snooping around in Bogotá?"

"They're still sufficiently sexist to think I couldn't possibly be any threat to them," said Nancy with a wry smile.

"They don't know her, probably," said Scott. "She speaks Spanish. If we send her in with fake documents . . . I don't like it one bit, but—"

"I want a fake passport," said Nancy. "Let us say Guatemalan. I can fly a plane, so I want a fake pilot's license from the same country. A driver's license. Whatever a citizen of that country would carry. Surely the CIA, if not Naval Intelligence, will know what I need. They can supply it too. I mean, I don't have to go to a New York novelties shop, do I?"

"We can supply whatever you need," said Admiral Buchanan. "Assuming we agree to this adventure. Are you thinking of going into Colombia alone?"

"If I expect to survive and achieve any success, I'm going alone," said Nancy with a smile, yet with firm determination in her voice. "I'm romantic enough to have read the accounts of many espionage operations from World War Two and since; and if you've read the like, you'll remember that most of what was done successfully was done by one agent, alone. I won't be rec-ognized. I speak the language. I—"

"I don't like the idea at all," said Scott. "We've argued the subject night after night."

"I've been thinking of something else and have discussed it with Scott. Suppose I am able to identify the aircraft and can get close to it. Couldn't we mount a transmitter in it, to send a signal our defense units can track?"

The admiral nodded thoughtfully. "I think that could be ar-ranged," he said. "Something like that."

"So?"

Admiral Buchanan glanced from her to Scott to Broughton. "Let us go so far, at this point," he said, "as to arrange for you to be thoroughly briefed. About Bogotá and the airport there. About the country named in your false documents. Then we'll see. We make no commitment right now."

"Another point," she said. "The CIA station chief must have strict orders to issue me suitable—*suitable* meaning 'cannot be traced'—weapons. I mean a pistol. No questions asked. Look . . . All I'm going to do is look. Watch. And maybe, somehow, put a little transmitter on an airplane. I don't want explosives or anything else dramatic. But I will want to be able to defend myself if it comes to it."

The admiral smiled weakly. "That's a condition, Miss Delacorte?" he asked.

"That's a condition," she affirmed.

Scott blew a sigh and shook his head. "I hope you won't accept it, Admiral."

"Buenos noches, Señor."

Scott winced. "Oh, my god!"

Nancy grinned. He had just knocked on the door of her room in the motel where they were living—the safe house in Chevy Chase—and she had opened the door and stood back to let him have a look at her as Idelia Santa Cruzada.

She'd had her hair cut: short on top, short on the sides, leaving barely enough to brush back. Spare wisps lay over the tops of her ears. At the back of her neck, her hair was shorter than his own. She was wearing dark-red lipstick, generously applied to give her lower lip a fuller look. She wore earrings, gold hoops the size of quarters.

Scott crossed the room to the drapes, closed them, and sat down in a small upholstered chair. "The briefing?" he asked dully.

"Bogotá is more than eight thousand feet above sea level," she said. "This means that aircraft cannot be fully loaded when they take off. What's more, they require a long runway. There are scars on the mountainsides, left by pilots who didn't understand this. They—"

"Yeah, sure. What about the politics of the goddam place?"

She smiled. "Odd. In France the local Mafiosi are referred to as *les Messieurs*. In Latin America they are called *los Señores*. It means the same thing. Sort of. But in Latin America they live like princes, without fear of government authority. Like *Union Corse* in Corsica. *Les Messieurs* are petty thieves by comparison. So, in some ways, are the Five Families in New York. The Five Families have always known that the government could, if it really chose, crack down. *Los Señores* have no such worry. In some of the smaller countries, they *are* the government. Where they are not, the government fears them."

"A name?"

She shrugged. "In Paraguay the name is Adolphus. They used

212

to say he was Adolf Hitler in exile. In Colombia . . . Obviously everyone knows. And no one says."

"The CIA?"

"Watching out for Communist influences, just like old times. Not much interested in the cocaine traffic, though the President has been urging them to take an interest."

Scott lurched from the chair and stalked to the window, where he spread the drapes and stared down at the mercury-vapor lamps blinking and slowly coming to life over the parking lot. He turned abruptly and looked at the person Nancy was trying to become for this mad intrusion into insanity.

"We could quit," he said wearily. "How the hell much—"

"Okay," said Nancy. "I can send a letter of resignation. I guess it's a little more complicated for a naval officer. But what the hell?"

"Sure . . ." he mumbled. "And we won't."

"No. I suppose not. Damn fools, you and I. Damn fools . . . Scott."

"I—I can't imagine the woman I love this much is . . . Nancy!"

She saw his tears and rushed to him, into his arms. "I'll resign if you will," she whispered.

"We won't. But afterward we damn well will. And never again! Never again!"

For fear of being seen with her, he could not go with her to the airport. She flew to Dallas, then to San Antonio, and from there to Guatemala. She was to be met by the CIA station chief, who would brief her about Guatemala before she flew on to Panama and then to Colombia.

"What you're suggesting, Captain, may be a little bit much. A five-thousand-foot runway? A tough landing."

Scott was talking to a man whose name was T. T. Buckley. The man had offered no suggestion as to what the *t*'s stood for. His business card read: "T. T. Buckley, Flight Planning Coordinator, Federal Aviation Administration." He had come to the task force office in Bethesda.

"I anticipated it might be," said Scott. "A tough landing."

They had been discussing the assessment Nancy had given Admiral Buchanan: The cocaine barons would very likely try to use the Whitney virus to fly a heavy jet transport aircraft into the United States. Another element of her analysis was that the aircraft was not likely to land on a major airport, even if it did come in undetected as a flight from South America, because of the difficulty of unloading it surreptitiously. It was more likely to land on a small airport.

"A fully loaded Boeing 707 can be put down on five thousand feet of runway," said Buckley, "assuming good conditions and a skilled pilot. He'll have difficulty taking off again, but he can land. To cover every airport in the United States that is within range of a 707 out of Bogotá . . . We're talking about—What? Half the airports in the United States?"

"An aircraft that can fly nonstop from London to New York can fly from Bogotá to—"

"New York," said Buckley. "Chicago. He'd have difficulty with the West Coast."

"The same thing would be true of DC-8s and, uh . . ."

"That generation," said Buckley. "They can be brought in on five thousand feet. Like I say, it isn't easy. But it can be done."

"So 727s—"

"Sure. And DC-9s, 737s. A little less runway. When you get down to five thousand you're asking a whole lot of the pilot and the airplane—with any of the big jets."

"So a five-thousand-foot runway—"

"Minimum."

"Minimum," Scott agreed. "What about weight? Not every paved runway can take the weight of a 707."

"True. I'm working on that. And some of the runways are too narrow. You wouldn't want to leave the wingtips on adjacent structures. Also, to get on some runways you have to drop in over obstructions. Take Pittsfield, Massachusetts. You've got your five thousand feet all right, but you could never drop a 707 in over the mountain ridges and get rid of enough altitude fast enough to touch down on the threshold. And threshold is what you've gotta hit on a five-thousand-foot runway."

"So it's not half the airports in the United States," said Scott.

"Still a great many, Captain. Still a third of them."

"You have some idea of how important this is."

"The matter has been sufficiently emphasized. We're working on it."

"Five thousand feet," Scott mused. He shook his head. "I know it's a lot of runways. Add another factor: isolation. The airport can't be one where major law-enforcement groups arrive in ten minutes."

"Gotcha," said T. T. Buckley. "Not too close to a big town."

Stepan Yanak sat in the bar in the TWA terminal at Kennedy Airport, talking to and skeptically appraising a balding blond man he'd been told to meet here. The man's name was Don Sumner.

"Not an easy problem," said Sumner. "I mean, man, that's asking for a hell of a lot."

"You flew them for—"

"Twelve years. How many years *can* a man have flown 747s? Yeah, I flew them. All over the friggin' world. For—"

Yanak put his hand on the man's glass of Scotch and water. "Until you decided something like this was more important."

Sumner shrugged. "What's important? They don't pay you much for jockeying sixty-five thousand tons of airplane and people through the skies. I got sick of bein' an aerial bus driver."

"Can you still do it?" Yanak asked.

"Like ridin' a bicycle," the man said. "You learn to do it once, you can always do it. Anyway, I still do fly 747s from time to time. Charters. Freighters. Some owners don't ask too many questions."

Stepan Yanak picked up his own glass and studied the man. A rogue pilot. Dismissed by Northwest Orient for drinking. Forty-five years old. His thin, fine hair had abandoned his ruddy scalp entirely. His ample belly was cinched in by his belt. Still, overall he remained youthfully, even athletically, compact and taut. He wore no eyeglasses over his cool blue eyes. Though he had a couple of Scotches in him, he impressed Yanak as alert and competent.

"You drink on the job?" Yanak asked.

"Not in the cockpit," said Sumner. "Not for ten hours before. I never did. Not back when Northwest was raising hell about it.

215

Lot of tension in the work. They should've been glad a man knew how to let himself down."

"Okay. Can you do what I'm talking about, or can you not?"

"I'll want to go out and look at the airport," said Sumner. "A 747 is almost two hundred feet, wingtip to wingtip. You're talkin' about a short runway. What about one that's too narrow? And what if the tarmac breaks down under the weight?"

"I told you before. We're not taking off again. You land it. That's all you have to do."

"You guys are going to *abandon* a 747?"

"Let *us* worry about that. It'll probably have to be disassembled and hauled out in pieces. But that's not your problem."

Sumner lifted his glass and took Scotch. "Five . . . thousand . . . feet," he said, shaking his head. "What's on the ends of the runway?"

"It's wide open on both ends, I promise you."

Sumner frowned and shook his head again. "You can't really do it," he said. "You'll blow the tires. The gear might collapse."

"I'm telling you, we don't care about that. You'll have no passengers. Just cargo. You can—"

"When? I'll want a hot summer day. On hot air, the 747 will sink fast and hit the pavement hard. On a cold day it would float, and you'd never get it stopped on a five-thousand-foot runway."

"In the next couple of weeks," said Yanak.

"And when do you tell me what airport it is?"

"Probably not before you take off."

"Umm," grunted Sumner through the final swallow of his drink. "This is gonna be one thousand percent illegal, right? How are you getting me out?"

"It will be done," said Yanak. "It will be taken care of."

"Umm. There's only one thing could be the cargo in this 747. So what do you plan to pay me?"

Yanak snapped his fingers at the bartender and pointed at Sumner's empty glass. "Question," he said. "You'll need a first officer and a flight engineer. Right? Can you provide them?"

"Sure. I've got a couple of friends ready to take a risk for the right money."

"Okay. We will pay you two million dollars, in whatever

currency you want. Two million. How you divide that up is your business. We will take responsibility for getting you fifty miles or so away from the airport. After that, you're on your own."

"You have the airplane?"

"Not yet. We *will* have it."

"And you won't tell me where we take off or where we land?"

Yanak smiled. "In good time," he said. "When you need to know."

"The identity of your client, Monsieur Poncet. I must know the identity of your client."

Jean-Claude Poncet melodramatically closed his leather-bound file case—the zipper making a loud *whupp*. "Then the conversation is finished," he said curtly.

Jean-Claude Poncet was a man of some seventy years, sepulchrally thin; his voice came out of him in a cigarette-ravaged croak, and his teary blue eyes were half hidden in concentric circles of loose flesh. His hair looked like an ill-fitting yellow wig—and maybe it was.

He and the harried businessman sat over tiny cups of strong black coffee on a hotel terrace overlooking Lake Lucerne. It had rained half an hour earlier, and a spectacular rainbow hung over the lake.

The businessman was Erwin Hegel, chief executive officer of a German company that, by reason of the long Teutonic words the initials stood for, was known only as DFG. He was in his forties: an apple-cheeked Bavarian, pudgy, bespectacled, and, today at least, beleaguered to the point of trembling.

"But, monsieur! How can I lease an airplane to an anonymous lessee?"

"How can you not, for the money I am offering?" Poncet asked coldly. "I believe your corporation is experiencing financial difficulty."

"Regulations, monsieur! Regulations."

"Everything will be entirely in accordance with all national and international regulations," said Poncet. "You will lease the aircraft to a Japanese corporation. Nothing in any regulation requires you to know the identity of the stockholders."

"Who will sign?"

"Officers of the corporation," said Poncet. "It is quite simple, Herr Hegel. Our charter will relieve you of three bank payments on the aircraft."

"The insurance—"

"No insurance."

"No—?"

"My clients will post a bond equal to the value of the aircraft. If any evil should befall it, you will receive the amount of the bond."

"But . . . liability . . ."

"There will be none. The aircraft will be totally in the control of my clients' corporation. The corporation will be exclusively liable. Your company will be relieved of all responsibility for the aircraft while it is under the charter and in the exclusive possession and control of my clients."

Hegel nodded skeptically. "My lawyers—"

"Promptly, Herr Hegel," Poncet cut in. "I have no time for lawyerly nitpicking."

"I suppose," said Hegel slowly and cautiously, "I should not inquire about what you expect to haul in the aircraft."

"That is rather obvious, is it not?" said Poncet. "Your 747 is configured to carry passengers. It is equipped with seats. My clients will be carrying Japanese tourists from Tokyo to the South Pacific."

"Ah," said Hegel, visibly relieved. "I have pilots, flight attendants. Do you need personnel?"

"We have pilots," said Poncet. "Do your flight attendants speak Japanese?"

Hegel shrugged and, for the first time, smiled.

"Ah, Idelia, how can you say no to me?"

The conversation was in Spanish. The young man was undeniably handsome: swarthy of complexion, his white vest undershirt displaying smooth muscles, of which he was noticeably proud. He grinned, showing strong white teeth.

"Because my husband would kill us both," said Nancy.

It was the answer she had used half a dozen times. So far, it had worked. The line boys and mechanics grinned when she said it and snapped out macho lines like *"Cuento incredíble"*—a cock-and-bull story; yet none of them, so far, had been brave enough to persist with his proposition.

He was a line boy, one of the hardworking young men who run out to each aircraft as it lands, to guide it into a parking space, to set chocks under the wheels, to offer fuel, washing, and other services. The airport at Bogotá was like every other airport. The line boys worked hard, and they got no tips.

He was a line *boy*. The mechanics were men. The pilots were men. When she arrived and began to show her Guatemalan pilot's license to aircraft operators in offices and hangars around the airport, she was bluntly told that girls who worked on the airport worked as waitresses in the restaurants; there was no other job here for a female.

A woman who flew airplanes? They laughed: No man would go as a passenger in a plane flown by a woman. She said she would fly courier runs: More laughs; who would trust an airplane and its cargo to a *muchacha*? She could give flying lessons: Guffaws; no, they said, ask at the bar in the terminal—a cute girl like you, you will make a good cocktail waitress.

Late in the afternoon of her second day on the airport, the elderly, palsied operator of a charter flying service grudgingly told her he would not object if she sat around his office and hangar. If he found himself short a pilot, then, maybe . . . If someone wanted to take flying lessons from her . . . He shook his head. It was not likely. But if she wanted to be there, he had no great objection.

On one condition. She had to fly with one of his pilots, to show she was qualified, that she really could fly. She would have to pay that pilot for his time, and she would have to pay for the fuel she used during this check flight.

She accepted. Unfair though the old boy's deal was, it established her on the airport. Having successfully completed the test flight, she was identified as a pilot—for god's sake, a *woman* pilot!—and had a valid reason for hanging around.

She arrived early every morning. She left only after sunset. She made herself conspicuous in tight, thoroughly faded jeans, with white T-shirts and a dark-blue nylon jacket. Her story—and she was often asked for one—was that she was the daughter of a well-off, well-connected Guatemalan family that disowned her for doing something as boorish as flying airplanes, and that she was married to a pilot who was now involved in flying mining equipment into the Brazilian outback.

Outside the passenger terminals all airports are much alike: vast expanses of concrete or tarmac bordered by ranks of grimly utilitarian line shacks and hangars. The commercial airliners move grandly in from the runways to the terminals and back out again, slow behemoths dominating all the smaller planes that, too, have their place in the business of air traffic. Big freighters—on this airport mostly old DC-3s—line up before the cargo terminals. Business planes hover around a smaller general-aviation terminal. And a hundred other airplanes sit on the pavement and in the grass around the shacks and little hangars of fixed-base operators.

The people on an airport are much alike too. Pilots, mechanics, line boys, and unattached aviation zealots, who hang around the ramps, wherever they are allowed, and talk like the pilots they never were and never will be.

Nancy had made a point of befriending two of these enthusiasts. They watched and they talked.

Her favorite was an American. His name was Bob Laud. He was the Colombian representative of a New York company that sent in one courier flight a day, carrying business documents in a Falcon jet that stopped in Bogotá on a run that also included Caracas and Quito. He was busy two or three hours a day and spent his free hours wandering around the airport, admiring planes and talking with any pilot who would give him the time. He made a proposition, took her brush-off in good humor, and returned from time to time to admire her and talk.

Some of his information was worth hearing.

He had no idea she understood English, so he spoke to her in heavily accented Spanish. "See that Lear? Want to know who it belongs to? Don't ask. That's a rule. Don't ask about that airplane."

"Why not?"

He answered with a nervous gesture of both hands, then said,

"The people who own it would want to know why you want to know. I asked. Some rough guys came to ask me why I wanted to know."

"Do you know?" she asked with a provocative smile.

"Ah-hah! Sure, I know. But don't ask."

Nancy—known to him as Idelia—was sitting at the controls of a Mitsubishi twin-turboprop. Though her forged Guatemalan pilot's license said she was qualified to fly this plane, she had never flown anything like it and had been studying the manual and identifying all the controls—in case she should be called on to fly it.

"*Roberto el tímido*," she teased.

He glanced around. "You can keep it quiet?"

She grinned.

"That airplane belongs to Plutarco Candelario," he confided.

She shrugged. "Who is Plutarco Candelario?"

"Not so loud! My God! Plutarco Candelario is one of the biggest men in South America. You've heard of *los Señores*?"

"Ah." She widened her eyes. "He is one of *them*?"

Bob Laud nodded. "A secret. We could get in big trouble talking about him. But that's who owns the Lear."

That afternoon Laud returned to the ramp where she hung out. She was sitting on a tattered aluminum-and-webbing chair, watching the runways.

"Look what's coming," said Laud.

She had already noticed. A strange 747 was landing. Not marked with the emblem of any airline, it was distinguished only by the dark-blue-and-white logo on its tail:

No matter how many times she saw a 747 land, Nancy never failed to be thrilled by the sight of the enormous aircraft majestically sinking toward the runway and gently touching its wheels to the pavement. She admired the skills it took to bring it in. She admired the engineering it had taken to design and build it. She was moved by the overall effect, of great power coupled with palpable dignity.

The great airplane rolled out and turned off the runway. It taxied past the passenger terminals and the general-aviation ramps, toward a ramp half a mile from the principal facilities of the airport.

"It's a combi," Laud said to Nancy as it taxied past them.

"What's a combi?"

"A convertible, you might say. The seats can be pulled out or put back in, so it flies as either a passenger plane or a freighter."

When, an hour later, Nancy saw them begin to haul seats out of the 747, she decided she was looking at something that needed to be reported to Washington.

She had a CIA contact.

The contact had been a surprise—the daughter of the commercial attaché at the United States Embassy. Emily Greenhouse had come to Bogotá with her widower father five years ago to help him establish a home for her younger brother and sister. Now the kids had returned to the States to go to college, but she had remained rather than leave her father alone. She was a handsome young woman, much in demand in the social life of the bored group of diplomats damned to what all but a few of them detested as a backwater posting and a frustrating setback in their careers.

Emily Greenhouse, too, was bored; and when the CIA station chief suggested she listen to the cocktail-party chitchat with more than a casual ear and report what she heard, she had been happy to cooperate. For a little more than a year now she had been an active agent of the CIA.

It was far better for Emily Greenhouse to be Nancy's contact, she had explained. Her cover was almost certainly intact. The station chief's was probably long blown.

After the initial contact, at the airport, the two women established a vegetable market as their meeting place. Emily Greenhouse was there every third evening. Every day she drove by Nancy's little hotel and glanced up at her window. A beer bottle on the windowsill meant that Nancy wanted to see her. Nancy left the bottle out, and Emily was in the market that evening.

"Two things," said Nancy. "First, who the hell is Plutarco Candelario?"

"A big man," said Emily. "The biggest man in Peru."

"Second to the president, I suppose," said Nancy dryly.

Emily laughed. She was a husky little woman, broad-hipped, heavy-breasted, compact, solid, and muscular. Her face was pretty, with regular features and striking brown eyes. She wore her dark-brown hair straight and long.

She and Nancy—in her Idelia persona—made a contrasting pair, a contrast that would be noticed by anyone who saw them talking together. Nancy, in her jeans, T-shirt, and jacket, with her short hair and exaggerated lipstick, looked like the audacious daughter of a prosperous local: a little defiant, not quite brazen but something like that. Emily was apparently determined to look like an American, in a loose white dress, the image of a suburban housewife in Houston.

"Are you kidding? Second only to the man he's second to: Virgilio Cordero. You've heard of *los Señores*? Those are two of them. That's where the cocaine comes from."

"Okay. A 747 arrived this afternoon. They're busy converting it from passenger to freighter configuration. I'm damned suspicious of it. The logo on the tail is DFG. We need to know what that means and who owns it, or has it under lease. I'd like to put the locator transmitter on board that 747. Where is it?"

"It's being converted. I think I can have it in the morning."

"Not tonight? In the morning may be too late."

"You think you can get near that plane?"

Nancy shrugged. "I don't know. Can I? I've made myself an airport character, as much as I can. I wander around—the Guatemalan pilot girl, nutty about airplanes. Whether or not I can get close depends on how nervous they are."

"If that plane has anything to do with Cordero's business, or Candelario's, you can get yourself killed, you know," said Emily soberly.

"I promised someone back in the States that I wouldn't play little tin-hero," said Nancy. "And I won't. But I want to get close to that plane and stick that transmitter on it."

"You need to go out there before dawn," said Emily. "I'll

have the transmitter for you by three this morning. In fact, this time, let's take a chance. My car's the green BMW. It's not locked. We'll leave here separately, and you get in the back seat. I'll take you where we can get a decent meal, and when the transmitter's ready, I'll drive you to the airport. Deal?"

"Deal," said Nancy.

Nancy would not allow Emily to drive her closer than the bus stop. There she left the BMW and walked toward the gate that led to the corrugated-steel shack that served as office and shop for the operator who let her wait around for her chance to fly an airplane.

A light rain fell out of a low overcast that hung over the airport and glowed amber from the lights. It was a cold rain, and she was immediately sorry she did not have a raincoat. The gate was not locked. Access to the ramp was easy enough. She went to the shack and tried the door, hoping to find a slicker inside. She had seen the line boys wear them. But the shack was locked. She took shelter under the wing of the Mitsubishi turboprop and surveyed the situation.

The suspicious 747 remained on the ramp half a mile from where she huddled and peered through the rain. It sat in front of the warehouse where she had seen the workmen storing the seats. The warehouse was dark. The plane was dark. No floodlights shone on the tarmac between the warehouse and the plane. Yet obviously the area was bustling with men and vehicles, all moving in the near-darkness; and it was easy to see, even from this distance and through the rain, that they were loading the 747 with cargo.

Nancy slipped out from under the wing of the Mitsubishi and began to make her way among the dozens of small airplanes lashed down on the ramp. Every airplane was anchored against being upset by a hard wind, with ropes or chains running from steel rings on the bottoms of the wings and on the tails to larger rings set in the pavement. She maneuvered around these lines and kept close to the airplanes, in their shadows.

She could not keep dry. Soon her T-shirt and blue jeans were soaked. She shivered. But she moved closer and closer to the 747.

She carried the transmitter and her pistol in a small canvas bag slung over her shoulder—under a clutter of makeup, tissues, chewing gum, and cigarettes: a clutter she hoped would discourage any casual investigator from digging deeper.

The untraceable pistol issued from the arsenal of the CIA was a Smith & Wesson automatic, only three and a half inches long. The transmitter was a problem. Since so much of an airplane was aluminum, magnetic attachment was not practical. If she couldn't get inside the airplane and stash it somewhere, then she had to attach it outside with two self-tapping screws. They had shown her how to do this. The sharp steel screws would penetrate aluminum, their threads would grab as they were turned, and with a few revolutions of a screwdriver the transmitter would be securely fastened to the airplane. She had been reminded that it had to be attached at an inconspicuous spot.

She reached the last airplane. From here there was an open hundred yards of tarmac to the 747.

And from here it was obvious that the big airplane was guarded. The guards were not policemen or soldiers; they were civilians in raincoats, with short automatic weapons slung under their arms.

The cargo going up the conveyors into the body of the 747 consisted of hundreds, maybe thousands, of boxes.

She could not get any nearer. Sneaking up to that big airplane in the night and attaching a transmitter was simply impossible. Getting near would have to be done some other way. She would have to walk up to the warehouse in daylight, with some story to justify her presence. She could, maybe, pretend to be a cleaning woman, carry a vacuum cleaner, and offer to clean out the cockpit. Something . . .

She returned to the Mitsubishi. It wasn't locked. She went inside, took off her clothes, and used the cleaning cloths from the luggage compartment to dry herself. She wrapped herself in one of the blankets provided for passengers and settled down in one of the seats to wait for dawn.

14
—∎-∎-∎-∎—

They had not given up the little house at Toiyabe Ranch, just outside Las Vegas. Stepan Yanak had arranged for some clean guys—that is, men with no criminal record, no warrants against them—to live in it from time to time, to see if the FBI was aware of it and would come to inquire when they saw somebody living there. No one seemed to pay any attention to it, and Yanak had reported to Cordero that apparently the house had not been associated with Whitney and that it was safe for him to return there.

So he did return, with Stepan Yanak. Allison remained in Bogotá—a hostage, as both of them clearly understood—and Darius came back, carrying the forged passport that identified him as the Irishman James McMurtry, through Madrid, Dublin, Montreal, and Chicago, to Las Vegas and Toiyabe Ranch.

He carried disks containing the programs he would use to activate the virus in the main ATC system and to infect a digitalizer. The computers that he and Allison had worked on in the Toiyabe house remained on their tables. The clean guys had not touched them.

He sat down at one of the computers, switched it on, and waited for it to go through the routines he had written for it, to configure it for the work he planned to do.

"This may take a while," he said to Yanak.

"What do you have to do?" Yanak asked.

226

"I want to see if they've built any new defenses," said Darius. "I want to know if they've detected the virus in the main system."

This time he entered the main ATC system through a contractor. He routed his telephone call through the FAA main office in Washington, and from there into the computer of a consulting firm in South Carolina. The consulting firm had a contract to redesign some elements of the system, so its computer had access to the ATC computers. The South Carolina computer innocently switched Whitney's call through, and, shortly, he was in the ATC system. If anyone noticed the connection, it looked like an authorized entry by the South Carolina contractor.

He required only minutes to check his virus. He had designed it not only to conceal itself and send out a delusive reading to anyone who detected it, but also to mark itself if anyone found it and tampered with it. What he'd had in mind was that someone might detect the virus and, instead of destroying it, might change it a little and leave it in place. Someone might alter it to make it betray the aircraft it was supposed to make invisible. Nothing like that had happened. The virus had not been modified. Almost certainly it had not been found.

Then he routed a call to Houston, and there entered the computer that digitalized the radar covering the southern and eastern approaches to Houston Intercontinental Airport. During the first two hours that he monitored that digitalizer, he did not detect a byte count. Then at three o'clock, which would be four o'clock in Houston, he saw the count. Apparently a new shift of controllers had come on, and they were starting their shift by checking their digitalizers for viruses.

Did that mean they did byte counts only three times in twenty-four hours? Apparently it did in Houston. He checked Boston. In the four hours that he monitored it, one byte count was performed on the digitalizer for the northeastern approach to Boston Logan.

Darius told Yanak to go into Las Vegas and call Bogotá. He could say that everything was as ready as it could be.

Don Sumner loved to drink, loved to eat, and loved—as he put it—to tomcat. But in the cockpit he was a crisp, humorless pro who disciplined himself and disciplined his crew. By the time

227

the sun appeared east of Bogotá, he had received his weather briefing and had filed his flight plan. In the red light of dawn he led his copilot and flight engineer up the stairs into the upper deck of the 747.

The seats and tables were still in place in the first-class lounge. You couldn't stow much cargo there. Anyway, this was where his passengers would fly: eight menacing fellows encumbered with guns. They were there exploring the luxurious lounge, settling in for a long flight. He saluted them and passed on into the cockpit. The flight engineer locked the door between the cockpit and the lounge, as Sumner had ordered. As far as Don Sumner was concerned, the gunmen in the lounge might have been hijackers. He wanted no contact with them.

He was dressed like an airline captain: in dark-blue coat with captain's stripes on the sleeves, in matching dark-blue trousers, dark-blue cap, white shirt, and black necktie. He put his coat and cap aside and sat down in the left seat. His shirt had short sleeves. The gold stripes on his dark-blue shoulder tabs also pronounced him a captain.

All that distinguished Sumner, his copilot, and his flight engineer from a regular airline flight crew was that they wore no airline insignia, only the insignia of their three ranks.

Preparing a 747 for takeoff requires the cockpit crew to go through a long checklist, testing every vital system, setting every control for takeoff. It is a time-consuming process, and the temptation to skip steps must be resisted. Sumner held the multipage list in his left hand, touched each item with the point of a yellow pencil, made each call, waited for the response, then moved the pencil to the next item.

"Rudder trim."

"Neutral."

"Nose trim."

"Neutral."

"Brake pressure."

"Two-fifty."

This 747-200B had a lot of years and cycles on it, and Sumner had seen airplanes better maintained. Even before they left Zurich for Bogotá, he had found a problem with the airplane. The hydraulic brake pressure indicated on the gauge had been marginal. It was good enough for the landing he would have to make in Bogotá, but sooner or later he was going to have to land this airplane on a very short runway. Immediately on landing at Bogotá, he had demanded work on the braking system. He'd had no confidence in the two Colombian mechanics assigned to that work, and he had stayed with them and watched everything they did. They had found no leaks and had just recharged the system.

He could see that the sun was up, but the overcast still hung low over the city, obscuring the surrounding mountains. At 6:00 A.M. local time he was ready to start engines and roll back.

He opened the door and checked the passengers. The gunmen were already into the liquor supply. But they said they were all aboard. He went down to the lower level and walked the length of the airplane, checking doors. The ground crew had proved competent, so he could be confident the cargo doors underneath were secure.

Returning to the front, he surveyed the cargo: something like forty tons of cocaine in paper cartons and plastic bags. The cartons were lashed in place with what must have been a mile of white nylon webbing. In the hold there were other hundreds of cartons. Somebody had used the figure $500 million for the value of this cargo. Someone else had mentioned $1 billion.

They started engines and unhooked from the airport electrical supply.

There wasn't a chance the airplane could take off again from where they were going to land. If for no other reason, that country airport would not have the equipment to restart the engines—not to mention that the bird would swallow more jet fuel than they brought onto that airport in six months.

The plan was that Sumner and his crewmen would fly away in a Cessna. That would be their escape. He was looking forward to that in a way. It had been a long time since he had flown a Skyhawk. But, like most pilots, he had always loved them and had fond memories of the four-seat, high-winged, fixed-gear little birdies. He'd have five-hundred-miles range in the middle of the night and could abandon the Skyhawk on some obscure airport and disappear in a rented car before the feds got out the word. He had a damned good chance to scram successfully with his $2 million. And that money retired him and his crew.

The 747 was not nosed up to a terminal and didn't need a tractor to move it out. Sumner began to talk to the tower, and the copilot taxied toward the runway.

Nancy sat inside the Mitsubishi and watched the 747 taxi for the runway. All she could do now was send word to Washington that it had left without the locator transmitter. No one need apologize for not being able to get it aboard. There was no way to get close to that airplane.

Her clothes were still damp, but she had to put them on. She stepped down from the Mitsubishi and went to her usual chair in front of the shack. She sat there shivering as the 747 roared down the runway, rose gracefully into the overcast, and disappeared.

"Hours of utter boredom punctuated by moments of sheer terror."

That was the pilots' cliché, the way they described their work. When Sumner and his crew leveled out at 35,000 feet, they were over Caracas and about to make their water jump, crossing the Venezuelan coastline for a four-thousand-mile flight over the North Atlantic to their first stop: Lisbon.

They had no view of anything below. All they could see was the tops of clouds. No matter. You couldn't fly the Atlantic by looking at what was down there.

They navigated by an inertial system, not by following radio tracks—although they watched those too. The inertial system was a set of gyros the pilots had set when they were on the ground, to the map coordinates for Bogotá and Lisbon. Once set, the system "knew" where Lisbon was, relative to Bogotá; it also detected every turn the airplane made, no matter how slight, and recorded that change in course in its internal computer; so it always "knew" exactly where the airplane was and automatically turned it in the right direction, constantly corrected for wind drift, and kept the big airplane steady on course, direct to Lisbon.

From time to time Sumner reported his position, in accordance with regulations. He knew he was tracked by radar, and controllers expected to hear from him at intervals. No problem. He was following a filed flight plan, squawking a transponder code; and even if he had lost track of where he was, Ground would know and could vector him.

It was routine. Even so, this was a long flight: Bogotá to Lisbon to New York. He and his copilot spelled each other, allowing each to doze—something they would not have dared do on a bona-fide airline flight. So far, in fact, all that was illegal about this flight—apart from their cargo—was the number of hours the crew was expected to fly.

"A 747? That reduces the alternatives a hundred percent. If its the right airplane."

"Scott . . ." cautioned Admiral Buchanan, "Where would they get their hands on a 747?"

Scott, in uniform, sat in the admiral's office in the Pentagon. "Sir," he said. "We are talking about men with all-but-unlimited access to money. Of course she could be wrong, but—"

"We sent her to Bogotá at the risk of her life," said Philip Broughton. "Let's not belittle the first piece of hard intelligence she's come up with."

"DFG . . . Who's DFG?"

"Deutsche Flugzeugwesen Gesellshaft—German Aviation Company," said the admiral. "We checked it out with NEXIS, that is, did a computer search of the European business journals. DFG is a small company. They own half a dozen jets. This 747 is the biggest and most expensive airplane they have, and it has proved a tremendous financial burden. They lease it wherever they can."

"Where can they land it?" Scott asked. "What's it take, seven thousand feet of runway?"

"Plus a hundred-fifty width," said Broughton. "And that's minimum. It reduces the number of possible airports to—"

"Wait a minute," said Admiral Buchanan. "The DFG 747 left Bogotá for Lisbon four hours ago. It's on a regular international flight plan, reporting from every reporting point. I'm sorry, guys, but I think Nancy's wrong."

Scott frowned over the report from the CIA. "She doesn't say it's for sure. She says it's a highly suspicious aircraft."

231

Broughton nodded. "Well, we've got a simple proposition. We track this 747 to Lisbon. We alert every North American airport that could receive it. You can't hide a 747."

Scott sat with Hal Miller in the office in Bethesda, a little before noon.

" 'You can't hide a 747,' they say. "Oh, *can't* you? If you have the kind of money somebody obviously has, you set every- thing up. You don't stupidly fly your 747 into a trap. If that airplane is loaded with cocaine, they're not taking any chances. Imagine the street value of what it could carry! A year's supply of the stuff! Got to be worth hundreds of millions of dollars."

Hal Miller sat surrounded by piles of computer printouts. "It's in here someplace," he said. "I mean, the virus. It's in here."

The sheets were covered with gibberish—with what would have been gibberish to anyone but a skilled programmer: kilobytes of source code, the programming for the ATC computers. To any- one not initiated, the columns of numbers and symbols were worse than obscure. A line of source code looked like this:

```
\^G<^O^^_^_ZûòE^A*Q¶^^cÖ}Aùr¶[0DOr_^^<¦Å^)0NU>_^_\*1
```

Miller had marked parts of it in red.

"I'm grateful for your detective work, Chief," said Scott wea- rily. "You've kept plugging, and I guess I haven't been much help with this part of things. And right now you know what's got me distracted, Hal. You know how it is between Nancy and me."

Miller's chin rose abruptly, maybe because he was surprised to be called Hal. "I know . . . Captain. A personal burden on top of everything else. I'm glad to keep plugging. That's what I'm here for." He slapped his hand down on the sheets. "I know it's in here. The damned virus is in here."

Scott picked up a few of the sheets and began to scan Miller's red marks. "I'll work with you for a while," he said. "And inci- dentally I got Broughton to send out an order for hourly byte counts on the digitalizers. Every airport in the United States. If the rogue

232

plane *is* a 747, it could come in from anywhere, not just through the south."

Miller nodded. "Anywhere. Everywhere."

It was roughly nine o'clock local time, and twilight, when Sumner let Bill Aridas, the copilot, put the 747 down on the runway at Lisbon. His attention was on the hydraulic-pressure gauge on the braking system. It had bled off during the flight, from 250 to 175. The leak was not major, but it slowly diminished the runway-stopping power of the airplane.

They could not call mechanics aboard in Lisbon. This was a refueling stop, strictly. No passengers off. No cargo unloaded. No customs or immigration officials on board. In and out.

He did not leave the cockpit. He spoke to the Lisbon controllers by radio. He was on his way to Kennedy Airport carrying passengers and a small load of cargo. His estimated time of arrival at Kennedy: 2:08 AM, local time. He filed a transatlantic flight plan. One hour and eighteen minutes after landing at Lisbon, the DFG 747 took off for Kennedy, New York, fully refueled and eight hours from its final destination.

"Kennedy. Not coming in through the south, then," said Scott. "Okay. Where in the northeast?"

T. T. Buckley, the FAA man assigned to checking airports, scanned his sheets. "Not many airports can take him," he said. "Excuse me, sir, but did you ever consider that the 747 flight from Lisbon might be a decoy, that the flight we're looking for might be coming in somewhere else while our attention is fixed on this 747?"

Scott nodded. "We've thought of that," he said. "We're not relaxing our surveillance of southeastern airports to concentrate on this one flight."

He had flown in the afternoon from Bethesda to Ronkonkoma, Long Island, to be in New York Center as the suspect plane approached the coast. Miller had stayed in Bethesda, still studying the source codes and trying to find the virus.

Admiral Buchanan was with him in New York Center. "Virus

or no virus, makes no difference," he said. "We'll pick him up on military radar and track him in. He'll have F-14s paralleling him from five hundred miles out."

Scott nodded at the admiral and said nothing. His thought was that if the Whitney virus worked, military radar would lose this 747 the same as ATC radar. In his judgment the Department of Defense was overconfident of its ability to detect any and all incoming air traffic. It didn't yet take the virus threat seriously enough.

His mind was on Nancy almost as much as on the approaching 747. Her dispatches from Bogotá could not include personal messages; and he had heard nothing except that she was alive and functioning effectively. That was all the CIA transmitted. That she had identified this flight was evidence of her presence in the vicinity of the Colombian airport. What risk she was taking was not suggested.

He walked through New York Center, nervously glancing at the radar scopes. None of them, of course, showed the incoming chartered 747. It was too far out. By the time it arrived, after 2:00 A.M., traffic would be light. That would make it easier to see.

"Sit down, Captain," said Admiral Buchanan. "Have a drink. We've got hours to wait."

A few miles away, in an apartment in Hempstead, Long Island, Darius Whitney sat at the kitchen table and tapped at the keys of a laptop computer—a small version of a desktop, with a fold-down screen and fold-up keyboard. A pair of small Hispanic men frowned and stared. Stepan Yanak sat at the table, too, sipping beer from a bottle.

The computer was attached to one of the apartment's three telephone lines with a pair of long, thin alligator clips. Darius had stripped the insulation from the wires with a small sharp knife and clamped the teeth of the clips onto the bare wires. He tapped number keys, then the Transmit key, and waited. A clutter of gibberish ran down the screen. Darius shook his head and tried another number.

"Can't get in?" Yanak asked apprehensively.

"I can get in any time I want," said Darius. "The point is to make it look like the connection is a telephone line from Cleveland Center, not a telephone line from Hempstead, Long Island. They've changed some things. Their security is getting tighter."

Yanak glanced at his watch. "Four hours," he said.

Darius kept tapping in numbers. The system continued to reject them.

"Hey. Won't they realize somebody is trying to break in?"

Darius shook his head. "Even if they do, it looks like calls coming in from Pittsburgh. To Cleveland Center. That won't alert New York. And if I detect problems, I'll go another way."

"Why not the South Carolina contractor?" asked Yanak.

"That would be a tip-off," said Darius. "The people down there don't work at night."

Yanak got up and paced nervously back and forth across the kitchen. "Hey," he said to one of the Hispanics. "Shouldn't you be trying the radio?"

The small man shook his head. "Not till the station goes off the air," he said. "Not till twelve o'clock. Anyway, the airplane is still too far out."

Nancy dozed in her hotel room in Bogotá—sleeping lightly, disturbed by buzzing mosquitoes and by bugs she imagined, or that really were crawling in her bed. She did not know where the 747 had gone. She had not dared ask. Even Bob Laud could not guess and dared not ask. Her signal had, maybe, alerted North American Air Defense Command. She hoped so. She hoped the word had gone on to Bethesda.

Last night, when Emily took her to pick up the transmitter, the CIA station chief had joined them in Emily's car. Nancy had mentioned to him the names Plutarco Candelario and Virgilio Cordero. He had responded that Cordero was a prominent businessman and an influence for political stability in Colombia. Candelario was the same in Peru. The station chief had acknowledged that rumors circulated about both men, but suggested she give no credibility to rumors. "When the Vice President visited Bogotá, he was invited to Señor Cordero's mountain villa for dinner. And he went. And enjoyed himself. Okay? Does that tell you who Señor Cordero is?"

* * *

"How's that brake pressure?" Don Sumner asked the flight engineer.

Sitting behind Sumner and to his right, the engineer put his finger on the gauge and read the number: "One-forty."

"How you figure? That enough?"

"If it holds above one hundred, there'll be enough."

"To bring a 747 to a grinding, screeching halt on a five-thousand-foot runway?"

"Yeah, if you've used enough reverse thrust to slow her down to forty, fifty knots. I'd keep pouring on reverse thrust. What the hell, we aren't taking off again, so if the bird gets bent in the process, the bird is bent."

"Right," said Sumner. He accepted it, but he wasn't happy. "Fuel?"

"Looks good. Enough to go to Plan B if we have to."

Plan B was to divert to Halifax, Nova Scotia, if anything went wrong. If it did, the fact that they were losing hydraulic pressure on the braking system could be a godsend. They could ask for a quick recharge, which could be done from outside the aircraft, and they could take on fuel too—and no one need come inside to see what they were carrying.

"You tuned to that frequency yet?" Sumner asked his copilot, Aridas.

Aridas nodded. "Too far out for it, but I'm tuned."

Sumner checked his watch. "One hour. And they'll be on time."

"Gotcha," said Aridas. "Twelve-oh-five, New York time."

"But we listen for an hour before," said Sumner a little sharply. "That's also where we get the emergency signal."

Bill Aridas switched the receiver to the cockpit speakers. Behind a chaos of static, a suggestion of music was just barely distinguishable. It was a New York broadcast station that would go off the air at midnight and leave its frequency clear.

Sumner scowled and reached for the switch that sent the noise back into the copilot's earphones. "Just keep listening," he said. "Something could come through before they go off the air."

* * *

"If he's your rogue 747, he's sure coming in normal, Captain," said Peter Langostina, shift supervisor at New York Center. We haven't picked him up yet, but he's reporting normally."

"What you have to watch out for," said Scott, "is a sudden disappearance off the scope. Suddenly he gets invisible."

"They can do that to us?"

"They did it to Miami."

"My god! In all our traffic, an invisible aircraft! He could—"

"Yeah, right," said Scott. "So keep an eye out. And do a byte count on the digitalizers."

"Again?"

"As often as you can. The byte count on the digitalizers is our only sure defense right now. We still haven't cracked the code in the main system."

In the kitchen of the apartment in Hempstead, Long Island, the last notes of "The Star-Spangled Banner" faded. For a moment the radio was silent, and Yanak and Whitney stared at it uneasily. Then the speaker filled with weak static. The station had gone off the air, and distant stations now put static onto its vacant frequency.

"Is ready," said the radio operator to Yanak.

Stepan Yanak walked into the kitchen. "We can send the new transponder code. Do you have one?"

Darius Whitney picked up a scratch pad and squinted over the numbers he had scribbled there. "Tell them six-one-six-one," he said.

At the transmitter in the living room the operator raised his eyes to heaven and asked for help as he prepared to send out a signal on an AM broadcast frequency—a most serious violation of the laws and regulations. If the Federal Communications Commission . . . ah, well, he was being generously paid. And it would be a one-time violation for only a minute. He looked at his watch: 12:05. He began to tap the key.

"Got it! Six-one-six-one."

Don Sumner nodded. He wasn't sure why he was surprised

at how this thing worked. Even so, he was surprised that it did. This was the age of the fuck-up. You couldn't order a pizza and have it come on time and be what you ordered. Nobody gave a damn anymore. But these guys did. They'd got an airplane. And all the rest of it. And now this: a new transponder code, right on time.

"Squawk six-one-six-one," he said to the copilot, Aridas.

"But what happens when our assigned transponder code disappears off—"

"It won't. Or so they tell me. Don't ask me how. I don't know. But we're not dealing with amateurs, buddy. Squawk six-one-six-one."

Sumner allowed his tension to subside a little. The radio signal had come in. The damned thing seemed to be working.

He glanced across the instrument panel of the 747 and saw nothing but normal indications on the gauges. His copilot was staring at the same gauges, and at the navigation indicators. Behind them the flight engineer was monitoring the thousand things he had to watch.

So far so good. Sumner could allow himself the luxury of staring out the windows, at the black sky above, at the stars, at the tops of the clouds, gray-lighted by the moon, all seen through the subdued glow from the instruments—what no one but a pilot ever saw. He tried to relax. What was tough came in an hour. It was well to relax now if he could.

"He's passed into U.S. airspace, Captain. Radar contact, Boston Center," said Langostina, the shift supervisor at New York Center. "Speed and altitude normal. Course as filed."

Admiral Buchanan took Scott by the arm and led him away from the scopes and the supervisor. "When that 747 lands at Kennedy, we'll have a look at him, but I think Nancy's suspicions are proving unfounded."

"Check with NORAD," said Scott. He meant North American Radar Defense.

The admiral nodded. "Why not?" He picked up a telephone and, after a moment, got through and began to talk. He talked and listened, talked and listened, then turned to Scott. "They've got him, too" he said. "No difference between what ATC radar is showing and what NORAD sees."

"Okay," said Scott.

"This is not the rogue airplane, from the look of it," said Admiral Buchanan. "I'm afraid Nancy missed this one."

"Maybe you won't mind if I make one more check," said Scott.

The admiral shrugged. "Of course not."

Scott walked back toward the scopes and Langostina.

"Captain. Telephone."

Scott went to the desk to which he had been summoned and picked up the telephone.

"Cap'n? Digitalizer room. Our byte count's off. Thought you'd want to know."

"I did want to know. Thanks."

He returned to Langostina. "Pete," he said. "Let's do something. Talk to Boston Center on the land line and ask them to send the 747 to a different altitude."

"DFG Flight Zero-zero-one. Boston Center."

"DFG."

"DFG, I have an Air Canada 1011 out of Logan that will be climbing through your flight path. Descend to and maintain two-six thousand. Report level at two-six."

"DFG, Roger."

Sumner nodded at Aridas, who had heard the exchange, and the copilot rotated the trim wheel to initiate the descent at the standard cruise descent rate of five hundred feet per minute.

"Dammit!"

In the apartment at Hempstead two small battery-powered radios monitored the frequency of New York Center and New York Approach Control. In another home in Boston an identical radio monitored Boston Center. They taped the chatter between controllers and pilots. The man in Boston had just called to report that Boston Center had called the 747 down to 26,000 feet.

"Whatta y'mean?" Yanak demanded of Whitney. "What's 'dammit'?"

"Tell Boston to call us back the minute they hear another word from Boston Center to our airplane," said Darius.

"Somethin' wrong?"

Darius looked up into the stern face of Stepan Yanak. His own face was white. "Could be very wrong," he said.

Langostina shook his head and spoke to Scott. "Boston Center says he's not descending to twenty-six. He responded, said he would; then he kept on flying at the same altitude."

Admiral Buchanan was listening. "Let's see where NORAD thinks he is," he said, reaching for a telephone.

"Damn," Scott muttered. "I know what they've done. They get better and better."

The admiral put down the telephone. "Analog radar shows him at twenty-six thousand feet."

Scott nodded. "Sure. The virus they used at Miami made their aircraft invisible to ATC radar. The aircraft disappeared when it began to squawk the transponder code that activated the virus. The new virus is more sophisticated. The aircraft disappears all right, but the screen display of its prior transponder code continues to fly course and altitude. What Boston Center is looking at is a false image. The 747 actually descended to twenty-six thousand and is flying at that altitude."

"I'm going to scramble the interceptors," said Admiral Buchanan.

Scott nodded. "Before he disappears off military radar too."

"He can't do that," said Admiral Buchanan.

"I'd like to think so," said Scott.

"Damn! I can't believe it."

The copilot switched the signal into the speakers. For a moment Sumner could hear nothing but static. Then the sharp string of Morse code beeps cut through, unmistakable: A-B. Again. A-B. Abort.

Something was wrong. They were being called off.

"Plan B," said Sumner decisively.

He picked up his microphone. "Boston Center, DFG Zero-zero-one."

240

"DFG, Boston Center. Go ahead."

"DFG has got a failure of hydraulic pressure. It's bleeding down rapidly. In another hour I won't have any braking power at all. I'm diverting to Halifax for repairs."

"DFG, Roger. I can clear you for an immediate left turn to, uh, nine-zero degrees. Contact Moncton on one-two-three-point-nine. Good luck, sir."

"He's broken off! He's telling Boston Center he's losing hydraulic pressure in his brakes and is landing at Halifax while he's still got some braking power."

Admiral Buchanan picked up the telephone. He punched in a number. "Cancel the interceptors," he said. "Our bogie is landing at Halifax."

Scott stood with his hands on his hips, puzzled and shaking his head. "Let me talk to Boston Center," he said. Langostina handed him a telephone. "What do you show for altitude for DFG Zero-zero-one?" he asked.

"Uh . . . twenty-three thousand. Descending."

"How'd he get down from thirty-five to twenty-three so quick?"

"I don't know, sir. I haven't been watching him since he diverted. He's in Canadian airspace now. Even so, that's dumping altitude pretty fast. I don't know how he did it."

"Well, I do."

"I beg your pardon?"

"Never mind. Thanks."

Lieutenant Bryan Wallingford picked up his telephone. "Yes?"

"Lieutenant, this is Captain Scott Vandenberg, United States Navy, chief of the Presidential Task Force on Airline Safety. My call was switched to you because I am told you are in charge of security tonight on the airport at Halifax."

"Yes, sir. Something like that. I'm the duty officer at this hour."

"All right. A 747 has just broken off an approach to Kennedy Airport and will be landing at Halifax shortly. He says he's got a hydraulic problem. We could be one hundred percent wrong, but we have reason to think he may be loaded with cocaine."

"I appreciate the warning," said Lieutenant Wallingford, looking out the window at the storm clouds, and lightning flashing through wind-driven sheets of rain. "We won't let him off-load it here."

"I doubt if he'll try that," said Scott.

"I can't prevent his landing, you know."

"No, of course not. We don't suggest it. We would like to know where he goes when he leaves you."

"Certainly, Captain. We'll keep an eye on him."

"Look at that," said Aridas to Sumner.

As they rolled slowly up to the ramp before a huge hangar, two military trucks took up stations to each side of the 747. They were covered with canvas, but Sumner's experience, added to his imagination, suggested to him that each one was equipped with twin .50-caliber machine guns under that cover.

"Have to bluff it out if we can."

He spoke to airport operations on its radio frequency. "I'm losing hydraulic pressure in the braking system. I'd like a recharge. The leak is slow, so I can make it on into New York, discharge my passengers without too much delay, and have it repaired there. Also, I'd like to top my tanks. I'd like to make as quick a turnaround as possible. Propose to stay buttoned up. Some of my people want to get out and stretch their legs, but I'm saying no."

A few minutes later he came down the stairs drawn up to the 747 and walked into the shack to pay for his fuel and hydraulic fluid. He paid with cash—American dollars—explaining that DFG was having credit problems.

"In from . . ."

"Lisbon," said Sumner to the young Canadian army lieutenant.

Lieutenant Wallingford stared at the 747. Sumner had switched on dim lights in the body of the airplane, and Cordero's gunmen were crawling over boxes to reach the windows and stare out one window after another.

"No passengers, no cargo coming off, huh?"

"Nope. They're madder 'n hell to be delayed."

Wallingford studied the big airplane. He saw no reason to

242

board it. After all, the American captain had not been sure about what it carried. Anyway, whatever it was, it was not coming off at Halifax, which would have made it his responsibility.

"Well, good luck, then. I'm glad I'm not going with you, out into this kind of weather."

"Only three miles of it," said Sumner with a grin. "Above fifteen thousand feet it's perfectly clear."

In the cockpit Aridas had taken a weather briefing and filed a new flight plan. "Cleared to Bermuda," he said.

After forty minutes on the ground they took off again. They flew south, along the sixtieth meridian. The farther south they flew, the more distance they put between the 747 and the North American coastline. When they finally turned west to return to Bogotá, they were outside the reach of the North American Air Defense system.

"How is this to be explained?" Virgilio Cordero asked Stepan Yanak.

"As close as I can figure—and he's explained it a dozen times—they have increased their security checks. He says you need an opening of about an hour in which they don't do what he calls byte counts. Better you should have two hours. He insists they've been doing them only about every eight hours. Then, suddenly, the other night, one every hour. And now they've gone back to one every eight hours."

"Gibberish," grunted Cordero. He spun around to face Yoshitaka Hara. "Does this mean anything to you?"

"Yes," said Hara. "Yes, it does. Frankly, Virgilio, I don't think what happened is Whitney's fault."

"Oh? Do I hear one technician defending another?" Cordero asked quietly as he lighted a small, thin cigar.

Hara ignored the question. "As you know, our people recorded all the radio chatter out of Boston Center for two hours. I've listened to it twice. There's something funny in it."

"In the circumstances, what can be funny?"

"Boston Center told Sumner he had an Air Canada 1011 climbing out of Logan Airport that would be crossing his flight path. So he told him to begin his descent early—descend to twenty-six thousand. But Center never talked to an Air Canada flight going in that direction for a whole hour before he gave that order to Sumner."

"And that means?"

"Whitney's program is designed not just to make our airplane disappear off the digital radar scopes; it keeps the image on the scope, following the same course and maintaining the same altitude, for twenty minutes—until our airplane is a hundred and fifty miles away. When Center ordered Sumner to descend, Sumner descended. He doesn't know about that element of the virus program. If he did, it wouldn't have made any difference; he'd have had to descend anyway. Sumner took our airplane down to twenty-six thousand. The radar image kept flying at thirty-five."

"This Air Canada 1011. An evil coincidence?"

"I'd like to think so," said Hara. "And I would think so if I had heard on that tape any talk between Boston Center and the Air Canada flight that was supposedly climbing into Sumner's flight path. No. I think it was a check. A test."

"Why?"

Hara glanced at Yanak. "I think we've got two problems," he said. "One, in that man Vandenberg we're up against one smart cookie. Two, I think the Americans knew about our flight from the hour it took off from here. I think Vandenberg and his people were watching our 747, from the time it left here, and tracked it all the way to Lisbon and back across the North Atlantic. As soon as it crossed into American-controlled airspace, they put it to a test. They had to be concentrating on that 747."

"You think we have a spy, then," said Cordero grimly.

"I don't think it's a coincidence that the Americans began doing hourly byte checks about the time our airplane was due, or that they faked a reason to order Sumner to change altitude. I think they knew what that flight was, from the time it took off."

"CIA?"

"Not within their jurisdiction," said Hara. "I'd guess we've got a narc in Bogotá. At the airport."

Cordero frowned. "Very possible," he said pensively. "Why did somebody take particular note of *that* 747? Unless somebody watched us load it? Damn."

The time of year had arrived when the heat and humidity became oppressive in Washington. What was more, the air conditioner didn't work in the motel room where Scott had to live. He had asked for a new unit, and they had installed one; but it wasn't new, it was just a unit from another room; and it groaned and rattled and dripped and barely managed to lower the temperature to 85°. He delayed returning to his room as long as he could and left early every morning.

Except Sunday. What could you do on Sunday? Nothing justified his demanding the staff come in to the office in Bethesda on this Sunday morning, and it would have been pointless for him to go there alone. He sat on his bed in his shorts, with the Sunday-morning *Post* spread out around him, sipped Coke—hot coffee would have added to his discomfort—and sweated.

The newspapers and television stations had not mentioned the 747 that had approached New York, then turned back. They didn't know about it. It had returned to Bogotá. Nancy had sent word through the CIA: the DFG 747 had landed at Bogotá some twenty-four hours after it took off. It remained on the airport.

She didn't know where it had been of course. He hoped she didn't try to find out. She was in danger down there, every hour of the day; and he was acutely conscious of it.

It was a wretched business, having to sit in the office in Bethesda, examining sheet after sheet of source code, marking minor changes that turned out to have originated in the system itself, searching for Whitney's elusive virus, with no great confidence they would ever find it.

Whitney was erasing it and reinserting it. Scott was sure of that. That was what he did with the smaller virus in the radar digitalizers. And he erased fully, leaving no trace.

Which raised a point. Whitney was not in Bogotá anymore. To do what he was doing, he had to be in the States. Unless somebody—possibly Yoshitaka Hara—had learned how to work the Whitney virus. But Hara *was* in Bogotá. FBI surveillance of him continued, and—at least ostensibly—he was in Colombia.

Nancy. Never again. That was what they had said. Never again. There had been three messages since she left for Colombia. Nothing personal in them. That they came through was assurance that she was alive. Functioning. So, okay.

He could send a message to Bogotá. But what would it say? Be careful . . . Don't take chances . . . Chuck it and come home!

He reached for the telephone. On a Sunday he could go out and see Judy. Sally couldn't object to that.

The day the DFG 747 returned to Bogotá, Nancy at last got to fly an airplane. The old man who ran the charter service shoved a dispatch bag at her, handed her the keys to a Piper Cherokee Six, and told her to fly the single-engine airplane to Quito, Ecuador, deliver the bag of documents, and bring the plane back that afternoon. Anticipating something like this—hoping for it in fact—she had been studying the charts and navigation aids. The flight was an adventure, happily most of it in clear weather, and she landed back on the airport at Bogotá in late afternoon, to spot the 747 on the ramp as she taxied in.

Oppressively hot days were unusual in Bogotá. Drenching rain was not. For the next two days Nancy sat in the line shack and stared out the window, most often at the DFG 747, which sat looking heavy and ungraceful on the ramp in front of the big warehouse most distant from the passenger terminal.

She cursed her ignorance. Before she left the States, she and Scott had talked about communication, how they would talk to each other while she was in Colombia. They had concluded that her stay would be short and that the embassy would provide all the link they would need—through the lines used by the CIA and the naval attaché. That had been a mistake. The CIA station had its function, and what she was doing was no part of it. CIA co-operation was a concession, given without grudge, but given none-theless with the understanding that she would not use their line any more than she had to and would reveal to the CIA itself no more than she had to—as it was going to reveal to her no more than it had to. The naval attaché, it turned out, had no special facilities of his own and relied on the CIA and the diplomatic pouch. The result was that communication to and from Scott had been infrequent and curt.

As much as she could, Nancy kept away from Emily. She was dangerous to Emily, and Emily was dangerous to her. She did not want to be identified with a young woman from the American embassy, even if no one knew Emily worked for the CIA. And Emily did not need identification with Nancy, even if no one suspected who she was.

The 747 sat isolated. Rain fell on it. It was powered down, without lights showing. Nancy assumed they had unloaded its cargo somewhere and that it was waiting here to take on another load.

Sure. It would take days, maybe weeks, to come up with enough cocaine to load that big airplane. They couldn't send that kind of load every week. Or every two weeks. She wished she knew if they had, for certain, penetrated United States airspace and delivered that cargo. She wished she knew for certain that the cargo had been cocaine.

Bob Laud, the American dispatch-service representative, came in out of the rain. For a minute or two he talked with the old man who had given Nancy her job. Just about the only personal exchange she'd had with the old man was to share their amusement over Bob's comic Spanish. The telephone rang, and after a brief conversation the old man pulled on a great yellow slicker and went out.

Laud shed his raincoat and ran the sleeve of his jacket over his pink bald head, rubbing off gleaming beads of water.

"Ho, Idelia. You can't fly any airplanes today. How about visiting a nice, warm, dry room and drinking a bottle of real French wine?"

"My husband would kill us both," she said, though she knew Bob Laud had seen through that little defense and took it for a joke now.

"*La virgen de aeropuerto*," he laughed.

She nodded toward the 747. "That one's still there," she said in Spanish.

"Forget about that. I don't even want to talk about it." The stress he put on his words was suggestive, not just of his strain with speaking Spanish but of dark fear. "And whatever you do, don't try to go near it."

"What's the matter? It belong to Virgilio Cordero?"

"Idelia! That's not funny. You must not drop that name around as if it were a joke."

She stared at the 747, its lines somewhat obscured by the rain. She tipped her head to one side. "I have never sat in the cockpit of an airplane like that. I wonder if the pilots would—"

He shook his head emphatically. "No one can get near it. It's guarded."

"How much do you really know about it, Roberto?" she asked playfully. "More than I do?"

"I had coffee with the pilot," he said.

"Ohh . . . *I* want to have coffee with him. You must arrange for me to have coffee with this pilot."

Laud shook his head. "It was by accident. I—"

"Take me to where you had coffee," she said. "Maybe he'll be there again."

Don Sumner *was* there, in the modest little *cantina* beside the general-aviation terminal. Laud introduced Nancy to him—as Idelia Santa Cruzada of course—calling her a Guatemalan girl-pilot who wanted to meet a man who flew a big jet.

Sumner was receptive. He asked her if she was really a licensed pilot; and when she said she was, he asked her how many hours of experience she had and what kind of aircraft she had flown. She answered him, and he liked the answer: that she really was a pilot, but that she had nothing like his experience. So they shared an interest, but she was in no way threatening to him. Also, he conspicuously failed to overlook her face and figure.

Conversation between them was all but impossible. Sumner could not speak Spanish, and Nancy could not admit she spoke English. The situation gave her an advantage.

"She says she'd like to see the inside of a 747," Laud translated.

Sumner shook his head. "Some other 747," he said.

Laud translated, Nancy spoke, and Laud translated again. "She asks what's so secret about this one. I'm sorry. I know she shouldn't ask. But she's innocent and does ask, and I guess she'd do just about anything to get to sit at the controls of a 747."

Sumner grinned. "What'll she do for pilots?"

Laud laughed. "I can ask her if you want. But I can tell you what the answer is going to be."

"Ask her if she'd like to spend the night with a 747 pilot."

Laud chuckled as he asked and translated. "She says her husband would shoot you both. I've heard that line before."

"Ask her if she would just have dinner with a 747 pilot."

Laud didn't need to translate Nancy's answer. She looked directly at Sumner, smiled, and nodded.

"There is no way you can hide the fact that a 747 has taken off," said Yoshitaka Hara.

He spoke to Virgilio Cordero in the library in the villa on the mountainside above Bogotá. Allison was there with them. They had coffee and pastries and fruit—breakfast in the library because it was raining outside.

"And if someone knows what it is—that is, what it's carrying," Hara continued, "they'll track it. If they do that, nothing Whitney can do is going to break it through their defenses. We talked about hiding an airplane. And we *can* hide one. But not one they're specifically looking for, not one that's been identified and—"

"Rationalization," muttered Cordero.

"But it's true," said Allison. "And something worse. That 747 sitting on the airport in Bogotá has been identified as a suspicious airplane. When it leaves again, somebody is going to report it has left. A spy on the airport? Yes, probably. But the spy's job is done. They *know* the airplane. Any CIA agent . . . anyone . . . could send the report now."

"Your suggestion, then?" asked Cordero haughtily, yet with a degree of respect for her intelligence.

"Off-load the stuff," said Hara. "Send the 747 back to Germany. Load the stuff on two or three 707s."

"Start over," said Cordero.

"And don't blame the technology," Allison protested. "Darius has created an almost-perfect program."

"Perhaps," said Cordero. "But so far it has not produced results."

"I think it has produced important results," said Allison. "If he hadn't rewritten the virus to detect a byte count and signal us that it was happening, you would have lost that 747 last week. Lost it and the whole cargo."

"You seem to be suggesting that no part of our failure is any fault of his," said Cordero.

"If Vandenberg and his crew hadn't known the airplane was coming and from where and when," said Hara, "they wouldn't have started doing hourly byte counts."

"Why don't they do byte counts all the time?" asked Cordero.

"Because it fouls up their radar," said Hara. "The radar is out of commission for two or three minutes while the digitalizers are switched over to the program that does the count."

"Somebody made another mistake," said Allison. "This flight came in after midnight, when traffic had slacked off. The next flight should come in during peak-traffic hours. They won't do byte counts so often then."

"You two think we should try again, hmm?" asked Cordero.

"That is my recommendation," said Hara.

"Would you be willing to go as passengers on the next flight?"

"Not a flight in *that* airplane," said Hara crisply.

"I'll go gladly," said Allison. "I have every confidence in Darius's work."

Yanak was tired of flying. For three days he had been aboard the Lear, flying to every airport of any consequence in South America, or so it seemed. As the Lear touched down yet again, he had to ask the pilots where they were.

"This is Asunción, Señor. Paraguay."

As the Lear taxied toward the ramp, Yanak scanned the aircraft on the field. A fool's errand. He'd been sent on a fool's errand. Cordero had been highly specific about what he wanted. But finding it—Not likely. After this, where would he go looking? In the States? Europe? There would be a hell of a lot more 747s on fields there than there were on the airports of some of these jerkwater countries of South America.

He raised binoculars to his eyes and scanned the ramps. Only two 747s on the field. One at the passenger terminal: PLUNA. Uruguayan. The other sat on the ramp in front of a hangar: CAS, yellow and orange stripes. He didn't recognize the letters.

Wait a minute! Maybe the fool's errand was about to produce results.

Half an hour later Yanak walked around the 747 marked with a long yellow-and-orange stripe and the orange letters CAS in a yellow circle. In smaller print beneath the logo were the words CORPORACIÓN AERONAVES SANTIAGO. One-third of the right wing, including the right outboard engine, was missing.

"A dispute as to who was entitled to the taxiway," said a man in response to his question. Whether the man was a pilot, a mechanic, or just an airport bum, Yanak could not tell. "Three weeks, they say, to get the parts, to install them. They are working on the engine in the hangar. It is not badly damaged. But the wing . . ." He shrugged. "Three weeks, they say. I expect to see it sitting here five weeks."

As the Lear taxied out, Yanak used a camera with a telephoto lens and took a dozen pictures of the damaged 747. On reflection he rejected the idea, but for a bit he had wondered if Cordero had sent a pilot to taxi under the wing of a moving 747.

Nancy sat in the lounge of a downtown hotel. It was by no means the finest hotel in Bogotá, but it was immeasurably superior to the hotel where she was living; and she was determined to get a memorable dinner out of this evening if nothing else.

She was wearing a simple, cheap, white cotton dress that she had bought in Guatemala. To keep her appearance consistent with her story of being the disowned daughter of a straitlaced Guatemalan family and the wife of a rarely employed pilot, she could have nothing stylish or expensive. Except for this dress, she had only blue jeans, T-shirts, a couple of nylon jackets, two pairs of cheap shoes, and dime-store underwear. The white dress was not out of place in this bar. Don Sumner wore a light-blue jacket over a white polo shirt, with dark-blue slacks. He smoked a tiny black cigar.

"I . . . do of the English a little," she said to him.

He grinned. "Thought you might."

She understood the implication out of the mouth of this self-confident American: that any girl on the make, or even one just looking for an adventure, would speak a little English. She was not certain she had the skill to fend him off and at the same time get a little information out of him. She tried to remember the gaffes of grammar and punctuation she had heard from Spanish-speakers struggling with English so she could duplicate them.

"I really am of the license for fly," she said, imposing a heavy accent on her words.

"Really? Seriously? What kind of airplane?"

"The . . . is call in English the Skyhawk. Yes? You know this? The wing on top. Very nice. And others. The Piper Cherokee Six this week. Big engine. Fly fast. Much difficult."

"Cessna Skyhawk, yes," he said. His eyes narrowed. He was not a subtle man, and she understood he was about to test her. "What do you think is the most difficult maneuver with a Skyhawk?"

"Man . . . oover?"

"How do you *not* like to fly? Is there some kind of flying you do not like?"

She grinned. "Yes. The . . ." She used her hands to describe the maneuver. "You fly too slow, airplane go up too slow. You know? Airplane"—She turned her hand over and indicated a plane falling—"Very afraiding. Bad. Must fly many time."

"Stalls," he said, obviously satisfied. "Yes. You have to fly stall practice. Many times."

252

She nodded. "Afraiding. Very bad."

It was difficult to believe he could not see the truth about her. A man is easily deceived who wants to believe he has come upon an exceptionally beautiful girl who wants to believe she has encountered some kind of superman.

"How many hours do you have?" he asked.

"Hmm?"

"How many hours have you flown?"

"Oh . . . *Doscientos*," she said. "Two 'undred."

"All in Skyhawks?"

"No, no. Others. Biggers . . . Littlers . . ."

"You fly for money?"

"Yes."

"What kind of flying do you do for money?"

"Fly . . ." She fluttered her hand as if she were searching for the words. "Look at the electric. You know. Man look down at . . ." She formed circles with her thumbs and forefingers and held them up to her eyes, to signify binoculars. "Look at the—down."

"You fly power lines, to let people inspect them from the air."

She nodded. She was glad she had once encountered a man who did just that: flew the routes of power lines and pipelines, carrying inspectors.

Summer ordered another round of drinks. She was accepting margaritas, fearful that drinking martinis would give her away.

"Why are you waiting around for flying jobs on this particular airport?" he asked.

"Don't like me fly here," she said. "My license no good here."

"Then why did you come to Colombia?"

"Ho-ho," she laughed. "Why you, Donaldo? Is good question, why anybody here?"

"I can fly anywhere," he said.

"You like copilot?" she asked with a grin. "*Doscientos.* Fly good."

"Talk to me when you've got *dos mil*," he said. "Talk to me when you've flown two *thousand* hours, not just two hundred."

She turned down the corners of her mouth and tried to look crestfallen.

"Hey!" he laughed. "I could teach you to fly the 747."

She looked up. "You will? I—I just . . . just sit in. You make for me sit in . . . where copilot sit?"

He frowned and shook his head. "Not this 747, Idelia. I can't take you aboard this one."

"Is why?"

"The people who own it don't want anybody aboard."

"But . . . you *pilot*. You chief man of airplane."

He shook his head firmly. "Not . . . I'm sorry, Idelia. I can't take anyone aboard."

She tried to pout. It wasn't easy; it was not a mien that came naturally to her.

"I'm flying away tomorrow," he said. "Will you spend the night with me?"

"Where you going, Donaldo?"

He shook his head. "Can't say. But, tonight—"

"No," she said quietly. "My husband kill us both."

He tipped his head and smiled skeptically. "Where is this husband of yours, Idelia?"

"He fly."

"Where?"

"Many place."

"Who's he fly for? What kind of planes?"

She turned her eyes away, down to her empty glass. "No talk of this," she said. "No talk."

She was conscious that Sumner's skepticism about her husband who would shoot them both had suddenly turned to suspicion. Also, he realized his evening was a flop. He sighed and glanced around the bar, and she wondered if he were not about to back out of his invitation to dinner. He couldn't take her to bed. He couldn't even talk with her very well. What kind of man was Don Sumner? She was about to find out.

"Well," he grunted. "You hungry? Want to go in to dinner?"

Nancy put the beer bottle in her hotel-room window. In the morning an encoded message went to Washington. When deciphered, it said:

DFG 747 will depart Bogotá today. Destination unknown. May mean another attempt to enter States. Alert
Vandenberg.

Overnight the cargo was off-loaded from the 747 and returned
to the warehouse. On Tuesday morning Summer and his crew
taxied out and roared off into fog and drizzle.

It was a short flight, only as far as Quito, Ecuador. They taxied
to a hangar on the side of the field opposite the passenger terminal.
On the ramp a dozen vehicles, four of them equipped with cherry
pickers, quickly surrounded the big airplane. Men swarmed over
it. Before Sumner and his crew got away from the airport, the work
was well underway. The 747 was going to be repainted.

The next morning, when Sumner arrived at the airport to have
a look, the job was almost finished. The 747 now had an orange-
and-yellow stripe. The DFG logo was gone from the tail. In its
place a new logo had been painted: CAS. And beneath the logo
the words *Corporación Aeronaves Santiago.*

The registration number had also been changed—totally illegally of course.

On Thursday morning Sumner flew the 747 back to Bogotá.
He did not return it to the ramp where it had sat before. Instead
he drew it up to a gate at the passenger terminal. Sumner and his
copilot and flight engineer were hurried away from the airport in
a small van. No one was to see them near the 747. No one was
to know that the Deutsche Flugzeugwesen 747 was back on the
airport.

Darius Whitney was back at the little house on Toiyabe Ranch.
A garrulous Spanish-speaking man had accompanied him on the
flight from Kennedy to Las Vegas. The man tried to talk so Darius
could understand, but communication between them consisted
mostly of smiles.

He was to remain here in the Nevada house until they made
the next at attempt to get the 747 into the United States. The word
was that he was to give his attention to the computers in the house
and work out whatever problems he could, since the next attempt

would almost certainly be the last—and Señor Cordero was in no forgiving mood about another failure.

For a while the happy Hispanic stood behind him and watched him work with the computer. After a while he became bored and walked away. Darius doubted he had understood much anyway.

Fine. Darius had another project in mind, and this day or two gave him time to work on it.

Cordero assumed apparently that Darius was not sophisticated enough to know that anyone who had the number could take the money out of a Swiss number account. But Darius did know that. He had toyed briefly, a few years back, with the idea of developing a program that would discover those secret numbers—until he found out that the numbers were written with fountain pens, not even with ballpoint pens, on little slips of paper, and were never put in computer memory. He knew something about Swiss number accounts: that they were not computer-managed and not accessible by computer.

On the other hand, maybe Cordero didn't know how you could withdraw funds from a Swiss number account by computer. Maybe he had never thought about that. Well, Darius had thought about it. He had thought about it before Cordero deposited $10 million in a Swiss account and given him the number. Cordero presumed, probably, that the money would remain in the bank in Zurich until Darius personally appeared to withdraw it. Personally. That was how you were supposed to withdraw funds from a secret account.

But there was another way.

Darius hummed a little tune as he worked on the program that would withdraw the money.

Because he was a computer illiterate, Cordero wouldn't suspect. Probably he wouldn't suspect, either, that the ATC virus included a README message. It was a simple little gimmick, but well hidden. The virus had to hear from Darius Whitney at least once every ten days. He had to transmit to it at intervals a number determined by a simple but obscure formula involving the squares of primes. If he didn't, the virus would display a message on the screen of every traffic controller in the United States: README. A message. Short, but telling everything, with names. Allison had helped him write it.

The damned fools didn't suspect.

Except maybe Hara. Yoshitaka Hara was a kindred spirit, another one of those men who had been seduced by the computer. Probably that damned Vandenberg was another. And seduced was the right word. The computer was for men like them—also for Allison—a subject of total fascination. It had won from them a literally mystic commitment. They had not yet discovered the limits of its power, but they knew they could use it to have power that was denied to others. The computer was generous. It shared its power. Like a god, it shared its power with its devotees.

16
—▮-▮-▮-▮—

Nancy had done what she could in Bogotá, she figured—and Naval Intelligence figured so, too. On a secure line between the embassy and Admiral Buchanan, she had received orders to come home. Scott had come on that line for a moment and had urged her to take no more chances, just come home.

She had returned the locator transmitter to the technician and had given the little S&W automatic back to Emily. The attaché had handed her a ticket on an Avianca flight going out at eight in the morning. He also told her that the embassy would advise Immigration in Miami that Idelia Santa Cruzada was to be rushed through procedures and helped to get aboard the first flight for Washington.

"What else can we do for you before you go?" Emily Greenhouse had asked.

"Take me where I can buy clothes," Nancy had said. "I don't want to get off a plane in Washington and have Scott see me dressed like this."

"Sure," Emily had said. "I'll take you where I buy my things. It's a little shop off the lobby of a hotel. They'll outfit you from the skin out. And if you've got any problem about funds, I'll charge it and you can send me a check."

Nancy recognized the hotel where Emily's favorite shop was. It was where she and Don Summer had eaten dinner together.

Walking into the lobby, she was self-conscious, concerned that the worn and faded blue jeans and the white T-shirt of an unemployed pilot were conspicuous, even offensive. It was not a fine hotel really, only what had once been called a commercial hotel, but people there dressed better than this; and she felt awkward.

"On the left," Emily said as they walked through the lobby over maroon carpet that was worn and showed yellow in paths where the heaviest foot traffic went.

On the far side of the lobby was the entrance to the cocktail lounge where Nancy had sat at the bar with Don Sumner. Up a carpeted flight of stairs was the restaurant.

"Look in the window," said Emily. "You can see—"

"Emily! Inside! Inside quick!"

Nancy shoved in the door of the shop and rushed clumsily inside.

"What the hell . . . ?"

Nancy quickly stepped behind a rack of skirts, crouched, and stared through the window into the lobby.

"*Señora?*"

"Nancy?"

Nancy silenced the saleswoman and Emily with an angry wave of the arm. "Jesus *Christ,* the whole damned thing makes sense now. Emily, the pilot there. The one in the blue suit and cap."

Emily peered out, then nodded.

"That's Don Sumner. Forget clothes. We've got to move! Quick!"

Emily forced the car through traffic. "You want to explain?" she asked.

"Yeah. The man I saw in the hotel is the pilot who flew the German 747. The plane is gone. He's supposed to be gone." She paused and sighed loudly. "Or is it gone? Two days after the Deutsche Flugzeugwesen 747 flew away, a 747 landed carrying the markings of Corporación Aeronaves Santiago. What do you want to bet it's the same airplane?"

"This makes sense to *you,* I suppose."

"All kinds of sense. Maybe. I've got to get a look at that 747.

Also, why is Sumner going out of the hotel dressed like a captain? Is he flying tonight?"

"The whole deal is on again?"

"Might be," said Nancy. "We've got to get back to the embassy and pick up the locator transmitter. Then maybe there's some way I can get it onto that plane."

In traffic it took an hour to stop at the embassy and reach the airport. There again Emily shoved the BMW into an illegal parking place. Nancy told her to stay away from her, not to let anyone see they were together; then she hurried into the passenger terminal to see if the CAS 747 still held a gate.

It did. A flight board indicated that a charter for Rome would depart at 12:30. The counter was not manned. The gate was not staffed.

Nancy found a window where she could peer out at the 747. It was being prepared for takeoff. A restaurant-service truck was shoved up to the front of it, the body scissored up to the level of the principal passenger deck. But what was being loaded was not meals and beverages. Square paper boxes were being passed into the body of the airplane by a crew of sweating men. Nancy watched for a minute. Obviously there was an urgency about the loading.

Were they loading cargo little by little, through the galley door? It was an inefficient way to load cargo, but it was also inconspicuous.

The cockpit was lighted. She could see the flight crew at work, reaching for switches, pulling on handles, twisting knobs—going through their pre-takeoff checklist, from the look of it. She could not tell if the man in the left seat was Don Sumner.

As she watched, the food-service truck pulled away. In a few seconds another one replaced it, and the loading of cartons into the 747 continued.

Nancy glanced around. The terminal was crowded. It was the hour when flights departed for early-morning arrivals in Europe. People were lined up at the ticket counters. The flight boards indicated evening departures for Madrid, Rome, Paris, and London. Bogotá was not one of the world's major airports, but five or six 747s were at the gates, or imminently expected. There was money in Colombia, and it enabled people to fly off to European destinations.

Emily had come to the window too. She stared out and pretended not to notice Nancy.

"I've got to get aboard that plane," Nancy said suddenly, speaking in a low voice and not turning her head toward Emily.

Emily shook her head. "Crazy. You can't—"

"I've got to get the locator transmitter aboard," Nancy insisted. "Scott told me on the telephone that the virus keeps getting more sophisticated and that he's not confident he can keep blocking flights. If that 747 gets through and lands in the States . . . There's gotta be—what?—twenty-five *tons* of cocaine aboard. Or more."

"The transmitter—" Emily began to say.

Nancy interrupted. "The beep from that transmitter may be the only way our people can identify that 747 and get a fix on it. I've got to get it aboard if there's any way. And I think I know how I might be able to do it. Where . . . Where's a mop-and-broom closet? Help me find a service closet."

"This is crazy!" Emily said in a frantic whisper. "The service closets are usually someplace close to the rest rooms. Over there. To our left."

"Okay. Now, remember, you don't know me. Watch from a distance. If I don't get on and off that plane in ten minutes, go back to the embassy and get the word through to Washington as fast as you can."

"This is crazy," muttered Emily one more time.

Emily was right about where the service closet was. The second door in the little foyer that led into the women's room was the door to a closet for cleaning supplies. Nancy opened it and found herself facing shelves crowded with the usual—rolls of toilet paper, packages of paper towels, cartons of soap. On the floor stood two mops in big buckets, two push brooms, and a vacuum cleaner.

She grabbed the vacuum cleaner and a plastic bag of rags and polishes and walked toward the gate where the CAS plane was being loaded.

"*Señorita . . .*"

261

Emily walked up, gestured as if asking directions, then furtively shoved the S&W automatic into Nancy's hand.

Nancy nodded, pointed toward a gate with her left hand, turned away, and dropped the automatic into the cheap little canvas bag she carried for her handbag.

Carrying the vacuum cleaner and supplies, Nancy walked toward the gate opening to the 747. From five yards away Emily coughed loudly. Nancy turned around, supposing that cough was a warning.

It was. Two men and a woman strode with grim purpose toward the gate. Nancy put down her bag of cleaning supplies and opened it, pretending to focus her attention on its contents. She glanced as often as she dared at the approaching men and woman.

She knew two of them from the photos the FBI had supplied to the task-force office in Bethesda. One of the men was the Japanese, Yoshitaka Hara. And the woman . . . my god! The woman was Allison McGuire. They marched up to the door opening into the jetway.

That door was not entirely unwatched. As Hara and the woman and the third man, who was unknown to Nancy, walked through, a man appeared and greeted them. He pointed, and they walked on through the jetway.

Nancy moved over to Emily. What she had to say to her was important. She would have to risk their being seen together.

"You have to send word to Washington," she said. "Tell them that Yoshitaka Hara and Allison McGuire are aboard that 747—which makes it the rogue airplane, for sure. For damned sure. You understand?"

Emily walked away. Nancy carried the vacuum cleaner and bag of supplies toward the door to the jetway. The man stepped out and blocked her way.

"*Limpiadora,*" she said. A cleaner. She nodded at her vacuum cleaner. "*Ordenado.*" Ordered.

The man looked at her with an evil skepticism that tempted her to retreat. As his eyes surveyed her, they softened from antagonism to scorn. What harm could there be in this cleaning girl dressed in faded old jeans and carrying a vacuum cleaner and her rags? He shrugged, sneered, and stepped aside.

Nancy walked along the corridor to the open door at the front of the 747. Inside she saw what she had never seen before, because she had never been inside a 747 configured to carry cargo. The long fuselage stretched away to what seemed like a limitless distance—packed tight with boxes strapped into place.

It was as she had suspected. They had been loading their cargo through the galley door. Stacks of those square cartons stood in ranks along the sides of the endlessly long body of the 747. Its capacity was beyond imagining. It could have carried half a dozen large trucks, or twenty automobiles, maybe more, depending on how you loaded them.

And this one was packed with boxes.

Cocaine? Only one way to be sure.

She turned right and walked down the narrow aisle between the piles of strapped-in boxes. She used the Swiss army knife that was part of her kit to cut a hole in one of the cartons. Then she slit the plastic bag inside, near the top. She thrust her hand through the slit and withdrew it, white with fine powder.

Cocaine.

Cocaine, my god, how much of it? This one box contained a fortune, street value. The ranks of boxes along the extent of this huge airplane . . . A pandemic of addiction!

Crack! Reduced to crack . . . how much?

If there was a way to . . . Well, what would you do? Blow it up in midair? How did you destroy this much? How, other than by destroying the airplane?

She did what she could. She took the little steel box, the locator transmitter, from her bag, pushed the sliding switch that activated it, and shoved it between two cartons of cocaine—as far back between them as she could reach, so it was out of sight.

She returned along the narrow space between the boxes.

"Ho! Who you?"

"*Limpiadora*," she said, feigning calm, even boredom, but doubtful that was how she sounded.

The man who confronted her in the narrow aisle between the boxes was Yoshitaka Hara. He faced her with a small pistol in hand. "Don't give me that shit," he said in English. "Who are you, sister?"

"*Limpiadora,*" she insisted.

"Toss that handbag to me," he said. "Let's see."

Don Sumner shook his head. "Figured she was somethin' funny," he said. "What the hell. Couldn't quite figure it out."

Nancy sat in one of the luxurious, leather-covered seats in the first-class lounge on the top level of the 747. She was bound to the seat by a white nylon strap, one of the straps they had been using to fasten the boxes of cargo in place. It was tight around her waist, like a seat belt, and was knotted behind and below the seat, beyond her reach. She might have been able to squirm around and finally reach the knot if she had been alone, but she was confronted not just by Hara, but by half a dozen armed men, who were settling into the lounge and pouring themselves drinks. Their hostile stares were less frightening than their leers.

The woman Nancy had identified as Allison McGuire sat across from her smoking a cigarette and staring at her with open curiosity. Nancy wondered where Darius Whitney was and if he would come aboard before they took off. That was unlikely, as she thought about it. He would be in the States somewhere, injecting his virus into the ATC system.

"You damned sure she's what you say she is?" Sumner asked, frowning at Nancy.

"Had a pistol in her handbag," said Yoshitaka Hara. "Besides which, she had an airline ticket for Miami. Sort of unusual, don't you think—a cleaning woman with a loaded pistol and a ticket to Miami?"

The pilot frowned at her, obviously reviewing in his mind how much he had told her, what if anything she could have reported to whomever she worked for. "You speak English, then," he muttered.

She nodded.

Sumner glanced at his watch. "What are we gonna do with her?" he asked Hara.

"For right now she's going with us. There isn't time to take her out to the villa. I don't want to think about how we'd take her through the airport. She has to come with us. She won't learn anything she doesn't already know."

Sumner looked at the belt that bound her. "Make damned sure she doesn't get away from you," he said.

Ten minutes later the 747 was pushed back from the gate and taxied away from the terminal. Emily, who had waited in the airport, now went to a telephone and called the embassy. A message went out to Washington:

> FAA agent Delacorte aboard 747 that departed Bogotá 21.35 local time. Probably a prisoner. People identified as Oriental named Hara and woman named Allison also on board. Flight ostensibly bound for Rome but left three hours early and without passengers. Will try to obtain more information.

"But *what* damned 747? How was it marked? Did they file a flight plan for Rome? He's been in the air an hour. Where the hell is he now?"

Clutching the decoded message in his right hand, Scott slapped it into his left.

Admiral Buchanan put down a telephone. "Bogotá is saying no such departure. A flight for Rome departed at 20:40 local. None since. They say they had various 747 departures, none at 21:35."

"A nonflying civilian on the airport might have called it 21:35," said Scott, "when it was 21:00 or 22:00, depending on what our civilian thought was a departure time. But was that the time of pullback from the gate or the time of lift-off from the runway?"

"The closest they had was a 21:55 departure for Caracas. That was a charter flight."

"Is Caracas expecting it?"

"We're trying to find out."

"What about Atlantic Control?"

The admiral shrugged. "The air is full of traffic. Tell them what flight we're looking for, they'll tell us where it is."

Scott sighed. He paced the admiral's office. "Nancy said this afternoon there was no rogue 747 on the airport. She must have gone out there and . . . and found it. And got aboard!"

"I'm trying to get a scrambled call through to the agent who reported that Nancy went aboard. She called the embassy from the airport, and then she went home. They've called her in to get on the scrambler."

"She?"

"Another woman. Not the station chief. She's done good work, they say."

"Nancy went *aboard*! How could she?"

Darius Whitney had slept four hours. He got up and sauntered into the living room, stopping in the kitchen on the way to start a pot of coffee, but he found the pot already steaming and half-empty.

"Guess who?"

Stepan Yanak was standing in the doorway between the kitchen and the attached garage of the little house at Toiyabe Ranch.

"I'm your new baby-sitter," said Yanak. "The Spic is gone. The Señor sent me special."

Darius nodded. He spoke no greeting. He picked up a bottle of bourbon that sat on the counter, poured, and drank a small shot.

"Asleep," said Yanak scornfully. "I was about ready to roust you out of bed. Isn't it about time you got those computers up and running?"

"I've got plenty of time," said Darius.

"You screw up this time, you know what's gonna happen."

Darius poured himself a cup of coffee. "I can guess," he said wryly.

He went into the living room and sat down at one of the computers.

A lot of time. He had a lot of time yet. The dead screen, the dead keyboard, were somehow disheartening. How many years of his life had he sat staring at glass and plastic? Was the computer really a powerful spirit he had won to his side? Or was he the drudge who . . .

He remembered a movie he had seen: *Little Shop of Horrors.* Every day, at first, the boy had fed a carnivorous plant drops of his own blood. Then the growing carnivore—called Audrey II, wasn't it?—demanded more.

Was this damned machine Audrey III?

He reached for the power switch, then withdrew his hand, reluctant to bring the electronic imp to demanding life.

Click-click!

He looked up. Stepan Yanak stood behind him. He had just pulled the slide on an automatic, as ugly as himself, and he pointed it at Whitney's neck.

"What?"

"I just wanta make sure you understand the deal," said Yanak.

Whitney looked into the black round muzzle of the automatic. He was terrified, but it didn't make much difference. Anyway, the son of a bitch wouldn't dare shoot him now. Not before the 747 was on the ground.

"Put the popgun away," he said. "If you accidentally kill me, the señor will boil you in oil." His voice was thin and wavering, but that didn't make much difference either; the words were brave enough. "We may not get the 747 into the States this time either. But Cordero knows one thing for damned sure: You'll never get it in without me."

Yanak shoved the muzzle closer to Whitney's neck. "My orders are to tell you this is your last chance. If the 747 doesn't make it in this time, you are a dead man, Whitney."

"I figured that."

"So it's gonna make it this time?"

Whitney nodded. "And then you'll kill me anyway. When you talk to the señor again, tell him I figured that. And tell him it wouldn't be a good idea. Tell him Darius Whitney is not the fool he thinks he is."

Yanak pocketed the automatic and walked out of the room.

Whitney flipped the switch and activated the equipment. He had twenty-four hours, almost, to activate the virus in the ATC system. Until then he had something else important to do.

Cordero had given him the secret number of a bank account in Zurich and had told him there was $10 million in it. Darius had wondered if that was a real number, giving access to a real account, and if it really had money in it. Now he would find out. He had been working on a way of transferring that money out of the Zurich account.

Breaking into a Swiss number account was all but impossible. The computer couldn't do it, because the accounts weren't computer-managed. But a London bank, receiving electronic orders from a New York bank—or thinking that was what it was receiving—could withdraw the funds from a Swiss number account and put them in a London account. Provided only that it was given the secret number.

Now he would find out if the number Cordero had given him was real. To make it look like a legitimate transaction in securities, he wouldn't transfer all of the $10 million from the Zurich account. He was going to transfer an odd number—like $9,136,542.56. And even if that computer illiterate Yanak stood over him and watched, he would do it.

Stepan Yanak never looked. He sat down across the room with his coffee and a drink and ignored Darius.

They had flown only a short time—and without climbing to a very high altitude—when the 747 settled down to a gentle landing.

"Where are we?" Nancy asked Yoshitaka Hara.

The Japanese shook his head.

But when the engines were shut down, Don Sumner came back into the lounge, and he was ready enough to talk. He said they had landed in Caracas. Everyone might as well try to sleep, he said. He was going to. They would be there a while.

He sat down in one of the leather-covered seats, and Hara handed him a cup of coffee.

"Well, you're not Idelia-the-Skyhawk-pilot," he said to her. He looked to Hara. "Have you found out who she is?"

"I haven't pressed the question," said Hara.

"I'll tell you," she said. She twisted her body to straighten her back. The constraining strap held her rather rigidly in one position, and she was beginning to suffer some pain in her muscles and spine. "My name is Nancy Delacorte. I'm an agent with the Security Division of the Federal Aviation Administration. Recently I've been assigned to the Presidential Task Force on Airline Safety."

"Under Captain Vandenberg," said Hara.

"Exactly," she said. "And you are Yoshitaka Hara."

"How do you know?"

"I've seen the pictures of you that they're going to put up in post offices," she said. She nodded at the woman. "Yours, too, Allison McGuire."

Hara nodded. "The information won't do you much good," he said.

"I'm probably in as good a position as you are," she said. "I'm aboard this flight by accident. Don's on it because he's the pilot. Your gunmen have their assignments, I've no doubt. But you, Hara, and you, McGuire, why are you aboard?"

"I'm in command," said Hara.

"Sure you are. If this plane gets shot down by interceptors, you're going down with it. If it crashes trying to land on some airport where it shouldn't be, you'll be aboard. And if it has to turn back like the other flights that tried this game, you . . ." She nodded toward the gunmen. "I'm surprised Whitney's not here. I guess he has to be on the ground in the States to do his dirty work."

"Nancy," said Sumner, "you talk too much."

She snapped her head around toward him. "What do you think's going to happen to you?" she asked.

"Has anybody offered the lady a drink?" asked Sumner.

Hara shrugged. "Why not?"

"Can you make a martini?" she asked.

"Of course. Tanqueray?"

"Beefeater, if you have it."

Sumner went to the window and looked down at a ground crew working around the outside of the 747. Bill Aridas, his co-pilot, was out there talking with them. They would top off the fuel tanks and charge that damned hydraulic cylinder again. They would be on the ground six hours, roughly. He wanted top pressure; then he'd check it again just before they took off.

"Is anybody going to tell me where we're hauling this load of poison?" Nancy asked.

Sumner smiled at her. "Be more fun to guess," he said. His smile became a grin. "I was dumb not to see through your act. Baby, you don't look like an airport bum, no matter how you try to play the role."

Emily Greenhouse was on the scrambler phone.

"She saw the pilot. That's what excited her. She saw the pilot of the 747. He had told her he was flying away, and the next morning the 747 was gone from the field, but there he was, walking out of the hotel. We drove to the airport. The 747 wasn't there. That got Nancy interested in another 747. She decided it was probably loaded with cocaine. She picked up a vacuum cleaner and was going to go aboard as a cleaner. Then she spotted the Oriental man and that woman named Allison. She said she was sure that plane was loaded with cocaine. Anyway she went aboard. I don't know what she told the security man, probably that she was supposed to clean inside the airplane. I waited for her to come out, and she never did. The flight crew went aboard, and some other men, and the plane was pulled back and went. It took off."

"How was that plane marked?" Scott asked.

"I don't know. I couldn't see it. It was out there in the dark. It was supposed to be a flight for Rome, according to what was on the board at the gate. Charter, I think. Anyway, not a regular airline."

"Okay. Your report said the plane took off at nine thirty-five. Did you see it take off?"

"No. I could see planes taking off, but out there in the dark I couldn't distinguish one from another, particularly since I never saw the markings on that 747. I allowed ten minutes for taxiing out and so on. It backed away from the gate at nine twenty-five, so I reported it took off at nine thirty-five."

"It could be there yet," Scott suggested.

A moment of silence on the scrambler. Then, hesitantly, "It could be."

"Can you find out?"

Another moment of silence. "I have to be careful. I'm not supposed to blow my cover. Someone else can go look. I couldn't ask questions in the airport, you know. I mean, that would have blown my cover for sure. If that airplane was what Nancy thought it was . . . you understand?"

"Right."

"Once she went inside that airplane, I couldn't do anything more for her. But you have to know something. She was carrying an airline ticket for Miami. For her morning flight. And I slipped her a pistol before she went into the airplane. If they found those on her, her cover's blown. She was carrying the locator radio. That's why she took the risk of going aboard, to hide the radio somewhere on the airplane."

Admiral Buchanan had accompanied Scott to the offices in Bethesda, and they were there at 12:30 AM. He had agreed that, for the time being, that office made a better command post than his office in the Pentagon, because of its computer equipment and personnel. Everyone—the civilian staff of Vandenberg & Associates as well as Hal Miller and the other technicians hired for the task force—was on duty. The admiral had also brought along a small team of communications technicians to give him and Scott access to scrambled telephones and radio communication with ATC and North American Radar Defense—NORAD.

The President had been notified at eleven o'clock that another attempt on the nation's air security seemed likely to occur within the next eighteen to twenty-four hours.

"I'm willing to make an assumption," said Scott to Admiral Buchanan and Hal Miller. "They'll come in the same way, toward New York. They've located an airport they think they can use. There aren't that many in the country—not many that can take in a 747, I mean. And this mystery airplane has got to come down someplace where it won't be immediately surrounded by law-enforcement people."

"Buckley reported again—the FAA guy who's checking airports," said Miller. He shook his head. "Nothing new."

"Otis Air Force Base has ninety-five hundred feet of runway," said Admiral Buchanan. "But it's an Air Force base. With Air Police. Suffolk County, on Long Island, has nine thousand. But it's in the middle of a heavy concentration of population. Quonset

271

State is right on the edge of Providence. Brainard is on the edge of Hartford."

"I thought about Stewart Air Force Base," said Scott. "There's plenty of runway for a 747. That's where they landed the Iranian hostages. But it's an Air Force base."

"Sir," said Miller to Scott. "I've been thinking about that plane. They need ten thousand feet, but pilots say they can put it down on six in an emergency. Suppose you were going to put one down and literally stand it on its nose with the reverse thrusters and brakes. I mean, bust the nose gear. Slide 'er. Maybe skid off the end of the runway. With what they're carrying, they can probably afford to bend a 747. It may be that they'll—"

"It may be," said Scott, "that they can land on some obscure little country airport. Is that what you're suggesting?"

Miller nodded.

"Okay. But they've made arrangements somewhere. They have to unload and scram, damned quick. I'd guess they're going to try to take over some airport. Temporarily. That takes some planning and preparation. So, I'd guess they're going to try to reach the same airport they were trying to reach before."

"I think you're right," said Admiral Buchanan. "But I wouldn't want to bet the store on it."

"I propose we move out to Ronkonkoma in the morning," said Scott. "New York Center. We'll have to cover other possibilities, like Miami, but I'm betting they come in from the northeast again."

Admiral Buchanan nodded. He spoke to Miller. "Any sign of an attempt to inject the virus?"

Miller shook his head. "We're pretty well covered, but I've started to believe the virus is already in the system and has been in for some time. All Whitney has to do is activate it. It's defying our best efforts to locate it."

"Keep looking, Chief," said the Admiral. "You two will excuse me. I'm going to check with my communications men."

"Yes, sir," said Miller respectfully. He glanced at Scott. "One more thing. The meteorology. The forecast is for a low ceiling tomorrow night. With rain. Trying to bring in a 747 without an instrument landing system . . ." He shook his head.

Scott dropped wearily into a chair. "Hal, I can't kid myself. I don't see any way Nancy is going to make it."

"The forecast can change before tomorrow night," said Miller quietly, his face grim.

"Sure," said Scott. "But if they come the way they came before, off the North Atlantic and onto the approach for Kennedy, what's the chance of a midair? A radar-invisible airplane entering the world's busiest air traffic. If they get through that, then they try to land on a short runway, in rotten weather. And let's assume it all works. Then . . ." He shook his head.

"Captain, there are a whole lot of possibilities."

Scott nodded. "Among which is the possibility they'll kill her. I mean, shoot her. Maybe they already have."

"I know you love her, sir . . . Scott," Miller whispered. "I wish there was something more I could do."

"You're doing the best things you can, Hal," said Scott. "Apart from plugging away, keeping at it, looking for that damned virus . . . apart from that, you're a good friend. I'm grateful to you."

Miller put a hand on Scott's shoulder. "Some way it'll work out."

Cecily Brockton-Browne had been at work an hour and was beginning to think of taking a break.

She frowned over the screen. Here was an odd one. Allied Industrial Bank in New York was asking Bank of the City, here in London, to transfer some funds from a number account in Zuricher Handelsbank to a new account to be opened here—the money to be transferred on to New York later apparently. Well, nothing unusual. Some American with hidden assets wanting to begin to recover them. Maybe he was actually going to pay his taxes.

To establish an account in the name of Mr. McMurtry. Mr. James McMurtry.

What was unusual was that the confidential number was in the order, right there on her screen. It might represent an opportunity to lay hands on a nice piece of money for herself. It would also represent an opportunity to spend a lot of time in the nick.

The amount in Swiss francs was Fr 63,874,911. She punched the secret number in, together with the codes to order the transfer.

The green numbers glowed on the screen. She checked them. They were correct. She sent the order.

She sat back and puffed for a moment on her cigarette while she waited for Zurich to respond.

Within three minutes Zuricher Handelsbank acknowledged the order and confirmed the transfer. Mr. James McMurtry now had an account in Bank of the City with more than five and three-quarters of a million pounds in it.

She left her station and went to pick up a cup of tea.

An hour and a half out of Caracas—about 7:00 A.M. Washington time—Sumner at last lifted the nose of the 747 and began the long climb to 33,000 feet. He had flown at a low altitude, wasting fuel, and in thick clouds and rain, all the way across Colombia and Venezuela; and now as he crossed the coastline over the Gulf of Paria, just west of Trinidad, he also made a sharp course change, to the north, which would carry him over the Windward Islands.

"Check that hydraulic pressure," he said to the flight engineer.

"Holding," said the engineer. "Hasn't slipped a pound."

"Fuel?"

"As planned."

The 747 climbed out of the clouds and into a wide-open sunlit day. The cloud cover seemed to be clinging to the continent behind them. It was broken to the north, then clear, and soon they could see the islands: Grenada, Saint Vincent, Saint Lucia, and Martinique.

Over Martinique, Sumner turned northeast. He was in radio contact with the ground now. He activated a flight plan he had filed by radio just after leaving Caracas. To the controllers he was a charter flight out of Caracas, carrying 357 vacationers to the Canary Islands and later on to Madrid and Rome.

In the first-class passenger lounge Nancy twisted uneasily under the nylon strap that held her to her seat. Of course she couldn't sleep. The others dozed, but none of them really slept. The tension was palpable and oppressive.

Hara and a couple of the gunmen had gone back down to the main deck of the airplane, where the cargo was.

She wondered if Scott knew she was on this plane. She wondered if he knew where it was and if he had any idea where it was going.

She had broken a promise to him. Coming aboard this 747 was exactly the kind of heroics she had promised him she would avoid. She could take satisfaction, though, in having planted the transmitter. If Emily had gotten word to the States, they would be monitoring the frequency. This plane might be invisible to radar, but the beep off that little transmitter would identify and locate it just as effectively.

Scott loved her. She loved him. She'd had no doubt about it for a long time. In the midst of everything that had happened since they fell in love, it had been difficult to find time to focus on each other. They had done it in fleeting moments. Now she had time to think about it—now, when the chances seemed heavily weighted against her ever seeing him again.

She wanted to live. More than ever before, she wanted to live.

But suddenly she felt the muzzle of a pistol pressed to her cheek. She looked up. It was Hara. He held the pistol in his right hand and the little locator transmitter in his left.

17

—❚-❚-❚-❚—

About 4:30 A.M. Hal Miller finally went to sleep, sitting in his chair in front of a computer. Scott Vandenberg saw him slump forward and for an instant was alarmed, until he heard Hal start to snore. Others were sleeping in the office, at their desks, one young woman on the floor. Admiral Buchanan and his technicians had left, ostensibly to arrange to move the Presidential-Task-Force headquarters to Garden City, Long Island, in the morning, more likely to get a few hours' sleep. When Miller finally fell asleep, he left Scott alone, still desperately studying every element of the ATC system program, still searching for the elusive virus.

He had scanned the printout sheets. During the last few hours he had entered the system and scanned screen after screen of the program code. Darius Whitney was a devil! A native genius. And maybe the most dangerous man in the world right now. If he could do this . . .

Scott shook off those thoughts and refocused on the screen in front of him. He reached for coffee. What was in his cup was cold. No matter. Coffee had begun to burn his stomach.

Coffee. Nancy loved it. Real coffee with all its caffeine. She liked everything real, in fact. No decaf coffee. No light beer. A stiff drink now and then. Rare beef. Bacon and eggs. Tough, emotional music. She liked challenging contemporary art. She had loved to drive the Porsche, and to swim. With her, pretending at life was not good enough. Only really living it.

And maybe she had died because she wouldn't be faced down, not by death any more than by life.

Or maybe she was alive. And if she was, her best chance of staying alive was somewhere in these infuriating screens of code.

He sighed. He stared. He flexed his shoulders and rubbed his eyes. Whitney had hidden . . . but wait a minute! If you couldn't find Whitney, could you flush him out?

"Hal. Chief. Wake up, man! Listen!"

Miller had not been sleeping soundly and was quickly awake and alert.

"Listen . . ." said Scott, his voice hoarse but rising with enthusiasm. "Look. Whitney is going to enter the system sometime today or tonight, to look for an unused transponder code. Right? I mean, his 747 will be approaching on a fake flight plan, using a transponder code Whitney lifts from the flight-plan data in the system computers. Right?"

"That's how he did it before," said Miller.

"All right. So he's going to be prowling around in the flight plans looking for a transponder code he can use. Okay, suppose we put in a message for him."

"Saying what?"

"Telling him that Allison McGuire is aboard the 747. I bet he doesn't know that. And I bet what Morgenstern told us is true: that Darius and Allison are lovers."

Miller frowned. "Supposing all that is true, what good does this message do us?"

Scott sighed. "Maybe none," he said, his enthusiasm ebbing. "But we're not getting anywhere with anything else we're doing."

"You have to figure the guys who are using Whitney will be watching him," said Miller. "They'll read the message too."

"We encode it," said Scott. "Put it in some form a computer-oriented person like Whitney will recognize and can read—and nobody else can."

"Assuming the people who are watching him can't read it," said Miller skeptically.

"Chief, you've been around computers and computer types so long you assume everybody is computer-oriented. Look—To Admiral Buchanan these sheets of source code are so much gibberish. They would be to Nancy also."

"What code?" asked Miller.

"Something simple," said Scott. "ASCII." He meant the American Standard Code for Information Interchange, a code that makes it possible for computers, which deal only with numbers, to read and write letters and symbols. "What you bet he can read it without a table?"

"It's worth trying," said Miller. "Let's write the message."

Scott nodded. "We'll write a short one first, one he can read and translate without having to copy it off—because he may not have a printer beside his computer. Then . . . a longer message."

Miller nodded. "Like, 'DW. AM is on 747.' Something like that."

"Good enough," said Scott. "In ASCII that's . . ."

Miller wrote it out:

68 87 46 65 68 73 83 79 78 55 52 55 46

Scott wrote a longer message: Whitney. Allison is on 747 with cocaine. Danger. Where will it land?

Miller wrote the ASCII code:

87 72 73 84 78 69 89 46 65 76 76 73 83 79 78 73 83
79 78 55 52 55 87 73 84 72 67 79 67 65 73 78 69 46
68 65 78 71 69 82 46 87 72 69 82 69 87 73 76 76 73
84 76 65 78 68 63

"Let's put a signature on it," said Miller, and he wrote, "Vandenberg":

86 65 78 68 69 78 66 69 82 71

"Chief," said Scott. "I don't know if this will do any good at all. But it's worth trying. We have to suppose he will be looking for a transponder code three or four hours before that plane is due on the East Coast. He won't try to come in before dark. Just to be safe, let's load this code into the flight-information display about four o'clock this afternoon. Okay?"

"Okay. What are we going to do about warning controllers that this code means nothing to their work?"

"They're smart enough to figure that out," said Scott. "But then you'll have to monitor the information display every minute, looking for Whitney coming back with a message. I'm going to Ronkonkoma. I'll ask you to stay here and watch for that message."

"Let's pray we get one," said Miller.

The Aeronaves Santiago 747 was about four hours out of Caracas and over the mid-Atlantic.

Nancy had managed to sleep a little. Sumner and Hara had removed the strap from around her middle. Instead they had looped and knotted nylon cords around her wrists and then to the arms of the seat, giving her enough slack to move her hands a little though not enough to bring them together. Then they had knotted the loose ends of the cords around the legs of the seat to make it impossible for her to untie any of the knots. She could change positions and had been far less uncomfortable the last three or four hours.

Allison McGuire looked as though she were sleeping. Nancy knew she wasn't. She was just keeping her eyes closed and dwelling on her thoughts, which were doubtless somber.

Nancy was a little surprised they hadn't hurt her when they discovered she had planted the locator transmitter. Hara simply didn't care, since he'd found it; and Sumner rather admired her for it. In fact they had suspected from the moment they caught her that she had brought a locator aboard, Hara said. She couldn't have come on this airplane just to see if it was carrying cocaine; she had to know that. The transmitter wouldn't make any difference until they approached their destination airport, so he had not begun to search for it until they left Caracas. He didn't think it would be hard to find, and it hadn't been. It would be near the carton she cut open, he said—if not actually inside it.

Awake now, she looked out the window. The Atlantic stretched away to the horizon, confronting the high-flying aircraft with a steely, blue-gray glint. The sun was to the right. They were flying east. Or northeast. To Europe.

Why?

She didn't know why. If she survived, she would learn why. If she didn't, then it didn't make any difference.

Then nothing would make any difference. Scott would mourn her. This wasn't what they had planned. Nothing like this. Life cut short. Scott left alone.

She signed and looked out the window again, trying to control the dread that threatened to overpower her.

"Hara," she said a few minutes later. She had noticed him looking at her. "Hara, I've got to go to the ladies' room."

Yoshitaka Hara nodded and spoke to one of the gunmen in Spanish, telling him to untie her. He himself opened the door of the head, looking in as if to assure himself she could not find a weapon in there.

"Allison," he said. "Stand in the door and watch her."

Nancy rose from the seat. Her legs were weak. Her feet were swollen. Her hands were tingly from the constriction around her wrists.

"Leave the door open," Hara said. "We won't stare."

They didn't. But they glanced in past Allison. All of them.

When she sat down in her seat again, they put the strap around her waist again. It wasn't so tight this time. Hara offered her orange juice, pastries, and coffee.

He spoke to her. "You say you've seen a photograph of me. You said it would be put up in post offices. Surely that is your little joke."

"The FBI is on your case," she told him. "Your suite in Las Vegas has been under surveillance for almost two months."

She saw fear distort the man's face. She wished her confidence in what she had just said were as well founded as his shock. If the FBI was doing what it had done before, it had relaxed surveillance as soon as it knew Hara was out of the country. But he didn't know that. So he had something to think about.

Hara sat down beside her. "Why am I wanted by the FBI?" he asked quietly.

"Whitney has been charged with serious computer crimes."

"I know. But I—"

"He has used your suite in Las Vegas, your equipment, and your telephone lines."

"How much do you know?" he asked.

"Personally?"

"The government."

"Just about the whole deal, I'd guess," she said.

He nodded sorrowfully. "I'm as much trapped in this plane as you are," he muttered under his breath, but loudly enough that she could hear.

Nancy stared at him curiously. She nodded cynically. " 'Had I but served God as diligently as I have served the King, he would not have given me over in my gray hairs,' " she said.

"Wolsey," said Hara. " 'Do not place your trust in kings.' "

"The quotation you have in mind is, 'No reliance can be placed on the friendship of kings,' which is even more apropos."

Hara shook his head. "Señor Cordero would know both quotations," he said. "And will have considered the wisdom of them in his calculations."

"Tough man," she said.

"Shrewd," said Hara. "And ruthless."

"Where are we landing?" she asked.

"Tenerife," he said. "Canary Islands."

"Then back across."

"Yes. And then comes the dangerous part."

In mid-afternoon in the Bronx a slight but muscular man dressed in black pants and a white vest undershirt stood at the grimy window of a third-floor room and watched the commerce on the sidewalk across the street. Wholesale and retail. To all kinds of people. It was amazing how varied they were. And how many.

Crack. Five years ago no one would have believed a whole new industry, a whole new commerce, could grow so fast. What else had grown like this? Computers? Nothing like. A kid on the street could make a hundred thousand dollars in a year. And kids were doing it right down there, right now, retail. The wholesalers . . . good god, the money!

It involved risk, yes. Risk and danger. But that was manageable. That was *his* job: to manage the risk, to minimize the danger.

Except today when he had to go out to Connecticut again. It made him nervous; it made the men who worked with him nervous—to drive up Interstate 95, away from the city, out to a different kind of country, where people were different, hostile, suspicious, and they would be conspicuous.

And this operation was dangerous.

He'd scouted it. He'd rehearsed it in his mind a hundred times. He'd rehearsed it with the others a dozen times. Then they'd gone out to try it and had been called off at the last minute. They'd had explosives in place. They'd been ready to go! In a few more minutes . . . then they'd got the word to call it off, and they'd had to disconnect everything and haul it away. Timing. If they hadn't got the word in time, they'd have set off the charges, and the operation would have been botched beyond ever putting it together again.

The only thing he had against the bosses was that to them everything looked so goddamned easy: Just go out and do it. Just go throw a rope around the moon and pull it down. How could it be difficult?

"Alfredo. *Todo listo.*" Everything was ready.

He turned away from the window, picked up the white shirt he had hung over a chair so it would not be wet and stained with sweat before they left, and walked out of the squalid room.

They had two new Ford vans. New cars would be less noticeable in Connecticut. Every man was well dressed. That was one of the things that was frightening about driving out through Westchester County and on up into Connecticut—that the police might stop you just because they didn't like the look of you. He hated Connecticut. He would never go back again after tonight.

Scott stood in the middle of the big control room of New York Center. He had arrived later than he had meant to. At six this morning Admiral Buchanan had given him a direct order to get a few hours sleep. Nothing much could happen before late afternoon or early evening, and then Scott would need to be alert and efficient, the admiral had said. They would wake him if anything developed.

Scott had stretched out on a cot and slept a little, on and off, but his sleep was filled with nightmares of what was happening to Nancy—what may have already happened.

Miller woke him at ten-thirty with the word that nothing had happened but that Admiral Buchanan had ordered breakfast, which was waiting on a table in the computer room. The Navy had entered his room in the safe motel and had brought him a change of clothes: a summer-weight khaki uniform, with a captain's eagles on the collar and a cap with scrambled eggs on the visor. Scott had eaten, then shaved, before they left for Garden City.

A man walked up to him. "Captain Vandenberg. We've met. The night before Thanksgiving, last year."

"I'm sorry."

"Oh, don't worry. You wouldn't remember me. In fact I wouldn't recognize you after just that short meeting, except that someone just now pointed you out to me. I'm Leighton Drake. I'm the senior FAA man here. It isn't my shift, but I thought it would be a good night to be here."

Scott did remember Leighton Drake, now that he was reminded. The gray man, a professional civil servant, had watched the nation's air-traffic system disintegrate the night the virus attacked LANCE.

"What's coming in tonight, Mr. Drake? Anything look unusual?"

Drake shook his head. "The usual traffic for a Thursday night in July. It'll be heavy. And the weather is deteriorating. One of those nights that separates the men from the boys—both in the cockpits and in the control towers."

"What about charters?"

"Lots of them coming into Kennedy and Newark. Coming in from Rome, Athens, Vienna, Paris, London . . ."

"Lisbon?"

"Lisbon. Madrid. Tenerife. Marrakech. Shannon."

"Are all those 747s?"

"Two-thirds of them. Height of the tourist season. Most of them will be turning around and going back."

"What about that weather?"

"Did you see it developing as you came in? We're going to have a beast. Thunderbumpers. Rain. Minimums."

A young woman came up. "Captain . . . Telephone. Bethesda."

Scott hurried to a telephone in a small office off the main floor of the center. Hal Miller was calling.

"For a minute we had an anomaly in the ATC system," said Miller. "I thought we might be looking at Whitney activating the virus. And maybe he did. But I still can't find it."

"Run the Whitney detector," said Scott. "Crude as it is, it might work."

"You think so? My impression is, he's quit doing Whitneys."

"I don't know," said Scott. "I suspect a man's design habits are like his fingerprints—they never change, no matter how hard he tries to disguise them. Anyway, if you're right and he's in, we have a new chance to try the Whitney detector."

"It'll take a while," said Miller. "Besides, if it's in there now, it's wholly inactive. Finding it—"

"What else are we doing?" asked Scott. "Anyway we may get a reprieve. The weather is going down and down."

"I noticed that," said Miller. "Puts another impediment in their way, doesn't it?"

"And another hazard in ours," said Scott, "if they decide to make a 747 radar-invisible in the New York traffic."

"Will you be calling course and altitude changes the way you did before?"

"Chief, I don't see how I can. With all that traffic out there in the murk—I don't see how I can."

"Then military radar won't be much help. It was that divergence between what was seen by ATC radar and what was seen by military radar that identified the bogie last time."

"It's hard to think they'll try it in the weather that's closing in," Scott said.

"Wishful thinking," said Miller.

"Have you put in the ASCII message for Whitney?"

"Actually that's why I was calling you. You ready to go with that now?"

Scott glanced at his watch. "In thirty minutes. Okay?"

"You got it," said Miller.

* * *

The 747 sat on the ramp at Tenerife, Canary Islands, and Don Sumner climbed the steps from the main cabin to the lounge and flight deck. He tossed his cap on one of the seats and ran his hand around the perimeter of his scalp, where the thin remnant of his hair remained. He had just returned from the terminal, where he had made a telephone call to Virgilio Cordero in Bogotá.

He glared at Yoshitaka Hara and shook his head. "Maybe *you* oughta go in and call Cordero," he said. "Maybe he'll listen to you."

"On what subject?" asked Hara.

"I've got the New York weather," said Sumner. "They're talking minimums. Do you know what that means? Not only am I expected to perform a feat of airmanship that in other circumstances would get a man a trophy; I'm now expected to do it in low cloud and rain. Besides which . . ." He paused and shook his head again. "Besides which, when this son of a bitch goes invisible, it's gonna be *really* invisible. I mean, in VFR conditions the pilots of other planes at least have a chance of seeing you, plus you have a chance of seeing them. But we're going off the radar scopes, and we'll be out there in traffic, in weather where you can't see your wingtips. On top of everything else, we're now going to face the real possibility of a midair!"

"And if the other plane happened to be another 747," said Nancy, "that would mean four hundred people or more."

Hara looked around at the gunmen, eight of them. They were listening. Some of them understood English.

"Would the Señor listen to you?" Sumner asked Hara.

"*Their* orders," said Hara, shifting his eyes toward the solemn enforcers Cordero had sent along, "are to make sure you fly this operation. No matter what. He said he's heard all the excuses he's going to hear. Including from me. No, he won't listen to me. And I don't think they'll let you leave the plane again."

"You guys'll be killed, too, if we screw up," said Sumner to the gunmen.

One of them, a man with steel-gray hair sternly combed, and gold teeth, shook his head. "You not screw up," he said. "Not

285

when you go down with rest of us. Señor say you might try chicken out."

Hara spoke to Sumner and to Nancy. "Cordero thinks Whitney has betrayed him. He—"

"Maybe he's right," Sumner interrupted. "That's something else Cordero mentioned. Maybe you'll know what this means. A Swiss bank account. It's empty. All but."

"He's always been smarter than any of you thought he was," said Allison bitterly.

Hara scratched his head, and a faint smile broke his somber mien. "That old bastard! He found a way to get into that account without going to Zurich!"

"Well, he didn't do *us* any good," said Sumner. "I'd say Cordero is hysterical right now."

The senior gunman didn't like that. He slapped the pistol in his holster. "You fly airplane, Sumner," he said. "Take good care of your life and mine, okay?"

"Peligroso," grunted the fat man. Dangerous. *"Estúpido."*

The fat woman who was watching him hook up the equipment shook her head. She glanced at her watch. It was four o'clock. She said what they were ordered to do was dangerous, maybe, but not stupid. They didn't get stupid orders. Anyway they would abandon the place and be gone from Hempstead, Long Island, long before anyone reacted. After all, no one was going to send a SWAT team with screaming sirens just because a short string of Morse code momentarily interrupted the inane music and chatter on a broadcast station.

That was what was ordered. The fat man couldn't wait until the station went off the air, as he had done before. Tonight he had to override the broadcast station and transmit the transponder number to the incoming 747. His Morse code beeps would sound over any music or talk on the station at that hour. Anyone who could read code could read the number, but it wouldn't make any difference; no one would understand its significance. Anyway that was what he was ordered to do.

He put on his earphones and punched a number into the telephone.

"Yanak."

"Hempstead. Is okay?"

"Everything's okay. Just be ready for my call. Don't let the old woman talk on this line. How's the weather look?"

"Looks bad. Raining."

"The equipment tested?"

"Tested."

"Okay. I'll call you about half an hour before we need you, to be sure you're awake. Be on the ball."

The man on the other end hung up.

The fat man looked at his wife. "Yanak . . ." he grunted. "*Yanak me cae en la nuca.*" Yanak gives me a pain in the neck.

"*Mal tiempo,*" said a truck driver to Alfredo. "*Tengo miedo de la tempestada.*" Bad weather. A frightening storm.

Alfredo looked at the sky. A storm was developing. Thunder rolled behind some of the thick gray clouds.

"You'll have to speak English tonight," he said to the driver. "Not all these men understand Spanish."

The driver shrugged and glanced scornfully at some of the men.

"We'll eat here." They had made their rendezvous at a truck stop with a diner. "Everything will be the same at the airport."

"I hope is not," said the driver.

Alfredo allowed a smile. "Tonight the airplane will land," he said.

"I hope."

"Yes. No drinking. Everybody will have to move fast. And smart."

The driver glanced again at the men standing in the rain around his four trucks. "I no like some of them much," he said.

"We'll take care of that when we have to," said Alfredo.

"Uhmm . . . *Sí.*"

Sumner frowned over his chart. Well, some things worked out. He'd had a little luck anyway. A rotten-looking low swirling over the Azores made his unusual northerly route from Tenerife to New York a reasonable choice. Otherwise, someone might have wondered just why he was swinging up to 45° to make this crossing.

Turning west, he had a place in the flow. There were other 747s out there, to his right mostly, a few to his left. They were streaming toward New York and Boston, into deteriorating weather. The difference was, *they* were going to land on airports with ten-thousand-foot runways, with full instrument-landing systems, while he was going to put this 747 down on five thousand feet, on a runway without strobe lighting and barely wide enough to take the wheels of a 747.

The other point was, would the Colombians back there kill him as soon as he shut down the engines? And his crew? And what about the woman?

His money was on deposit. He knew that. It was in half a dozen banks, from Savannah to Des Moines. They couldn't get at it. Only he could withdraw it. But how much difference did two million bucks make to this crowd? They were sacrificing a 747. If he didn't bend it, it would be confiscated by the feds. So what difference did another two million make? The gunmen already had their orders—kill him or not kill him. They knew. He would find out.

Hours of utter boredom punctuated by moments of sheer terror.

"He *can't* come in tonight, Captain," said Peter Langostina. He was the shift supervisor who had worked with Scott the night the 747 turned back to Halifax.

It was after six o'clock. You couldn't see the weather from inside the closed precincts of New York Center, but Scott had stepped outside half a dozen times in the past two hours, staring nervously at the low overcast and the drizzle.

He and Langostino had charts spread out before them on a large table and were looking at airports. "He's going to have a six-hundred-foot ceiling, rain, gusty wind," said Langostino. "That limits a 747 to New York, Boston—"

Scott picked up a telephone and talked to Philip Broughton at the FAA office in Washington, where he would remain on duty until this situation was resolved. He asked him to increase security on the likely airports.

Turning to Langostina, whose statement he had interrupted by picking up the phone, Scott said, "That's assuming he's coming in where we've got this weather. Maybe I've guessed wrong. Maybe he's coming into Florida or Texas . . . or California."

Langostina looked at his watch. "The heavy traffic will be making the landfall about now. Newfoundland. And thereabouts. If your 747 is in the stream, you should see some evidence of him pretty soon."

"If we see any evidence of him at all," said Scott. "If he isn't sneaking in without our seeing him."

"That idea frightens me half to death," said Langostina. "As that traffic converges on Boston and New York, separation diminishes. We won't have planes wingtip to wingtip, but having an invisible aircraft in that traffic is a terrifying prospect."

Admiral Buchanan was in New York Center, having established a temporary office in what was ordinarily the staff canteen. Scott spoke with him. "We should have an aircraft available so we can make a quick flight to whatever airport is involved tonight—assuming it is an airport in this area."

"I'm one ahead of you," said the admiral. "We've got two Lears ready, also a pair of helicopters. On MacArthur Airport. Also, we've got a police escort standing by to take us there."

"We may need a combat team."

The admiral nodded. "Waiting on MacArthur Airport."

Ten minutes later Hal Miller called from Bethesda. "I'm looking at a couple of Whitneys, Captain. A couple of Whitney signatures. In the ATC system. What's more, they look like stray programming. I can't see any function they have in the system."

"What if you erase them?" Scott asked.

"Well . . . They might be something useful. I'm a little nervous about tinkering with the system at a heavy-traffic hour."

"They could be the code that calls out his main program when he activates it," said Scott.

"Yes, they could be that."

"Keep watching it," said Scott. "You may be looking at the key."

When Scott put down the telephone, Admiral Buchanan asked for an explanation.

"The program we developed to look for characteristic Darius Whitney problem-solving has come up with what we're calling Whitneys," said Scott. "It may mean nothing. It may mean we're beginning to find him. Miller knows where to look anyway. I doubt if the virus has been activated yet. It's hiding somewhere. Right now we've got just a couple of Whitneys. If a dozen more show up in the next hour, we'll know the virus has been called out and activated."

The first time they tried to bring a 747 into the New York area unseen, Darius Whitney had worked with a portable computer in an apartment not far from New York Center. This time he was working with the more complete equipment in the house at Toiyabe Ranch. He would have better control in case something began to go wrong.

The sun was still brilliant over the mountains and desert outside Las Vegas.

"Now what?" asked Yanak aggressively.

Yanak had been drinking more than he usually did, Darius noticed. Yanak said it calmed his nerves. It made him louder anyway.

On the screens of two computers Darius Whitney was displaying the traffic analysis New York Center was seeing—not a radar image but a list of incoming flights: estimated times of arrival, arrival routes, altitudes, speeds, transponder codes.

"It's getting heavy," said Darius. "Look at it. That's the incoming evening traffic."

"Has our boy shown up?"

"Not yet. He's coming in on the tail end of it."

"Because he wants darkness," said Yanak.

Darius glanced at another screen. "Some airports are doing hourly byte counts on their radar digitalizers," he said.

"You're active? The virus is in there and ready to run?"

"Of course," said Darius. "It's hiding, waiting for the call. I won't activate it until absolutely necessary."

Yanak nodded and walked out of the room. "I'm going to check New York," he said. "Some of our guys there have been getting nervous during the afternoon."

While Yanak talked to someone on the East Coast, Darius turned to another computer and read the results from the program that monitored the New York and Boston digitalizers for byte checks. Hourly was as often as they could do, wasn't it? What if they—?

Yanak returned. "Weather. Weather, weather, weather! You know what those idiots in New York want me to do? Call Bogotá and get authority to scrub the operation again! If I called and said that, the señor would—Jesus! Is everything okay? We don't have a hell of a lot of time."

"I won't activate till I have to, till I absolutely have to," said Darius. "Don't worry. We've got time."

Yanak had begun to carry the pistol again. He used it to gesture. "What the hell are you doing now?" he demanded.

"Watching the time pattern on their byte checks. They're smart, but they're not doing them at irregular intervals. When the time comes, we can wait till I see one, then we activate everything."

"Your orders are—"

"I don't give a damn what my orders are. My job is to make this thing work."

"Smart guy, aren't you, Whitney?"

"Me and the pilot," said Darius caustically. "You and Cordero will have to leave it in the hands of the smart guys now. A billion dollars, isn't it? In *our* hands."

"Don't get too cocky. Guys who do have a way of winding up in big trouble."

"Like dead?" asked Darius.

Yanak pressed the muzzle of the pistol to Whitney's neck. "Careful how you talk, old man," he snarled. "The señor knows you looted the Zurich account. I don't know what his orders are gonna be, but—"

"You let Cordero know he's going to need me for the rest of his life," said Darius.

"Crazy old man," muttered Yanak. "You better start looking for your damn transponder code."

"That's what I was doing when you interrupted me," said Darius.

Yanak stalked into the kitchen to pour himself a drink. Darius returned to the computer that was monitoring the display of air traffic entering the Boston-to-New York area.

Traffic was heavy. Bad weather did not interrupt big jets heading for instrument-landing airports. He looked at the numbers for a BA flight:

```
BA003 LHR JFK ETA0240Z 3495 SAY1
```

British Air Flight 003 from London Heathrow Airport to John F. Kennedy Airport was expected to arrive at 0240 Zulu—that is, 8:40 Eastern Daylight Time, squawking transponder code 3495 and making a Saybrook 1 approach to Kennedy.

Then . . . What the hell—?

```
68 87 46 65 68 73 83 79 78 55 52 55
```

He translated it directly from the screen: "DW. AM is on 747."

Then there was more. He pressed the printer keys and took a copy of the string of code, which he had to concentrate on for a moment to read.

```
87 72 73 84 78 69 89 46 65 76 76 73 83 79 78 73
83 79 78 55 52 55 87 73 84 72 67 79 67 65 73 78
69 46 68 65 78 71 69 82 46 87 72 69 82 69 87 73
76 76 73 84 76 65 78 68 63 86 65 78 68 69 78 66
69 82 71
```

Whitney. Allison is on 747 with cocaine. Danger. Where will it land? Vandenberg.

In one sense, Alfredo decided, the bad weather was an advantage. All the small airplanes on the airport were tied down near the terminal building and hangars. The parking lot was all but empty. Reflections of the runway lights glistened on the pavement of the main runway. He wondered if they would close the airport and switch off the runway lights. If they did, would he know how to switch them back on?

He didn't know much about how airports worked. He knew there was no control tower here. He knew those lights were necessary. He knew there was some kind of radio system the pilot would need to bring in the 747. A beacon or something like that. It was part of his job to see that the operators here didn't turn everything off and leave.

Because of the storm, setting the explosives was going to be a miserable job. But it would also be dark earlier. He could send the crew out to work on that before he and his team moved in and seized the airport operations room.

He had come just for a quick look, but he decided to stay. The airport was his already. He and his crew had now taken their Uzi submachine guns out from under the floor panels of the vans, and they had enough firepower to eliminate any possible interference.

As he sat in the van in the parking lot, a pair of bright lights appeared in the sky. A twin-engine airplane broke out of the ragged bottom of the clouds and sank toward the runway. It seemed to hang out there in the air for a long time; then it touched down with a shriek. So—they *did* fly in this weather.

"CAS Zero-zero-two, continue as filed to a Saybrook Two arrival. Cleared to Flight Level Thirty-one."

Sumner put the microphone close to his mouth and responded, "Zero-zero-two, Roger. Descending to thirty-one."

The exchange was laconic. His copilot was already putting the nose down for the descent to 31,000 feet.

They were still well above the weather. But they knew what it was: worse.

He glanced over his shoulder. "Brake pressure?"

"A little off," said the flight engineer. "Still in the green."

"It's got to hold another hour and a half," said Sumner to himself as much as to the engineer. He spoke to Aridas. "Tune the ADF to that stupid station. We're too far out for it, but we don't know when they'll give us our transponder code."

"What's down there, Don?" asked the flight engineer.

"Land," said Sumner. "Nova Scotia."

18

It was 8:45, and Scott Vandenberg had taken a call from Hal Miller in Bethesda.

"Hey! We've got Whitneys! The program has identified eight of them in the last five minutes."

Scott looked at his watch. "Okay, Chief," he said to Miller. "That confirms it. They're coming in tonight. And in what? The next hour?"

"Hour. Hour and a half."

"Where are these Whitneys?"

"Where you'd expect," said Miller. He could not subdue the excitement in his voice. "In the component of the program that maintains the record of incoming flights—identity, altitude, speed, course, transponder code . . ."

"Okay. Keep watching it," said Scott. "Don't interfere with it. I'm going to call an alert here. We don't dare do anything that could foul up the traffic pattern. Watch for anything that would identify the flight. Look for a charter. Or a nonsched. It's hard to think it could be a scheduled airline flight."

"We're on it down here, Captain. Keep us advised."

Scott put down the telephone. He turned to Leighton Drake. "Order a byte count on the digitalizers," he said. "Here and Boston."

"Will do."

"I'm going in to talk to Admiral Buchanan."

Darius Whitney was alerted by the movement of lines on one of his screens. He watched the numbers and symbols rolling down the tube. It was what he had been looking for, even hoping for: a byte count. Not just a byte count. An early byte count. He might have expected one at 9:00, New York time—that is, on the hour—but here was one that had started eight or ten minutes before the hour.

And Boston too.

He wasn't monitoring byte counts everywhere, just in New York and Boston.

Okay, so they were alert. Fine. They were on to the game. He would still outsmart them. He would still show Captain Scott Vandenberg a thing or two about system design. However this whole thing came out, they would remember him.

"Yanak!"

"Yeah? What now?"

"Here's your transponder code. Tell your radio people in the east to send three-zero-seven-nine."

Yanak checked the time. "So soon? It's early."

"The plane is less than an hour from the airport."

"Okay. Three-zero-seven-nine."

"Tell them to transmit it every ten minutes from now to nine forty-five."

"Any problems?" Yanak asked.

"Every goddam kind of problem you could think of," said Whitney. "But the pros are gonna get that load of cocaine down on that airport. Like I told you. If it's screwed up, it'll be screwed up by your side, not by me."

"CAS Zero-zero-two, cleared to Flight Level twenty-one."

"CAS Zero-two, Roger. Descending to twenty-one."

Boston was off to the right. Going down to 21,000 feet brought the 747 almost to the top of the overcast. One hour and thirty minutes from landing.

The overcast wasn't the problem. The tall cumulonimbus at about 220° was. It was full of yellow flashes, and it stood to something like forty thousand feet. The cockpit radar was full of it and showed it at about one hundred miles, a little more. It was between them and their airport. Also, the 747 was equipped with a Ryan Stormscope that displayed lightning activity. The quarter of the Stormscope where the big thunderbumper stood was full of blips, every one a stroke of lightning.

"Contact," said Aridas. "Morse code over the inane chatter on that idiot radio station. Squawk three-zero-seven-nine. Got it? Three-zero-seven-nine."

"Not yet," said Summer. "I want to stay on the Saybrook Two approach as long as possible. We've got to go around to the south of that goddam thunderhead. About Block Island we'll cut away."

No one could leave now. They didn't need to know it, but no one could leave. Alfredo's men surrounded the dimly lighted terminal building. Silently they had moved into position, crouching in the surprisingly cold rain.

"Alfredo . . ."

"*Sí* . . ."

"The explosive charges are set. Here is the controller."

Alfredo nodded. "A few more minutes," he said.

Scott had been called to the side of a young controller and stood looking at her radar scope. She stared at it with marked anxiety and listened intently to the talk in her earphones.

She looked up at Scott, her face flushed. "We've lost a 747!" she whispered. "CAS Zero-zero-two! He'd just come up on the edge of my scope, then—he must be down! I mean, he's gone, like he blew up! One second he was there. The next—"

"He's not down," said Scott. "This is what I've been looking for. Where was he when you lost him?"

"Out over the water, like between Martha's Vineyard and Block Island," she said. "I don't understand. How could it—?"

Another telephone was handed to Scott. "Urgent!" the man muttered.

"Miller, Captain. We've got a system full of Whitneys now. I took it on myself to shut them down, sir. And—"

"And a false target just disappeared off the scopes," said Scott, nodding to the still-distraught young woman.

"I'd think so," said Miller.

Scott stepped into the canteen, where Admiral Buchanan was on the telephone to Washington. The Admiral put the telephone down.

"Sir," said Scott. "Our bogie just disappeared off the scopes. He's off course out there in that weather, headed for god knows where."

The admiral punched another number on his telephone. Scott stepped back out to the control room. For a moment he leaned against the wall. Out there in that weather, headed god knew where . . . With Nancy.

Darius Whitney saw his program begin to collapse. They had found it. They were shooting at it. Element by element, it was disappearing. A virus doctor was sanitizing the ATC system before his eyes.

But maybe they were too late. The digitalizers were still blinding their radar to the true position of the 747, and within thirty minutes it would be on the ground.

Anyway there was nothing more he could do. He lifted himself from the chair where he had sat for hours staring at screens and touching keys. He was stiff. He walked through the suite toward the kitchen. Did he have to tell Yanak? Or would it be better to wait and see what happened? He would have a drink. If the 747 didn't make it, maybe he could fool Yanak, tell him everything had worked fine. Maybe he could get away from him before Yanak learned different.

If he didn't get away before Yanak learned the virus had failed again, Yanak would kill him.

The Colombians waiting for the 747 on the airport would know what happened, immediately. If it were twenty minutes late, they would know it had not made it. Where would they call first? Here? Or Bogotá? Would Yanak wait for the order from Cordero, or did he have authority to kill without any special order from the Señor?

Yanak was bent over the open refrigerator, looking for something. The 9mm. automatic he had pressed against Whitney's neck was lying on the table beside his half-empty drink.

Whitney stiffened. His chin rose. Then he moved decisively. He stepped quickly to the table and picked up the gun.

"Hey!"

Whitney fired just once. Yanak flopped back into the refrigerator and with both hands desperately clutched at bottles of salad dressing, at milk and beer, then at vegetables and jars of jelly, as if they contained the blood to replace what was coursing in gouts from his upper chest or could supply the breath he could not draw through his ripped trachea. He slipped to the floor, glaring balefully at Whitney. He lunged weakly toward him but fell short and lay face down, fists opening and closing as long as they could.

Whitney left the room and sat down again at the computer. Allison was on that airplane, in dreadful danger—not just of a midair collision or a crash but, worse, that Cordero's thugs would kill her, if for no other reason, than because he, Darius, had emptied the Zurich bank account. His fingers raced over the keys, sending a rapid string of characters to the Air Traffic Control computers in New York before they identified his telephone line and shut him out.

"Captain!"

Scott trotted across the floor of Center. A controller was gesticulating wildly. He was pointing at a computer screen, not a radar scope, and a young woman was frantically copying something off the screen:

87 65 84 69 82 66 85 82 89 45 79 88 70 79 82 68
46 68 87 46

Scott read the ASCII code. "Waterbury-Oxford. DW."

Waterbury-Oxford? They had studied the chart for Waterbury-Oxford and had judged it an unlikely choice. It had only five thousand feet of runway, and a power line hung across the south end of the main runway. On the other hand, it had an instrument landing system. It was the only airport in the northeast with an ILS and no control tower—an extremely unusual combination. What was more, it was in a rural setting.

Waterbury-Oxford made sense. Whitney might have sent the message to throw them off, but it made sense to think that was where the 747 was going.

Scott raced into Admiral Buchanan's temporary office. "We've heard from Darius Whitney," he said. "He's calling it Waterbury-Oxford, and I'm ready to believe it."

Alerted by calls from the radios in the police cars that had rushed Scott from Center to MacArthur Airport, two Lear jets in Navy markings were waiting on the ramp, turbines spinning, ready to go. Two helicopters carrying two combat teams had already taken off for Waterbury-Oxford Airport.

"Center has cleared us direct, sir," one of the pilots said. "They've got three 747s in holding patterns to make way for us."

"Admiral Buchanan has advised you are in full command, Captain Vandenberg," said a lieutenant. "Your orders, sir?"

"Let's go, Lieutenant. We're racing a 747 to that airport, and he's not very far out."

"Want to fly right seat, sir? I understand you are a fully qualified pilot. Since you know the mission."

"Not a bad idea," said Scott, and he took the copilot's seat.

Within two minutes the Lear roared off MacArthur and turned north.

Waterbury-Oxford Airport, approximately fifty miles north of MacArthur Airport, serves the people of the city of Waterbury, Connecticut, a place with about 100,000 population, plus the 25,000 of the town of Naugatuck. The airport lies closer to Oxford, a hamlet of 6,000, than to Waterbury—which explains its name. The airport is also only twenty miles, roughly, from Bridgeport and about thirty miles from New Haven.

It lies on a hilltop, 727 feet above sea level, surrounded by farmland and woods. The main runway extends north and south. A shorter runway intersects it toward the north end. A small, modern terminal building stands to the west of the main runway, about midpoint. No airline uses the Waterbury-Oxford Airport, but many corporate aircraft do. Usually twenty to fifty private planes will be found tied down on the ramps or pulled inside the hangars.

"Excuse me, sir," said a young man in fatigues who had come to the front of the Lear. "I'm Sergeant Burke. I was told to be sure you were equipped with weapons."

Scott looked around. "Okay."

"Thought you might like this, to start with," the young man said. He was black and wore the insignia of a buck sergeant of Marines. "You probably qualified with it."

He handed Scott what had formerly been the regulation side-arm for officers of all United States services: a Colt .45 automatic. It was in a holster wrapped in a web belt.

"As a matter of fact, I did qualify with the .45," Scott said. "You had to, to be commissioned."

"Yes, sir. Suggest you strap it on, sir. You'll find two extra magazines in the pouch on the belt. Also, sir, right here behind your seat"—He patted it to show Scott where it was—"is an M-16. It's what the other members of the team will be carrying."

Scott glanced at the menacing black automatic rifle. He had seen many of them over the years. He had never fired one, but he had handled them and knew what they did. The long magazine sticking out of the bottom held thirty rounds, but you didn't fire long bursts because it loosed seven hundred rounds a minute.

"And finally, sir, under the M-16 you'll find combat fatigues. I respectfully urge you to wear them, sir. All of our people will be wearing them, and if there's a firefight in the dark, the uniform may be what distinguishes our people from the baddies."

Scott nodded. "We'll be damned embarrassed if there aren't any baddies, won't we, Sergeant?"

"Negative, sir. *You* may be. I won't."

Scott turned in his seat and looked into the youthful face of the Marine. He grinned. "I never met a Marine sergeant with any hesitation about speaking his mind," he said.

"I hope you never do, sir," said the sergeant.

Scott returned his attention to the instrument panel. They had climbed only to three thousand feet. The Lear was enveloped in heavy cloud. They could see nothing outside but flashes of the wingtip strobes reflected by the dense mist. The airplane's receivers had already picked up the Waterbury instrument-landing signal. The autopilot was linked to one of those receivers, and the Lear was descending. The needles on the VOR head were centered for course and altitude, meaning the jet was coming precisely down the slot toward Runway 36.

Weather radar showed a massive thunderstorm thirty miles to the east, moving east. Residual rain from that storm smacked hard against the windshields.

"Five minutes, sir," said the lieutenant.

Time enough to change uniform. Scott left the seat long enough to pull off his suntans and pull on the camouflage fatigues. He fastened the web belt around his middle, and the Colt .45 hung on his right hip.

Nancy felt the 747 turn into a sharp right bank. She looked out the window but saw nothing. For a long time now she had known from the sound of the engines and the nose-high attitude of the airplane that it was descending. She had felt spoilers and flaps go out, though she couldn't see them. This turn, a sharp turn, could only mean that Summer had intercepted his approach course and was within twenty-five or thirty miles of some airport where he expected to land. She could not guess where.

Out the window to the right she could see red flashes of lightning. Also, she had been feeling turbulence. Big as it was, the 747 had shuddered and bounced as it flew through the edge of a major storm.

She had confidence in Don Sumner. He was no fool. He was taking this airplane where he judged it should not go, but she guessed he could make it in safely if anyone could.

She was cruelly bound now. The senior Colombian had tied her wrists tightly to the arms of her seat. He had tied her ankles together and then to a rear leg of the seat ahead of her. The nylon strap lay loose on the floor behind her, but he had fastened her seat belt, and she could not reach the buckle.

Yoshitaka Hara sat glum and silent across the aisle from her, glancing at her from time to time.

Allison McGuire stared at the back of the seat in front of her.

She smoked nervously, grinding out a cigarette in an ashtray and immediately lighting another. Nancy saw her shudder.

The Colombian gunmen sat hushed and afraid in their seats, staring out the windows. Even the senior Colombian was plainly apprehensive. His bold talk on the ground at Tenerife—about how Sumner would land safely to save his own life—did not sustain his courage now.

The 747 bounced heavily as it struck turbulence, after which it wallowed sickeningly as the autopilot worked to level it and return it to the glide path. It had lost altitude, and the engines spun up with a whining roar. One of the Colombian gunmen began to pray.

Alfredo and his men walked into the terminal. The three men there, who had unknowingly been prisoners for the past half hour, were easily subdued. One was a night watchman. The other two were technicians, radio operators. Alfredo demanded to know if the instrument-landing system was operating. The operators assured him it was.

He left the three men sitting in an office, under the muzzle of an Uzi submachine gun in the hands of a man who spoke only a few words of English. He walked outside. The gate was open, and the trucks that would carry the cocaine were passing through and moving up the taxiway to the north end of the runway.

Everything was in order.

Except the power lines that hung over the approach to Runway 36: They were out of the way for the airplanes that landed here, but the big 747, which had to touch down on the first twenty yards of runway, would come in lower. The power lines might—just might—be in the way.

Alfredo's instructions were to wait until he saw the landing lights of the 747, then detonate the charges in the towers that carried the lines. He wasn't sure who would lose power when those lines came down. He had been assured they did not supply the airport's electrical power.

He walked out into the rain, out onto the ramp, and took shelter under the high wing of a small airplane. He peered into the gloom to the south. Landing lights—Wait till he saw landing lights.

On the Navy Lear, flaps were down, gear was down. Scott shifted his attention back and forth between the needles and the darkness ahead. Very shortly they would be at the missed-approach point: the point where, if they did not see the runway lights, they were supposed to break off the approach and go around for another try.

"Well . . . If we can't get down, *he* can't get down," said the lieutenant in the left seat.

"Except that he's a fool," grunted Scott.

"What you want me to do, sir?"

"Go on past the MAP. There aren't any obstructions. Take 'er down to 750 feet. If we don't see anything then, break off and climb out."

"Yes—Uh—Radio."

They were using a frequency reserved for them, not the usual ATC frequency.

"Captain Vandenberg, this is New York Center. Respond, please."

"Vandenberg."

"Sir, the digitalizers are still screwed up. We don't know where that 747 has gone. Military radar hasn't got him. He must be low and slow and over land. He may be in our LaGuardia and Newark approach routes. We're trying to hold back traffic. But we've got two corporate jets for Teterboro and a 727 that could be factors. The corporate guys have been holding outside for an hour, waiting for that storm to move, and are short of fuel. They've got to go into Teterboro no matter what. The 727 has a heart attack aboard and insists on going through to Newark. The approaches to Teterboro and Newark are just north of Waterbury-Oxford. They're high, but they could be right in position for a midair if the 747 thinks he can't make it at Waterbury and tries to execute a missed approach. If he climbs out hard, he could hit any of them. Same thing is true for you, sir."

"Understood, Center."

"Something else, sir. Mr. Miller called from Bethesda. He wanted to know if you had seen the message from Mr. Whitney on the ATC computer screens, and we told him you had."

"Okay, thank you, Center. We're about a mile from MAP."

Landing lights! Alfredo saw the white glare of landing lights. He fired the charges. Four bursts of flame glared in the darkness. Then a display of blue sparks. The lines were down.

"What the hell?" asked the Navy lieutenant in the left seat of the Lear.

"I'll be damned if I know," said Scott, "but there's the runway. Just beyond whatever that was. Got it?"

Four red balls of fire had appeared and disappeared, followed by a fireworks display of sparks like the sparks from an arc welder. But beyond that, barely visible through the rain, were the two parallel strings of yellow lights, the runway.

The Lieutenant took control away from the autopilot. He pulled back his throttles, raised his nose, and let the Lear drop onto the pavement.

The jet rolled down the runway, past the midpoint and the terminal. It was three-quarters of the way to the north end before the pilot braked to a stop.

"Trucks up there ahead," the Lieutenant said to Scott.

The trucks faced the runway, their headlights glaring, trying to give the expected 747 a clear mark as to where the runway ended.

"Taxi onto the cross runway," said Scott.

The lieutenant turned left and rolled a hundred feet to the west of the main runway. With the plane turned, they had a view back to the south. Another set of landing lights burned through the mist and rain. Closely set. Not the 747. Those were the lights of the second Navy Lear.

"Everybody out!" Scott yelled to the seven marines in the rear. "Lights out, Lieutenant. Sergeant, you in charge of the combat team?"

"I am, sir."

"Assume those trucks are hostiles. Assume there are others in the terminal. Do your thing, Sergeant, You're the combat officer."

The Sergeant ordered his men to take up posts around the Lear. He would get oriented and let the other Lear land before he moved.

Alfredo watched wrathfully as two small jets landed and pulled off onto the cross runway. Who? What the hell were they doing?

He put his walkie-talkie to his mouth and warned the truck crews that this might be trouble. Then he ordered four of his men to join him in a van, and he sped out the taxiway toward the two intruding airplanes.

The second small jet had pulled up behind the first, and Alfredo could see men hurrying out of it and deploying like soldiers. As his headlight beams reached them, he saw they *were* soldiers. He braked to a skidding stop. Screaming at his men to jump from the van, he leaped out, threw himself to the ground, and opened fire with his Uzi. He'd be damned if he'd let a little group of tin soldiers ruin an operation as big and important as this.

The other four followed.

Sergeant Burke and his men were deployed. The Colombians had not seen them; their attention was focused on the second combat team piling out of the second Lear. The second team was caught in the streams of fire from five Uzis. All of them dropped to the tarmac.

Scott could not tell if some were hit or if they were only throwing themselves to the ground to take firing positions.

He himself was still beside the first Lear. Whining slugs chopped through the tail of the aircraft. He dropped to his knees behind the landing gear and took aim with his M-16.

The Marines were returning fire. The fire from the Colombians slackened as they jumped behind their van or scrambled away into the darkness.

Sergeant Burke rose and tossed a grenade.

Alfredo saw it bounce across the ground without realizing what it was. He would never know. It exploded in a furious short burst of fire, hurling a storm of steel pellets like a thousand small bullets. A hundred or more pellets bored through Alfredo, chopping him apart. He died instantly. Another Colombian was caught in the torrent of little steel balls and managed only to crawl a few feet before he died. A third man was wounded and began to shriek.

Scott fired a burst from the M-16. He had aimed at the van, thinking there was no point in leaving an escape vehicle intact. The van rocked under the shock.

He could not see the two Colombians on the other side of it, who had been running toward it. They saw it shudder, saw the slugs penetrate the steel body and disable the van. They crawled away toward darkness and toward the terminal.

Two Marines had been hit, one badly in the legs, the other superficially.

Sergeant Burke moved to talk to another sergeant, the one in command of the second combat team.

"Look out for the big trucks," Scott called to the sergeants. "Those are hostiles too."

The Marines deployed in a wide skirmish line and began to move toward the trucks.

"Sergeant Burke!" Scott yelled. "Hold it!"

To the south, two wide-set lights blazed in a spectral white glare coming out of the rain and mist. The commanding low roar of immense jet engines followed the lights.

"Jesus Christ!" whispered the young lieutenant who had piloted the first Lear. "He can't—"

He could and he was. Don Sumner had taken control away from the autopilot a moment before and had dropped the 747 twenty feet or so below the glide path. The path led to a touchdown point two hundred feet or more beyond the threshold of the runway. He didn't have an extra two hundred feet and meant to touch down as soon as there was pavement.

Aridas was glancing back and forth between the view ahead and the altimeter. The runway was at 727 feet above sea level. The needle passed through 800, still rapidly unwinding.

"Flare!" yelled Aridas. Flare was the term for lifting the nose and dropping the aircraft abruptly onto the runway.

Sumner nodded and raised the nose to an angle of attack that gave the 747 maximum drag. At the same time he pulled the throttles all the way back.

The sixteen wheels of the main gear touched the pavement.

Sumner reversed thrust and shoved the throttles forward. The engines roared: a furious, penetrating howl that blared through the night and for the first time alerted towns miles away that something extraordinary was happening at Waterbury-Oxford Airport.

Scott was not aware that his mouth hung open as he watched the enormous airplane hurtle down the runway. The blast from the reverse thrust blew up a hurricane of water ahead of it and in the glare of its lights. The pilot held the nose high, using drag to slow the 747. He had used two-thirds of his runway, even so, and was still moving fast. Scott heard an angry screech from the gear. The pilot had hit the brakes, hit them all the way, as hard as he could.

Smoke trailed the landing gear. The nose wheels dropped to the runway and hit with a shock that threatened to collapse the nose gear. The 747 passed the cross runway and barreled into the last thousand feet.

Then—then something odd. The pilot had just cut back his reverse thrust and was relying on his brakes—and was decelerating at a rate that looked like it would bring him to a stop just about at the end of the pavement—when abruptly his deceleration ceased and the 747 went on rolling. Liquid spewed from the open left wheel well.

Hydraulic fluid! Excessive pressure on the brakes had ruptured a major component of the hydraulic system! Scott had seen it happen before, on fighters making carrier landings.

The 747 rolled off the pavement at thirty or forty miles an hour. The nose wheels dug into the soft wet earth, and the nose gear collapsed. The tail went up, and the nose of the big aircraft came down. The sheet metal of the nose collapsed, too, and dug into the mud. The 747 did not skid forward but came to a violently abrupt stop that wrenched the left wing loose.

Nancy was thrown forward. Because her wrists were bound, she could not cover her head or face with her hands, and her forehead slammed into the back of the seat in front cf her. Stunned, she hung forward and wondered woozily if she were injured.

Yoshitaka Hara sat open-mouthed, also stunned, perhaps mentally as much as physically.

Allison McGuire wailed in terror and held her face in her hands, weeping.

The Colombian gunmen had left the upper deck during the final minute of the approach and were somewhere below—except for the senior Colombian, who had stayed in the lounge. Thinking apparently to move fast, as soon as the 747 stopped, he had unfastened his seat belt and stood up as the plane rolled down the runway. When the gear broke and the nose struck the ground, he had been thrown off his feet to sprawled in the aisle, and now lay dazed, his head bleeding. His Uzi submachine gun lay on the floor in front of him.

The cockpit door burst open, and Don Sumner rushed into the lounge. He and his crew had been held in place by crossed shoulder belts and lap belts and had suffered no injury.

The Colombian struggled to crawl forward and grab his Uzi, but Sumner jumped toward him and kicked him hard along the side of his head. The Colombian made another try to reach the Uzi, and Sumner kicked him again, full in the jaw. The jaw was broken, likely, and the Colombian dropped to his face on the floor.

Sumner picked up the Uzi. He leveled it on Hara. "How 'bout you? Which side you on?"

Hara shook his head. "Don't worry. There are no sides left."

Bill Aridas knelt beside Nancy and began untying her.

"You hurt?" Sumner asked.

She had begun to believe she wasn't, not seriously anyway, and she shook her head.

Sumner took a station at the top of the curving stairway and peered down into the lower level, holding the Uzi ready, looking for the Colombian gunmen.

The Marines ran to the 747, outrunning Scott, who came trotting after them. He wanted to remind Sergeant Burke that there might be hostiles around the big trucks, but as he approached, he saw they were abandoned. The trucks could not leave the field except by driving down the taxiway to the terminal, and the Marines held that ground. The drivers and loaders had retreated into the night.

The overhead clatter of helicopters distracted him. They had caught up with the jets and were bringing in two more combat teams, probably more heavily armed.

The Marines, climbing onto the left wing of the 747, approached a door. Scott watched Sergeant Burke attach a shaped explosive charge to it. The Sergeant stepped back, crouched, and a small explosion blew the door off its hinges.

Sergeant Burke was the first man in. Scott heard the rip of automatic fire. He ran forward and got the help of two marines in lifting him onto the wing. He was the fourth man inside the 747.

"Secured, I think, sir," said Sergeant Burke. "Look—"

Boxes had broken open. Plastic bags had ruptured. Cocaine had spilled to the floor. Colombians lay in the white powder.

"Some of 'em must have been prowling around," the sergeant said. "When the plane crashed, they were thrown against the crates, against the bulkheads. Two were up and ready to fire."

The two who had been up and ready to fire lay in cocaine made red and sticky by their blood.

A moment later Scott climbed the circular stairs to the upper deck of the 747. Don Sumner, who had dropped the Uzi to the floor, stood apprehensively at the top of the stairs, his hands held apart from each hip.

Scott held his Colt .45 in a tense grip, aimed at Sumner's belly.

"Scott!" Nancy rushed into Scott's arms. "Oh, Scott . . ."

"Captain Vandenberg, I presume," said Sumner dryly.

One Year Later

One year to the day after the 747 landed on Waterbury-Oxford Airport, Scott and Nancy Vandenberg played golf at Saint Andrews, in Scotland. They had flown their Beech Baron across the Atlantic—Newfoundland, Greenland, Iceland, the Orkneys—and were received as honored guests, allowed to play in spite of the fact that they had begun to learn the game only during the past year and chopped too many divots out of the royal and ancient course.

They had spent more time than they wanted to spend before congressional committees and on television news shows; and now they had fled their celebrity status, hoping it would ebb during a long vacation in Europe.

Darius Whitney was missing. So was Allison McGuire. It was presumed that they were together. No one was sure where, and no one was looking very hard.

Within hours after the 747 nosed over into the Connecticut mud, the proprietors of NEXIS, a computer-based information service offering access to the back files of hundreds of newspapers and magazines, discovered a bogus newspaper article in their system. Ostensibly it was a feature article from the *Los Angeles Times*. In fact it was the product of a virus—inserted in a system that had, until now, been supposed to be 100 percent immune from viruses.

The article was a sort of Whitney confession—though written in the third person as though by a reporter—telling in detail how and why Darius Whitney had caused the Thanksgiving Eve debacle; how he had been contacted by the Colombian cocaine baron Virgilio Cordero; how he had written and used the viruses that had almost succeeded in bringing forty tons of cocaine into the United States; and even how and why he had shot Stepan Yanak.

Before the proprietors of NEXIS could clean the fake story out of their computer, it had gone out over the wires to hundreds of their customers. Within hours it was picked up by the Associated Press and put on the AP wire—with of course an explanation of what it was. The next day the Whitney story appeared in every major newspaper in the United States and in hundreds of papers in other countries.

The last word in Whitney's story had been that he was retiring, coupled with a promise never to create another virus. He omitted mention of a virus he had *already* created, which he had activated the same night. When the Bank of the City opened in London, a dozen electronic transfer orders were waiting, and by noon the millions in the James McMurtry account had been transferred to accounts in various names in eight banks in the United States.

By the time investigators identified McMurtry as Whitney and traced the accounts, all but two of them had been closed. A little more than $1 million remained. The rest was gone.

Criminal charges remained pending against Darius Whitney, although no actual indictments had been returned.

One year after Waterbury, Yoshitaka Hara was back in his suite at The Sands. He had served eleven months of a three-to-five-year term at Danbury and was released early as a reward for his cooperation in the investigation of the cocaine trade.

Hara, too, testified before congressional committees.

Donald Sumner and his copilot and flight engineer were missing. Nancy had suggested to Scott and the Marine sergeant at Waterbury that Sumner had perhaps saved her life by subduing the Colombian with the Uzi—and, anyway, he was a competent pilot and, overall, a good fellow. A few minutes later Sumner and his crew had taken off in a Cessna Skyhawk. Nancy had suggested that Allison McGuire be allowed to go, too. She had been the fourth person in the Skyhawk.

Little Judy Vandenberg was at home in Bethesda, more than a little annoyed that she had not been allowed to fly to Europe in the Baron with Daddy and Nancy. In this she did not have her way. She'd had her way at the wedding, though, when she had stood beside her father, not as ring bearer or flower girl, but in the role she had thought was appropriate—maid of honor.

In spite of the confessions of Whitney and Hara, in spite of the testimony the Vandenbergs gave before congressional committees and a grand jury, the United States had found it impossible to prosecute Virgilio Cordero. (Some suggested the government didn't much want to, in light of Cordero's notoriously friendly relations with the Vice President.) The government of Colombia officially announced he had fled the country and could not be located. He was traced to Paraguay, then to Chile, finally to Panama.

Whatever problem he represented, it came to an end one April morning on a beach not far from Agua Dulce, Panama, where the bullet-riddled body of Virgilio Cordero washed ashore. He had generated a quantity and quality of publicity that *los Señores* could not forgive.

In the first six months after the landing of the 747 at Waterbury, the importation of cocaine into the United States declined—according to estimates—by 23 percent. In the next six months it increased—again according to estimates—by 211 percent.